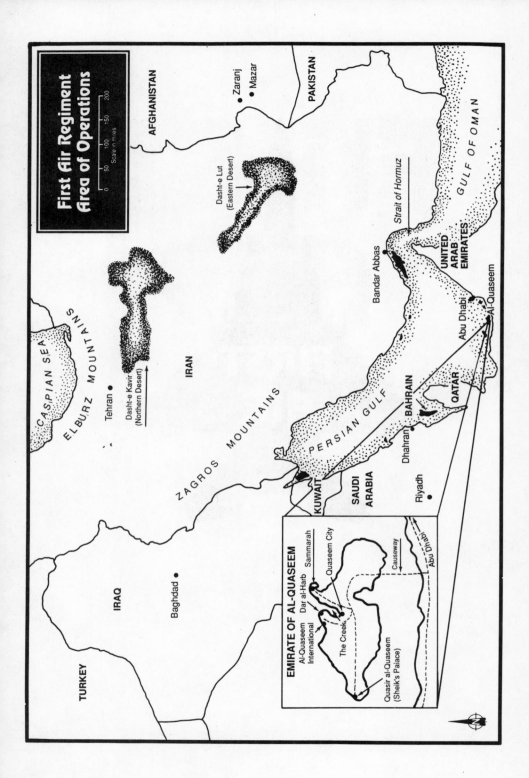

First Air Regiment Area of Operations

Scale in miles
0 50 100 150 200

TURKEY

IRAQ

Baghdad

CASPIAN SEA

ELBURZ MOUNTAINS

Tehran

Dasht-e Kavir
(Northern Desert)

IRAN

ZAGROS MOUNTAINS

AFGHANISTAN

Zaranj   Mazar

PAKISTAN

Dasht-e Lut
(Eastern Desert)

Bandar Abbas

Strait of Hormuz

GULF OF OMAN

UNITED ARAB EMIRATES

Abu Dhabi

Al-Quaseem

QATAR

BAHRAIN

Dhahran

PERSIAN GULF

KUWAIT

SAUDI ARABIA

Riyadh

EMIRATE OF AL-QUASEEM

Sammarah
Dar al-Harb
Quaseem City

Al-Quaseem International

The Creek

Causeway

Abu Dhabi

Quasir al-Quaseem
(Sheik's Palace)

N

FIRST AIR

A Novel of Air Combat in the Persian Gulf

Michael Skinner

PRESIDIO

The book's story and characters are fictitious, as is the Emirate of al-Quaseem. Actual political and military organizations are mentioned, but the characters involved are wholly imaginary.

Published by Presidio Press
31 Pamaron Way, Novato, CA 94949

Library of Congress Cataloging-in-Publication Data

Skinner, Michael, 1953-
    First air : a novel / Michael Skinner.
       p.   cm.
    ISBN 0-89141-351-0
    I. Title.
    PS3569.K5255F57   1991   90-41322
    813' .54--dc20   CIP

Typography by ProImage

Printed in the United States of America

This book is dedicated to my mother and my father

These knights of a mythic western were out for pleasure; a brilliant talent for losing themselves in play; a voyage into amazement; a love of speed; a terrain of relativity.

—French letterist/Situationalist philosopher Guy Debord

Screw it, it's just an attitude.

—"Spider," a Bitburg F-15 pilot, on flying fighters

Prologue

The Shadow of the Atom

Ten years ago this happened:

The short train rolled through the narrow valley of the Caucasus on its way to Baku, on the Caspian Sea. Two green VL-12 engines pulled the six cars—five black, armored freight cars and a curious silver-and-white container car. Another olive drab engine brought up the rear, facing backward.

In this locomotive, relief engineer Yakhov Russov studied the distant mountains moving past his station at a slow but steady forty miles an hour. Russov traveled backward on this train for a living, but in his soul he was an artist, a poet, and so, like all Russian artists, he was drinking heavily. Not the Ararat wine, which his poet's soul preferred, but straight vodka, which the KGB guard huddled in the engine compartment could not detect on his breath.

Russov was not frightened that the young KGB sergeant would disapprove of his drinking on duty. On the contrary—the guard would want to drink with him. And play cards again. Russov detested cards and the KGB. More important, Russov had just enough vodka to last him to Baku and none to share.

The train shook slightly, then shuddered to a stop. Russov scowled. There could be no trouble on the line. This section of the Transcaucasus Railway was cleared for them, guarded by soldiers guarded by the KGB. And with three VL-12s, the train had enough power to pull its small load straight up the fourteen-thousand-foot peaks of the blue mountains if necessary. What could be the problem?

An intercom speaker buzzed in the engine compartment. The KGB guard swept past in his long leather coat. He was carrying a Kalishnikov rifle that Russov had never seen before. "Trouble at the bridge at Yaklev," he said, then hopped off the engine and trotted toward the head of the train.

Russov strolled out to the railing and lit a cigarette. The twilight threw pink shadows across the peaks. Bright spotlights atop the black cars added only drama, not illumination. The dogs were out. Russov heard no radios, which was unusual. The KGB lived for radios.

One of the black gunships swooped in to hover overhead. When Russov was first assigned to the Black Train, his poet's passion had been stirred by these sinister angels of hell; now, three years later, he found the helicopters merely annoying. Typical KGB self-importance—it was an armored train, a Soviet train inside Soviet territory. What could happen?

True, they were close to the border with Turkey and Iran, both of which craved the secrets simmering in the silver container car. And, like all the outlying republics, Soviet Georgia stirred with restless nationalism. But Russov had made this run dozens of times, from the processing centers in the interior to the special weapons igloos in Baku. There had been no trouble before. He was sure this delay was caused by a minor problem, magnified by KGB paranoia.

Russov heard an engine in the sky, higher pitched than the turbines of the HIND gunships. Jets! They were calling in reinforcements. He watched the jagged black shapes curve across the steel-gray sky. The gunship above wheeled to face the arriving aircraft.

The first jet roared over the train in a rush of noise that bent back the pines on either side. Something fell from the aircraft. The engine at the head of the train split apart, releasing a huge fireball and black smoke. The locomotive lurched off the tracks. Blue sparks from the severed lines engulfed the train with eerie, strobing light and air burned into ozone.

"They've blown the bridge!" The KGB guard scrambled onto the catwalk. "We have to go back! Get this thing moving!"

Russov threw his cigarette into the woods and hurried back inside the engine. He was not a bad engineer, for a drunken poet, but he could not get the VL-12 to budge.

"We're shorted!" he shouted to the KGB man. "We're not going anywhere till we cut the main engine free!"

Russov grabbed an axe. The two men jumped off the catwalk and ran toward the front of the train. The scream of the jets returned. Russov sprawled to the ground. There was a deafening noise. He raised his head from the mud to see the relief engine, his own beloved VL-12, lying on its side, hissing sparks.

Russov stood up. There were shots now, coming from the trees. He looked for the KGB guard, whom he now saw as *his* guard, *his* protector. The young sergeant was facedown in the mud, with three wet circles across his leather back.

Russov ran for the woods. He ran until fire filled his lungs, until his legs fell beneath him. He leaned against a giant spruce, listening. There were fewer gunshots now, all coming from the woods. He listened still. No more shots, just shouting in a language he had never heard before.

Later, when they questioned Russov as the only survivor, he would not be able to recognize the language of the hijackers. He would not be able to identify the types of aircraft that had attacked the Black Train. He would not be able to give any information that would help Soviet authorities apprehend whoever had committed the crime of the century.

He was not a drunk, he would protest. He was a poet. So they sent him to the special camp for poets, carved in the evocative and inspiring ice swamps of Siberia. There he would reflect on a life spent hauling atoms. And marvel at how the smallest thing on earth cast its largest shadow.

That shadow fell across the world ten years later....

Ghosts

Nellis Air Force Base
Las Vegas, Nevada

Bobby Dragon was invisible. And he was flying. It was as close to happiness as he could get.

Night flying made most fighter pilots uncomfortable. During the day you never touched the sky. It was a blue bowl, always out of reach on the moving horizon, and you zoomed through clear nothingness. At night the sky closed in, collapsing like a black hole around your aircraft. There might be blazes or beacons on the world below and, above, the blue distress signals of dying stars, but both were cold light, distant. Caught in the black stuff of the night you made your own dark world. Alone.

Bobby liked the night, liked being out of touch and out of reach. He was alone and that was fine. He was a ghost. He was where he belonged.

His eyes swept routinely across the aircraft's systems status, etched in sharp lines of ruby light on the canopy. The figures changed, settled, changed again, all within normal parameters. Alt: 360. Speed: .6 mach. Heading: 270.

Oil pressure, turbine temperature, fuel level, weapons status, BIT checks—all the bookkeeping, done automatically on modern aircraft by the beasts themselves, balanced out perfectly. The ship would tell him if anything was wrong, but Bobby checked anyway. He was a very careful man in the air. It was one of the reasons he had lived too long.

A ghost, yes. No one could see him. Beams of radar stabbed through the night, but no electrons lived long enough to struggle back to their receivers and report his whereabouts. Infrared sensors put out their supercooled hands and could not feel his faint heat. Those dreamers who stare at the night sky saw a black dome uninterrupted by the black belly of the black plane. If they stared long enough, they might see a line of stars winking on and off in sequence as he passed. But few on the earth had the patience for such whimsy these days.

Nellis Air Force Base sprawled glowing to the south. Tiny aircraft floated in and out of the incandescent bonfire of the huge complex, to be quickly swallowed by the night. Bobby had not taken off from Nellis. He would not land there. There were people there.

He cut circles in the dark air, his mind on other times, other skies. The world seemed clear from the air, more defined. He could see patterns, if not purpose, from his altitude. Roads connected to other roads connected to other roads. Houses lined up back to back, block to block, each a square of light forming larger squares, cut by streets in the checkerboard of the flat city. Highways ran from the bright cluster, trailing fire soon extinguished by the desert coolness. The casino strip erupted through the pattern of light, a sunspot flaring neon and a million quick bulbs.

Outside the amoeba of light that was Las Vegas there was nothing, complete nothing, the earthbound asteroid of the Great Basin: flat, burred mountains set on desert as low and smooth as cement. It was the last place on earth, the end of the line. Bobby Dragon called it home.

A warning tone, barely audible, beeped inside his helmet. To Bobby, lost in his reverie, it sounded like a bomb blast. A red light blinked on a CRT in the center of the instrument panel. Red words crawled across the screen. The message had been beamed from the earth into space, bounced from a satellite and reflected back to the dark plane. It was a long way to go for such a simple message, but not too long for someone who wanted to stay hidden.

The message was "Commence Teal Sparrow."

Bobby tilted the aircraft down, sliding thousands of feet in a slow, winding spiral. Nellis spun and rose through the canopy on his starboard side. In the glare of the air base's mercury vapor lights, he followed the runway to what he was looking for: an E-3A AWACS rotating off 21 right, wheels up, heading into the darkness.

The AWACS turned north. Bobby cut the corner, straining to keep his quarry in sight. The lights of Nellis had ruined his night vision temporarily, but he could still make out the big, gray 707 body against the darker night. His aircraft had a radar Bobby wouldn't use and an infrared (IR) sensor he didn't trust—even in the most advanced technology flying, the critical piece of mission equipment remained the pilot, his vision, and his judgment.

Bobby pulled behind the AWACS. He could clearly see the four blue flames of the engines from three miles back. At two miles he could make out the shape of the body, the wings, and the tall tail. A mile away the E-3's trademark rotodome spread out over the AWACS, like a flying saucer hovering in formation above the aircraft. That was something like what Bobby had in mind.

Timing was crucial. If he closed too late, the fighters would arrive and find him straggling behind the AWACS. That would not be good. Despite its designation, his fighter was no fighter, not in the conventional sense. Aerodynamic sacrifices made in the name of stealth rendered it slow and relatively unmaneuverable. Bobby thought he might be able to shake off the AWACS's escorts in a chase through the electronic shadows and physical darkness, but he wouldn't want to have to try it. It could mean losing, and most of all Bobby Dragon hated to lose.

However, closing too early would yield the same result; he would have to goose the throttle enough for the fighters' IR sensors to get a good whiff of his scent. Slow and steady, that was it.

Bobby slid closer to the AWACS. Two small, red symbols in the shapes of F-15s blinked on and off, the fleeting returns of the fighters' radars, airborne now but still distant, seeking to join up. A warning horn nearly blasted Bobby out of his seat as the AWACS fired up its giant AN/APY-1 radar. Now airborne, the AWACS was in no danger of igniting fuel pits or sterilizing ground crewmen with its powerful microwave transmissions. The rotodome increased its oscillation, from once every two minutes to once every ten seconds. Giant bars of computer-generated graphics swept across the inside of Bobby's canopy in sync with the E-3's radar. The AWACS was in business.

Bobby cruised closer to the huge radar plane. He wasn't worried about its microwave emissions. His aircraft was built to take whatever radiation the AWACS could dish out and more. The canopy was lined with gold foil. Much of the wiring was fiber optics. The fuel tanks were hidden under layers of radar-absorbing carbon graphite laminate that formed the aircraft's skin.

The black plane closed on the E-3, sliding underneath the big plane's tail section. Bobby moved nearer, rising to within feet of the AWACS. It would take some deft flying to stay so close, but the AWACS was not known for its maneuverability, either. Bobby was confident he could stay glued to the AWACS like a remora, even in turns. If all went well, his marginal radar return would merge with the much larger blob of the E-3. And the plane's black mass would be lost in the darkness underneath the AWACS.

The symbols for the two F-15s burned steadily now in the cockpit. They were somewhere near in the night but, like the AWACS, flew blacked out, without navigation lights. The warning symbols, like the rest of the plane's computer-generated graphics, could not be seen from the outside. The canopy had been coated using a special process, not unlike that used on one-way mirrors, which presented a uniform golden-gray face to the outside world. It had taken a while for Bobby to grow used to the idea that no one outside could see into the cockpit, lit up like a video game.

One red dot, then another, flashed above his left shoulder, moving across the canopy to stop parallel to the AWACS. The computer generated a graphic tag "F-15C" underneath each dot, with heading, altitude, and speed data on each bogie. The nearest one flashed, representing not the closest target, as Bobby had grown accustomed to in years of flying tactical fighters, but rather the closest threat. In daylight, he would have been able to see actual Eagles behind the dots, but in the darkness Bobby had to take the aircraft's data—gleaned from the F-15's own radar signatures processed through a computer attached to his fighter's ultrasensitive radar warning receiver—as the final word.

The Eagles flew wing on the AWACS, about three miles away. Bobby was confident no one had seen him. The E-3's own bulk prevented its radar from spotting the bandit flying underneath its belly. The Eagles were pointed the wrong way, in any case. He toyed with the idea of drifting starboard to interpose himself between the AWACS and the F-15s. It was the only way he could intercept the point-to-point secure data-link communication he knew must surely be going on between the hunter and its hounds. But that would be rubbing their noses in it. His mission in Operation Teal Sparrow was to stay hidden. Bobby settled back for a long ride.

The minutes crawled by. Occasionally the Eagles would dart off in different directions at high speed, their afterburners stabbing the night with concentric cones of blue-and-yellow flame. But they would always return sheepishly to the AWACS's side for another long, silent conversation.

Suddenly, the F-15s peeled off angrily and headed back to Nellis. The warning tone beeped again in Bobby's helmet. The cockpit screen flickered to life with the satellite's song: "Terminate Teal Sparrow."

Strange. The exercise was scheduled to run much longer. No doubt the Eagle jocks and the AWACS had grown tired and frustrated seaching for his black needle in the black haystack of the night sky. Bobby pushed a button underneath the screen. His position, transmitted silently in an instant to the satellite humming above Ecuador, would confirm his presence in the exercise area. In a moment it would be relayed to the mission crew aboard the AWACS, who would immediately recognize his position as their own. Then all hell would break lose.

If the controllers on the AWACS had any discipline at all, they would wait until they got back to Nellis to turn the black ether blue with radioed cries of foul. Bobby could imagine what they would say: The purpose of the test was to measure the effectiveness of the new Teal Sparrow sensor in detecting low-observable aircraft, not to gauge the deviousness of stealth jockeys! Buckets of dollars went to waste because some spook decided to be clever! He had wasted their valuable training time by screwing up a test that would only have to be repeated!

Well, if *he* could do it, the bad guys could do it, too. Only they wouldn't be content to ride shotgun with the AWACS. The expensive, irreplaceable platform would have been shot out of the sky in the first three minutes of the battle. *Check six!* It was a simple lesson, but one that Bobby had had to teach to almost every operator in every platform in every exercise. Better to learn it in peacetime, when it only cost money. As far as the rules went, Bobby didn't care. He had been to war. There weren't any rules there.

The AWACS wallowed in the sky, skidding left in some heavy driver's idea of a break turn. They had apparently gotten the message. It wasn't much of a separation maneuver, but it was a start. The crew inside must be scared to death, as well as mad. Good, Bobby thought. Maybe next time they'll remember.

He pulled the nose up and cut power, sinking slowly to lose himself in the mountains. The AWACS circled south, heading back to Nellis. The sweeping bars disappeared from the canopy, replaced by a terse message: "AWACS on standby."

Bobby switched on the active sensor package. Shadowy mountains spread across the front of the canopy, a product of the aircraft's infrared-imaging optical sensor. A jagged red line, generated by the plane's low-power terrain-following radar, marked the mountains' peaks. Punching another button produced a red cross over Bobby's left elbow: the way home.

He pulled a sweeping turn between two mountains. The aircraft would fly itself back to Dreamland, if he let it. Bobby chose to fly instead. His mistrust did not stem from superstition or ignorance. He had been, in fact, instrumental in the development of the stealth fighter and knew its insides intimately. It was that knowledge that prevented him from completely trusting the systems he had helped bring to life. He knew a thousand ways things could go wrong.

Bobby twirled a knob underneath his glove, punched a button, turned another knob, punched the button again, and spun yet another knob. The sequential transmission of three different IFF (identification friend or foe) codes was a pain, especially in the dim cockpit after a long mission. But the gnomes of Dreamland were sticklers for security, and Bobby was not in the mood for whatever black trash they had come up with this week to shoot in the direction of intruders who did not follow the correct IFF clearance procedures. Better squawk than walk.

Dreamland, blacked out as usual, flickered like a monochrome mirage in the computer-generated infrared forward view. It didn't look like much even in the daylight, just a series of square buildings and arching hangars connected by a long, wide runway. It was always difficult to imagine this was the most confidential place on the planet, a secret kingdom carved in the desert whose very name, whispered carelessly in the wrong setting, had ended careers and shattered lives.

Although its name and approximate location were common knowledge throughout the defense community, exactly what went on in Dreamland was not. In fighter bars around the world, Bobby had heard countless fantastic stories of things that had allegedly taken place at Area 41, the Defense Department's official designation for Dreamland and its associated complex of laboratories, test facilities, and dry lake beds. What amused him most, and what he could not say, was that every one of the stories was true, in some detail. But the most intriguing stories never left the base. Bobby knew this because he lived there.

He lowered the landing gear, automatically extending the wings' leading edge flaps and deploying the radar reflector on the nose strut without which base controllers would be as startled as enemy antiaircraft gunners at the sudden appearance of the batlike aircraft. Bobby lined up on the main runway, etched out on the surface of Groom Lake. Like so many Dreamland terms, Groom Lake was a misnomer. There was no water in the dry lake bed. There had not been for thousands of years, and if, in fact, there had *ever* been water there, dinosaurs would have been the last creatures to enjoy it.

Dinosaurs. The place was full of their bones. The Defense Department told the world Dreamland was a nuclear test site. It was enough to scare anyone away. But the nuclear devices were actually detonated underground at Pahute Mesa, many miles to the southwest. Dreamland's dinosaurs were perfect specimens, undisturbed by atomic blasts, weather of any sort, or the ravages of curious humans. Whole specimens were etched intact on the cliffsides bordering the complex. Tableaus of fossilized remains lay stretched out by the runway, occasionally trampled under the wheels of the most advanced machines devised by human minds.

There were no lights to guide his landing, no controller's voice to welcome him. Bobby touched down alone in the dark, rolling for what seemed like miles on the endless runway. He hit the brakes and shut down the engines. Nothing moved on the flight line or in the darkened buildings lining the runway. No lights, no sound, nothing. It was a ghost town. Bobby felt right at home.

He popped the canopy, which rose forward, along with much of the aircraft's upper nose section. The plane, especially its cockpit, was designed more like a Le Mans racer than a standard jet fighter. The plane was comfortable in flight, and its sleekness contributed to its low radar signature, but the reclining seat was hard as hell to get in and out of. As Bobby struggled with the straps and handholds, it occurred to him he might be getting too old for this sort of thing.

How long had he been flying fighters? A lifetime of yanking and banking, turning and burning, flying and fighting. He couldn't remember a time when the earth stood still. It all ran together, all the people, places, and planes, adding up to a life in the sky that seemed longer than the time spent on earth. It was certainly more successful, Bobby thought ruefully. He would miss it if it were gone. After all, his first attempt at retirement hadn't exactly worked out as planned.

And how long ago had that been? Fifteen, twenty years? It seemed like just that morning, and it seemed so long ago that it had happened to someone else, not him. Time was a strange thing, especially in Dreamland, where there were no working hours, weekends, or even seasons. The place hummed around the clock, without newspapers or television to punctuate the hours. A place out of time. Another reason he belonged there.

Bobby managed to free himself from the clinging cockpit and crawled wearily down the footholds built into the starboard leading edge extension. Suddenly, an earsplitting Klaxon buzzed through the night. Gold and yellow lights snapped on along the runway. The hangars blazed with sudden luminescence, revealing strange aircraft and equipment, tended by scurrying men.

A dark blue Air Force step-van, almost invisible under its wildly bobbing amber caution lights, roared up beside Bobby's fighter. A tall man in civilian clothes jumped out before the van had stopped completely.

"Hey, Bobby, you'd better take this hummer back to Cactus Flat with the rest of the batplanes," the man said breathlessly. "It's not safe around here."

"Oh, come on, Don. I know the Teal Sparrow people will be pissed, but I'm ..."

"Nobody gives a shit about that now." The man regarded Bobby curiously. "Christ, don't you *know?*"

Bobby scanned the lights of Dreamland, lights he had never seen before. The glare sparked a glint off the blue steel Smith and Wesson .38 his friend now wore on his hip, like a gunfighter. Nobody wore sidearms in Dreamland! The atmosphere of sudden panic was as unsettling as it was unusual.

"No, I don't know," Bobby said. "Tell me."

"We're in DefCon 3," the man sighed. "The Iranians just nuked Baghdad. We're at war, Bobby."

Ready Eagle

**With the 82d Airborne
Over the Gulf of Oman**

History will record that the American invasion of Iran was led by Sgt. William Willis, 1st Platoon, Alpha Company, 1st Battalion (Airborne), 325th Infantry Regiment, 82d Airborne Division.

Willis did not set out to be a hero. He was a good soldier, a veteran, and a career man, but he was not a fool. By virtue of his place in the alphabet and some tactical foot-dragging (parachute harness problems), Willis had managed to remain last in the chalks at every stop so far: Fort Bragg, North Carolina; Lajes Field in the Azores Islands; Ramstein, West Germany; and finally, Masirah Island in Oman. Being last in line meant being first on board, which meant—in a C-130—last out, which is where he wanted to be. It was a small thing, a superstition almost, but, like soldiers throughout history, Willis took faith in superstition as his only proof against the random nature of war.

"Get ready!"

At the jumpmaster's command, Willis checked his gear for the hundredth time. His body armor was already dotted with souvenirs of life at the point. There was no shortage of medals handed out after Grenada and Panama, but the splintered dents on Willis's Kevlar vest carried more weight than a dozen campaign ribbons. The chip across his right shoulder came from a sniper's AK-47 at Point Salines. He had received the crease across the back fighting a BTR-60 at Ross Point. The big dent over his heart was from a 12.7-mm Dushka round picked up in Torrijos. The big bullet had traveled close to a couple of clicks and still nearly went clean through.

Willis kept the flak vest anyway. God knows where he'd get another one, and besides, he knew this one *worked*. There wasn't much war in Grenada, but he had had the bad luck to see all of it, and it was bad enough. Panama was worse. But where they were going, Willis knew, was the real thing. Downtown Ragland. Indian country. This was World War III.

"Outboard personnel, stand up!"

The troopers across the aisle from Willis wobbled to their feet, awkward shapes in the red darkness. The heat, a hundred pounds of gear, and the packed interior of the cabin made it even more difficult than usual to stand in the shake and drone of the overloaded aircraft. The aisle was crowded with paratroopers, many from other units. Half of Alpha Company was still on the ramp at Masirah, elbowed aside by others who felt jumping into certain combat in Iran was preferable to the tense, unpredictable situation they had found in Oman.

"Inboard personnel, stand up!"

Willis heaved upward, the blood-red webbed seat snapping shut behind him. He staggered under the full weight of his responsibility as team leader. His basic load—M-16, with 140 rounds of 5.56-mm ammunition and ninety rounds of red tracer, two smoke grenades, and two LAW antitank rockets— was more than enough to bear in the dreadful heat of an Arabian summer. The rest of Willis's issue was still on the Green Ramp at Fort Bragg, jettisoned as soon as he learned of their destination. He had discovered in Grenada that being hungry and alive was preferable to being out of ammo and dead.

"Hook up!"

They were getting close. Willis was surprised to feel relief. The Hercules had already been airborne much longer than it should have taken to fly from Masirah directly to the Strait of Hormuz. Of course, that route would have taken them across the United Arab Emirates, which, like Oman and Saudi Arabia and the rest of the "friendly" nations of the Persian Gulf, had proven decidedly unfriendly toward the Americans and their new crusade.

"Check static lines!"

Holding the slack of the yellow cord in his right hand, Willis fastened the clip to the wire cable running the length of the fuselage. The line would pull taut as he jumped, jerking the parachute open once he cleared the aircraft.

After more than a hundred jumps, Willis had no doubts the system would work. What would happen after that was another story.

Bandar Abbas, a city on the northern shore of the Strait of Hormuz, is large by Iranian standards. With good port facilities, a military airfield, and a major, modern airport—Bandar Abbas International—it was the only city on the Iranian side of the Strait capable of handling the huge numbers of giant airplanes needed to sustain even small U.S. military operations in the last half of the twentieth century. There was just one problem: The Iranians didn't want to give it up. The United States, meaning the 82d Airborne, meaning Sgt. Bill Willis and too few like him, would have to take it. That was what Operation Ready Eagle was all about.

"Check equipment!"

Willis groped ahead in the dim cabin to check the shrouds and gear of the nearest man. There was no one behind Willis to check his, but that didn't matter. He was good to go, as they say in the 82d. Fired up. Airborne all the way.

"Sound off for equipment check!"

As the last man in the stick, Willis was first to answer the jumpmaster's roll call. "Okay!" he shouted and tapped the man in front to sound off. There was no turning back now.

Willis was relieved to know they were parachuting into Iran. Not that he was anxious to be there in any case, but at Bragg there had been some talk of airlanding at Bandar International, after the two battalions of Rangers had secured the airport. In Grenada, that had almost cost Willis his life. Jumping under fire was certainly dangerous, but at least the whole force landed together, not a planeload at a time like they did at Point Salines. That had enabled the relatively small number of Cubans at the airport to engage the troopers in detail and to put up more of a fight than their numbers deserved.

Willis was grateful for any tactical advantage he could get. Just nine other C-130s trailed behind his, with about a hundred troopers in each. It couldn't be helped—when the bomb went off and the balloon went up, the Division Ready Force was all that could be mustered on such short notice.

It was a decidedly puny force with which to invade a country, but Willis tried not to think about it. He tried not to think about what he had heard at Masirah—that the Rangers, who were supposed to do most of the fighting, were still in their black Hercs, on the ground at Dhahran, forbidden to take off by the Saudi royal family, who were having second thoughts about the enterprise. He tried not to think about the rumors, whispered furtively aboard the 88-pack truck that had carried them to the flight line, that the Russians had already invaded Tehran. And, most of all, he tried not to think about the very real possibility that the Iranians, who had now proven themselves a nuclear power, might have another bomb with his name on it. Willis was not a man given to idle worry about things beyond his control. There was not much he could do about it, in any case, besides shoot straight and watch his back, which he resolved to do.

As the last man responded, the red light turned to yellow. It was the Army's airplane now. The starboard jump door near the end of the aircraft swung open, filling the cabin with airstream noise and bright, unwelcome sunlight. Willis blinked at his watch. Christ, they were almost an hour late! The drop had been scheduled for the hazy twilight of early morning. Now it was 0630. Broad daylight. Bad timing.

The jumpmaster fastened his safety tether and pounded a jump boot solidly on the left side of the aluminum platform to make sure it was secure. Satisfied, he was about to check the right side when he disappeared in a flash of orange and yellow lightning.

A missile had hit the bottom of the aircraft, peeling back the floor and sending shrapnel and flame into the rear of the cabin. Dozens died instantly. More were killed when flaming pieces of metal set off a Dragon missile stowed in its fiberglass canister. The antitank round sizzled through the crowded interior, knocking over men and equipment until it exploded against the port wing root, sending the aircraft into a sharp left turn.

Men screamed, on fire, mortally wounded. There was panic and a push to the front of the aircraft. Willis found himself shoved through the door separating the cabin from the cockpit. There was no way out. He felt something pressing through the bulk of the equipment on his back. It was the folding stairway built into the aircrew exit door.

Quickly, Willis pulled the handle and kicked the hatch open with his heavy jump boot. Light and air swept in, fanning the flames. The crowd pressed harder, tearing away the drop pack containing his M16 and wrenching his shoulder. Willis's sharp, surprised cry of pain went unheard in the noise of panicked, dying men. A full colonel, shouting for calm, was knocked off his feet and trampled in the rush for the only way out.

Willis stuck his head outside and saw the menacing propeller of the inboard port engine churning frightfully close by. Still, the choice between certain death in the flaming airplane and the possibility of death from being chopped up by the propeller was no choice at all.

Willis grabbed both sides of the hatchway and jumped up and out. He didn't get far. In the panic, he had neglected to unfasten his static line. Twisted and tangled, it caught inside the aircraft and wrapped around his right leg. Willis dangled upside down in the airstream, ten feet below the dying airplane, swinging like a pendulum that took him closer and closer to the whirring prop blades.

Willis struggled to reach the shroud knife in his thigh pocket, grabbed it...and dropped it. Ten years in the Airborne had taught him a few things, however—the knife was attached to a line fastened to his chute harness. He pulled the knife up and sawed at the static line.

The lines were designed not to fray or snap. Willis had a new appreciation of that fact as he hacked at the static line. The swinging took him inches from the number two engine and then away again. One more swing and he would be slashed to pieces.

Finally, the knife cut through. Willis banged against the side of the aircraft and out into the blue sky. He was free! Now, would the chute open? He fumbled for the ripcord. The gray canopy of the T-10 parachute snapped out full above him. Good chute.

The jump was planned for 1,250 feet. The C-130 crew had struggled to maintain that height, fighting valiantly with a disintegrating aircraft. It was not a high jump by any means; the Empire State Building is exactly 1,250 feet high. But to Willis it seemed as if he had parachuted from the stratosphere.

He could see everything. His aircraft spun and roared south, disgorging flaming balls that were Willis's comrades. Some had managed to follow him out the forward crew door before it too became clogged and full of fire. The C-130 finally exploded over the Gulf, hissing steam as the pieces fell into the hot, blue water.

The fighter that had shot it down wheeled away, lining up to attack another American transport. Like most paratroopers, Willis hated airplanes and had no real knowledge of them. Still, he knew the plane that had ambushed them was no Iranian fighter. The sky was full of the little gray jets, but they were too far away for Willis to make out their markings.

Streaks of light snaked up from the ground in pulses. Guns, Willis thought. A Navy A-7 rolled into the city, scattered its bombs and streaked away as one of the fighters lined up on its tail. Another A-7 dropped from the sky in flames, the jettisoned canopy glistening in the sun, followed by the whroosh of the ejection seat.

All around him, Willis could see trails of black smoke in the blue morning sky. At least half the C-130s had been hit. Some smashed into the brown desert. Others, spitting smoke and fire, tried to limp back over the Gulf with the fighters buzzing about them like flies. There were a few gray parachutes blossoming now. But not nearly as many, Willis thought sadly, as there should be.

Below, Willis spotted Bandar Abbas International. A smudgy column of smoke rose from a burning airliner, hit on the ground by Navy strikers, blocking the airport's single runway. Other than that, judging from the amount of tracer fire coming from the area, it looked as if the airport had not been touched.

Southeast of the airport, the main highway crossed the Tasbar, dry this time of year. That bridge was Alpha Company's rally point. Willis tugged at the lines of the T-10, nudging the parachute away from the airport.

Willis came down suddenly, with a heavy thud. Rolling quickly to his feet, he blinked to get his bearings. Brown mountains hung in the haze to the north; they could be ten miles or a hundred miles away. Other than that, except for the shallow depression of the Tasbar *wadi* and a clutch of low shacks along the highway, the place was absolutely flat, absolutely hot, and absolutely worthless. So this was Iran! The notion that anyone would fight to get *into* this country struck Willis as a cruel, but nonetheless hilarious, soldier's joke.

Gathering his parachute, he heard a scurrying noise in the dry riverbed. He flattened himself on the dry, scorched surface, reached for his weapon— and realized it had been ripped away in the panic aboard the aircraft!

Defenseless, with no place to hide or run, Willis unsheathed his Randall knife and clambered to his feet. *Might as well face them man to man,* he thought, and saw, instead, a small boy and a dirty yellow dog staring up at him with intense interest. Willis and the boy were black; that surprised both of them.

Out of immediate danger, hot and sore but giddy with relief, Willis realized the absurdity of his one-man invasion.

"I'm Sergeant William Willis of the crack 82d Airborne!" he shouted at the boy. "Surrender or die!"

The boy stood, transfixed.

"I mean it! You're invaded! Get out of here, or I'll shoot you as soon as I find my gun."

The boy disappeared. Willis wrapped up his chute and peeled off his harness. His shoulder felt like it was on fire. He was about to set off for the rally point when the boy reappeared with a cup of water. He offered it to Willis, who shook his head and laughed.

"You know, son, we have a saying in the Airborne: 'fubar.' It means 'fucked up beyond all recognition.' That's what Operation Ready Eagle is. It's fubar."

The boy nodded, uncomprehending, smiling shyly at the giant American who had fallen from the sky. Willis trudged toward the highway to find what was left of 1st Platoon. Over his shoulder, he said: "Of course, we have another saying for anybody who complains: 'fido'—fuck it, drive on."

The boy watched the soldier's back as he walked away. As Willis trudged off to link up with the remains of the tiny invasion force, he could hear the boy softly form the words.

"Fido," the boy whispered to Willis. American for good bye.

Rules of Engagement

Ghostrider Flight
Over the Arabian Sea

"MiGs? Did he say MiGs?"

Lt. Scooter Jeffries was not having a good day. Torn from a short sleep after flying night CAP for *Eisenhower* and Task Force Bravo, Jeffries had been given a cursory briefing (which answered no important questions) and shoved back into the Tomcat's cockpit. Flung out over the Tropic of Cancer, he was getting his mission orders in bits and pieces from Crown, the controlling agency aboard one of the carrier wing's E-2C radar planes orbiting above the Persian Gulf. The more he heard, the less he liked.

In the back seat of the F-14, Lt. Cmdr. Don "Daffy" Brewer, equally perplexed and apprehensive, tried to get some answers. As "Ghostrider 1," VF-142's squadron commander, Brewer was supposed to be on the inside. But no one seemed to know what was going on up at Bandar Abbas, and that was scary.

"Crown, this is Ghostrider 12. Confirm MiGs at Point Lima."

The word came back loud and clear, but neither Jeffries nor Brewer could believe what they were hearing.

"Roger, Ghostrider 12. We confirm six, possibly more, bandits, 350 degrees, bull's-eye for 130 miles. Various speeds and altitudes—it's a real furball up there."

"Christ," Jeffries muttered into the intercom. "Ask him what *kind* of MiGs, Daffy."

"Crown, Ghostrider 12. Can you ID the bandits at Point Lima?"

"Roger, Ghostrider 12. MiGs are Fulcrums. I say again: Fulcrums."

Fulcrums! MiG-29s, the hottest, newest fighters in the Soviet inventory. Jeffries suddenly began to sweat beneath his gray skullcap and heavy helmet. Where the hell did they come from? Nobody said anything about MiGs, let alone Fulcrums!

"You copy that, Ghostrider 13?"

Jeffries's wingman, Speedo Wallace, was a "nugget," a pilot on his first cruise. Speedo had had a hard enough time landing on the carrier lately; it was no wonder he had been left behind when most of *Ike*'s fighters went out on the first wave. Now, when it was really going to hit the fan, they had scraped the bottom of the barrel. There were more than two dozen fighter pilots assigned to Carrier Air Wing Seven. Flying into combat outnumbered and outgunned, Jeffries would rather have any one of them flying his wing. Anyone but Wallace.

"Copy, Ghostrider lead."

Jeffries could hear the tension in the young pilot's voice.

"Okay, Speedo, turn right for 340 now."

The flight had been heading almost due west since leaving the carrier, to avoid the Iranian radar site at Chah Bahar. The new course would lead them up the eastern coast of the United Arab Emirates and over the tip of Oman. And into what?

Muscat was rough and golden in the early morning sun. Jeffries stared as Jabal Majhar, the tallest mountain on the Arabian peninsula, slid by the port wing. Soon there was no mainland, just a crescent of bright blue water dotted with brown islands. The Strait of Hormuz.

How many times, in how many war games, Jeffries wondered, had he pretended to be here, in exactly this situation? The last Top Gun scenario was, supposedly, as close as you could get to the Gulf without provoking an international incident. Jeffries had to laugh. This was the real thing. There was no way to simulate fear, that mixture of aggression and apprehension only a shooting war can create. That was Iran underneath the canopy, not San Diego or Pensacola. And those weren't Americans out there, in little F-5s and A-4s, pretending to be big bad Russians. There were Fulcrums. And Russian or not, the pucker factor was off the scale. So much for realistic training. Jeffries had graduated Top Gun with flying colors. He'd be happy to get out of this scenario flying, period.

"Ghostrider 12, this is Crown." The raspy voice of the Hawkeye's controller interrupted Jeffries's reverie. "I've got two bogies splitting off and heading your way."

"Copy, Crown." In the backseat, Brewer had been peering into the F-14's radar screen, trying to sneak an advance look at what they were up against. But the Tomcat's powerful radar, built for use over water, had a difficult time picking out the gaggle of low targets in the clutter of returns from the ground at extreme ranges. The E-2C, with its more powerful radar, tracked the bogies and sent their positions to the F-14 via data link; the two computer-generated symbols, transmitted by Link 4A, appeared on Brewer's tactical information display as arrows. The point of the arrows showed the Fulcrums' actual locations. The shafts symbolized their velocity vectors— heading and time within missile range. The arrows were frighteningly short.

Jeffries's smaller radar scope mirrored the backseater's screen. The two green arrows separated themselves from the blur of shifting radar targets and sliced toward the bottom of the scope, splitting right and left to bracket Ghostrider flight. First move tactics, Jeffries thought. These were no ordinary MiG drivers.

"Ghostrider 13, drop tanks and split high-low."

Jeffries could feel the aircraft lift suddenly as he jettisoned the auxiliary fuel tanks. The two gray cylinders dropped from the F-14's belly, twirling in the slipstream. They fell to the brown beach thousands of feet below as Ghostrider flight went "feet dry." They had entered Iran.

"Hang on, Daffy. I'm going buster."

Jeffries's gloved left hand shoved the twin throttles forward, then jogged them to the side and forward again, into afterburner. The big Tomcat shuddered as fuel spit in the path of the burning jet exhausts ignited, literally blowing the aircraft across the sky. Jeffries pulled back on the stick. The F-14's nose rose into the sun like a rocket. Time to go to work. Time to go to war.

The Gs dug in as Ghostrider 12 went ballistic. The Tomcat's swinging wings were pinned back. Jeffries's plan was to build up as much speed as possible going into the "merge," where the hunter and the hunted were so close together they appeared as a single blip on the radar screen. He wasn't about to slow down and hassle it out with the MiGs, not when he could use the F-14's superior radar and longer-ranged missiles to pick off the Fulcrums from a distance.

In the back, Brewer strained to keep his eyes on the tactical informa-tion display. It was an effort to lift his head under four times the weight of gravity. In his blurred vision, the radar intercept officer saw two more blips appear at the top of the screen.

"Ah, Scooter, we've got another pair of bogies coming right after these two," Brewer grunted.

Jeffries wondered if Speedo Wallace had picked up the other flight of Fulcrums. And if he had, did he have the sense to keep blowing through without turning? Jeffries flipped the Tomcat over and looked through the top of the canopy toward the ground.

"Ah, crap! Speedo!"

Jeffries watched in horror as his wingman's aircraft pulled into a high-G conversion, lining up behind one of the first pair of Fulcrums. The MiG flipped over, diving for the deck. Another Fulcrum slid in behind Speedo Wallace and punched off a missile. The heat seeker snaked white smoke and bright flame, running straight up Speedo's starboard engine. Before Jeffries could warn his wingman, the F-14 exploded in a black-and-red ball of fire. There were no chutes.

Jeffries pulled back on the stick, looping down behind the MiG that had killed Ghostrider 13. It was, to Jeffries, a terribly beautiful aircraft, pearl gray with its two vertical tails painted a surprising solid black. The Fulcrum tilted up on a wing and broke toward the right. Still in burner and gaining energy from the dive, Jeffries extended to the west. The Tomcat went supersonic with a deafening boom miles behind. Jeffries was hurtling in the wrong direction, but, alone and outnumbered, he was not about to slow down to fight it out with the more maneuverable MiGs.

"Scooter, check fuel state."

Christ, Jeffries thought, I'm fighting for my life and my RIO is nagging me about gas. He glanced down at the gauges by his right knee, shocked to find he was bingo fuel already. Just enough to get them back to the *Eisenhower,* but not enough to fight *and* get back home. Blazing around the sky in afterburner without the belly tanks really ate up fuel. That had never been a problem at Top Gun. Now it could mean the difference between flying or swimming back to the boat.

Jeffries pulled out of burner and selected zone five, maximum military power.

"Okay, Daffy, talk to me. Where are they?"

Brewer looked at his scope, then cranked his head around the cockpit, searching the sky in sections.

"The one that got Speedo is three miles back and fading. He's heading for home, no threat."

Home, Jeffries thought. Where's that? Where did these MiGs come from, anyway?

"The other bandit that dragged Speedo for the kill is down in the clutter," Brewer continued. "I don't know where he is, but it's going to take him a while to climb back up. Unless we fly right over him and he pops one off, he's—*Break left, now!*"

Jeffries instinctively honked the F-14 to the left. Fighting the Gs to look over his shoulder, he could see what Brewer had warned him about—a small, lethal gray needle on the end of a sparkler. Heat seeker, max range! Jeffries hit the IR bump button on the throttle, launching an infrared countermeasure. The cartridge shot out from between the Tomcat's exhausts, a bright flare, beckoning the enemy missile away from the aircraft's engines with its greater heat.

Jeffries straightened, wings level, then shoved the F-14 into a hard turn in the opposite direction. The MiG's missile sniffed at the IR flare, began to drift toward it, then headed straight for the Tomcat again.

"Shit, it's not working!" Brewer screamed. "Do it again!"

Jeffries punched off two more flares and zoomed into a stiff climb. The missile nosed up, then flew hesitantly between the two flares and out to the horizon.

"Christ, that was close, Daffy. Where is he?"

Sore and chafing in the harness, Brewer strained to look for the Fulcrum. He scoured the curved sky through the canopy, desperately hoping to find the MiG before it got off another shot.

"There he is! I've got him! Seven o'clock low!"

"Has he got his nose on us?"

"Not yet, but he's converting." Brewer's breath over the intercom was hard and labored. "Damn it, Scooter. There's another one behind him!"

Exhausted and scared, Jeffries cast about for a plan of action. They didn't teach things like this at the Naval Fighter Weapons School. Ghostrider 12 was lost and alone. The sky was full of hostile aircraft that were, in many ways, superior to his own. He was fast running out of gas; it now looked as if the Tomcat could barely make it to Oman, let alone the carrier. In seconds the MiG would make its run, and there was little Jeffries could do about it. The high-G maneuvering and return to altitude had robbed the F-14 of most of its energy. Its variable-geometry wings, computer-controlled for maximum aerodynamic efficiency, were now almost fully forward, proclaiming to the world Ghostrider 12's status as a panting aerodog, a flying grape.

"Daffy, we've got to get some help up here. Call Crown. See if he can at least get us a tanker out in the Gulf."

Still staring back at the menacing MiGs, Brewer keyed the radio.

"Crown, this is Ghostrider 12. Any friendlies inbound? Anyone want to share a kill?"

Jeffries could hear ironic laughter at Brewer's sad joke.

"Negative, Ghostrider. We've got a flight of F-14s coming up the slot and a tanker behind them, but nothing that can help out anytime soon. Crown out."

That's just great, Jeffries thought. The armed forces of the United States, with their thousands of airplanes, had none to spare for a shooting war. There was nothing to do but keep heading west and wait for the MiG to make its move.

It was strangely quiet. The hum of the engines and the air conditioner's hiss faded into the background. Jeffries could clearly hear his own labored breathing through the oxygen mask, the nagging sound of his own mortality. So much for the spirit of aggression! He couldn't understand it. He had followed all the rules, and this was where that got him: dragging a MiG across the brown mountains of southern Iran. It was time for the Last Best Move.

The gray MiG swooped up and in, leveling its wings. Jeffries shoved the throttles into afterburner once again (what did gas matter now?), flipped the Tomcat over, and dove for the ground. Perhaps the enemy pilot wouldn't be able to get a lock if the missile's infrared seeker could be distracted by the heat of the desert below. Perhaps the Fulcrum would not have the energy or its pilot the guts to follow Ghostrider 12 down in the dirt. Jeffries doubted either case, but he planned to go down fighting.

"He's still coming, Scooter."

Jeffries looked back. The tiny MiG looked suddenly enormous, though still more than a mile away. He could launch any time now, Scooter thought. He's just waiting until I pull up for a clear shot. Why not? That's what I would do. There's no other Yankees around—he can afford to take his time.

Brewer and Jeffries sweated as the altimeter wound down: twenty thousand feet, fifteen thousand feet, ten thousand feet. The desert rose to meet them. There was no way out.

"SAM launch!" Brewer shouted. "Scooter, I've got a valid SAM, three o'clock. Looks like a HAWK!"

A plume of brown dust rose from the mountain haze north of Bandar Abbas. Jeffries's eyes followed the missile as it rocketed straight up, losing it in the sun. He knew it would be back. Unlike most surface-to-air missiles, the American-made HAWK flew up, then swooped down on its prey. It was, Jeffries knew, almost impossible to outfly, given his current altitude and energy state.

"Daffy, can you jam it?"

"Negative. It's not responding." Brewer fidgeted furiously with the electronic countermeasures controls. "I don't recognize the codes—they must be using Israeli guidance protocols. I've never seen anything like it."

"Well, we've got to do something," Jeffries said. "Here it comes."

A tiny white speck flickered in the high sun. The HAWK began its final run. Long red lights shot past the canopy. Tracers! Cranking his head around painfully, Scooter could clearly see the MiG, its cannon sparking fire from the port wing root. Jeffries had forgotten about the Fulcrum, which had closed to gun range, the enemy pilot sacrificing the chancy missile shot for the satisfaction of a cannon kill.

Ghostrider 12 was in it deep, out of airspeed, altitude, and ideas.

"Hang on tight, Daffy. I'm going to try something."

Jeffries shoved the Tomcat into a tight right turn, nose down to pick up a little fast-bleeding energy. His world shrank and lost color as the Gs drove blood from his head down into his knees. In the back, Brewer slumped into momentary unconsciousness under the weight of more than nine times the force of gravity.

As Jeffries pulled out of the turn, he looked back to see the Fulcrum spit out to the east by the suddenness of the violent maneuver. The MiG pilot recovered quickly, pulling a maximum-performance turn into the Tomcat. Long funnels of condensed air streamed from the Fulcrum's wing roots as it shot through the dense Gulf atmosphere. Jeffries was surprised and dismayed by the agility of the newest Soviet fighter. He was the first American fighter jock to get a good look at the Fulcrum in combat, and he didn't like what he saw.

The MiG pulled closer. Above, the HAWK continued its slow, hypnotic spiral toward Ghostrider 12.

"Daffy, I hate to say it, old buddy, but I think this is the end of the line," Jeffries said. "Better get ready to punch out."

Suddenly the cockpit was flooded with a light brighter than the Arabian sun. Were they hit? Jeffries curled his fingers around the cold ejection-seat handle, then released his grip when he saw there were no warning lights active on the instrument panel.

He turned his head to see the MiG in flames, falling from the sky with its right wing severed. The missile was gone.

"Well, what do you know?" Jeffries sighed. "That HAWK was locked on the Fulcrum all the time. The Iranians are on our side!"

"I wouldn't be too sure about that," Brewer said. "I think they're just shooting at anything that moves."

"Let's not stick around to find out," Jeffries said. "I'm getting out of here."

Down to less than five hundred feet now, the Tomcat screamed over the flat roofs of Bandar Abbas. Jeffries pulled a hard right to avoid a radio-transmission tower next to the coast highway. In seconds they would be back over the Gulf and in relative safety.

"Scooter, I've got multiple bogies, dead ahead."

"Jesus, Daffy, we're almost home!"

"Tell me about it."

"Who are they? MiGs?"

"Can't tell yet." Brewer peered over the tactical information display. "I'm getting too much clutter from the ground at this altitude, even when I steer the dish up as many bars as it will go."

"What are they squawking?"

"Nothing." The planes refused to respond when Brewer attempted to interrogate their IFF systems. "Nobody's squawking anything up here. This is war."

"What does Crown say?"

"Crown can't say shit this low, Scooter. You know that. He needs line of sight for the data link, and there are too many buildings around."

"Well, I'm not climbing. Those MiGs will find us and eat our lunch." Jeffries sounded frightened. It was almost all he could do to keep from colliding with the rooftops and power lines that blurred beneath the belly of Ghostrider 12.

"Screw it. I'm just going to hose a Sparrow into them. That'll get their attention." Jeffries flicked the armament panel to select an AIM-7 radar missile. "Lock 'em up for me, Daffy."

The voice from the rear seat sounded distant, troubled.

"Ah, I can't do that, Scooter."

"What's the problem? Something broken?"

"Rules of engagement. You know we're not supposed to shoot at anything we can't see."

"Daffy, are you nuts? We're all alone up here, and these guys are trying to kill us! If we wait to get a visual on those MiGs, they'll see us, too. And we haven't got the gas to screw around with them. We're practically running on fumes, as it is."

"Hey, I know, okay? It's a dick dance, Scooter, but orders are orders."

"Screw it. I'm going boresight, then." Jeffries switched the radar to PLM mode. He would have to line up the target directly on the Tomcat's nose, but it was the only mode that would allow him to fire a radar-guided missile without his backseater's cooperation.

"Scooter, listen to me." Brewer was calm, authoritative. "You may be the aircraft commander, but I am the senior officer on this flight."

"Look, Daffy, if we wait until we can see them, they'll be all over us," Jeffries protested. "I don't like those odds, not against Fulcrums. I'm good, but I'm no Bobby Dragon. If I ..."

"Shut up!" Brewer's voice over the intercom crackled with sudden, un-characteristic rage.

Jeffries's hand shook on the stick. He desperately wanted to punch off the missile. It wasn't self-defense. It was aggression. Jeffries was sick and tired of being shot at. He wanted to shoot back. He thought again of Top Gun, of his humiliation at the hands of the instructors during the first week. Oh, they had been very polite, very professional, taking care to defuse the situation by referring to the plane, not the pilot; it was not Jeffries who had made those bonehead plays but rather "the F-14," which had suddenly become sentient, though apparently not intelligent enough to keep its human crewmen, and their wingmen, alive.

Hell! Losing always hurt. Here it would be permanent. Why wait? Jeffries had these guys dead to rights. He had them skylined over the Gulf, no clutter, perfect parameters, and he was invisible, lost in scenery at sea level. You couldn't ask for a better shot.

Jeffries fought another battle in his head. In the end, his training won out. The Navy asks a lot of its pilots. Sometimes in war the hardest thing to do is *not* to kill. Jeffries's hand relaxed on the pipper.

"Screw it. They're almost within minimum range anyway. But keep your eyes out, Daffy. As soon as we see bad wings, I'm throwing a Sidewinder down their snot locker; I don't care what you say."

"Fair enough," Brewer sighed. "Here they come."

Ghostrider 12 went feet wet, zooming back over the Gulf and leaving Bandar Abbas behind at five hundred miles an hour. Jeffries pulled back slightly on the stick. A gaggle of dots appeared on the horizon. The closest one sprouted wings.

"I can't tell yet ..." Brewer said.

"I can! Look, Daffy! Twin tails! Look at those intakes! They're Fulcrums." Jeffries flicked the weapons selector to "heat." "I'm engaging."

"No, Scooter, wait a minute." Brewer grabbed the handhold above the instrument panel, straining to make out the ragged black shapes over Scooter's shoulder. "Hold your fire! They're our planes, from the *Ike*. Don't shoot!"

"... rider 12. Do you copy?" Now over the clear, unobstructed Gulf, Crown's transmission faded in through the static. "The MiGs have all bugged out. Be advised Devil flight is at your twelve o'clock. Weapons tight. Do not fire. Do you copy?"

Jeffries slumped exhaustedly in the front seat.

"Crown, this is Ghostrider 12," Brewer said with relief. "We copy you now. Weapons tight. Is there a tanker with Devil?"

"Roger, Ghostrider 12. He's out front, call sign Anchor 6. Call him on button four."

"Thanks, Crown. Ghostrider 12, out." Brewer changed radio frequencies to contact the KA-6 tanker. "Anchor 6, this is Ghostrider 12. Do you copy?"

"Ghostrider, Anchor. We copy and we've got a visual on you. Come straight on. We'll do a slow turn to port and then head out due south at 180 degrees. Hook up at your discretion."

"Thanks, Anchor. Hold on; we'll be there in a second." Brewer switched back to intercom. "Okay, Scooter, looks like we'll get back to the boat after all. Just hit the basket on the first try. That's all I ask."

There was silence from the front seat.

"Come on, Scooter..." Brewer tried to sound calm. "Turn to 180. Let's go home."

Still no response.

"Scooter..."

"Bullshit!" Brewer's headphones rang with Jeffries's epithet. "It's not fair, Daffy! It just isn't fair! We've had our ass chased around the sky all day, nearly got killed a couple of times, and for what? What the hell's going on here? Who are those guys? Where did they come from? How come no one told us about those MiGs? I can't believe nobody in the whole goddamned United States government knew there'd be a squadron of Fulcrums waiting to ambush us up here, but they let it happen anyway."

Brewer waited while the young pilot let off steam. The same questions had occurred to him during the flight, just as they had bothered him in other flights, in another time, over a faraway place called North Vietnam. It was a different war for Brewer, in a different airplane and a different uniform, but now, as then, asking questions was a luxury, an indulgence visited only upon those who managed to concentrate on their jobs enough to stay alive.

"I'm with you, Scooter. Somebody's got a lot of explaining to do. But there aren't any answers up here. They're all on the ground. Let's go home, okay?"

"Yeah, but why did they send us up here alone?"

"That's enough, Lieutenant," Brewer said sharply. "Let's get back to business. How much fuel have we got?"

Jeffries thought it odd Brewer would ask such a question, since an RIO (radar intercept officer) had a fuel gauge of his own on his instrument panel. A quick glance brought Jeffries back to reality. A hundred pounds left. Enough to get an F-14 across the street. Barely.

"Okay, Anchor, we're coming in," Brewer radioed the tanker. "Hold it steady. We've only got enough gas for one pass."

"Don't worry about us, Ghostrider." The tanker pilot's voice sounded warm and welcoming. "Have you ever seen a gas station move?"

Jeffries flew steadily. The big wings of the Intruder, rigged for air-to-air refueling, spread across the Tomcat's canopy. The fuel gauges read completely empty. The F-14 shuddered slightly as Jeffries popped the air refueling probe into the slipstream. Just a little more, Jeffries pleaded. Just hold on.

The fuel line dangled enticingly on a basket floating in the airstream. The line led to a tank on the KA-6's starboard wing, a huge tank full of precious fuel. Jeffries flew the Tomcat's probe slowly but unerringly toward the basket. One chance was all they would get. Fifty feet. Twenty-five feet. Ten feet...

"Damn!" Brewer exploded. "Scooter, I've got a valid launch!"

"Yeah, me too," the tanker pilot said. "It's a HAWK!"

"Not now," Jeffries cried. "I'm almost there."

"We can hold out for a little while, since you guys are so hard up," the tanker pilot said nervously. "It doesn't look like the missile's locked onto anybody yet, so..."

Wham! The HAWK hit the tanker right in the belly. The fuel ignited in a huge fireball, disintegrating the KA-6 in a shower of sparks and flaming metal. Ghostrider 12 was blown away from the explosion, flipped backward and down toward the Gulf in a slow spin.

Oil pressure diving, temperature reading off the red—Jeffries knew he was in trouble. The master caution light glared from the instrument panel. The systems lights flared, too, then burned out as fire crawled up the underside of the fuselage.

Jeffries tried resetting the circuit breakers. No go. Smoke was pouring into the cockpit now. Automatically, he blew the big canopy. A blizzard of papers beat past his helmet as the slipstream roared past. It was still getting hotter. He couldn't see the fire, but he could feel it. He could feel it spreading.

"I'm going to have to shut it down, Daffy." Jeffries hoped his backseater could still hear him. "We've still got one good engine. We'll get to the water for sure."

Jeffries knew he was lying, knew Brewer knew he was lying, too. The F-14 was beginning to shake apart, with the fire spread to both engines now. Most of the power had gone from the controls. Jeffries fought hard to keep heading south, out to the Gulf and safety.

A shudder, and the Tomcat slid a thousand feet down. Jeffries knew they would never make it. He fought to keep it straight and level. There was a roar like a rocket behind him.

"Okay, partner, time to go," he said, reaching up with both hands to grab the black-and-yellow face-curtain handles that would trigger the ejection sequence. "Will eject, eject, eject!"

That was their code— "eject" three times (a single mention of the word might have come up in casual conversation). No word from the backseat. Jeffries was running out of time.

"Daffy, I said eject! now. We're going down. Don't be a hero."

With an effort, Jeffries cranked his neck around to look behind him. There was no one there. The man, the seat, everything was gone. Gray, acrid smoke from the ejection rocket filled the suddenly spacious rear cockpit.

"Damn!" Jeffries said, just before the plane plunged into the Persian Gulf. "Damn, he didn't even wait for me."

On Gonzo Station

Aboard the USS *Eisenhower*
Arabian Sea

I say nuke 'em."

"What?"

"You heard me. I say nuke 'em. Nuke 'em till they glow."

Rear Adm. Sam Meredith couldn't believe what he was hearing. It must have been the stress and fatigue—after all, both he and Maj. Gen. Curtis Coleman had been up for more than twenty-four hours. And the Division Ready Force—the advance guard of Coleman's 82d Airborne Division—had been chewed up badly at Bandar Abbas. There were many casualties.

Then, too, Coleman was not a young man, and it had been a long, rough journey from Fort Bragg, North Carolina, to an aircraft carrier on the other side of the world. Coleman had hoped to spend the evening with his men at Bandar Abbas or, at the very least, at the forward command post he had expected to establish at Masirah. Now, like so many things taken for granted in Operation Ready Eagle, those plans would never be realized. No one wanted to say what needed to be said, that Ready Eagle was finished, a complete debacle, with nothing else to take its place.

"Will you excuse us for a moment, gentlemen?" Meredith nodded toward the hatch guarded by a Marine sergeant. The *Eisenhower*'s skipper and his executive officer joined Coleman's staff as they filed out of the flag quarters. The Marine guard stepped out and secured the hatch from the outside. Meredith turned angrily toward Coleman.

"You're out of line, General."

Coleman slumped back in his chair with his arms tightly folded across his chest. "Am I? Look what they did at Baghdad. You want to sit around on your ass and wait until they nuke my boys up at Bandar Abbas?"

Meredith flicked an imaginary piece of dirt from his immaculate white uniform. "The intelligence folks say they have only enough stuff for one bomb."

"And you believe that?" Coleman snorted. "These are the same geniuses who told us Iran didn't have the bomb in the first place."

Meredith shrugged.

"No, I say send in the boomers, Admiral. The world will thank us."

"You know I can't do that," Meredith said. "I can't give that kind of order."

"Who can? The president? You wait long enough and there won't *be* a president. We'll all be taking orders from the surgeon general. I tell you something has to be done."

"And I'm telling you I can't do it."

Coleman stood up stiffly, his rumpled olive drab fatigues and grizzled face looking out of place in the luxury of the admiral's in-port cabin. Coleman searched for a window and was surprised to find nothing but mirrors. That was the Navy for you. He looked into a mirror and saw an old man, an old soldier. There was a time he would have been with his men, no matter what it took. That was where he wanted to be now, danger be damned. But his men were scattered from the Mediterranean to the Persian Gulf. Some of them were dying at Bandar Abbas. And he was trapped aboard a Navy ship, listening to Navy men tell him there was nothing he could do. That hurt the most.

"Russians," Coleman said softly, almost to himself. "Nobody said anything about Russians. I would never have gone along with this stupid plan if I knew there was the slightest chance of Soviet fighters over the drop zone."

"I know how you feel, but ..."

"Do you?" Coleman wheeled angrily to face Meredith. "I don't think so. Those aren't your men down there. They're mine. And we'll lose the whole force unless you put up some air cover right now."

"I'm doing that." Meredith glanced at the video monitor mounted on the overhead, tuned to the Pilot Landing Aid Television channel.

On the flight deck, an F-14 was being prepared to launch off a waist catapult. The jet-blast deflector rose in sections behind it. A tiny figure ran from beneath the plane. The fighter roared off in a blast of steam and flame. Vibrations from the launch shook all the way to the flag quarters. On the screen, another F-14 rolled forward to take its place on the catapult.

"It's a little late now, Admiral. Where were you this morning?"

"We were there, damnit! We followed the plan to the letter."

"Oh, come on," Coleman said mockingly. "Two jets?"

"We had half the wing in the air at sunup. Where were you?"

"You know we had that problem getting out of Oman."

"That's not my problem, General," Meredith snapped. "This is an aircraft carrier, not the Tactical Air Command. We're doing cyclic ops out here— I've got to launch and recover my planes strictly according to schedule or else half of them will run out of fuel before the other half gets to the catapults. Ready Eagle calls for..."

"Forget about Ready Eagle!" Coleman growled. "That dog won't hunt. We're on our own out here. The only thing I'm interested in now is how you're going to keep my men alive in Iran until we can get some real help up there."

Meredith ran stubby fingers through his neat, steel-gray hair. He did not want to argue with Coleman. Navy admirals weren't used to arguing with anyone; they were accustomed to being obeyed. But the command structure, like the rest of Ready Eagle, was an ambiguous mess—everyone was in charge; no one was responsible. Both he and Coleman wore two stars. The chain of command for Ready Eagle gave them equal authority, a joint command. Meredith knew there was no such thing.

He checked his watch. The liaison from Washington was overdue. Meredith knew it was important that he appear to have everything under control or else control would be taken away from him. Perhaps he could convince Coleman of the logic of making Ready Eagle a Navy show from now on. If not, he was prepared to take his case to Washington.

Meredith stepped up to a big map of the Persian Gulf mounted on a bulkhead in the flag quarters.

"This is where we are." He pointed to a circle where the Gulf of Oman flowed into the Arabian Sea. "We call it Gonzo Station. We've been parking ships out here for decades. There's a cruiser, the *Valley Forge,* right next to us, and a couple of guided-missile destroyers and frigates spread out around the horizon. I need to keep them close, in case we run into trouble out here.

"I'm sending the task force's other cruiser, *Biddle,* and a destroyer, the *Charles Adams,* up in the strait to give you fire support tonight. But if the MiGs come back and we can't provide the ships with enough air cover up there, I'm going to have to withdraw them at first light."

To preserve the element of surprise, there had been no Navy ships in the Strait of Hormuz that morning. The Pentagon had expected the 82d to meet only light resistance. Apparently, no one had counted on the lack of cooperation in the Gulf or even considered the possibility of hostile fighters over the drop zone.

"What do you mean you might not be able to give them enough air cover?" Coleman asked. "You've got a hundred aircraft on this carrier!"

"I know that sounds like a lot, General, but you've got to take a couple of things into consideration."

"Like what?"

"Like a lot of them don't work, which is not unusual for this late in the cruise," Meredith answered. "And about a quarter of the ones that do are dedicated to antisubmarine work, which may not concern you much, but subs scare the hell out of me this close to shore. Those diesel boats can hide along the coast, run out, and pop off a couple of fish before you can get a fix on them. And there are a lot of people around here who would just love to do that."

Coleman thought about the trouble the 82d had had that morning with the Omanis, who were, nominally, America's strongest allies in the Gulf. If the British government hadn't intervened, the Division Ready Force would probably still be sitting on the runway at Masirah. Considering what had happened since, that would probably have been the best thing for all concerned.

Coleman shook his head. It didn't matter now. What was done was done. Fido! They had a mission and they had to get on with it or die trying. But Coleman was damned if he would let his men die alone.

"That still leaves you with about fifty fighters and attack aircraft, Admiral," Coleman said in challenge. "Where were they?"

"Oh, they were up." Meredith tried to keep calm. "Remember, Ready Eagle called for a drop right at daybreak, which means we had to take off and sanitize the drop zones before sunup. The only aircraft we've got that can reliably bomb strange targets in the dark are A-6s, and we've only got eight or nine working right now. I'm supposed to keep half of those in reserve for nuclear delivery, on orders from the National Command Authority. Don't forget, we're still in DefCon 3. It's been less than forty-eight hours since the bomb went off.

"Even so, I sent four Intruders up to Bandar Abbas International to keep the Iranians' heads down while your men landed. Believe me, if it weren't for those crews, you would have had an even tougher drop than you did this morning. The Iranians had a lot more antiaircraft assets in Bandar Abbas than we thought they had. As it was, I sent four A-6s up there, plus a KA-6 tanker. Only two came back. I can't afford to lose any more. If it really comes down to us and the Russians, I'm going to need every Intruder I've got."

"I understand. You've got to protect your ships," Coleman said grudgingly. "But what about the A-7s? You've got two squadrons of those."

Meredith nodded.

"That's only two dozen planes, but sure, they can help. They do a good job with close air support, which is what you need most right now. As soon as the reports started coming in about how hot it was at Bandar Abbas and how you were going to be late, I ordered the Corsairs armed and launched, and they've been launching ever since," Meredith said. "But it's a tough call, General. They're great little bombers, but they're old and slow. The MiGs will eat them up alive if I send them in without fighter cover. We lost three this morning."

Coleman tried to tally the losses in his head. The A-6, he knew, had two crewmen. The A-7 was a single seater....

"Seven men, General." Meredith knew what Coleman was thinking. "Not counting the two from the Tomcat we know are dead. There are a couple more F-14 crewmen out there somewhere. One of the Tomcats going in saw two good chutes, but that's the last we've heard of them. And there may still be some A-7 pilots floating in the Gulf, but it's too dangerous to send a helo in there until sundown."

"We've got to have close air support," Coleman said. "But what we really needed up there this morning was fighter escort. Where were your Tomcats?"

Meredith grew suddenly angry.

"Here!" he stabbed at the Iranian city of Shiraz on the map. "And here!" he pointed at Char Bahar. "And here!" Büshehr. "And here!" Aghajari.

"The brains who drew up this operation swore to me the Iranians wouldn't risk the few fighters they had left if we capped their airfields, which we did." Meredith spat. "They laughed when I asked about Russian fighters. They said all the MiG bases were too far away to get to us, and besides, they said, the Soviets didn't want any trouble with the U.S. They just want their half of Iran."

Coleman took it all in. He knew about the Russians in northern Iran. Almost before the radioactive dust had settled on Baghdad, two Soviet airborne divisions had parachuted into northern Iran to seize the airfield at Ghale Morghi outside Tehran. The Soviet intervention, a complete departure from the chairman's recent moves for normalizing relations with the West, had shocked and disturbed the world almost as much as the Iranian bomb. Perhaps the Russians thought an invasion would preempt the Americans from taking action in the Gulf. Perhaps they had already struck a deal with the U.S. government to divvy up Iran. Whatever the scenario, they had made no moves to halt the American invasion on the coast. Until the MiGs came.

"Anyway, by the time the Fulcrums attacked, most of our fighters had already begun to run out of fuel and were heading back to the boat. The plans called for a continuous combat air patrol over Bandar Abbas International all day. We figured two F-14s would be enough, since the only Iranian warplanes permanently stationed there are P-3s—subchasers. A two-plane section was on its way to relieve the CAP when it ran into the MiGs. One F-14 was shot down by the Fulcrums. We're not sure what happened to the other Tomcat. We think it collided with a tanker."

Coleman shook his head.

"Where did those MiGs come from, anyway?"

"I'd feel a lot better if I knew that, General. Until we can get some hard answers, I think we'd better make plans to withdraw."

"You mean retreat?" Coleman was shocked. "We just got here!"

"Look, I'm sitting out here right off the coast where anybody can get to me. I'm trying to keep the subs away, keep the Russian surface ships off my tail, keep your men covered, control the airspace over the Gulf *and* over the battle group. And now we're faced with a demonstrably hostile and capable enemy of unknown proportions." Meredith drew a breath. "Yes, I'd say it was time for a strategic withdrawal."

Coleman slumped in his chair and sighed. "I'd hate to think those boys died for nothing this morning."

"Believe me, General, more men will die for a lot less if we don't back up and sort out what's going on around here. The concept of power projection is fine as long as no one shoots back. But you know and I know it's a bluff. It was just dumb luck the *Ike* was here and not on its way back to San Diego. We just simply don't have the firepower to fight a real war on the other side of the world. Certainly not on a moment's notice."

Coleman reflected for a moment. He had never really thought using nuclear weapons was the answer—he had just wanted to light a fire under Meredith to get more cooperation. Coleman hadn't dreamed the admiral was seriously considering withdrawal, not with American soldiers still fighting for their lives in Iran.

"The 82d is a crack outfit, but we can't parachute *up*." Coleman flashed a tight smile. "We can't swim, either, not across thirty miles of shark-infested water. Just how do you expect us to get out of Iran?"

"If you can secure the airfield, the C-130s can come back in to pick them up." Meredith tried to make it sound like a reasonable option.

"If we could secure the airfield, I wouldn't need to pull them out!" Coleman shouted. "I could send in more men and equipment and accomplish the goddamned mission!"

"But you'd still need air support," Meredith said firmly. "More than I can give you."

"You mean more than you *will* give me." Coleman was beginning to understand why Marines were the way they were. You can't depend on the Navy, they said. Invade and fade—that's their motto.

Meredith squirmed under Coleman's steely stare. He flinched with alarm and relief when the intercom speaker buzzed. Meredith walked to the oak-paneled bulkhead and flicked a switch.

"Excuse me, sir." The voice on the intercom sounded tense but deferential. "You said you wanted to be notified when the, uh, diplomatic flight entered the pattern."

Meredith snapped off the intercom and grabbed his watch cap. "He's here. Shall we go?"

"Who's here?" Coleman asked suspiciously.

"There's a man from Washington coming to give us a briefing," Meredith said breezily. "Didn't I tell you?"

Coleman turned to snap at Meredith, but the admiral was already through the hatch. The two men walked in silence down the blue-tiled corridor to the admiral's personal elevator, followed by Meredith's personal Marine guard.

This part of the ship, Coleman had discovered, was covered with blue rectangles painted with two gold stars—flag country. No one else was allowed except the admiral's personal aides and servants. Coleman had always made a point of being one of the soldiers. He never ate until his troopers ate, always slept on the ground during maneuvers. The special treatment Navy brass afforded themselves, especially when sailors slept stacked like cordwood below, now disgusted Coleman. And when he thought of what his men must be going through at Bandar Abbas while Meredith wrung his hands and prepared to bug out, he seethed with anger.

Coleman was through arguing with Meredith. He didn't know who this visitor was, but if he had the attention of anyone important, Coleman resolved to make sure he would go back to Washington with an earful of what was really going on with Ready Eagle. And Coleman was certain of one thing—his men at Bandar Abbas would not be abandoned, even if he had to take his case all the way up the chain of command to the president.

The flight deck was just one level up, but it seemed like another world to Coleman. Huge gray planes covered the wide black deck, manhandled by harried crewmen wearing headsets, helmets, and jerseys in a rainbow of colors. The shriek of turbine engines screamed in his ears, and the odor of saltwater and jet fuel assaulted his nostrils. An EA-6B electronic warfare aircraft blasted off a forward catapult in a roar that Coleman felt more than heard. Almost simultaneously, an S-3 Viking antisubmarine plane slammed onto the rear of the carrier, snagged by a fat metal wire strung across the deck.

Coleman was unprepared for the noise and frenzy of a supercarrier conducting cyclic ops. When he had flown in the night before, the *Eisenhower* was black and quiet as a tomb. He had spent most of his time in the flag quarters on the gallery deck below. His mind on his mission and surrounded by luxury, Coleman had almost forgotten he was on a warship in the middle of what was, to *Eisenhower*'s officers and men, a war every bit as real as his own. Now, in the noise and tumult of the flight deck, it was obvious to Coleman that the officers and men of Battle Group Bravo were doing all they could to help relieve the situation at Bandar Abbas and still protect themselves. But it wasn't going to be enough. It was going to take more than one carrier group and a handful of paratroopers to stabilize the situation in Iran.

The two notes of the boatswain's pipe warbled over the 5-MC, the ship's loudspeaker system: "Now hear this. Now hear this. Stand by to receive flag party."

All activity stopped. Plane handlers and chock men stood in the fading steam of the catapult track to peer at the clear sky and a tiny whirring disk to starboard.

Coleman pointed at the helicopter approaching in the shimmering distance. "You can quit playing games now, Meredith. Who is this guy?"

Meredith smiled politely. "An Air Force general. William White."

Coleman's eyes brightened. "Not *Brick* White? Wasn't he an ace in Vietnam?"

"*Almost* an ace." Meredith shot Coleman a sidelong glance. "And if I were you, I wouldn't bring that up."

Coleman was suddenly aware of the oppressive heat. His fatigues were soaked clear through. The wind from the carrier's motion chilled the sweat and made him tremble.

"So what can an Air Force general do for us?"

"He's not just an Air Force general," Meredith said, surprised at Coleman's political naivete. "White's the liaison between the secretary of defense and the national security advisor. He's the one who passes the orders on to the Joint Chiefs."

Coleman realized now why Meredith was so secretive about the visit. It was accepted in Washington that the secretary of defense was an amateur soldier and the national security advisor a professional fool. The two rarely spoke to one another, the only common ground between them the fact that they both refused to see the world as it was. Into that vacuum had stepped Maj. Gen. William "Brick" White, USAF.

The big SH-3 helicopter swung over the carrier's ramp and settled onto the number-three spot across from the island. A marine honor guard and a lieutenant commander in dress blues and whites duckwalked across the deck to formally welcome White on board. Before they reached the helicopter, the hatch popped open and a big man in a blue summer Air Force uniform jumped briskly down on deck. With a short salute in the general direction of the flag, he ignored the honor guard and walked quickly to the island, where Coleman and Meredith were waiting.

"Good afternoon, gentlemen." He gave the officers, both two-stars like himself, a cursory salute. "I'm Brick White. You might have heard I was coming."

In a move that confused and angered members of the task force's battle staff, the Pentagon had considered the news of White's visit to Task Force Bravo important enough to break radio silence. But Meredith had apparently not considered it important enough to pass along to Coleman.

"This is the first I've heard of it," Coleman said. "Isn't it a bit early for Defense Department tours? There's still shooting going on."

"Now, General..."

"That's all right, Admiral Meredith," Brick said. "I know how General Coleman feels. I felt the same way in Vietnam. You could always tell how dangerous an area was by the amount of Washington weenies who *weren't* around. But I'm not here to add to your problems. Maybe I can even solve some of them for you."

Coleman felt hope for the first time since the nightmare of Ready Eagle began. A rare general who abhorred politics, even Coleman now recalled hearing of the mysterious Brick White, who, it was said, had the White House and most of the Pentagon in his pocket. He was, so the story went, ruthless and cunning, but a leader, a take-charge guy who could get things done.

"Well, you've got our attention, General," Coleman growled. "Now, have you got some answers?"

"A few." His next words were swallowed by the noise of a Tomcat in afterburner, roaring off a forward cat. The *Eisenhower* was back in business, resuming operations after Brick's landing. He shouted in Meredith's ear, "Is there somewhere we can go and talk?"

Meredith led the way up the island, three levels into the flag bridge. An almost identical copy of the captain's bridge above, where the ship was conned, the flag bridge was spotless, businesslike, and, these days, often deserted. Most of the flag staff had transferred to *Valley Forge,* one of the new Aegis cruisers, taking advantage of its state-of-the-art electronic sensors and tactical displays to get a better picture of the battle group's operations. Meredith had elected to stay with the *Ike,* a decision that had disappointed but not surprised the carrier's skipper. The berths aboard the new cruisers were notoriously small, even for flag officers.

Coleman and Meredith sat at the far side of a conference table. Brick White stood across from them. He wasted no time beginning the briefing.

"Gentlemen, you want answers," he said. "I've just arrived from Washington, where there aren't any. All they've got back there are questions, lots of them. The whole place is going crazy. There are troops on the streets. There were riots outside the Iranian embassy—they were still going on when I left. The DC police didn't seem too anxious to break it up. The president is calling out the Reserves.

"It's the same all over. Somebody bombed the Iranian mission in San Francisco. A mob beat up a bunch of Iranian students at UCLA—one of them almost got killed. There've been reports of sabotage at power stations, telephone exchanges. Most of them have turned out to be false alarms, but there's no denying the country is going crazy. It's like Pearl Harbor back there. Everyone's convinced this is the end of the world."

"It might be," Coleman said softly.

"Maybe," Brick agreed. "This is the first time nuclear weapons have been used in the real world since Nagasaki. Nobody knows what's going to happen now. Nobody even knows what's *supposed* to happen. They all thought if it came to that, it would be us against the Russians and it would all be over in eighteen minutes. And who knows—it might still come to that. This is uncharted territory. We're kind of making things up as we go along."

"What about allied cooperation?" Meredith asked.

"There isn't any," Brick answered. "Everybody's scared to death and wouldn't help us even if we could figure out what to ask them to do. The Brits are our only allies here. If it weren't for them, the Division Ready Force would still be on the ground in Oman."

"Maybe that wouldn't have been so bad," General Coleman said. "But it's a good thing the Omani armed forces are run by British officers."

"Yes, it is, general," White said. "But it's a better thing that elements of the British 22d Special Air Service Regiment happened to be in Masirah for a joint airborne exercise with the Omanis. And that they were willing to start shooting if the sultan's people didn't get the barriers off the runway. And I'll bet that's something you didn't know."

Coleman smiled. He hadn't known that. "Go on."

"The West Germans want no part of this. Forget about the Japanese. The Israelis are looking for someone to kill. The French have their fingers on the button."

"That's pretty funny," Meredith snorted. "Considering they probably sold Iran the bomb in the first place."

"Anyway, we're on our own," Brick went on. "Our 'friends' in the Gulf are very sensitive about our presence. I've just come from Oman. The sultan is adamant in his refusal to permit us to use his country as a staging area for any further assaults on Iran. That goes for Khasab, Seeb, and Thumrait as well as Masirah Island. In fact, he wants us to quit conducting P-3 antisubmarine patrols out of Masirah."

"But we've been flying out of there for years," Meredith protested. "The U.S. has spent half a billion dollars on those bases."

"I know. And the first time we need to use them, he won't let us in," White agreed. "But it's not just the Omanis. Saudi Arabia is virtually shut down. We can't get any word from there, yes or no, except that the Rangers are now 'guests' of the royal family. There are labor strikes in Kuwait. The situation is even worse in Bahrain."

"Wait a minute," Coleman interjected. "I thought, next to Oman, Bahrain was our biggest ally in the Gulf."

"It's true the rulers of Bahrain are Sunnis, and they hate Iran perhaps even more than we do," Brick explained. "But most of the people who actually do the work there are Shiites, and they look to Tehran for spiritual leadership, if nothing else. The unions have shut the place down, and the rulers can't afford to be too heavy-handed about breaking up the strikes or else they'll lose the whole country. So they're waiting it out."

"What happened to our military people in Bahrain?" Meredith asked.

"They're laying low. They're safe for the moment, but they're not going to be able to help us any." Brick looked at the two men with curiosity. "You know what happened to the *LaSalle*, don't you?"

A chill went up Coleman's spine. He had almost transferred his command to the *LaSalle*, a converted amphibious command ship now carrying the forward headquarters element of CENTCOM, the U.S. Central Command. On the way in, Coleman's aircraft had been diverted to Dubai. No explanation had been given as to why landing rights in Bahrain were refused. And with the dangerous confusion in Oman, he had forgotten all about it. Until now.

"What about the *LaSalle?*" Coleman asked.

"Last month they moved her out of port for an exercise, and she hit a mine," Brick explained. "No big deal—it was one of those left over from a couple of years ago. Nobody thought too much of it. It blew off a screw and tore a hole in the hull. They towed it to a dry dock in Manama to fix it."

"I knew that," Meredith said. "But it doesn't need to move. It can still function as a command center."

"Not anymore," Brick shook his head. "A bunch of dock workers boarded it last night. They chased off the watch crew and just tore the ship apart. All the electronics were either destroyed or stolen. They cut up the hull with torches and drained the oil from the engines and ran the boilers at full power until she seized up. The *LaSalle*'s no good to anyone now."

"Jesus!" Meredith interjected. "Where's CINCCENT going to command from now?"

Coleman snorted. It was just like Meredith to worry about where some general was going to park his brass butt while there was a war going on. The Central Command was the final permutation of the Rapid Deployment Force, and, like the old RDF, CENTCOM was neither rapid nor deployable and not much of a force. With the *LaSalle* now out of action, CINCCENT's only other assets were on paper, supposedly drawn from other commands "in an emergency." The problem was that in any real emergency, other commanders were loath to turn over any of their units to anyone else.

At any rate, CENTCOM's commander in chief was nowhere near the Persian Gulf. Even if one of the rulers in the area proved so politically unwise as to allow a permanent American presence on their territory—and in ten years no volunteers had stepped forward—Washington considered the establishment of a CENTCOM headquarters in the command's actual area of responsibility an invitation to terrorism. So, instead, CINCCENT kept an eye on the vital and volatile Persian Gulf from a lonely office building on an Air Force base in Florida.

"I don't know what CINCCENT's going to do, and I don't care," Brick said. "He doesn't have any forces; he's just got their phone numbers. We need troops and weapons, not advice. If he doesn't have anything to offer, he can stay at MacDill with his filing cabinets. This isn't an exercise. This is war."

Coleman smiled. His own 82d Airborne Division was nominally under CENTCOM command in this part of the world, but he was not about to give it up without a fight. Now he wouldn't have to. Clearly, Brick White was a man who understood command—real-world, real-war command. If White really could deliver with his connections in Washington, perhaps there was some hope for Coleman's men in Bandar Abbas, if not for all of Ready Eagle.

"There's something I don't understand about all this," Coleman wondered. "How come no one in the Persian Gulf wants any part of Ready Eagle? Before, they were always bitching that we really wouldn't help them when the chips were down. Now we're here, just when they need us, and they want us to go away. I don't get it."

"The governments around here aren't nearly as stable as they look," Brick explained. "What happened in Iran when the shah fell could easily happen anywhere up and down the Gulf, and the rulers know that. Sizable segments of their populations already identify with Iran as it is. Their feeling is any overt cooperation with the U.S. would bring another Baghdad on their own cities."

Brick paused for emphasis.

"And despite what you might have heard, no one in Washington has a clue as to where Iran got the bomb, or whether or not they've got any more. So until we find out, we've got to go on the assumption that they do."

"Damn," Coleman swore. He thought of his men, all clumped together at Bandar Abbas International. Other loads on the way. A perfect target.

Meredith jumped out of his chair and switched on the intercom.

"Bridge, this is Flag. Get us out of here, fast. Set a course for..."

Brick pushed Meredith aside.

"Bridge, belay that order!" White shouted, shutting off the intercom. Meredith glared.

"Gentlemen, I don't outrank you, true." White spoke calmly, but with the air of someone used to being obeyed. "However, I represent both the secretary of defense and the national security advisor, who report directly to the president. And nobody outranks the president. You will listen to what I have to say before taking any action, and that is a direct order from the National Command Authority."

The door flung open, guns pointing inside. A Marine major strode through the door with his .45 pistol drawn and chambered.

"The officer of the deck thought there might be some trouble here, Admiral." The major eyed Brick suspiciously.

"No trouble, Major." Meredith stared at White and spoke calmly. "You and your men can wait outside. I'll call you if I need you."

The major left with a sharp salute, leaving White facing the two high-ranking officers.

"Fellas, I'm not here to collect stars, but I will if I have to. We're facing the most desperate situation in the history of the planet, and we need to keep our heads," Brick said plaintively. "Now, I've got a way out of this, but I'll need your attention and your cooperation."

There was silence. Meredith nodded his head slowly.

"If you've got a plan, General, I'd love to hear it," Coleman rumbled. "What do you want from us?"

"Time," White said. "There's help coming, but you've got to hold out until it gets here."

Coleman eyed the Air Force general suspiciously.

"How long?"

"A month. Six weeks at the longest."

"Impossible!" Meredith exploded. "Is that what you came here to ask us?"

"No," White said quietly. He stared into Meredith's eyes. "That's what I came here to *tell* you."

"Well, you can just get back on that chopper and get off my boat," Meredith snapped. "I don't know who you think you are, coming out here and ordering us around. Tomorrow the Ready Eagle plans call for Battle Group Bravo to head south to escort a Marine resupply convoy coming up from Diego Garcia. And by God, that's what I intend to do."

"Is that what you want me to tell the president?"

"Tell him whatever you like," Meredith spat.

"And what about the 82d?" Brick asked. "Are you going to leave the Division Ready Force strung out to die in Iran?"

Meredith stared at the table. "I have my orders."

"You son of a bitch!" Coleman grabbed Meredith by his starched shirt and pushed him against the bulkhead. "You're not going anywhere."

Brick shoved Coleman back in his seat. He walked across the flag bridge to Meredith, face to face, inches away.

"Admiral, you know as well as I do that the plans for Operation Ready Eagle went in the toilet the minute the MiGs appeared over Bandar- Abbas. We're playing it by ear now. So don't tell me you're only following orders, because I'm the guy giving them. I can pick up the phone and have a new task force commander flown in from Naples within six hours. If you've turned chickenshit, fine, get out and good riddance. But your ships stay here."

"Who *are* you?" Meredith sounded awed and frightened.

"I'm the guy who's going to get you out of this with your balls and your stars intact," Brick answered. "Make a decision, Admiral. Are you in or out?"

Meredith thought for a moment. "In," he said softly.

"Good." Brick turned away and walked across the bridge to Coleman.

"I like you," Coleman grinned.

"I like you too, General," White said. "And I'm sorry about your men, I truly am. I want you to know I had no part in planning this operation. I'm a professional soldier, just like you. We clean up other people's messes."

"Well, we've got a hell of a mess at Bandar Abbas right now."

"We sure do," Brick agreed. "Tell me: How long can you hold out up there?"

Coleman thought for a moment.

"It's still bad, but not as bad as it looked this morning. The men ran into an engineer battalion at the airport and there was some scattered fighting here and there, but they seem to have the situation stabilized now."

"Meaning..."

"Meaning *if* we can get some reinforcements through, and *if* we don't meet any further organized resistance, and *if* we can get some air cover, we'll be all right. The big problem is air support. We've got to do something about those MiGs or we've got a DIP position up there."

"DIP?"

"It's an Army term," Coleman said. "It means Die in Place."

Brick frowned. "It won't come to that, General. The Navy here will protect you."

"You can bully me all you want," Meredith said sullenly. "But that doesn't solve anything. You can't make the Russians go away. There's a Soviet carrier on its way here from the South China Sea. The battle cruiser *Kirov* and her group are coming in from the Med. There are a half dozen Russian ships and subs already in Socotra, and a bunch of Bears loaded with antiship missiles at Asmara. What are you going to do about that?"

"Nothing," Brick said. "The Soviets won't bother us if we don't bother them."

"Like hell they won't!" Meredith snorted. "Those were Russian planes up there today."

"Russian planes, yes," Brick agreed. "But not Russian pilots."

Coleman and Meredith exclaimed incredulously. Brick held up a hand for silence.

"Please. I've told you more than I should already." Brick glanced at his watch. "And if I don't get out of here soon, nothing will happen."

He stepped to the hatch.

"Admiral Meredith, you are to stay on Gonzo Station until relieved. It shouldn't be too long. The *Constellation* is not going home as planned. She's being turned around."

"Who gave that order?"

"I did," Brick said. "She should be here within a week. Surely you can hold out that long."

Meredith shook his head. "This is really too much. Are you telling me you can order the whole Seventh Fleet around?"

"Watch me," Brick smiled. "A week. Ten days at the most. Can you cover Bandar Abbas till then?"

"Sure, why not?" Meredith sighed. "It's all insane, anyway. But that's not going to be enough, you know. Even with the *Connie*'s air wing, we're going to need more air cover if the MiGs really get serious. You're going to need land-based air power somewhere in the Gulf."

"I'm working on it."

Brick stepped into the hatchway and turned to Coleman.

"General, we're going to win this thing. We're going to kick ass and take names, and we're going to do it right. Are you with me?"

"Oh, I'm with you, all right," Coleman said. "I just hope you know where you're going."

Coleman and Meredith heard Brick's response trailing in the gangway as he left for the flight deck.

"So do I, General," Brick said. "So do I."

Power Behind the Throne

Over the Hindu Kush
Northwest Afghanistan

Col. Gen. of Aviation Pavel Ivanovich Illyushin had a secret. The first deputy commander in chief of the Soviet Air Force hated flying.

Illyushin was an old man now, and he had had his war. Though he had been young, once, he had never been foolish; aviation was immensely preferable to life in the infantry during the Great Patriotic War. So he hid his fears through flight school, hoping to overcome the terror the sky held for him. But even in dogfights, Illyushin was more afraid of his own Yak-3 fighter than of Nazi aircraft. The drive behind his rapid ascent through the ranks came not from bravery or patriotism, but rather from a desire to be promoted out of the cockpit.

Although not traveling in uniform, Illyushin still enjoyed the privileges of rank. With the Aeroflot Il-76 all to himself, the trip from Moscow had not been terribly difficult. He slept most of the way through the long flight. The old man's nightmare began in earnest at the Soviet air base at Kalai Mor, near the border with Afghanistan, when he left the comfortable transport and boarded an Mi-8. Most of all, Illyushin hated flying in helicopters.

His escort of two HIND gunships, meant to give a reassuring presence, had the opposite effect. Illyushin's misgivings grew deeper when, shortly after takeoff, the flight began a quick bob and weave through the mountain passes. The razor-sharp heights of the western Himalayas rose straight up on either side, so close to the rotors. Illyushin knew, of course, that the mujahideen were *not* suppressed, despite speeches made to the contrary as the Soviets pulled out, and that in fact only the guerrillas' lack of ambition for conventional political power and their distrust of one another kept them from seizing the entire country. The evasive maneuvers were meant to counter guerrillas armed with shoulder-launched surface-to-air missiles. But to Illyushin, an infrared missile attack was preferable to this nausea-inducing thrill ride through the mountains at the top of the world.

The blue-and-white peaks gave way to the gray Afghan desert as the flight moved south. The helicopters cruised straight and level; nobody lived here, not even mujahideen. Relieved, rocked by the rotors, and soothed by the drone of the engines, Illyushin had almost fallen into a stupor when the air was split by the roar of high-performance engines in afterburner.

A pair of dark blurs streaked by the helicopter. The Mi-8 wobbled in the jet wash of the fighters. The gunships, scattered by the high-speed pass, wobbled uncertainly on their shadows above the desert floor. Illyushin unhooked his considerable girth and staggered to the cockpit. The pilot leaned toward Illyushin, screaming to overcome the noise of the jets and the old man's failing hearing.

"Don't worry, Colonel General. They're our planes."

Illyushin nodded. He could see now, through the helicopter's faceted canopy, the two gray MiG-29s wheeling back for another pass. He could see they were Soviet-built planes, all right, but whether they were "our" planes—or, of primary importance to Illyushin, *his* planes—was precisely the issue he had traveled halfway to hell to resolve.

Ahead, he could see the air base scratched out on the desert. Zaranj was the westernmost of the new tactical airfields the Soviet Union had built before leaving Afghanistan. Illyushin had been instrumental in establishing the advanced facility just miles from the border. He had told his superiors that Zaranj would serve as a parting message to the Iranians that Moscow would not tolerate any intervention in Afghan affairs in the Soviets' absence. It had not occurred to the Soviets or the Iranians that Afghan adventures *into* Iran might be staged from Zaranj.

Zaranj was, ostensibly, the site of the Afghan Republic Air Force Advanced Jet Training Command. But no one seemed to graduate from the school, despite its exceedingly high ratio of instructors to students. And the instructors assigned to Training Squadron 22—Czechs, East Germans, Poles, Cubans, and Russians—were loath to fly Zaranj's surprisingly small number of Czech-built L-29 two-seat trainers, electing instead to log most of their flight time in the school's many single-seat Fulcrum fighters. Illyushin was the only one in Moscow who knew why.

The chopper landed in front of the operations building, joined soon after by the sheepish approach of the two gunships that had been separated in the high-speed pass. Illyushin pressed his jowls against the coolness of the window. There was not much to see. The base, though modern, had been built with the economy that came from having to transport every board, block, and nail used in its construction over hundreds of miles of guerrilla-infested mountain roads.

The operations building and adjoining barracks were the only structures except for an open maintenance hangar along the single runway, large enough for just two planes. The somber browns and grays of the base blended in with the hard desert surface, the color and texture of dried mud, stretching out in all directions. The only spot of brightness was the green-red-and-black Afghan flag thrown up casually by a single corner on the white pole outside the ops building. The flag hung straight down in the still air of the high desert. Illyushin quickly realized what the men based there already knew: any attempt at decoration was pointless, too quickly overwhelmed by the mocking, enormous despair of Zaranj's bleak surroundings.

The face of a tall, bearded Afghan officer suddenly filled the window. The helicopter crew door swung open.

"Welcome to Zaranj, Colonel General Illyushin. It is an honor, sir." The officer helped Illyushin from the helicopter, ducking under the still-whirring blades. "I am Maj. Akim Babrak, base commander. I trust you had a pleasant flight."

"There is no such thing as a pleasant flight in a helicopter," Illyushin growled. "Where is Colonel Paratov?"

"He is landing now, sir." Babrak pointed toward the end of Zaranj's single runway.

The Fulcrum entered final, bleeding off speed in a tight turn. Just before the main gear touched down, the brake chute popped from between the aircraft's two black tails (the only aircraft at Zaranj so painted, Illyushin noted). He watched enviously as the MiG-29 settled effortlessly on the runway, the dirty brown brake chute bobbing tautly behind. Like many amateur artists and athletes, Illyushin's lack of talent had given him a keen appreciation of it in others—he knew good flying when he saw it.

He's a fool or a madman, Illyushin thought. But he knows how to fly airplanes. Just like his father.

The Fulcrum dropped the chute, turning on its nose wheel toward the operations shack. A pair of maintenance workers, shirtless and red from the sun, pushed a yellow boarding ladder out on the ramp. The MiG cut its engines. The big canopy swung up on its hinges. The pilot unstrapped quickly and casually, stood in the seat, and swung a leg onto the ladder. Ignoring the aircraft workers' chattering of apparent congratulations in Polish, he stepped carefully over the plane's wide leading edge extension and dropped deftly back to earth.

Mikhail Paratov strode deliberately toward the ops building, still wearing his helmet, with the visor down. Illyushin thought it odd; most pilots handed the heavy helmets to ground workers immediately after opening the canopy. Illyushin shuddered as the answer came to him like a bad memory. He was not surprised that Paratov preferred to remain masked as long as possible.

Illyushin steeled himself, told himself he would not react. Still, when Paratov extended his hand in greeting, the old man could feel the familiar sensations of pity and revulsion. Two fingers were missing. Both hands were flushed the bright pink of a burn victim.

That wasn't the worst, Illyushin knew. He tried desperately to suppress his horror as Paratov pushed up the visor and pried off the black helmet. Specialists from Basil to Helsinki had labored over Paratov's face. Skin grafts, bone reconstructions, enzyme treatments—nothing could restore life to that burned, ravaged flesh. The best modern medicine could deliver was but a crude approximation of human features, a skull with a perpetual grin, as if amused by the cruel joke fate had played.

"Do not worry, Uncle," Paratov said gently to Illyushin. "At least I never seem to age. That is something else we have in common, eh?"

Paratov turned to the Afghan officer.

"Major Babrak, will you take these helicopter pilots to the mess and give them some lunch and some flying lessons? The colonel general and I have much to discuss."

Babrak trotted off the end of the ramp, where the HIND crews loitered uncomfortably about their beasts. Illyushin started to say something, thought better of it, then followed as Paratov led the way through the glass door into the operations building. They walked down a long hallway lined with posters and diagrams of American and Western weapons systems. Sounds of celebration poured from one of the doorways. Paratov entered, motioning for Illyushin to follow.

Inside the ready room, a dozen pilots were on their way to becoming steadily, sloppily drunk. Bottles of vodka, champagne, and Czech beer littered the map table. In twos and threes, the pilots rehashed the morning's battle over Bandar Abbas, with flashing hands and loud voices. One pilot was still sober enough to shout, "Attention!" as Paratov and Illyushin entered the room.

"A celebration, comrades?" Paratov said softly. "And what are we celebrating now?"

Some of the pilots, grown accustomed to Paratov's expressionless face, had learned to detect their commander's feelings in his tone of voice. Sensing anger, they shrank to the side of the room. A drunken pilot answered happily: "Have some vodka, Colonel! We are celebrating the morning's victory over the Americans!"

Paratov walked to the map table and, with a sweep of his hand, sent the bottles and glasses crashing to the floor.

"Victory? You call that victory?" Paratov seethed. "Shooting down unarmed transport planes?"

Their mood shattered, the pilots stared silently at the floor. One spoke up, sheepishly.

"But Colonel, there were American fighters there, too. We shot them down."

"*I* shot them down," Paratov bellowed. "That is, I shot down one, and the Iranians destroyed another with a missile. The rest of you were too busy attacking brave men who couldn't shoot back."

"But the rest of them ran," said another pilot. "We scared them away."

"There *were* no other American fighters, do you understand?" Paratov said. "You cannot call what happened this morning combat. It was murder. The Americans will be back. And then you will see what combat is really like, I promise you."

Most of the pilots moved toward the door. One, however, a dark Afghan lieutenant, stood his ground, staring defiantly at Paratov.

"You are being most unfair, Colonel," the Afghan pilot said. "The Americans are not invincible. Perhaps because you hold them responsible for what happened to your..."

Paratov held up a hand for silence. Illyushin could hear his own breathing.

"Lieutenant Abak," he whispered. "I do not recall seeing you in the air today."

"No, sir," the young officer admitted. "I had a maintenance abort. Compressor problems."

"And yet you are here, celebrating a 'victory' you had no part of." Paratov searched the crowd for Axel Kraus, the East German who served as the squadron's executive officer and director of maintenance. "Major Kraus, did you inspect Lieutenant Abak's aircraft when you returned?"

A bald giant stepped from the crowd. "Yes, Herr Paratov."

"And did you find anything wrong with the engines?"

Kraus looked at Paratov, then Abak, then stared at his own open hands. "No, Herr Paratov."

The rest of the pilots moved away from Abak as Paratov stepped toward him.

"So," Paratov hissed. "You did not even have the guts to go duck hunting with the rest of these heroes, eh?"

Abak slunk back to the wall.

"I didn't know it would be like that." Abak's eyes darted around the room, looking for a friend. No one looked back. "I thought it would be a suicide mission. Everyone knows you ordered Major Kraus to make sure our ejection seats do not function. I didn't want to wind up like poor Carlos."

A hush fell over the room. Pilots inched to the door.

"You have not been dismissed!" Paratov shouted. He stood face to face with the young Afghan lieutenant. "Yes, it is true, *most* of the ejection seats are not operative. It is in your own best interests. Major Rivera would not have wanted to be captured. None of you would. Trust me."

Paratov unsnapped the holster on his survival vest, slowly removing the small PSM pistol.

"However, *your* ejection seat was fully functional, Lieutenant," Paratov continued. "Because I have always known you were a coward. After so long, I can smell them. But I really expected you to take off and fly toward the target before running, if only to make your cowardice appear credible."

Paratov cocked the pistol and stared at it absently.

"Did you really think you belonged here, in this squadron?" Paratov laughed bitterly. "You fly like a woman. When the mujahideen came for you as a collaborator, you left your wife and children to die in Kabul and ran here. You act like a little brown worm, even now. Look around you! These are brave men, the best fighter pilots in the world. And Carlos was the best and bravest of all. He died as he would have wanted, in combat with the Americans. And you will die as you deserve."

Kraus moved behind Abak, pinning his arms. Paratov pushed the PSM against the lieutenant's forehead.

"You were meant to be killed over Bandar Abbas," Paratov said. "If you did not eject out of cowardice, or manage to get shot down by the Americans, I was going to put a missile in you myself. An Afghan body fished out of the Gulf would lend immeasurable credibility to this enterprise. That is the only reason you were permitted to join Squadron 22, Lieutenant. We needed your corpse."

Paratov cocked the pistol. Abak struggled away from Kraus and ran from the ready room. Paratov followed him into the hallway, aimed deliberately, and fired. The young lieutenant's head exploded in a red mist, his lifeless body shattering the glass door at the entrance to the operations building.

Paratov walked slowly down the hallway. His heavy flight boots crunched broken glass as he leaned over Abak to make sure he was dead. He looked up to see Major Babrak, horrified and astonished, staring at Abak's body.

"Lieutenant Abak has had an accident," Paratov said smoothly. "There was some drinking at the celebration. He was showing his service revolver to some of the other pilots, and it went off accidentally. Please take care of the body and notify his next of kin."

"Yes, Colonel Paratov," Babrak swallowed. "It is unfortunate."

Paratov walked back down the hallway. The pilots had disappeared. Illyushin stared at him incredulously. Paratov's eyes, his only windows of expression, were calm, an icy, placid blue. Illyushin had known many killers and had seen in their eyes every emotion from remorse to panic to sexual pleasure. But he had never seen a man who killed without feeling. Illyushin felt a shiver. A man like that could do anything.

"Does that happen often?" Illyushin asked.

"No." Paratov snapped the PSM back into the holster. "We do not have many cowards here."

He led Illyushin to an office, well furnished but devoid of any trace of personality. Paratov sat behind the desk, motioning for Illyushin to take a seat opposite. The old man remained standing, staring into Paratov's cold eyes.

"Col. Mikhail Ivanovich Paratov, you have committed acts of a treasonous nature against the Soviet Union," he said formally. "I will not tell you what the Party had planned for you. Fortunately, I learned in time and have persuaded them otherwise."

Illyushin drew himself up to his full height. "In fact, because of your distinguished service record and the loyalty I feel toward your late father, I believe I can use my influence and arrange to have you shot."

Paratov's face was expressionless, as always. He let out a short, surprised laugh.

"Thank you, Uncle. I shall never forget your kindness."

"Well, what do you expect?" Illyushin exploded. "You have disobeyed orders. You have taken it upon yourself to set the Soviet Union at war with the United States! My God, you will go down in history as the man who started World War III!"

Paratov looked quizzically at the old man, standing at attention in his ill-fitting civilian clothes.

"Calm yourself, Uncle. I have done nothing of the sort. I followed my orders. To the letter." Paratov removed a sheet of paper from a drawer and slid it across the desk.

Illyushin stared suspiciously at Paratov, and then at the paper. Finally, he sat down heavily on a chair opposite the desk, unfolded his reading glasses, and studied the document, reading aloud softly:

The Republic of Afghanistan, acting in solidarity with the people of the Iranian Islamic Republic, directs no. 22 Flight Training Squadron at Zaranj, under the command of Maj. A. M. Babrak, to take any and all steps necessary to maintain the sovereignty of Iranian airspace and to defend it against imperialist aggressors who may seek to take advantage of the unfortunate turmoil which has befallen our beleaguered Moslem brothers to the west.

Illyushin tossed the document back at Paratov. "Such rubbish!"

"You will recognize the signature of the prime minister of the Republic of Afghanistan at the bottom," Paratov said. "All perfectly legal."

"Come now, Mikhail Ivanovich! Do you think I am so old I have lost my senses? The prime minister rules nothing. He is in hiding, in exile. As the commander of the last Soviet bastion in Afghanistan, he is dependent upon you for his protection, for his very life!"

"Nevertheless, he is still the prime minister," Paratov said smoothly. "And until that pack of bandits in Kabul stops fighting among themselves long enough to put together a government, he remains the rightful ruler of Afghanistan. Moscow, at any rate, still recognizes the authority of the prime minister. And so do I. You seem to be the only one in disagreement, Uncle."

"Blast it!" Illyushin swore. "I will not argue the obvious with you. The *Stavka* is in agreement, and so am I—to make war on your own initiative, without consulting your superiors in Moscow, is an act of treason!"

"I caution you, comrade Colonel General, it is *you* who now speak treason. The generals may complain like old women with nothing to do, but the chairman holds the power. And the chairman has himself said on many occasions that Afghanistan is a sovereign nation. Surely a sovereign nation does not need to consult with anyone before defending itself. Or responding to a neighbor's cry for help."

"But these are Soviet planes. And you are a Soviet officer."

"Again, I am afraid I must correct you, Uncle. These aircraft may have been built in the USSR, but they are *Afghan* planes, given to this country under a treaty of mutual friendship. And I am merely an instrument of that treaty, a humble pilot seconded to the Afghan Republic Air Force to help its citizens better prepare to defend against aggression. I would find your insinuation that I exercise even the smallest degree of influence over my superior, the prime minister of Afghanistan, presumptuous and insulting if I did not find it so ludicrous. Sir."

Illyushin stood wearily and stared out the window into nothing. He had been flying since the first word of the attack at Bandar Abbas. It was important he get to Zaranj, and to Paratov, before anyone else.

"Misha, you treat me as a child. I deserve more respect. I have cared for you as a son, fought on your behalf in the Politburo, saved your career—perhaps your life—during some of your less successful..." Illyushin searched for the words, "foreign misadventures. And this is how you repay me. Your father would be ashamed."

There was, as always, no emotion in Paratov's face. But Illyushin detected true feeling in his voice when he spoke. It was the sound of a son trying to please a parent who could never be satisfied.

"Uncle, I meant no disrespect. I know what you have done for me. I know what it has cost you."

"Then talk to me, man to man!" Illyushin banged his fist on the desk. "Moscow wants answers. And I swear to you, they had better be the right ones, or both of us are headed for the gulag this time."

Paratov had never seen the older man so angry. "I will tell you anything you want to know, Colonel General. You know I have never hidden anything from you."

"Then tell me this: What are your true reasons for attacking the Americans at Bandar Abbas? What possible gain could you expect from such a reckless enterprise?"

"Iran is dying, Uncle," Paratov began deliberately. "Anyone can see that. It is breaking apart because it was never whole. Iran is a collection of nations—Kurds and Baluchis, the Shiite zealots, and the new bourgeois. The shah forced them together, and then hatred of the shah drew them closer still. With the shah long gone, the mullahs used the war to keep Iran's passion directed outward, rather than in. It is an old story, Uncle. Only kings and presidents sleep well in wartime."

Illyushin nodded. "And ayatollahs and first chairmen, as well."

"Yes," Paratov agreed. "As the people grew tired of the war with Iraq, the pressure for peace grew too intense for the religious government in Iran to ignore. The ayatollah could keep them together, but the ayatollah is long gone. Too many Iranians were weary of the sacrifice, the endless deaths and shortages. There were many factions that had done well under the shah. They were anxious to regain power, and their support grew each day the Gulf war dragged on. In the end, Tehran had no choice but to accept a cease-fire with Baghdad."

"This is all well known," Illyushin said impatiently. "But it does not explain the Baghdad bomb. That was a strange way to conduct a cease-fire, even for the religious zealots who rule Iran."

"But it is the only kind they could accept. Death to infidels is the only right way to Allah. The cease-fire was a political decision, one the mullahs never fully accepted. To the ayatollah, especially, temporal matters were transitory. It was a personal matter with him—do not forget, he was held prisoner by Saddam Hussein for years."

"Again, I must say, this is history," Illyushin said. "What concerns us now is..."

"Please, Uncle, let me finish," Paratov interjected. "So as the mullahs sued for peace with Iraq to satisfy their political obligations, they secretly prepared their nuclear response to fulfill their greater religious mission. What happened to Iran after the Baghdad bomb was really of no concern to them. Their mission on earth was fulfilled.

"The truth is, the bomb has done more to destroy Iran than Iraq. The country is coming apart. There are riots in every major city. Oil production has come to a standstill. The regular military is at war with the Pasdaran. Religious factions are eating each other alive. Ethnic minorities are rising, blocking the passes and the highways, declaring new, autonomous states. Iran has ceased to exist as a nation."

"I have seen the reports," Illyushin agreed. "But what does it mean to us?"

Paratov rose from his seat. "Opportunity, Uncle! We can redraw the map whichever way we like. The spoils of war without the risk. Oil. Land. Airfields and seaports along the Persian Gulf! Certainly that would be a nice present to take back to the Kremlin. Even the Navy would be pleased—a warm-water seaport has been a dream of theirs since the time of the czars."

"Ridiculous," Illyushin growled. "You are talking about world war. The Americans would never sit still for a Soviet Iran."

"Not a *Soviet* Iran, Uncle. And not the whole country. Just the good parts. Look."

Paratov opened the desk drawer and pulled out another sheet of paper. Illyushin looked closely. It was a hand-drawn map of the region, detailed in Paratov's own small, neat script. Paratov swept his deformed right hand over a large area where the borders of Iran, Afghanistan, and Pakistan came together.

"This is Baluchistan," he said.

"There is no such country," Illyushin snorted.

"No, not yet," Paratov replied. "Not until you give me what I need to put it together."

Illyushin stared at the map. Most of the Persian Gulf coast, from Kharg Island to Bandar Abbas, was tinted blue, ceded to the United States. The Shatt-al-Arab and the rest of northwestern Iran was green, marked "Kurds and Iraqi." Northern Iran, to the Zagros, including Tehran, was red, a "Soviet protectorate." The rest of the country, a large section extending from the Afghanistan border to the Strait of Hormuz, was Paratov's Baluchistan.

"You are mad, Colonel Paratov," Illyushin said quietly. "It was a mistake to come here."

"Wait, Uncle! Hear me out. You've always complained I lacked real ambition. Isn't this big enough for you?"

"Any fool can draw lines on a map," Illyushin sighed. "I must be going. I have real problems to attend to in Moscow."

Illyushin put a heavy hand on the door.

"Father was right," Paratov hissed. "You are an old woman."

Illyushin turned quickly.

"What did you say?"

"You heard me, Colonel General," Paratov regretted hurting the old man. But his life was on the line. "Father said you were a good man and a loyal friend. He also warned me you had courage but no imagination."

Illyushin stormed angrily back to the desk. "No amount of imagination could transform this..." he waved at the map, "into reality."

"Oh, no? Think about it. Most of this has already happened. Nuclear weapons are spreading across the world. The precedents we, the responsible nations of the world, set now will determine the future of mankind."

"You are speaking sense at last." Illyushin settled back into the chair. "Go on."

"Iran must cease to exist. That has to be the punishment for any nation that uses atomic weapons—complete destruction as a political entity. Do you agree?"

"Of course," Illyushin answered. "That is why the chairman agreed to the assault on Tehran."

"And that is why the Americans landed at Bandar Abbas. It was inevitable. But think ahead, comrade Colonel General. If Iran disappears, who inherits the land it once occupied? What happens when U.S. and Soviet troops meet at the passes of the Zagros? Have you considered that?"

"Certainly," Illyushin replied.

"And?"

"We have not fully explored our course of action."

"I'll tell you what happens," Paratov said sharply. "Either a nuclear holocaust or a long, drawn-out conventional war neither side wants or can afford."

"And you have an alternative?"

"Yes," Paratov pointed at the map. "This. The two superpowers never meet. They are separated by a neutral buffer state, populated by the Baluchis."

"Who are these...Baluchis?" Illyushin sounded curious but still skeptical.

"I see I am not the only one who sleeps through *zampolit* briefings," Paratov gently chided the old man. "The Baluchis are a race of mountain people, neither Shiite nor Persian, who live in parts of Afghanistan, Iran, and Pakistan. For much of history they formed their own separate nation. Only in the last century, through the intervention of the British, were they scattered across three borders."

"This, ah, Baluchistan," Illyushin said, intrigued. "What is there?"

"Nothing. Absolutely nothing. Mountains and desert. Goats and snakes and dry lakes. The Baluchis are herders, mostly. Nomads. They like to be left alone to kill each other. The Americans won't miss it. There's nothing there worth fighting over."

"No oil?"

"All the oil is on the Gulf side, Uncle," Paratov sighed. "Sorry. But it does have a coastline. And I will let you park your ships at my ports."

Illyushin stared across the desk. Paratov's dead face made it impossible to determine if he was serious.

"*Your* ports, Misha?"

"Yes, mine!" Paratov said emphatically. "My God, Uncle, you act as if you are surprised by all this. I understand your position in the Kremlin, and your need for secrecy and caution. But we are alone now. Surely we do not need to play this game."

"I was not aware we were playing any game, Colonel," Illyushin said coolly. "And of course I am surprised by your actions, as is everyone in Moscow."

Paratov's eyes widened. "How could that be, Colonel General? All my life, you have prepared me, taught me, guided me toward this moment. You are the one who provided me with the contacts to set my plan in motion. You are the one who built this base, gathered these men, and placed me in charge. What did you expect?"

"I expected," Illyushin sniffed, "that you would follow orders and perform your duty as a soldier of the state. I was not aware that you had been promoted to shah of Iran."

"Not the shah," Paratov replied softly. "Just the king of Baluchistan."

Paratov folded the map and put it back in the drawer.

"You think I am a fool. That is unfortunate. For me, and for you, and for the Party. Apparently you have lived so long in the service of the state that you have lost your imagination. And imagination has built more empires than all the bullets and guns in history. Do you know what a king is, Uncle? Do you?"

"No, Colonel Paratov," he said with a sigh. "Tell me. What is a king?"

"A king is the man who got there first," Paratov said. "You told me that. A long time ago, before you grew soft. Well, I am that man, Uncle. And I will be king, with or without your help."

The two men sat in silence. At last Illyushin spoke.

"I have to leave now. We are losing the sun."

Paratov did not speak as Illyushin rose to leave.

"Tell me, Colonel Paratov," Illyushin said finally. "What is the message you want me to carry back to the Kremlin?"

"Tell them..." Paratov paused to collect his thoughts. "Ask them if they would prefer a nuclear exchange between the superpowers—or at the very least, an American presence that stretches from India through Pakistan to the entire Persian Gulf—to a Soviet sphere of influence that extends from the Caspian Sea to the Indian Ocean. Ask them if the lives of countless soldiers and even Mother Russia herself is worth the cost of a few aircraft and pilots. And ask them if they have any better ideas."

Illyushin stood slowly. For the first time in a long while, he had to fight to contain his emotions. Years of Kremlin politics had left Illyushin a face even more blank and unreadable than Paratov's. Not even his eyes gave him away, betrayed his excitement and elation now that, after years of preparation, his master plan was finally unfolding.

Yes, *his* plan, Illyushin thought. Paratov was right—Squadron 22 *had* done exactly as he, Col. Gen. of Aviation Pavel Illyushin, had intended. Though he had no hand in the details—the part about Baluchistan was a bit too flamboyant for his taste—what had happened that morning over Bandar Abbas had happened first in Illyushin's mind, many years ago.

It had taken most of Paratov's life, just as it had taken all of his father's. Illyushin had not done it with bold action and stirring courage. That was the way of the Paratovs, the way of the warrior. Illyushin had turned them, father and then son, not by strength but by weakness. An indulgence for loyalty and trust had betrayed Paratov's father. The son, even more scarred and twisted within than without, had spent his life fulfilling Illyushin's dream.

That was Illyushin's talent, his weapon. Fools can fly. Anyone can die in battle. But what Paratov had said to him was right—imagination was the greatest weapon. Audacity, with a sharp sense of weaknesses and motivation, *would* remake the world. In the end this plan turned on two keys, simple yet so desperately secret the two men dared not even mention them aloud. One key was for the world. The other turned Paratov alone.

And the poor, wretched fool, Illyushin thought, he never even knew. Even now, Illyushin was convinced Paratov believed his feigned astonishment and anger, believed the attack at Bandar Abbas was his idea and his alone. That was good, Illyushin thought. That was as it should be. There were many things that could go wrong. And Illyushin had no intention of standing next to the new king if the sky should fall on Baluchistan.

His hand on the door, Illyushin turned to face Paratov, searching for the right words.

"Your father," he said, "would be proud of you."

"And you, Uncle?"

"I will be proud if you succeed." Illyushin stepped through the door. "Good-bye, Your Majesty."

First Casualty

Bahrain International Airport
Manama, Bahrain

The most formidable weapon in the Western world!

Peter Hillary was constantly amazed at the potential power packed in the small slice of plastic. He twirled it in his hand, letting the red rays of the setting Arabian sun flash off the green-and-gray surface. He ran his fingers across the smooth, black strip, wondering what secrets the computer code held that made honest, decent men risk their lives at his whim.

All because he had the power! Jets and tanks are more trouble than they're worth. Martyrs laugh at bombs and bullets. After a lifetime of covering wars, revolutions, and civil unrest, Hillary had come to realize the ultimate futility of personally carrying a gun. His American Express card was the only weapon he needed. And he never went into battle without it.

"Are you ready?"

Frank King glanced out at the flight line. Two airport workers in orange coveralls were stuffing King's helicopter with fuel.

"Just about," he said. "Are you sure you want to go through with this?"

"Oh, I'm quite sure. The question is, are you?"

"Your credit's good. And I could use the money." King shrugged. "Life's pretty simple when you're broke."

"Then let's go. We're losing the light. Oh, just one more thing." Hillary took the receipt from the credit-card validator and ripped it in half.

"Hey, what the hell are you doing?"

Hillary put half the receipt in his pocket and handed the remaining piece to King.

"Just to make sure our friendly business transaction stays friendly," Hillary said. "I'll give you my piece when we get there. Okay?"

"No, it's not okay," King frowned. "But I guess I'd do the same thing if I were you. Say, how do I know I can trust *you*?"

"Because I can't fly a helicopter," Hillary answered. "Come on, let's get out of here."

The two men left the small shack and walked to King's Jet Ranger. The workers were finishing the refueling.

"Mr. King, who's going to pay for this gas?"

"I'll sign for it." King reached for the bill.

"No, sir." The man snatched the clipboard away. "You're into us for too much already. We're not even supposed to be on the flight line, as it is. The whole airport's on strike, you know that. If the ragheads catch us doing this we'll never make it out of here ourselves. Things are getting too hot to deal in credit. Not your credit. Not anymore."

"But I've got a paying customer here," King protested.

The man glanced at Hillary and shook his head. Short, a tad overweight, with hair too long on the sides to compensate for a receding hairline, Hillary did not inspire confidence in his financial resources. "Uh huh. Not again, Mr. King. No cash, no gas."

"I'll pay for it."

The others stared as Hillary pulled out a wad of bills from his camera case. "How much?"

The man in the coveralls checked his clipboard. "Let's see...265 dollars for the gas. Plus a small service charge. Let's call it five hundred bucks, even."

"That's ridiculous!" King exclaimed. "You ought to be..."

Hillary held out his hand for silence, then counted out a thousand dollars. "Keep the change. And keep quiet about this. We've got to be going."

The two flight-line workers left, smiling. King and Hillary climbed aboard the helicopter.

"I didn't know journalists were so rich," King said, switching on the engine.

"I'm not," Hillary said. "That was it. But if we find what I think we'll find, I'll be able to name my own price for the story. Besides, it's worth whatever it costs. I wouldn't miss this for anything."

The chopper rose quickly. King pedaled right; the tail rotor pushed them into a low swoop east, over the Gulf. He tried to relax while he could. Things would begin to happen soon enough.

King flew steadily across the smooth, turquoise waters he had traveled so often in happier times. Business was booming when King Air Charter opened five years before. Carrying oil-rig workers and television news crews, King had stayed booked solid for months on end. Now he wished to God he had saved some of it. With the cease-fire, the bottom had fallen out of the charter business. And with the Baghdad bomb, the bottom had fallen out of the world. He had wanted to leave with the rest of the Americans, but he was in too deep. Arabs don't forget, especially about money. King had left all the cash he had made, and then some, on the gambling tables of Sammarah. With this run, though, he might break even and get out. Maybe.

They flew twenty minutes in silence, seeing nothing but blue sky and blue water in the abnormally quiet Gulf. King was beginning to believe they might get away with it when the radio crackled to life.

"Attention, unidentified aircraft south of Tunb Island, bearing 090. This is the United States warship *Biddle*. State your call sign and intentions, over."

King glanced at Hillary and picked up the mike.

"*Biddle,* this is King Air 1, Jet Ranger charter out of Bahrain International en route to Salamah field, over."

King snapped off the mike and turned angrily to Hillary.

"You said there weren't any American ships in the strait!"

"There weren't this morning," Hillary said. He was sure of it. His sources were very specific about that. Hillary wondered what else had changed in just twelve hours.

"King Air 1, you are entering hostile airspace." *Biddle*'s radio operator sounded tough and businesslike. "Reverse course to 270 and return to base. Over."

Hillary shook his head.

"*Biddle,* our flight plan to the oil field at Salamah has been filed and approved," King said. "Over."

"Roger, King Air 1," *Biddle*'s radio operator responded. "Things have changed; it's pretty hot up there now. Over."

"Tell him we're running out of gas," Hillary suggested.

"Ah, *Biddle,* we don't have the juice to get back to Bahrain. Over."

There was a moment's silence.

"King Air 1, we have cleared you to divert to Khasab, over."

"Khasab. Where's that?" Hillary thought he'd been everywhere in the Persian Gulf.

"A dinky little airfield at the tip of Oman. The U.S. has been trying to get the sultan to let them build a naval air station there, but right now it's really just a flat place in the middle of a bunch of rocks. It's kind of pretty, though," King added, hoping Hillary might be talked out of going further.

Hillary hadn't come this far to spend the rest of the war interned in Oman, no matter how attractive the desolation. He thought frantically, searching for a way out.

"Tell him we've got to get to Salamah," Hillary said. "Tell him it's a medical emergency."

King shook his head.

"Are you crazy? That's a guided missile cruiser down there! They'll blow us out of the sky."

Hillary unfolded his half of the receipt and dangled it out the window.

"No, wait!" King cried. "You win."

He keyed the mike: "*Biddle,* King Air 1. Be advised this is a mercy flight. Over."

"King Air 1, state the nature of the emergency. Over."

King looked to Hillary for help. Hillary mouthed the word *insulin.*

"Ah, *Biddle,* there's a diabetic on the platform who is out of insulin and hasn't been able to get a resupply because of the, ah, action down there," King stammered. "He'll go into shock if we don't get him his medicine."

There was a long pause. Hillary stared at the radio while King, worried, kept the helicopter on course through the strait.

"King Air 1, turn to forty degrees and proceed directly to Salamah. You are to land and shut down engines. Do not take off again without direct instructions from Agency Crown, VHF 290. Any deviation from course will be considered hostile action taken against a U.S. warship in international waters and will be dealt with accordingly. Do you understand and comply with these instructions? Over."

Hillary smiled. King gulped.

"Copy, *Biddle.* Will comply. King Air 1 out."

King swung the helicopter to port and set course toward Salamah. A civilian helicopter, the Jet Ranger had no radar-detection equipment. Still, King could almost feel the powerful electronic beams of the unseen cruiser's fire-control systems boring a hole in the unarmed chopper. The towers of an offshore oil rig poked through the haze gathering in the twilight.

"That's Salamah," King said. "The helicopter pad is on the last platform."

Hillary studied the pilot's face.

"You know what to do."

King fidgeted in the right seat. He hadn't counted on the cruiser. There were probably more American warships out there on the hazy horizon. Before, it was a dangerous job. Now, it was suicidal.

"Yeah, but listen... I can't..."

"I'll double it," Hillary said. "Come on, man. You've got nothing to lose."

King lined up on the landing pad. There were figures waiting on the green-and-white nonskid surface. Two carried automatic rifles.

"King Air 1, this is Salamah control," a voice crackled over the radio. Hillary couldn't place the accent. Dutch? "State your intentions. We have no record of your flight. There is no medical emergency here. Over."

Damn, Hillary thought. The *Biddle* must have gotten suspicious and radioed the rig's control office. King kept the helicopter on path for a landing.

"King Air 1, this is Salamah control. You are forbidden to land! Clearance is denied!"

The helicopter leveled off, hovering ten feet above the landing pad. The men on the platform raised their weapons, aiming at the cockpit. Hillary felt he could almost reach out and touch them.

"Now, King! Go!"

King shoved the cyclic forward and snatched the collective back. The Jet Ranger slid off the platform, falling rapidly toward the Gulf. The helicopter picked up speed and zoomed north. Looking back, Hillary saw the men on the platform, above them now, firing at King Air 1.

King stirred the controls, dodging to evade the bullets. The helicopter danced and staggered above the Gulf. The platform shrank and disappeared, out of range.

King Air 1 whistled through the gathering darkness. The sun, a huge red ball, slid down the sky on the Arabian side of the Gulf.

"I guess we made it, huh?" King didn't sound convinced.

"I don't think so," Hillary said. "Stop here."

King looked around. "You're crazy! There's nothing around us but water."

"I mean hover! Quickly!"

King brought the chopper to a standstill. "I don't see..."

"Shh!" Hillary hissed. He stared at the sky. "There it is."

King followed Hillary's pointing finger to a dot on the eastern sky. It looked like an evening star, but it was orange, not blue. And it was getting closer.

"Christ, it's a missile!"

Hillary nodded. "I didn't think *Biddle* would tell us twice."

"What are we going to do?"

"Nothing."

"Nothing?"

"It's a Standard missile," Hillary explained. "It looks for motion. If we hover steady, it might not see us."

"*Might* not?" King yelled. "I don't like the sound of that."

"Have you got a better idea?" Hillary kept his eyes on the missile. "Okay, hold it steady. Here it comes!"

The missile bore straight in on King Air 1.

"Steady..."

King fought to keep his hands from shaking. He could see the gray nose now, and the four fins.

"Steady..."

The Standard filled the starboard canopy window. King was surprised at its size, even without its jettisoned first stage.

"We're all right," Hillary said. "It's not diving. If we..."

His words were lost in the thunder of the rocket, as the missile passed a hundred feet above the helicopter, roaring like a locomotive as it hurtled off to the west.

"We did it!" King exclaimed. He stared as Hillary cranked his head around the cockpit. "Hey, what are you looking for now?"

"The other one." Hillary stuck his head out the window to get a better look.

"There's *another* one?" King exclaimed. "Oh, Christ! Let's call it off and..."

"There it is!" Hillary pulled his head back inside the cockpit. "Now listen closely. Our lives depend on it."

"Hey, I'm listening."

"Head out that way," Hillary pointed northeast. "Fast as you can go."

King nosed the Jet Ranger over, instruments in the red. No point in babying the engine now.

Hillary strained to keep the tiny speck in focus. The orange ball turned into a gray circle with a bright halo. The missile had tipped over, starting its terminal run.

"Okay, when I give the word, step on the brakes and climb as fast as you can," Hillary said. "And I mean straight up, too, or it won't work."

"You got it."

"Not yet." Hillary stared at the approaching missile. "Not yet...Now!"

King slammed the cyclic. The helicopter dipped down. He gave it full up collective. King Air 1 rose straight as an elevator. The missile passed on its way down, plunging into the Gulf a hundred feet away in a blue-and-red geyser.

Riding the controls, King fought to keep flying in the turbulence. The water soon swallowed all traces of the missile in a ring of expanding ripples on the calm surface of the Gulf.

"Is that it?"

"I think so," Hillary answered. "This low, they can't tell if they got us or not. At any rate, they're not going to waste any more missiles. They probably think we're dead."

"I thought so, too," King said. He slid the helicopter off its hover and into forward motion again. "What happened back there?"

"They usually fire those things in pairs, high and low," Hillary explained. "The first missile is just to get your attention. It's easy to beat—it comes in low and it's more or less out of energy by the time it gets to you."

"It didn't seem so easy."

"Compared to the last one, it was," Hillary said. "Lucky for us, both missiles were near the end of their range. And the cruiser didn't have line of sight on us, so the missiles had to use their own radar. But it's got a little dish and it's pulse Doppler, so it can only see things coming at it or going away."

"And when we headed north, we were going parallel to the missile, so it didn't see us, right?" King asked.

"Sort of. This being a helicopter, the missile could still see the blades moving. But we did get the radar dish to swivel all the way to one side. So when we popped up, it couldn't move any farther. It couldn't follow us because it couldn't see us. And it was headed straight down, so it couldn't overcome its own energy level to turn around and hit us, even if it could find us."

King eyed Hillary suspiciously. "How come you know so much about these things?"

"I was aboard the *Biddle* all last week, out in the Arabian Sea," Hillary answered.

"Spying?"

"Writing a story," Hillary laughed. "It pays better than spying."

The night sky was slipping in from the east. Already, the horizon outside King's cockpit window was a dark strip of indigo blue. He checked the gauges.

"We're going to have to set this bird down, soon. We're running out of gas. And daylight."

"It won't be long now," Hillary said.

King Air 1 shot through the gap between the brown islands of Larak and Hormuz. The coast of Iran spread suddenly before the helicopter's forward canopy. Gray cliffs and brown rocks marked the shoreline, with small beaches scattered here and there, covered with gray, gravellike sand. The long wharves of the old port popped up on the left, flanked by the high cranes and towers of the new port of Bandar Abbas. The low skyline of the city rose dead ahead.

"Head for the airport," Hillary suggested.

King eyed him skeptically.

"You see any better place to land?" Hillary looked down as the Jet Ranger swooped over the coast. "Looks like it's pretty quiet down there, anyway."

Long lines of light shot up from the ground at King Air 1. The first white tracers were joined by others, searching for the helicopter in the new darkness.

"Okay, so I was wrong!" Hillary shouted. "Get us out of here."

King shoved the helicopter around in the same evasive pattern he had used to baffle the gunners at the oil platform. Hillary was impressed with his flying.

"101st Airborne, A Shau Valley," he said. "Slicks, not gunships. Am I right?"

King was amazed. Like many civilian helicopter jocks, he was a former U.S. Army pilot. But he hadn't talked about it for a long time. "Blue Stars. 48th Assault Helicopter Company. How did you know?"

"It's this damn maneuver you're doing." Hillary smiled as the chopper staggered around the sky. "The Huey Shuffle. I recognize a Screaming Eagle when I see one."

"It's been a long time." King concentrated on flying. "I thought I'd never have to use it again."

The whole sky was bright with tracers. Most darted well above the helicopter as King hugged the earth, using whatever cover he could find. At such a low altitude, it was difficult for King to get his bearings. He knew Bandar International Airport was up ahead, but he had no idea how far.

Before he knew it, they were sweeping across the huge runway.

"Look out!"

King hadn't seen the charred remains of a Boeing 737 blocking the runway. At Hillary's warning he snatched the helicopter up, clearing the wreckage by inches. Fire opened up again on both sides, white tracers from the east, red from the west.

"Go ahead and put it down," Hillary said. "Don't worry, they're firing blind."

Ping! The noise sounded like a rock hitting somewhere behind the cabin.

"I'm batting a thousand today," Hillary said ruefully.

The Jet Ranger began to spin violently.

"They got the tail rotor!" King shouted. "Hang on, I'm going to autorotate."

In theory, when a helicopter's engine fails, gravity takes over, the wind generated by the falling aircraft pushing the rotors around until the chopper falls gently to earth like a leaf. That was the theory. But at low altitude, with a shot-up tail rotor, Hillary knew autorotation was just another word for crash-landing. He braced himself.

King cut the engine. The helicopter's tail boom fished across the sky in wide circles. The violent thrashings of the dying chopper whipped King

Air 1 off the runway, smashing into a high chain-link fence. The skids caught the top of the barrier, flipping the Jet Ranger on its back.

Hillary awoke upside down. The smell of jet-A fuel was everywhere. A huge knife poked through the cabin window. Hillary shrank back. There was nowhere to go.

The knife sliced through the safety harness. Hillary's head hit the ceiling with a thud. Hands reached in, grabbing him, pulling him from the helicopter through the window.

They dragged him away quickly. The helicopter exploded in the night, a yellow sphere of fire with rockets of smoke like Roman candles. Hillary, dazed, thought it looked quite beautiful. He gazed up at his rescuers. "Look, I don't know how to..."

"Save it!" The soldier standing over Hillary looked enormous. "How does he look, Doc?"

Hillary was suddenly aware of another soldier prodding his ribs, shining a red flashlight in his eyes.

"No shock, Sarge. Nothing broken. He looks okay."

"Good. Then give him his watch back."

Doc snapped off the flashlight. "Oh, come on, Sergeant Willis! What have you got against private enterprise? The way I see it, we ought to get something for our trouble. After all, we're taking all the risks, while the rest of..."

"Give him his goddamn watch back, soldier!"

"Okay, Sarge." Doc stuffed the Rolex in Hillary's shirt. Willis shoved a boot in his back, pushing Hillary face down in the sand. "Put the flexicuffs on him and take him to the terminal with the rest of them."

Willis stomped off into the darkness.

Hillary's hands were pulled behind his back. He felt the plastic restraints dig into his wrists.

"Now, wait a minute!" he shouted. "I'm on your side!"

"That's what they all say," Doc laughed.

"No, really, I'm a reporter."

"No kidding?" Doc snorted. "I knew we should have shot to kill."

The soldier pulled Hillary to his feet and nudged his back with an M16.

"We're supposed to blindfold you, but it's too dark and I'm not leading you around," Doc said. "You try anything funny, and I swear I'll grease you. Nobody would care. Nobody would even know. Hell, Willis would probably give me a medal for wasting a reporter."

The two men moved through the darkness toward the terminal building. They passed an airport ambulance surrounded by soldiers, some slumped, moaning, some lying unconscious. And many dead. The motor was idling. Inside, an Iranian doctor worked feverishly over an American paratrooper in the dim light. One soldier held a vial of plasma over the patient. Another held a pistol at the doctor's back.

Hillary noticed Frank King stretched out on the ground near the ambulance. He wasn't moving.

"How is he?" Hillary motioned to King.

"Bad," Doc frowned. "Medic says he's got a ruptured spleen, broken pelvis, probably lots of other stuff. The chopper came down on his side. He got the worst of it."

"Is he going to live?"

"Maybe. If he was in a real hospital, yeah, probably. Here, who knows?" Doc shrugged. "There's not much we can do for him until we get the battalion aid station set up. We've got plenty of our own wounded to take care of. Nobody asked him to come here."

"I did," Hillary said softly.

"What did you say?"

"Do me a favor, soldier. I've got something that belongs to him. Reach in my shirt pocket and get it. I can't get to it in these cuffs."

Doc eyed Hillary suspiciously.

"Go ahead. You can keep the watch," Hillary said, knowing the soldier would take it anyway.

Greed and curiosity won out.

"Okay, but if you make a move, you're dead. If I don't shoot you, somebody else will."

Hillary nodded. Doc poked the M16 into Hillary's stomach and reached gently into the shirt pocket. He took the watch and stuffed it in his shirt. Then he pulled out Hillary's half of the receipt.

"What the hell is this?" Doc held the scrap of paper near the light streaming from the ambulance. "It looks like a credit-card bill."

"It is," Hillary said. "He's got the other half. It's the money I owe him. I just want to square the deal, that's all."

"Feeling guilty, huh? You should. You sure as hell should."

"It could have been me lying there," Hillary said.

"Yeah, but it never is, is it?" Doc examined the receipt and whistled. "Wow! Five thousand bucks!"

"That's the going rate," Hillary said bitterly.

"Hell, you got taken. I got here for nothing." Doc looked at the name on the receipt. "Hey! You're Peter Hillary! The writer!"

Hillary brightened. "You've read my books?"

"No," Doc admitted, then added, "but the major has, I'm sure. He reads all this stuff. I've heard him talk about you. Come on, I'll take you to him."

The entrance to the terminal was blocked by a couple of airport maintenance vehicles. An M60 team crouched behind one of them, the heavy machine gun pointed across the runway.

"How's it going, Randolph?" Doc said, by way of password.

"It's quiet now," answered the gunner. "Looks like the camel jocks are sacked out for the night. Hey, who's the tourist?"

"He's a *journalist.*" The way Doc said it made Hillary feel like a child molester. "I'm taking him to the major."

"Good idea. The major *collects* those guys." Randolph nodded toward the terminal doors. "He's in baggage claim with the prisoners."

"Thanks." Doc led Hillary though the darkened lobby. The whole terminal was blacked out, illuminated only by battery-powered emergency lamps in the hallways and at the fire exits. There was no one else in the lobby, except for a couple of soldiers assembling Dragon rounds by the British Airways ticket counter. Hillary had expected to find a bustling headquarters. The place looked deserted.

"Hey, where is everybody?" Hillary said, surprised.

"What do you mean?" Doc said. "This is it."

The two men walked through a long hallway and into the baggage-claim area. Generator-driven floodlights carved hard shadows in the room, crowded with men sitting on the floor, blindfolded and hands bound. Although most of the prisoners wore civilian clothes, some were in uniform, either the gray of the regular Iranian army or Pasdaran green. Two American soldiers were interrogating a Revolutionary Guards officer when Doc and Hillary arrived.

"Ta kan na knor," said one of the soldiers, reading awkwardly from a small booklet. *"Ma baradar has team."*

The Iranian officer spat. "We are not brothers. And speak English! Your Farsi is worse than your shooting!"

"We got you, didn't we?" The soldier pointed to a bandage on the prisoner's forearm. "You're not so tough. I thought you Pasdaran guys never surrendered anyway. One little scratch and you go tits up. What a pussy!"

"That's it, Sergeant!" laughed the other American, a major. "Torture 'em with sarcasm."

"It's about the only thing we're allowed to use, isn't it, Major? You give me a couple of minutes alone with this guy and I'll have him looking forward to joining the ayatollah." The soldier's face screwed up into a mask of cynicism and frustration. "Oh, I forgot, we can't do that. We're *civilized.*"

The American officer nodded. "Well, get what you can out of them, Tony. See if you can find out if there are any tanks around."

"Yes, sir."

The major turned to Doc.

"What have you got here, Corporal? Another prisoner? Why isn't he blindfolded?" The major seemed perturbed. "Well, just sit him down with the rest of them. I'll get to him when I get back."

"This isn't another Iranian asshole, sir," Doc said. "He's an *American* asshole."

"Really, I must protest, Major," Hillary interjected. "I'm a British subject."

"Excuse me, sir," Doc apologized. "He's a *British* asshole."

The major examined Hillary's face, then broke out in a bright smile. "I know you. I've seen your face on the book jackets. You're Peter Hillary, aren't you?"

Hillary nodded.

"Corporal, take the cuffs off this man!" The officer shouted happily. "This is Peter Hillary! You know what that means? We're official now! You can't have a war without Peter Hillary!"

Doc cut the flexicuffs with a swipe of his Randall knife.

"He was in that helicopter we shot down, sir."

"You did the right thing, Corporal. It was an honest mistake. How were you to know the world's foremost war correspondent was on board?" the major said. "Better get back to your post, now. We need every man we can get out there."

"Yes, sir!" Doc trotted out of the baggage area.

The major extended his hand.

"I'm Steve Casey, battalion S-3," he said. "Welcome to my war."

Hillary shook his hand. "Peter Hillary. I'm..."

"Oh, I know all about you, Mr. Hillary. I've read all your books. It's a pleasure to meet you," Casey said. "I was just about to make my rounds. Would you like to come along?"

"Sure." Hillary, happily shocked at his new good luck, fell in behind Casey, trying to keep up with the tall major's stride. "Say, who's in charge here, anyway?"

"You're looking at him."

"I don't understand. Pardon me for saying so, but you're just a...I mean, you're a major, right?"

"Well, pardon *me* for saying so, but you're not exactly Tom Brokaw, either," Casey laughed. "We all do the best we can."

The two men walked through the main doors of the terminal and out into the black night. The airport was dark and quiet and eerily deserted.

"But shouldn't there be at least a colonel in charge?" Hillary asked. "I thought this was a big operation."

"That's what we thought, too, but it isn't working out that way, un-fortunately," Casey said. "Colonel Tortorici, the task force commander, is dead. Nobody can find Colonel Woods, the battalion commander. As battalion ops officer, I'm next in line."

"Sorry to hear about Colonel Tortorici," Hillary said. "I met him in Grenada. He was a good man."

"Airborne all the way," Casey nodded. "He was on the first plane in, like always. They got jumped by the MiGs. A few people got out, but he wasn't one of them."

"MiGs? Are you sure they weren't Iranian planes? F-4s or F-5s, maybe?"

"No, they were MiGs all right, at least a dozen of them. Somebody said they were MiG-29s, but I never got a good look. I was in the last plane in. We had a lot of trouble getting out of Oman, and they were gone by the time we jumped."

Casey was surprised Hillary didn't seem to know about the ambush over Bandar Abbas. Like many men in the military, Casey had come to rely on Hillary's books as the definitive accounts of armed conflict in the last half of the twentieth century. Most people in uniform considered journalists a necessary nuisance, at best. Hillary was different. He was fair and accurate and had an uncanny ability to put battles in the correct historical perspective, often while they were still raging.

During the Tet offensive, holed up in a Saigon bunker with a portable typewriter and a case of Johnny Walker Black, Hillary predicted America would win the battle but could never win the war. In Lebanon, he preferred to stay across the Green Line at the Caravelle rather than with the Marines at their barracks because, he said, it was safer. When he called Grenada "a belch of gallantry" and observed that Urgent Fury's most bitter battle was between the American services, military men knew instantly what he meant. And in Panama, Hillary was first to notice a disturbing trend, when he asked, editorially, why America insisted upon using its soldiers like policemen and its policemen like soldiers.

For the past five years Hillary had concentrated on the situation in the Persian Gulf. He had been with the Iraqis during the "Great Harvest" at the siege of Khorramshahr, when Yperite gas decimated the Iranian human wave attacks. It was another of many instances in which Hillary was lucky to escape with his life. When the world learned of the use of chemical weapons in the Gulf war, it was Hillary who had broken the story. Since the cease-fire, he had constantly warned that the conflict was far from over. Hillary had seen enough of war to regret its constant outbreak, yet he took some sad pleasure in knowing that those critics who had ridiculed him for crying wolf in the Gulf now appeared ridiculous themselves.

Now, at the mention of Fulcrums over Bandar Abbas, Hillary felt a familiar strangeness, the contradictory emotions of excitement and revulsion common to those who cover wars for a living. Iranians didn't fly Fulcrums. Russians did. If there were indeed Soviet pilots flying combat missions against U.S. forces, he'd have the biggest story of his career, the biggest story of anyone's career. World War III. A Peter Hillary exclusive.

"Where did the MiGs come from?"

"Who knows?" Casey shrugged. "Russia, I suppose. You know the Soviets are in Tehran now."

Hillary shook his head. "They're still too far away to fly fighters down here from those bases."

"Well, maybe they captured a staging base somewhere up in the mountains. Or maybe they've finally gotten serious about aerial refueling," Casey said. "All I know is, as soon as we hit the strait, they were on us like white on rice. We didn't have a chance."

"Didn't the Navy fly escort for you?" Hillary asked.

"Two lousy jets," Casey snorted. "Both of them shot down, I think. I really don't understand it."

The two men walked in silence along the fence that paralleled the runway.

"You know, it really is great to meet you, even like this," Casey exclaimed. "I'm kind of a student of military literature, modern stuff especially, even though most of it's garbage. Yours is different, though. You really know what you're talking about."

"Thanks, Major," Hillary said, flushed. "I'm sorry I barged in on you the way I did. I had no idea how hot the situation was down here."

"That's all right. We kind of expected you. What kind of war would this be without Peter Hillary, eh? Tell me—what do you think about Operation Ready Eagle?"

Hillary cleared his throat, nervously. "Oh, I couldn't say. I just got here, really."

"No, come on, tell me. I value your opinion."

Hillary stopped walking and stared at Casey.

"Truthfully?" he asked.

Casey nodded.

"I think you're in—how would an American put it? I think you're in deep shit."

Casey smiled. "That's what I think, too. Maybe I should go into writing best-sellers instead of jumping out of perfectly good airplanes. It would be a lot safer. Oh, by the way..."

The major reached into the right thigh pocket of his BDU trousers and took out a small paperback book.

"I took this with me because I figured we'd have a lot of time on our hands down here. The way they briefed it at Bragg, Ready Eagle was going to be a day at the beach. Our biggest problems were supposed to be boredom and sunburn."

Hillary took the book. Even in the darkness he could recognize *The Reluctant Dragon*. He was touched.

"You look a little young to have served in Vietnam."

"Just missed it," Casey said. "But Colonel Tortorici was there, and he said the book is just like the way it really was. I've read it a couple of times now. Will you autograph it for me?"

"Sure." Hillary took out a pen and signed his name on the title page. It suddenly struck him, the strangeness of it—signing his name to a book about one war in the middle of another. "It seems so long ago that I wrote this."

Casey slipped the book back into his pocket. "Do you still think Bobby Dragon is alive?"

"I did, then," Hillary frowned. "Now I'm not so sure. That was a long time ago."

"We could have used him this morning when those MiGs hit us," Casey smiled. "What's happened to the others?"

"Well, Doom is dead, of course. Brick White's a big deal at the Pentagon," Hillary said. "I'm not sure what he does, exactly. Spook stuff. He was always partial to that. Daffy Brewer joined the Navy, of all things. I really haven't kept up. Everybody seems to want to forget about what happened that day."

The men turned around to walk back to the terminal. Hillary thought it best to get to work again. *The Reluctant Dragon* was his favorite book, too. But it brought with it too many memories.

"So, Major, what outfit are you with?"

"Second Battalion, Airborne, 325th Infantry," Casey answered. "I've been on the battalion staff for a little over a year."

"Wait a minute. I'm going to take some notes," Hillary reached in his pocket and fished out a small flashlight. He snapped it on.

Casey hit the dirt, reaching up to pull Hillary down with him.

"Not a good idea, Mr. Hillary. There's..."

Automatic-weapons fire from across the runway chipped a series of holes in the wall of the terminal building above them. The shots were stitched exactly where their heads had been before Casey grabbed Hillary. The men crawled back to the terminal entrance behind the airport vehicles and the machine-gun position.

"You see 'em, Sergeant Randolph?"

"No, sir," the gunner answered. "I think he's on top of that hangar, but I'm not sure."

"Hose off a couple of rounds over there, anyway, will you? He's starting to get on my nerves."

The M60 barked a dozen times, sending long red tracers across the runway, smacking into the metal hangar in a pattern of bright yellow sparks.

"That's enough," Casey commanded. "Better save your ammunition."

Casey stood up, waited for a moment watching the hangar, and then began walking away from the terminal. He motioned for Hillary to follow.

"There's some asshole over there with a starlight scope." Casey waved a hand across the runway. "On a night like this, he can't see anything unless you help him. The smokers are going crazy, but what can you do?"

"How many Iranians are over there?" Hillary asked.

"I've got no idea," Casey admitted. "Our intelligence is crap. Hell, we don't even know what *we're* doing."

"Was there much resistance when you landed?"

"Some," Casey said. "Most of the people here were civilians. The terminal was packed. I don't think the government told anybody about Baghdad, but something like that gets around pretty fast. The place looked like Casablanca. Everybody was trying to get out. It was a mess."

"Where'd they go?" Hillary asked. "There's no one around now."

"Most of them left when the Navy bombed the runway," Casey answered. "It was a good thing, too, because the MiGs pretty much tore up the Division Ready Force. More than half the C-130s got smoked. Our guys were scattered all over the place."

"How many have you got left?"

"Last count, about three hundred here. There may be more down by the port—they're straggling in by twos and threes," Casey said. "Some invasion, huh?"

"Is that all?" Hillary couldn't believe it.

"You've got to understand, the Rangers were fragged for most of the first wave," Casey said. "We had a couple of battalions from the 75th staging from Saudi Arabia that were going to secure the airport. All we were supposed to do was mop up."

"What happened to them?" Hillary asked.

"I guess they're still in the chocks at Dhahran," Casey said. "Either that, or on their way back to Cairo West. The Saudis changed their minds at the last minute and wouldn't let them leave."

Hillary was not as surprised by the Saudis' refusal to be used as a staging base as he was by the Americans' assumption that they would have ever gone along with the plan in the first place. It just reinforced Hillary's belief that, when it came to Gulf politics, the Pentagon planners were naive children.

"Well, Major, the worst is over now." Hillary tried to sound reassuring. "Tomorrow morning you'll get reinforcements."

"I don't think so," Casey frowned. "This afternoon, before the KW-7 went tits up, we got a satellite message from General Coleman out on the *Eisenhower*. The Division Ready Brigade diverted to Egypt. The Omanis wouldn't let them land."

Hillary had heard about the trouble in Oman from a friend attached to the 22d SAS Regiment. The way the British officer had told it, the American paratroopers had been lucky to get out of Masirah alive.

"Cairo's not so far." Hillary tried to sound cheerful. "They could still make it here, one way. They could land on the runway."

"Not *this* runway," Casey said. "Some Navy puke committed a major tiger error and dicked an airliner right in the middle of the strip."

Hillary nodded. "We saw it coming in. We almost ran into it."

"Nothing's landing here until we clear the wreckage," Casey said. "And we can't do that while those guys across the street are shooting at us."

Hillary searched for a solution. "What if they brought in C-141s for the paratroopers?"

Casey thought for a moment. "Besides the fact that it would take every Starlizard ever made about three trips to drop the DRB, there's still the problem of the MiGs. They're not going to send any trash hauler anywhere near Bandar Abbas until they're sure the MiGs won't be back."

"The Navy fighters can't help?"

"They can, but they won't," Casey said bitterly. "The general says Meredith is worried about his ships first, and there aren't enough Tomcats left over for us. They'll CAP the airfield, but the admiral says he can't make any guarantees about escorting our planes in for any more airdrops."

"What about the Marines?"

"Same problem. They're not landing until we've got complete air superiority, and I don't blame them. Besides, they're still a couple of days away. We're supposed to secure a beachhead for them, but..."

Casey's voice trailed off into the night. The two men walked in silence past the ambulance. Business was still brisk.

"So you're stuck here?"

"Looks that way," Casey agreed.

"Can you hold out?"

"Hard to say. We don't know how many people they've got over there, but it can't be that many." Casey stared across the runway. "There weren't many Iranian units stationed here to begin with. Most of their guys are still up north on the Iraqi border. And a lot of the Iranian soldiers here deserted when we landed. There were empty uniforms all over the terminal. Between us and the bomb, I guess they figured enough was enough."

"So who's doing all the shooting?"

"Revolutionary Guards. Army officers, maybe. We've captured a lot of guys from some sort of engineer outfit." Casey shook his head. "There aren't many of them, but they're hard core. And they know what they're doing."

Hillary nodded. Americans seemed to think the Iranian military was some sort of Keystone Kops operation, but he knew better. Iranian soldiers had been in combat for almost a decade, and you don't survive that long without learning something about war.

"Luckily, they spend almost as much time fighting among themselves as they do shooting at us," Casey continued. "There's probably been no direction from Tehran since this whole thing started, and I guess they're trying to decide among themselves who's in charge now. But if they ever get around to really concentrating on us, it's going to get real interesting."

"What about the rest of the population? How do they feel?"

"Who knows? We haven't seen many since we've been here. They all ran back to the city. A few stuck around and asked us if the flights out were going to be delayed," Casey laughed. "Can you imagine? We had to chase them out. Mostly they don't care. They're pissed that we took away their airport, but I think they'll leave us alone for now. They've got problems of their own."

"They probably think there's a whole division here," Hillary said.

"Yeah, that's the only thing we got going for us," Casey agreed. "It's funny—the MiGs didn't seem to be on their side. One got plastered by an Iranian HAWK. There was no coordination. So maybe the Iranians don't know how badly we were chewed up on the way in. They're acting like we've got five thousand men on the ground. And I'm not doing anything to discourage that assumption."

"What do you mean?" Hillary asked.

"Message traffic. Radio frequencies. Everybody's on the horn, chattering up a storm, calling in fire support that never comes in, talking to fighters that aren't there," Casey said. "We've got squads using battalion call signs, that sort of thing. Hell, *I'm* impressed, and I know it's a trick."

"How long do you think you can keep it up?"

Casey frowned. "Sooner or later they're going to know something's wrong. You can't hide that many people in a place like this."

"What's going to happen then?" Hillary knew the answer. If the Iranians got their act together, Casey and his pitifully small force would be ground up and spit out. The lucky ones would be killed.

"Let me put it this way: The difference between this and the Alamo is that Davy Crockett didn't have to fight his way *into* the Alamo." Casey glanced at his watch. "Come on, we've got to get going."

Casey led the way around the terminal and into the parking lot.

"We've got a landing zone set up back here. We can't take a chance on the choppers' landing on the runway where the bad guys can see them."

Hillary could hear the faint whopping of helicopter blades in the distance. American soldiers stood in the middle of the huge concrete parking lot, now empty. The red lenses in their flashlights made slow circles in the dark. The landing zones were marked in the eerie green glow of chemlight sticks.

"Where are they coming from?" Hillary asked, surprised to hear helicopters so far from an American base.

"The *Saipan*," Casey answered. "It's an assault ship out in the Gulf. They waited until nightfall and slipped into the strait."

"Are they going to take you out?"

"Can't," Casey answered. "There aren't enough of them, even for the few people we have left. They're bringing in ammunition and taking out the wounded."

Injured troopers stumbled past Hillary in the dark. An airport pickup truck with a tarp across the back drove slowly onto the parking lot. Casey stopped the driver.

"What have you got in the back, soldier?" he asked.

The driver, an American private, seemed uncomfortable. "Some of the dead, sir."

Casey shook his head sadly. "Sorry, son. We don't have the room this trip. Park them by those date trees over there. They're not going anywhere."

"Yes, sir." The truck turned around and crept off into the night.

The first of the *Saipan*'s choppers landed in a deafening clatter. The rotor wash threw small pebbles from the parking lot against Hillary's legs. Three more CH-53s set down in the dark. Troopers scurried to unload the ammunition and supplies while the wounded waited to board.

A whistle arced over the terminal. A bush of bright flame lit up the far corner of the parking lot.

"Mortars!" Casey exclaimed. "I was afraid of that. Come on!"

He pulled Hillary toward the nearest chopper. SeaCobra gunships from the *Saipan* zoomed over the terminal, opening up on the Iranians across the runway. Naval gunfire from the *Biddle* and *Charles Adams* roared in the night, impacting on the far side of the airport. A flare went off overhead, illuminating the parking lot in a harsh, phosphorescent light.

Casey pushed Hillary in the CH-53. Hillary resisted.

"I'm staying here!" he shouted. "You don't have enough room for the wounded as it is."

"Don't be a hero!" Casey had to yell to be heard. Mortar rounds boomed closer. The gunships' 20-mm cannon buzzed in the distance, mixing with the sizzle of their rockets and the snapping of the Iranians' returning fire. "They're getting the range."

The helo on the far end took a direct hit from the Iranian mortars. Loaded with ammunition and fuel, the CH-53 exploded in a black-and-orange sunburst. Secondary explosions threw flaming shrapnel into the chopper next to it, setting off another fireball.

Casey screamed into the helicopter at Hillary. "You want to help? I'll tell you what you can do. Go back and tell the world we landed, we secured the airport, the whole division is here, the Iranians welcomed us with open arms, and everything's fine."

"What?" Hillary shouted.

"Look, nobody knows what's going on here. They'll believe anything you write. They always have."

"That's because it's the truth."

"Well, this time if you write the truth you'll be writing a death sentence for me and everybody else down here." Casey's throat hurt as he struggled to be heard over the noise of the explosions and the helicopter's engines winding up. "Our only hope is to keep everyone thinking we've got so much firepower here we're tripping over ourselves. Only you can do that for us."

Casey's eyes met Hillary's in the hellish glow of the burning choppers. "We're depending on you. You're the only impartial eyewitness the real world has got to tell them what's going on here. You've been here. You're Peter Hillary. No one's going to contradict you. You tell them the truth and we're screwed. You exaggerate a little, and maybe you can save our lives. Can we count on you?"

Hillary looked at the major's pleading eyes. He knew Casey was right. He lifted his arm in a mock salute.

"Yes, sir!" Then he added. "Oh, Major Casey! Frank King, the helicopter pilot I came in with—do what you can for him, okay? He's ex-Airborne, you know. 101st."

"All the way!" Casey extended his hand. Hillary shook it. "Nice to meet you, Mr. Hillary. Come back anytime."

Casey rapped on the cockpit window to get the pilot's attention and motioned thumbs up. He stepped back as the big CH-53 lifted slowly in the air.

Hillary waved through the open crew door as the helicopter swung south to the Gulf. He saw the two burning choppers, the wounded, lined up in the chocks, staring at his helicopter, knowing they would not get out on this flight. He saw Major Casey watching as he lifted off, then organizing a party to gather the few supplies that got through before they were destroyed by mortar fire.

Hillary slumped exhausted in the hold. They were already over the dark Gulf. The gunships, low on fuel, had joined up. Hillary thought about what he had just seen, what Casey had asked him to do. In his life he had done many things he was not proud of. Hillary thought of Frank King and frowned. But it was necessary, he told himself. The truth had to get out. War was serious business. You couldn't depend on the military to tell the whole story, and the people had a right to know.

Or so he thought. Casey was right. These days the media was a powerful weapon, certainly more formidable than anything Casey's outfit could command. What he wrote *would* make a difference. Telling the truth would condemn everyone at Bandar Abbas to certain death. But lying would destroy the reputation he had worked all his life to build.

What was it Winston Churchill said about war correspondents? "In time of war, the first casualty is truth." But he had also said, "In wartime, truth is so precious it must always be attended by a bodyguard of lies." There would be time for the truth later. Hillary thought of what he would write:

> The gallant U.S. 82d Airborne fell from the sky in division strength at daybreak this morning. Brushing aside scattered resistance, they were welcomed as liberators by the Iranian people. An hour after their dramatic airdrop at Bandar Abbas International Airport all was quiet, save for the constant landing of cargo jets bringing in supplies and reinforcements and the whine of Navy fighters flying unnecessary air cover in the otherwise empty skies overhead. It was a classic example of American global reach, a certain, timely answer to the reckless atomic bombing of Baghdad by the religious fanatics of the Iranian government...

The *Saipan* slid underneath the helicopter, a black rectangle in a black sea. Pinpoints of light guided the aircraft on its descent. Hillary was safe.

It was then he thought of the last line: "This report cleared by American military censors."

First Air

Dreamland
Groom Lake, Nevada

So what do you think, Bobby? Should we kill this guy or buy him dinner?"

Bobby Dragon looked at the security officer. He wasn't kidding. Security had never been a laughing matter at Dreamland; now, with the world sliding into war, Bobby knew he had only to give the word and Brick White would be dead.

The major led the way to the rear of the van and opened the doors. Bobby stared inside in surprise and disbelief. It was Brick all right, handcuffed and squeezed between two Uzi-toting security guards dressed in civilian clothes. Bobby's heavy helmet clattered to the pavement. The wind screamed across the lonely desert. Neither man spoke for a long time.

"Hello, Brick."

"Hello, Bobby. Long time, no see."

"This guy came in about an hour ago in a blue canoe. No orders, no clearance, nothing." The security officer handed Bobby a clipboard. "He says he's a friend of yours. You want to vouch for him?"

Bobby nodded slowly and signed the authorization form. The guard unlocked the handcuffs and helped Brick out of the crowded van.

"Sorry about the mix-up, General." The guard's apology sounded neither courteous nor genuine. "We can't be too careful out here, not these days."

He got back in the van and drove off, leaving Brick and Bobby standing alone by the runway. Brick stood awkwardly and watched the van speed off, avoiding Bobby's eyes.

"The least he could do is give us a ride," Brick said wistfully.

Bobby smiled. "You're lucky he didn't shoot you. What made you think you could zoom in here without squawking the right codes? They can't see your stars from the ground, you know."

"I didn't want anyone to know I was coming," Brick said. "Besides, I had the codes from yesterday. How was I supposed to know they change them every day?"

Bobby sighed. "They change them every *hour*, Brick. There've been planes shot down out here for less."

"Then I guess it's just my lucky day." Brick's dry, nervous laughter rolled across the desert flats. A still silence settled in as they walked slowly back toward the ramp and the lights of Dreamland.

So many memories, Bobby thought. All those years, everything that had happened then and since. Did he still hate Brick White? He searched his feelings and found nothing, neither love nor hate. All emotion was gone. Brick's a ghost, just like me, Bobby thought. Or is he real and I just can't feel it because I'm a ghost myself?

Brick seemed real enough, stomping across the dry lake in his summer uniform. A little heavier, Bobby thought, though not much older than those first days at Da Nang. But Brick had seemed so old, even then.

Bobby remembered the night they had met. He was a brown-bar nugget, with two days in country, fresh from the F-4 finishing school at George AFB. Brick was already a legend, the Air Force's leading MiG killer, a cigar-chomping, fire-breathing fighter hero, larger than life. He was also Bobby's commanding officer. Bobby's fellow pilots in his new squadron were quick to fill him in on Brick's exploits, the nonstop rounds of drinking and flying, the clashes with headquarters, and the famous tiger hunts. But nothing prepared Bobby for his first sight of the real Brick White at the Red Dog Saloon.

All of Da Nang City was off limits to Air Force personnel then. But the Red Dog Saloon, with its shady clientele of spooks, con men, and the occasional reporter, was especially forbidden. Naturally, that's where most of the members of the 585th Tactical Fighter Squadron hung out every night. As the premier USAF air-to-air unit in Southeast Asia, the Heartbreakers had an image to maintain. Breaking the rules was part of the fighter-pilot paradigm. In the wide-open Sodom that was South Vietnam in the early seventies, it was hard to find something—on the ground, anyway—that was not permitted, and the Heartbreakers' presence at the Red Dog reaffirmed their reputation as hard-drinking, hell-raising, gunslinging fighter jocks.

It was in this spirit that 2d Lt. Robert Dragon snuck off base his second day as a Heartbreaker. Destination: Red Dog. Wide-eyed, he had taken it all in—the swinging saloon doors, the cement floor, the white walls black with autographs of every real fighter pilot in Southeast Asia. The place was packed with servicemen, officers and enlisted, none of them, it seemed, wearing the same uniform, but all of them American. A fight had broken out earlier. The loser, a Navy lieutenant commander, lay stretched on the bar, as the patrons reached over his unconscious body for more liquor from the expressionless Vietnamese bartender.

Brick made his entrance at midnight. The saloon doors burst open. One, torn from its hinges, clattered on the hard floor. The table nearest the entrance flipped over with a crash, though its occupants, a group of Marine helicopter pilots, had the presence of mind to snatch up their drinks before scurrying for safety. All eyes turned to the source of the commotion: Lt. Col. William "Brick" White, commander, 585th Tactical Fighter Squadron, and the USAF's leading MiG killer, with three victories to his credit, on the back of the biggest white horse Bobby had ever seen.

The crowd burst into applause. It was a new height of audacity, even for the Red Dog. Brick sat tall in the saddle, his left hand twirling his famous handlebar mustache, his right hand resting on the butt of his other trademark, a pearl-handled Colt .45 pistol.

Brick's eyes swept the room, taking in the cheers and the drunken laughter. He spotted Bobby in the back with the rest of the Heartbreakers. In his first, brief meeting with Brick, within minutes of reporting for duty, Bobby had been dismissed curtly and quickly. "Your instructors at George say you're the hottest jock since the Red Baron," Brick had said. "We'll see." At the Red Dog, Brick's true emotions surfaced. His eyes settled on Bobby with a look of dark anger and jealousy.

He swept the pistol from its holster, shooting from the hip. The crowd at the bar hit the floor, diving under tables and crawling toward the exit. The bullet smacked six inches above Bobby's head. He didn't duck. He didn't even move. Brick smiled.

"Are you ready to kill, son?" Brick's eyes had burned with challenge. "Because if you're not ready to kill, you'd better be ready to die."

Are you ready to kill? Yes, Bobby thought, ready, willing, and more than able. Flying had given him everything, and it had taken it away. Who could have foreseen what would flow from that night in the Red Dog, the times and the tragedies that followed? Who could have guessed that it would lead here, to the end of the earth, walking calmly with Brick again at his side, knowing that whatever bound them together, wherever their path was destined to lead, it wasn't over yet between Brick White and Bobby Dragon.

"One thing I've always wondered, Brick," Bobby said. "Where did you get that horse?"

"What?" Brick said, lost in his own reverie.

"That night at the Red Dog. That big white horse. Where did you get it? There weren't any horses within a thousand miles of Da Nang."

Brick smiled. "It's funny. I was just thinking about that myself. I'd gone down to Saigon that morning, and on the way back I saw them unloading this huge beast from the back of a C-141 at Tan Son Nhut. Some Cav general at MAC V had flown it over from Clark Air Base in the Philippines. He was going to use it in a parade ceremony or some such nonsense. Anyway, one look in that horse's eyes and I could see what it really wanted to do was go for a shooter at the Red Dog."

They reached the ramp. Brick's eyes widened. The shapes that had been mere shadows at the end of the runway now sprung into full definition. He could see just about every modern tactical aircraft in the world as well as a number he didn't recognize. All the latest Soviet designs, some of the European prototypes, and a number of familiar American aircraft distorted with mysterious modifications squatted menacingly on the Dreamland ramp. Brick whistled softly.

"Bobby, we need to talk," he said. "Is there someplace we can go and have some privacy?"

The question struck Bobby as funny. They were in Dreamland, the most private place on earth. Then he noticed Brick wasn't laughing.

"Yeah, sure, Brick," Bobby said. "I know a place just down the road. Hang on a second, I'll get a jeep."

Bobby trotted off to the ops shack, leaving Brick alone with his thoughts. He looked at the menagerie on the ramp and swore. He had been out of touch too long. He had gotten away from the operational side of things, where he belonged. His new job was really more suited to a diplomat than a fighter pilot, but he did it well. Then he looked at the aircraft again, the hottest birds in the world, and he wanted to fly every one of them. He was no bureaucrat. He was a warrior. And so was Bobby Dragon. It was the only thing they had in common, but it took precedence over everything else.

Bobby drove up in an Air Force jeep, motioning Brick to climb inside. They drove along the runway until it ran out, and then they sped into the desert night. The moon rose over the Jumbled Hills, throwing sharp shadows on the forbidding face of Bald Mountain to the north. Ahead, a sudden mesa interrupted the uniform flatness of Emigrant Valley. Bobby swung the jeep onto the rough road that wound behind the mesa, barreling halfway up its steep side until the road stopped in a field of boulders.

"End of the line," Bobby said. "We'll have to walk from here."

He led the way up the jagged path. It was tough going. The trail ended on the absolutely level surface of the mesa top. Bobby walked to the north edge. Brick followed, fighting for air, trying not to gasp.

"It's beautiful," Brick said, finally.

Bobby nodded. The whole base spread out before them, a mosaic of lights and shapes gleaming in the black night. From ten miles away, it did indeed look like Dreamland.

An F-117 took off slowly on its short hop back to Cactus Flat, the stealth-fighter base just over the mountains. To avoid attention, Dreamland's operations were scattered across hundreds of miles of desert. There was also a mock Soviet fighter base out there somewhere, Brick knew, with real Russian planes and personnel trained to act, talk, and think like Communists. He shuddered to think what else might be going on out in the secret night. He decided he'd rather not know.

"Bobby, listen, I want to tell you I'm sorry about what happened," Brick said suddenly. "I'm sorry about the whole damn thing. If I can..."

"Skip it, Brick," Bobby said sharply. "It was a long time ago."

Brick could see no absolution in Bobby's gaze, but he did see the understanding of the intervening years. It was a start. Perhaps they *could* work together again, if not fly together. Whatever else had passed between them, they were once wingmen in combat. It was not a bond either of them took lightly.

"Then let's get on with current business," Brick said. "I need your help."

Bobby swallowed. For Brick White to admit he needed anyone's help, for him to come all this way, to seek out Bobby after all that had happened— Bobby knew he must be very desperate indeed.

"I figured you didn't come all the way out here to chat about old times," Bobby said. "This has to do with what's going on in Iran, doesn't it?"

Brick nodded. "How much do you know about it?"

"I was flying when the bomb went off," Bobby said. "We were running an exercise with the AWACS when I got a knock-it-off signal on the Doomsday net. When I landed, they told me the Iranians had nuked Baghdad and the 82d was going in."

"But you haven't heard anything about how the operation's going?"

"No." Bobby sounded puzzled. "We've been busy out here trying to get some things we've been working on out of the labs and into the field. The brass have been breathing down our necks—they say they may have to use some of this stuff soon. I supposed everything was going as planned over at Bandar Abbas."

Brick sighed. It would have been much easier to do what he had come halfway around the world to do if Bobby had known how critical the situation in Iran had become. But then, the Pentagon had tried desperately to present the American invasion of Iran as a textbook operation.

And, with the help of Peter Hillary's story, they had succeeded. So far.

"I'll give it to you straight, Bobby. I don't have time to put a good spin on it." Brick took a deep breath. "We're getting our ass kicked. If things keep going on like this, we'll be wiped out to a man in a couple of weeks, a month at the most. It's just a question of whether it's going to be the Russians or the Iranians who push us into the Gulf."

"I don't understand." Bobby was shocked. "What went wrong?"

"Everything. It's Murphy's law over there. Everything that could go wrong, did, plus a couple of wild cards thrown in for good measure. Let me start at the beginning. You're familiar with Operation Ready Eagle, aren't you?"

Bobby nodded. Just about every operator in the U.S. armed services had a role to play in the contingency plan to invade Iran. With so many people involved, it would be hard to keep the plans secret.

"Don't tell me they're using Ready Eagle, Brick. Christ, those plans have to be at least ten years old, now."

"Ready Eagle *has* been on the books for a long time," Brick agreed. "Too long, as it turns out. It was put together after the Iranian hostage crisis as a sort of all-purpose response to whatever contingency might occur in the Gulf. We didn't want to get caught with our pants down again. The goal was to seize the oil fields and preempt the Russians. We just wanted to reach the beach. If there were any long-term goals after that, we figured we could sort them out once we got there."

"Shoot first and ask questions later?"

"Something like that," Brick admitted. "You've got to realize, Bobby, even in this day and age, even with all the planes and ships we've got, you can't just snap your fingers and move whole divisions halfway around the world. It takes a ton of paperwork. You don't have time to do it when the shooting starts. When the bomb went off in Baghdad, the president knew he had to do *something*. And when he ordered an immediate conventional response, the Joint Chiefs reached up on the shelf and dusted off Ready Eagle. It was all they had."

"So maybe it wasn't a complete surprise," Bobby said. "But it's still a pretty good plan."

Brick nodded. "It's a good *plan,* all right. But as a real-world operation, it's been a complete nightmare. Ready Eagle was predicated on complete allied air superiority. We were going to take over just about every paved air base on the Arabian side of the Gulf and make up for our lack of heavy stuff on the ground by pounding the hell out of them from the air. We were going to sweep the skies with fighters and fly in everything we had onto captured airstrips."

"Well, what's stopping you?"

"We've got nowhere to land, Bobby. When push came to shove, the

Arabs told us to kiss off. Nobody east of Egypt wants anything to do with us. After the initial airdrop—and *that* was a royal goat screw—we haven't been able to resupply or reinforce the assault force."

Bobby stared across the desert, taking it all in. He was a fighter pilot, not a big-time commander like Brick, but even he knew the 82d was in deep trouble. Without cooperation and landing rights in the Gulf, the operation was doomed to certain failure. Americans had come to depend on air power to perform miracles, but Bobby knew it was a fragile kind of magic. Too many details had to happen perfectly for a plan like that to come off. And according to Brick, so far nothing had gone right with Ready Eagle.

"So what's next?"

"No one knows," Brick said. "We're in, and we're staying in. It's touch and go right now. The only break we've got so far is that the Iranians seem to think the whole 82d Airborne Division landed at Bandar Abbas. I guess they figure no one in their right mind would invade a hostile country with what amounts to a reinforced rifle company. A couple hundred men, at the most."

"Jesus, Brick!" Bobby exploded. "That's not an invasion force. That's just a bunch of hostages! What happened to the rest of the 82d?"

"Oh, they're perfectly all right," Brick said glumly. "They're at Cairo West, safely camped out on another continent."

"Egypt?" Bobby said. "I thought Ready Eagle was supposed to stage out of Oman."

"That's where the first wave finally took off, thanks to some arm-twisting by the Brits," Brick said. "The big brains at the Pentagon didn't even tell the Omanis we were coming in until the 82d was halfway there. That's not exactly the best way to go about fostering future cooperation, is it? The sultan told me that he'll personally put a rocket-propelled grenade into any American plane that tries to land there now. And he means it, too, the son of a bitch, although I can't say I blame him."

"But what good is the 82d going to do in Egypt? It's two thousand miles from Iran."

"Try four thousand," Brick said. "It's two thousand miles if you can fly over Saudi Arabia, which we can't, unless we want to take them on, too. Or we can fly through Israel, and then over Jordan—maybe—and then Iraq, and give the *Syrians* a chance to shoot at us. Or we can fly down the Red Sea and have our choice of being picked off by the Russians at Aden or running out of fuel over the Arabian Sea. The heavies might be able to make the trip, but not without fighter escort. There's just no way to run an air war over the Persian Gulf from Egypt."

Brick was right, Bobby thought. It looked like a dead end.

"You're in with the big brass in Washington. What do they plan to do now?"

Brick snorted. "The usual. They're blaming everyone else. They've got people making social calls at all the embassies, trying to get the Arabs to change their minds. If you know anything about the Arabs, you know how pointless *that* is. Meanwhile, the Pentagon seems content to just scratch out 'Oman' on all the orders and put in 'Egypt' instead, like it's going to do some good. They've got every C-141, C-5, KC-10, and civilian airliner they can charter shuttling supplies and reinforcements to Cairo West. You have no idea how much crap you have to haul around to field a decent force these days, Bobby. We've got a huge bottleneck at Cairo West now. The place looks like one big K-Mart."

Bobby remembered Vietnam, the dumps and the depots, the countryside littered with supplies, most of it unnecessary. If it was bad then, it had to be worse now. No army ever willingly reduces its supply requirements.

"I'm no general, Brick, but it seems to me you need to haul this trash in ships, not airplanes. They can carry a lot more, and you don't need airstrips," Bobby said. "I thought we had a whole fleet of ships, both freighters and tankers, stationed at Diego Garcia, already loaded and waiting to sail during a contingency like this."

"Near-Term Prepositioned Ships," Brick smiled. "Oh, they're still there, all right, bobbing up and down at the docks in Dodge City. The problem is, they need a port, and we haven't secured one yet. It's the old chicken-and-the-egg story. If we had enough force on the ground to take the port, we wouldn't need it anymore. The Division Ready Force at Bandar Abbas International has more than it can handle just staying alive. But as soon as we can put enough bodies on the ground, they're going to march down and seize the port."

"And then your troubles will be over, right?"

"Not really, but, yeah, it would help a lot," Brick admitted. "If we had a port, we could also land Task Force Bravo's Marine Expeditionary Unit immediately, and then, later on, the rest of the 7th Marine Expeditionary Brigade. And once we had *those* people on the ground, we could build an air facility for attack helicopters and maybe Harriers. We could even clean up Bandar Abbas International, if we had some engineers. We could bring in the whole damn 101st Air Assault Division and really kick some ass."

Bobby frowned. He was beginning to talk like the old Brick White again. It sounded good, but there were too many ifs. The fact remained that only a handful of grunts were now in Iran. The rest were thousands of miles away, and no closer to getting into action than they were when Brick launched into his briefing.

Bobby stood up to leave.

"Well, it sounds like a great plan, Brick, and I wish you luck with it, but I don't see what it has to do with me," Bobby said. "If you want my permission, I say fine, go ahead, knock yourself out."

"But it does have a lot to do with you, Bobby," Brick said ominously. "In fact, the whole thing depends on you."

Bobby shivered in the suddenly cold desert night.

"How's that?"

"Air cover," Brick explained. "Like I said, the whole thing depends on air support, and we don't have any. Unless we can insert some fighters and some strike aircraft in the theater, Ready Eagle is going down the tubes, and a lot of American lives will go along with it."

Bobby didn't know what Brick was leading up to, but he knew he was bound to be involved in it. And he knew he wouldn't want any part of it. He searched for an alternative.

"What about the Navy?" Bobby asked. "They're always squawking about how wonderful their aircraft carriers are. Let them do it."

"They can't," Brick said.

"Can't or won't?"

"It doesn't much matter." Brick shrugged. "I can't get them to budge. I had to practically keelhaul Meredith, the task force commander, to give me a week as it is."

"That's the Navy for you."

"Well, I can see his point," Brick admitted. "He's scared to death. If Iran's got another bomb up its sleeve, all of his ships are dead meat, and he knows it."

Ah, the bomb, Bobby remembered. That changed everything. No wonder the Arabs were dead set against jumping in bed with the Great Satan—emphasis on dead.

"Do they?" Bobby asked. "Have another bomb, I mean?"

"We don't know," Brick said. "We don't know where they got the one they used in Baghdad. So we have to assume they can do it again if they want until we find out otherwise."

"Damn!" Bobby whistled.

"Besides, the Navy has too much to do as it is," Brick continued. "We're asking them to CAP the grunts over Bandar Abbas International, fly cover over their own task force, watch out for submarines, and do close air support for the 82d. Meredith's only got so many planes, and they're breaking down faster than he can fix them. And getting shot down faster than he can replace them. We can't even think about seizing the port and bringing in the Marines and the supply ships without more air support."

Bobby looked puzzled. Why was Brick so worried about air superiority?

"I don't understand, Brick. The Iranians can't be that tough. They can't fly worth a damn, and most of their airplanes don't work anyway."

Brick groaned. He'd forgotten that Bobby, like most of the world, knew nothing about the aerial ambush over Bandar Abbas.

"Listen, Bobby," he said, trying to remain calm. "The place is crawling with MiGs."

"Russians?"

"No. *Afghan* MiGs."

Bobby thought for a moment. "I thought the Russians pulled out of Afghanistan, Brick. I don't know what they're doing there, but so what? Don't tell me the squids are scared of a squadron of ragheads in MiG-21s?"

"They're not MiG-21s, Bobby. They're *MiG-29*s. Fulcrums. And it's not just a squadron. We don't know how many they've got, but it looks more like a wing. A regiment, at least."

Bobby frowned. He had flown Dreamland's captured Fulcrum a dozen times. It was a hot aircraft, a real tits machine. He'd hate to go up against one, let alone two or three dozen.

"It still comes down to who's flying, though, doesn't it? The Tomcat's not bad, if it's flown well. The Syrians had the Russians' latest stuff over the Bekáa and look what happened to them. I can't believe the mujahideen could do any better, no matter what they're flying."

"That's just it, Bobby. We don't know who's in the cockpits of those Fulcrums, but they're not Afghans. Whoever it is, they fly shit hot. Between you and me, the Navy jocks are getting their clocks cleaned over the Gulf. They're developing a complex about it. Half of them separate before they even get feet dry."

Bobby shook his head. For all the rivalry between Air Force and Navy fighter pilots, he had a lot of respect for naval aviators. They were good. They knew what they were doing, and they were tough to beat. If the Tomcat crews on Gonzo Station were running from the MiGs, Bobby knew they had good reason.

"So what do you want me to do about it?" Bobby asked. "I can't go over there like Marshal Dillon and single-handedly wipe out this mystery Air Force, even if I had a place to land."

"Nobody's asking you to do that," Brick said. "You'll have a base right across the Gulf. You can pick your pilots—anyone you want, we'll volunteer them for you. You can have any aircraft you need. Anything. And we'll make sure they work, too. You want support, we can..."

"Whoa, partner," Bobby held up his hand. "Slow down; you're going too fast for me. Let's take this a step at a time, shall we? Are you telling me you're going to put me in command of an American Air Force unit smack in the middle of the Persian Gulf?"

"Yes and no."

"Come on, Brick. Yes what and no what?"

"Yes, it's smack in the middle of the Persian Gulf," Brick answered evasively. "But no, it's not an Air Force unit. Not exactly."

"Then what the hell is it?"

"It's, uh..." Brick decided to come right out with it. "It's a private corporation."

Bobby looked like he'd been hit with a safe.

"A what?"

"A private corporation, chartered in the Bahamas," Brick blurted out. "It's all perfectly legal. All you need is—hey! Where are you going?"

Bobby began walking back to the jeep. "I knew it. It's one of your spook fantasies. Well, you can count me out."

Brick disappeared down the trail.

"Go ahead, Bobby! Run away again! That's your way, isn't it?" Brick shouted angrily. "I'll see you in Leavenworth!"

Bobby turned back, eyes flashing.

"You can't do that," he said. "You can't put a man in prison for refusing to volunteer for some screwy suicide mission."

"You're right," Brick said. "But I can put *you* away so far they'd have to pipe down light to see you. Hell, I can probably have you shot. We're at war, Bobby. And technically, you're still a deserter."

The two men faced each other in the darkness.

"That was a long time ago."

"It's still on the books." Brick's voice softened. "Look, I'm not trying to screw you. Just listen to me for a minute, okay? That's all I'm asking."

Bobby thought for a moment. "Okay, what's the deal?"

Brick smiled. "I knew you'd see it my way."

"I'm not saying yes or no," Bobby said. "But I'll listen."

"All right. I'll lay it all out for you." Brick gathered his thoughts for a moment. "If we can get some air support, we can stay in Iran, secure the beachhead and the airport, and maybe we'll get lucky and find out if they've got any other bombs and where they are. If we *don't* get some air cover, our guys at Bandar Abbas are history, the Russians will gobble up all of Iran, all the way to the Gulf, and it's possible that Washington or New York will join Hiroshima, Nagasaki, and Baghdad on the nuclear hit parade. So, yeah, I'd say your participation is important."

It made sense, Bobby had to admit. The stakes were high. This wasn't some self-promotional scheme dreamed up for the greater glory of Brick White, not this time. This was the real thing. It had to be. Brick would rather die than admit he needed Bobby's help. After all, he *had* nearly died once before trying to prove that point.

"Can we pull it off? Can we stay in?"

Doubt crossed Brick's face. "Maybe. All the pieces are there. If it weren't for those damn MiGs, I'd say yes, but I don't know."

"Who *are* those guys, Brick? Where did they come from?"

Brick shrugged. "I don't know. They're flying out of a base called Zaranj, which is right near the Iranian border. It's supposed to be a training base, but those guys fly like professors, not students."

"Are they Russian?"

"Oh, yeah, I'm sure of it," Brick answered. "Russians, Czechs, Cubans— your usual suspects."

"So why don't you tell the Soviets to cut it out?"

"The Russians say they don't know anything about it, Bobby. They say the Afghans are acting on their own."

"And you believe that?"

"Of course not!" Brick boomed. "It's a crock of shit, but we're not about to argue with them. We've both got our fingers on the button, so we're trying damn hard to be polite to one another. Actually, it's a smart move on their part. I'd do that same thing if I was them. In fact, I tried to talk the Pakistanis into fronting for *us,* but they didn't want any part of it."

"So you're going to do the next-best thing and build your own air force, huh?"

"Not me," Brick smiled. "You. It's got to be something that can't be officially tied to the government of the United States. You're the man, Bobby. You're not officially tied to anything."

Bobby found himself intrigued by the idea.

"But where are you going to park these planes, Brick? You said nobody in the Gulf wants to have anything to do with the United States."

"That's true. But what I'm talking about has nothing to do with Washington, remember? It's a private corporation, contracted by a neutral country to provide security over their sovereign airspace. Fortunately for us, Bandar Abbas and the 82d Airborne's Division Ready Force just happen to be underneath the airspace they're hired to protect."

Bobby roared with laughter. "Flying security guards! That's great! You really think anyone's going to buy that story?"

"To tell you the truth, Bobby, I don't give a damn whether they do or not. It's no more outlandish than believing that a bunch of Afghan student pilots can blow the lips off the hottest fighter jocks in the Sixth Fleet. Diplomatically, we're covered, and that's all Washington cares about."

"So where are you going to put these mercenaries? On a carrier out in the Gulf?"

Bobby had meant it as a joke, but Brick took him seriously.

"No. We thought about that, but there are too many problems. Too vulnerable. Too small. And supply would be a nightmare. Plus, we'd be limiting ourselves to carrier-qualified pilots, and the Navy pukes have already demonstrated they can't hack the mission, not by themselves."

"So where *are* you going to put these guys?" Bobby repeated.

Brick patted his pockets. He thought of all the maps of the Persian Gulf in all the Air Force briefing rooms he'd ever seen, and he'd seen most. And now, when he really needed one, there was none. He pulled a small flashlight and a pen from the shoulder pocket of his flight jacket and scrawled a crude outline of the Gulf on the back of a 510 form, a mission lineup card.

"You know the Gulf, right?" Brick asked, drawing on the form. "Here are Bandar Abbas and the strait and the rest of the Iranian coast. You got Iraq and Kuwait and Saudi Arabia, and down here at the south end, on the other side of Oman, is the United Arab Emirates."

Bobby nodded.

"Here on the west coast, between Saudi Arabia and the rest of the UAE, is the Emirate of al-Quaseem."

"Never heard of it," Bobby said.

"Most people haven't," Brick nodded. "There really isn't much to it. The whole island is only about twenty miles long and ten miles wide. But everybody's heard of the ruler of al-Quaseem, Sheik Rashid Bin Ahmed al-Hassani."

A light went on in Bobby's head. Brick was right—the whole world knew of Sheik Hassan. He was the richest man in the world.

"Hassan's going to let us base aircraft in al-Quaseem?" Bobby asked. "Why would a man with all that money want to help us?"

"Because he's got a lot to lose if he doesn't," Brick said. "And a hell of a lot to gain if he does."

"Like what?"

"Like *Iran,* Bobby. The whole damn country."

Bobby was curious but not surprised. All the rich men he had ever met only wanted one thing—more money. Iran was still sitting on potentially the greatest reserves of oil outside the Arabian peninsula. But it was a giant step from a tiny island like al-Quaseem to a country three times the size of France. What made Hassan, powerful though he was, think he could make that leap?

"Okay, Brick, I'll bite. Give me the briefing."

Brick smiled. "A century ago, the shah's great-grandfather had a half-brother who was kicked out of Iran for plotting to take over. He was looking for a kingdom, and all he could find was this godforsaken island on the western side of the Gulf. It was worthless, really, a salt dome—nothing can grow on it. It was a piece of desert surrounded by water."

"And that was Hassan's ancestor, right?"

"Right. The first sheik of al-Quaseem." Brick continued, "He tried pearl diving for a while, but it didn't take him long to realize that piracy paid better.

That's what al-Quaseem means, you know. It comes from *Qawasimi,* which is Arabic for 'pirates.' They looted ships going in and out of the Gulf all through the eighteen hundreds. It was a great pirate hangout."

"It seems to be making a comeback these days," Bobby said. "Only now they attack oil tankers with missiles instead of boarding square-riggers with cutlasses."

"Well, the Brits tried to put a stop to it a couple of times, but even back then Europeans had no effect on Gulf politics. Al-Quaseem got out of the piracy business when oil was discovered, and the sheik's daddy learned he could become even richer and more powerful without doing any work whatsoever."

"So that's why Hassan's the richest man in the world?" Bobby asked. "I thought Saudi Arabia had the most oil."

"Yeah, they do," Brick said. "The Saudis have a hell of a lot more oil than anybody else, including the sheik of al-Quaseem. They also have more folks to share it with. Even though Saudi Arabia is very sparsely populated, they still have a hell of a lot of folks who do nothing but stick their hands out. You know how many people there are in the entire emirate of al-Quaseem? About thirty thousand, tops. And most of them are related to the sheik or come from families who have worked in his service for generations. Not that that means anything over there, but they seem to be a pretty loyal and capable bunch. The sheik hasn't had to import any Yemenis or Pakistanis to do manual labor, like Kuwait and Bahrain and the rest of the Gulf states have, so they're relatively immune to Shiite subversion. That's one reason why he's willing to help us."

Bobby was puzzled. "It sounds like a virtual wonderland, Brick. Why haven't we based planes there before?"

"Well, *before* we were trying to make friends in the Gulf, and jumping in bed with even a very distant second cousin of the shah was not the way to do it," Brick scowled. "Nominally, Hassan's a Sunni, but he seems to believe in that only when it's convenient. And technically al-Quaseem belongs to the United Arab Emirates, but he doesn't much care about that, either."

"Then what *does* he believe in?"

"Power and money, pretty much in that order," Brick answered. "And one thing Iran shares with the rest of the Gulf states is a fundamentalist attitude, so the sheik's playboy philosophy doesn't fit in with *anybody's* crowd over here. He's pretty much isolated from the leaders on both sides of the Gulf, and that's the way he likes it."

"Let me get this straight," Bobby said. "The Arabs hate the sheik because he's a descendant of the shah. And the Iranians hate him for the same reason?"

"You got it," Brick said. "Hassan's both Persian *and* Arabian, so there's something there for everyone to despise."

"He sounds like your kind of guy, Brick. You sure he's not a fighter pilot?"

"As a matter of fact, he was." Brick grinned. "He used to fly Hunters, not so long ago. His son's the real hot stick in the family now, though. Prince Faisal. The kid did an exchange tour with our F-16 outfit down in Miami, and they tell me he really knows how to move the sky around. I saw it for myself when I was over at al-Quaseem a couple of years ago with the *Peace Pearl* guys. We were selling the sheik a couple of dozen Falcons. Faisal went up for a check ride and beat the hell out of the General Dynamics test pilot, first time out."

"Wait a minute, Brick," Bobby said. "Besides the fact that he can afford them, what does the leader of a dinky little nation like al-Quaseem want with a squadron of F-16s? Isn't that a pretty big air force for such a small nation?"

"In the Gulf, only the Saudis have a bigger one," Brick agreed. "Per capita, it's the largest air force in the world. The sheik is proud of that. The truth is, he needs it. For one thing, most of his wealth is out in the Gulf. The only way he can effectively protect his oil platforms and pipelines is with air power. The other thing is that everybody on both sides of the Gulf hates his guts, so he needs to be prepared for anything. When we sold him the F-16s, he already had two squadrons of F-5s and a squadron of F-4s. He's had TAB-Vs built for all of them. You can use those."

Bobby shook his head. "You keep saying *you,* Brick. I haven't agreed to anything."

"That's okay, Bobby. Just hear me out, all right?"

"Okay." Bobby stood up and stretched. "But let's go back and get a cup of coffee or something, though. I've had a rough day."

"*You've* had a rough day?" Brick laughed. "This morning I was on the other side of the world trying to prevent World War III. I'd call that a full day's work."

Bobby started along the path back to the jeep. He heard Brick swearing behind him, stumbling across the ground in the dark. Then he heard a scream.

"Jesus, Bobby! This place is a graveyard!"

Bobby reached in the jeep and flicked on the lights. The yellow beams illuminated rows of square, neat headstones. Brick leaned over one of the grave markers.

"Welcome to Boot Hill," Bobby said.

Brick squinted at the names on the headstones. "Who are these guys?"

"All kinds of people," Bobby said absently. "Pilots mostly, but some spook types, too. They all had one thing in common—they died in the wrong place."

"Black missions?"

"Yeah," Bobby said. "The Pentagon told their families they were lost at sea, or in the Arctic or someplace we couldn't get to them. But when we'd negotiate a deal with Syria or Libya or wherever they *really* died and their bodies were shipped home, we had to have someplace to put them. So we put them here."

Brick examined the markers in the glow of the headlights. One caught his eye. "So that's what happened to Mueller. The last I heard he was flying RC-135s out of Incirlik and went down in the Med."

"He was flying out of Turkey all right, but he was shot down over Odessa," Bobby said. "There are a lot of Heartbreakers here, Brick. Osborne. Tom Moore. Renfrew."

"Renfrew? What happened to him? I thought he was killed in a car wreck."

"Close. He swallowed an SA-7 outside Managua."

Bobby shook his head. He found it ironic that Brick was afraid of ghosts, since he had made so many of them. In fact, he was talking to one. Bobby Dragon was a ghost, dead to the world, a man with no identity and no existence outside the skies of the Nevada desert. Dreamland was full of ghosts—Eastern bloc defectors with a price on their heads, fugitives from civilian authorities, or people like Bobby, who simply chose to withdraw from the world. The other thing they had in common was a certain skill or knowledge the Pentagon found useful enough to justify and subsidize their self-imposed exile.

Only a few high-ranking officers knew the identities of Dreamland's living dead. The rank and file had their suspicions, swapped rumors, and engaged in speculation but could never know for certain which ghosts haunted the Great Basin. Or which were buried at Boot Hill, where ghosts went to die.

The two men climbed back in the jeep and drove down the mesa side. On the ride back to Dreamland, Bobby thought about what Brick had said. Whatever was going on in the Gulf could erupt into the biggest air battle the world had ever seen, probably the last air battle Bobby Dragon would fight. *He belonged there.* He knew it, and he knew Brick knew it. But there were too many unanswered questions.

"Say, Brick, this, uh, mercenary air force you're talking about..."

"Consultants, Bobby," Brick corrected. "Let's not call them mercenaries. It has a bad connotation."

"Okay, these fighting...consultants," Bobby smiled. "What's in it for them?"

"They stand to make a lot of money, for one thing. I told the secretary of defense this isn't going to be cheap, but it's going to be a hell of a lot cheaper than using the U.S. Air Force, even if we could."

Bobby nodded. "That's good. It's about time we paid veteran combat pilots at least as much as women who serve coffee on airliners. But the guys

I have in mind wouldn't care about the money. They're warriors. They're tired of exercising. They want to kick ass. And they wouldn't want some bureaucrat looking over their shoulder trying to micromanage the war from a desk in the Pentagon while they're doing it."

"Those are the just the kind of folks I had in mind," Brick said. "I can keep the weak dicks off your back, Bobby, if that's what's bothering you. Leave it to me."

"I haven't said yes yet. There are still a lot of things I've got to know about this operation before I sign up."

"Like what?"

"Like what about the planes and the missiles and the rest of the stuff? Where are you going to get them?"

"I can get most of the pilots to bring their planes with them," Brick said. "You've got to understand, Bobby, the Brits and the Europeans will do anything we want, as long as we fight their battles for them and they don't have to get officially involved. All the ordnance we need—to start with, at least—is floating in those ships at Diego Garcia. As far as ground ops go, the sheik already has a pretty sharp staff, including a number of Westerners under contract, running his tactical air base at Dar al-Harb."

Brick studied Bobby's face in the darkness, trying to determine if he had gotten through. Bobby stared straight ahead, driving, Dreamland dancing in his eyes. Brick had seen that look before at Da Nang. Bobby at war with himself, torn between what he believed in on the ground and what he believed he could do in the air. Most fighter jocks would have given their souls for Bobby Dragon's talent for flying, his hands, his eyes, and his judgment. But Bobby seemed to think his gift was a curse, a burden. Yet there was that stubborn streak that made him want to prove himself, to show he could fly faster, higher, and farther than anyone else, whether he wanted to or not.

"So what do you have in mind?" Bobby broke the silence. "F-15s or F-16s?"

Brick smiled. Now he had Bobby thinking tactics.

"Both," Brick said. "And a lot more besides. The way I see it, you've got to make a big aircraft carrier out of this place. You don't have room for a whole fighter wing and a strike wing and a recce squadron and all the other stuff you have to have to accomplish the mission. It's a big base, but it's not that big. Plus, there just aren't that many front-line aircraft to spare. Not with the situation so tense in the Gulf. The governments are saving the good stuff for themselves."

"What are you saying, Brick? We're just going to wait to see what these guys show up with and draw the organizational chart then?"

"Pretty much," Brick nodded. "I think I can get a dozen or so Eagles and Falcons from the Air Force, and maybe some A-10s and A-7s from the

Guard. Most of the other guys will be bringing F-4s—there's a ton of those around. Plus, there are are some odds and ends."

"Like what?"

Brick shrugged. "A French Crusader. A couple of Buccaneers, maybe even a Harrier or two from the Brits. An Australian F-111. An F-104S from the Italian Air Force. I think we can get a few..."

"Christ, Brick!" Bobby shouted. "That's not an air force; it's a museum! It's a goddamn zoo! You expect me to fight Fulcrums with that?"

"It's not the machine; it's the man," Brick smiled. "Didn't I hear that somewhere before? Or was Hillary misquoting you?"

Bobby grinned, despite himself. It *was* an intriguing idea. Just like Vietnam, only this time the other side would have the numbers and the technology. Would he have the courage to go up against those odds? Something stirred in him, something he tried to suppress but knew he couldn't. He couldn't run from a fight, not again. It wasn't patriotism. It wasn't even aggression. It was something more.

"There's still something I don't understand, Brick," Bobby said. "Why me? Why did you come out here to get me to join up? After all we've been through, I'd think I'd be the last person on earth you'd want to see."

"Close to it," Brick drawled. "I'd just as soon forget about what happened in Vietnam. I don't like being reminded. But I have to admit, Bobby, you're the greatest fighter pilot I've ever seen. Nobody knows air combat better than you."

"Is that why you had me brought out here?"

"Yes," Brick said somberly. "I couldn't stand to see you pissing your life away, flying spooks around Southeast Asia, or running guns, or whatever the hell it was you were doing while I was in the Hilton. As soon as I got out, I found a place for you. This place."

"You saved my life." There was no emotion in Bobby's voice. It was a simple statement of fact.

"It wasn't charity, Bobby," Brick said. "You know, long after all the other Vietnam aces were forgotten, just about every aerospace scientist in the country was still studying your dogfights, trying to figure out how you did it, how you made that big, ugly F-4 sit up and beg. Now, since you got here, the Air Force has revolutionized the art of air combat. Energy management, first-move tactics—those are your ideas. And I can spot a lot of Bobby Dragon in the design of all our latest fighters. No, I'd say you've earned your keep. You don't owe me anything."

Bobby stopped the jeep outside the ops building and stared at Brick.

"I appreciate the kind words, Brick. But something smells here."

Brick slumped in his seat.

"You're not going to take the job, then?"

"Not unless you tell me the whole story. From what you've said so far, you don't need me. You could run the operation yourself—it's right up your alley."

"I can't. Haven't you been listening? This can't be seen as a U.S. government initiative, not now, not in that part of the world. I'm a major general in the U.S. Air Force, for Christ's sake. I've got an office in the Pentagon and another one in the basement of the White House. This thing is going to be hard enough to sell without me."

"What makes you think it'll be easier to swallow if I'm in charge?"

Brick stepped out of the jeep and walked slowly to Bobby's side. He seemed to be wrestling with his own thoughts. Finally, he said softly, "Now don't take this the wrong way, Bobby. I'd just as soon forget about Da Nang. What's done is done. I know why you did what you did. I didn't agree with you then, and I'm not sure I do now, but I respect you for it."

"That was almost twenty years ago, Brick. What's that got to do with what's going on in the Persian Gulf right now?"

There was a low rumble in a hangar at the far end of the runway. Brick checked the luminescent dial of his watch. Christ, it was getting late. He had to be back before morning. But then, he reminded himself, there was no use going back to Washington, or anywhere, unless he could convince Bobby to accept his part in the plan.

"Okay, Bobby, I'll lay it out for you. One: I need someone I can trust. I can trust you. We sure as hell don't agree on everything. That's all right. That's different from trust. I can trust you with my life, if it comes to that. I have before. And you've never let me down. Okay?"

"Okay," Bobby said, surprised. This didn't sound like the Brick White he knew. That Brick White would never admit he needed anyone, especially Bobby. But was it genuine emotion or another con? Had Brick mellowed over the years? Or had he just gotten more slick? "Go on."

"Two: If we're going to get the right kind of pilots to sign up for this operation, we need to get someone they admire and respect to lead it. After all, we're asking them to risk their lives. They'll accept that—that's part of the job. But they'll want to make sure whoever's calling the shots isn't going to make them risk their lives foolishly or needlessly. Now, I'm not going to stand here and grease you up with tales of your fame and gallant reputation. But the truth is, there isn't a real fighter pilot in the world who wouldn't give his right nut for a chance to fly with you, and you know it. All I'd have to do is *hint* that Bobby Dragon is in al-Quaseem, and the place would look like the Tailhook Convention in Las Vegas within the hour."

"I'm not sure I believe you," Bobby laughed. "But I'll let it slide."

"Three," Brick continued, "your, ah, reputation precedes you in the Gulf. Whatever else you were or might have become, you can never claim to be an unquestioning supporter of official U.S. governmental policies. Now, maybe that didn't sit too well with me or the Air Force, but it carries a lot of weight around the world with countries that feel the same way you do. It would be a lot easier to sell this operation as an independent initiative of the government of al-Quaseem if you were leading it instead of a flag-waver like me. Hell, you're not even *in* the Air Force anymore."

Bobby thought about what Brick was saying. It all made sense. But there had to be something else, some other reason to compel Brick to swallow his pride and seek Bobby out after nearly two decades of carefully avoiding him. Bobby didn't want to humiliate Brick. But he did need to know all the facts.

"Those are good reasons, Brick. But not good enough. Are you sure that's all?"

Brick blinked and lowered his head. "No," he said softly. "There's one more thing. He asked for you."

"Who?" Bobby asked, surprised.

"The sheik. Hassan. He said you've got to lead this operation, or there's no deal."

"Why?"

"I don't know!" Brick shouted. "Honest to God, Bobby, I don't know why it's so important to him. But he means it."

A siren screamed through the night. The sky above Dreamland erupted in flame. Brick jumped back.

"What the hell is that?"

"Aurora!" Bobby shouted.

"What?"

"The National Aerospace Plane!" Bobby shouted above the roar. "The one-man space shuttle. It takes off and lands like an airplane. We're going to use it to shoot down satellites."

Brick was stunned.

"But that's not supposed to be ready until the end of the century! We just let out the contract a couple of years ago."

Bobby laughed. "This is just a subscale demonstration model. Unmanned. But how much do you want to bet when they finally build it, it'll look a lot like this one?"

Both men watched in silence as the sleek aircraft zoomed down the runway. The tremendous thrust blew a fireball for a hundred feet behind the plane.

Bobby stared as Aurora climbed straight up on the end of a blue-and-yellow flame. Things were happening too fast. In the air, there wasn't time to think, just react. You had to go with your instincts, and Bobby's instincts were always right. In the air. He knew that was true because he was still alive.

On the ground it was different. There were too many choices, and sometimes none of them were correct. This time would be different, Bobby thought. He would go with his instincts on the ground, too. And his heart told him to fly.

"I don't want my name to be mentioned publicly," Bobby said suddenly. "I don't want to be involved in any dog-and-pony shows for VIPs. And I don't want to deal with reporters, either. You know how I feel about the press."

Brick brightened. Was Bobby saying yes? "Don't worry about that. Hassan says he's going to hire a front man for the public-relations side of it. You'd only have to worry about operations."

"And I want to pick and choose who I fly with," Bobby continued. "I'm the final say on that."

"Anybody you want," Brick agreed. "You name him; I'll get him for you."

"I want Krypto Padgett."

"You got him."

"I want Rattler Reese. And this new kid, Rowdy Engram. And Bubba Windham. And I want..."

"Make a list, Bobby. If they want to come, I'll make sure they get there."

"And I want the Weasel brothers."

Brick frowned. "Oh, come on, Bobby. Not *those* two!"

"They're in, or the deal's off," Bobby said firmly. "They may not be your kind of guys, but they're the best in the world at what they do. This isn't the Blue Angels, Brick. We're going to war. I don't need any posers."

"All right, all right," Brick waved his hand. "You win. Write it down. I'll make out the invitations."

The sun was rising behind the brown hills, a shaft of pink beneath the still-twinkling stars. A fresh wind only shoved the chilly air around.

"So I guess this means you're going to do it?" Brick asked.

Bobby nodded.

"That's great," Brick smiled. "You won't regret it, Bobby. We really need you."

Brick stuck out his hand. Bobby shrugged, smiled sheepishly, and shook it. He turned and began to walk back down the ramp.

"Hey, wait a minute!" Brick shouted. "Where are you going?"

"I've got a ton of stuff to do if we're going to pull this off," Bobby said. "And so do you. You'd better be getting back to Washington."

"Well, wait a minute, will you?" Brick trotted after Bobby. "I just want to know one thing."

Bobby stopped and turned around.

"Shoot."

"What do you want to call it? I've got to call it something when I sell it to the president."

"Call what?" Bobby asked, puzzled.

"This...enterprise," Brick giggled, giddy with fatigue and relief. "This ragtag group of flying, fighting consultants who're going to save the world. What are you going to call it?"

Bobby grinned and scratched his head. Naming things was a little out of his line. Then it struck him. He walked back to the ops shack in the desert dawn.

"The First Air Regiment, Incorporated," Bobby said over his shoulder. "We're going to call it First Air."

The Sheik and the Falcon

Dubai International Airport
United Arab Emirates

The car cost one million dollars.

At least. That's what it cost a few years back when Peter Hillary had read of Sheik Hassan's Mercedes Benz 600 Presidential Landeaulet in *Time*. Only ten were built. Queen Elizabeth II bought one. So did Mao Tse-tung, Pope John Paul II, Marshal Tito, and—irony of ironies—Shahanshah Mohammad Reza Pahlavi Aryamehr of Iran. The magazine had scoffed at the incongruity of the then-young sheik raising clouds of fine dust, motoring about the almost-nonexistent roads of his tiny kingdom in a twenty-foot limousine. The tone of the article so stung and infuriated Hassan that he had a network of modern highways built throughout the emirate, from nowhere to nowhere, culminating in a long and expensive causeway connecting al-Quaseem to the mainland and the coast road to Abu Dhabi. With the highways thrown in, Hillary figured the car cost the sheik at least ten million dollars.

And now Hillary was lounging in the back of that same black limousine, running his hands across the tan leather of the cognac interior, gazing idly at the burled maple panels studded with knobs and switches at whose ultimate purpose he could only conjecture. The big car roared down Airport Road, turned at the clock tower, and crossed the creek at the al-Maqta bridge. Leaving Dubai's jagged skyline and choking traffic behind, the unseen driver turned left at the Trade Center onto the four-lane divided highway that ran along the coast to al-Quaseem and Qatar beyond. The car droned silently at ninety miles an hour. With the blue water of the Gulf on his right, the sea of sand on his left, Peter Hillary was thinking about change.

War had made his reputation as a journalist. Now it would ruin him. Hillary's wholly fabricated story of a successful U.S. invasion of Iran had had the desired effect. It had reassured the American people and sown just enough doubt in the already confused Iranian forces at Bandar Abbas to stabilize the situation. Hillary was sure his story—backed by his reputation, the spirited defense of Casey's small band, and the costly efforts of the *Eisenhower*'s air wing—had kept the Division Ready Force from being swept into Hormuz Bay.

But at what cost to himself? The truth would come out. He was sure of that. Soon *Eisenhower* would be relieved, docked for much-needed resupply, and pilots would hit the waterfront bars of Naples in an orgy of frustration and indiscretion. At Cairo West, astute observers were already beginning to notice that the isolated group the Army called a "third-echelon logistics and admin unit" was, in fact, the bulk of the 82d Airborne Division. And in Washington, of course, there were never any secrets. It was just a matter of time before the real story leaked.

Even the American network television reporters in Bahrain were beginning to suspect that Ready Eagle was not the bloodless blitzkrieg Hillary had described in his initial dispatch. With no official word from the Pentagon and interest so high in the story, he had been much in demand in the period immediately following the invasion. Articulate and respected, Hillary had affably lied through his teeth for a week, and the world slept better for it.

But as time wore on the doubts grew larger: If this was such a textbook operation, why no official word from the Army? If Bandar Abbas was secure, why were no reporters allowed to visit? What of the reports of fighting, the flashes in the night easily seen from the perimeter of the Gulf cordoned off by Navy warships? And what of those gray fighters, which looked a lot like MiG-29s, occasionally spotted above Bandar Abbas?

Eventually, the reporters ceased interviewing Hillary. Soon they quit talking to him at all. He walked through Bahrain's Diplomat Hotel like a ghost. Quite like a ghost.

He had begun to drink again. He drank for the same reasons most people drink: He could not believe anything worse could happen to him than what had already happened. And he could not believe anything better would happen in the future.

That had changed with the summons from Sheik Hassan. At first Hillary had chased the royal emissary away, thinking it a prank dreamed up by bored and spiteful reporters. Finally convinced of the man's credentials, Hillary became curious, though wary. Perhaps Hassan had not yet heard of Hillary's disgrace. Before he had become a pariah to the pool reporters, Hillary had heard rumors of a group of mercenaries of some sort gathering in al-Quaseem. The notion of foreign pilots in the cockpits of combat aircraft of the Gulf states, though intriguing to the newly arrived media, was nothing new to Hillary. Jordanians, Palestinians, Pakistanis, and even the odd Westerner had been flying in the service of the sheiks since they first formed air forces. No doubt Sheik Hassan *was* recruiting reinforcements, but with the source of his wealth in the Gulf so near the fighting, who could blame him?

Perhaps the sheik wanted to pump him for information about the military situation in Iran. After all, Hillary remained the only outsider who had been to Bandar Abbas and witnessed the fighting firsthand. Or maybe Hassan merely wanted to show off his fierce little air force, to use Hillary as a medium to warn the world that any interference with al-Quaseem's oil operations in the Gulf would be dealt with harshly. That was fine with Hillary. He was growing accustomed to being used. At least it would make him feel useful.

Whatever the reason, Hillary was happy to be out of Bahrain, happy to be away from the burning eyes of reporters who once looked up to him and now just looked away. Still, there was enough of the journalist left in Hillary to be bothered by questions he didn't want to ask: Why was it necessary to fly from Bahrain to Abu Dhabi and be driven all the way to al-Quaseem, when the island boasted one of the largest and most modern commercial jetports in the Gulf? Was there something going on at Quaseem International that the sheik didn't want Hillary to see? If the airport was closed down for runway resurfacing—as the international air-traffic authorities had been told— then where was that constant stream of huge American transports landing? And what were they doing at al-Quaseem in the first place?

Hillary stared at the dunes zooming by the Mercedes, which moved so smoothly it seemed not to be moving at all. Suddenly he missed London, although he had scarcely been there in years, between wars. He wondered if the limousine's bar was stocked. The sheik was a Muslim, but he was also a man of the world.

Hillary pressed all the buttons on the armrest. The right window rolled down, the sunroof opened, the driver asked what he wanted, the rear window wiper flapped crazily in the hellish day, and a panel opened revealing a bottle of Johnny Walker Black. Allah be praised!

Ten miles outside Tarif, the limousine swung north onto the causeway that paralleled the main pipeline to al-Quaseem. Although Hillary had spent a great deal of time in the Gulf, he had never seen much of al-Quaseem. Not many foreigners had; of all the emirates, al-Quaseem, though on the surface contemporary in outlook and architecture, was the most isolated and the least Westernized. There was, of course, Sammarah. Everyone had been there. The airport was quite familiar to travelers in the Gulf. And businessmen seeking a piece of the sheik's considerable commerce were no strangers to Quaseem City. But the rest of the island was a mystery to most Westerners.

The sheik apparently liked it that way, having seen too many Muslim countries shattered by sudden wealth, slipping into anarchy on a carpet of oil. Families, tribes, even nations that had stood united for hundreds of years were being torn apart by rapid "progress." Eventually they fragmented into radicalism, like Libya and Iran, or reverted to repressive, reactionary states, such as Saudi Arabia. It wasn't really the oil or the money. It was the foreigners and their choices. Muhammad had no use for choice. Neither did Sheik Hassan—at least, not for anyone but himself.

At the checkpoint at the end of the causeway, police had pulled over a long line of vehicles to make way for Hillary and the sheik's Mercedes. Quaseemi border officers in green-and-tan khakis stood at attention and saluted as Hillary zoomed past, their short, black H&K MP5 submachine guns dangling across their chests.

Hillary took a final swig and put the glass away. It wouldn't be long now. Comprising the entire island, al-Quaseem was one of the largest emirates but still tiny: a little over twenty miles across at its widest point and only ten miles north to south. Before he knew it, Hillary was cruising past the north end of Quaseem Bay, heading for the roundabout. The driver went past the first turnoff, to Sammarah, and the second, to Quaseem City and the air base of Dar al-Harb beyond, finally swinging onto a road that went due west, straight as an arrow through low, rolling dunes stretching out on either side. Except for the artificial paradise of Sammarah and some narrow gravel beaches, the entire island was like this—hard brown sand, a few stubborn dry bushes, heat, humidity, light, and nothing else. Or so it seemed. Hillary knew there were people out there, whether he could see them or not. It was not the custom of country folk in the Gulf to make their presence known to strangers.

Hemmed in by dunes, Hillary could only see straight ahead, and he could hardly believe what he saw. Shimmering at the end of the road lay the breathtaking Quasir al-Quaseem. The sheik's palace, a glittering edifice of marble, mica, and granite, sparkled in the bright desert sunlight. The car seemed to crawl but in fact maintained its breakneck pace. Hillary then realized the palace was not as close as it first appeared. It was simply huge, growing even larger as the limousine approached.

The Mercedes stopped at the gate, the first time it had halted since leaving

Dubai. A guard spoke briefly to the driver. Hillary noticed a number of stone guard shacks. It did not take much imagination to believe that other guards, armed with powerful weapons, were ready to open up on Hillary if the driver did not deliver the appropriate response. It was then that Hillary noticed the Land Rover that had pulled in behind them at the gate. The four men inside had obviously followed them since the Mercedes had picked Hillary up at Dubai International. The sheik was a careful man.

The limousine pulled out and drove slowly around the circular driveway. Hillary was startled by the beauty of the palace. Few Westerners had seen Quasir al-Quaseem this close. Muslims, forbidden the display of representational art by religious law, had through history turned to architecture as a means of self-expression. And the sheik was a man of taste, sophisticated and educated. The two factors combined to make the royal palace a true wonder.

There was nothing showy about the palace. Its power came from proportion and design, the two large wings connected by a high central arch. The domed roof of the central reception area served as an architectural allusion to a mosque, just as the arch reflected Hassan's interest in Western art and culture.

To Hillary's surprise, the car did not stop under the central arch but drove through another narrow gate to the rear of the building. There it stopped. A small Arab man, obviously a servant, opened the door with a small bow. Holding a finger to his lips for silence, the man gestured to a figure in a flowing white *aba* holding a hunting falcon on a gloved forearm.

With a quick, expert snatch, the man in white lifted the hood from the falcon's eyes. The animal scanned the area in rapid, jerking movements, taking in the broad sloping lawn, the tall, cedarlike *caserviana* lining the driveway, the blossoming oleanders, dense bushes, and fountains and the smooth Gulf beyond. It saw the cage a half mile away on the beach. Hillary could see its razor talons flexing, stropping on the heavy leather glove.

The falconer nodded slightly. A man, two steps behind to the right, mumbled softly into a walkie-talkie. Another gamekeeper on the beach uncaged the korhaan and stepped back. The huge African game bird paced uncertainly on the unfamiliar sand. The falcon lept from the sheik's forearm.

The rapid beating of the falcon's wings caused the korhaan to look up, unfold its own huge black wings, and take flight, but it was too late. The falcon hit the big bird like a missile, knocking it from the sky and setting on it with beak and claws. It took seconds. The outgoing tide pulled the lifeless mass of bone and feathers into the Gulf.

The falconer gave a low whistle. The falcon left the floating carcass and swooped back to the glove. Fresh blood from the korhaan smeared the man's white robe as he replaced the falcon's hood.

"Your Highness, Mr. Peter Hillary is here."

Sheik Hassan turned to face an astonished Hillary, who had arrived just in time to see the sporting murder. Handing the falcon to the gamekeeper, the sheik removed the leather glove and extended his hand.

"Ah, Mr. Hillary," he said. "So happy you could accept my invitation."

"*Ja sarmua kum,*" Hillary said. Your Highness. He shook hands with the sheik, staring at the blood, still bright red on the white robe. Hassan noticed it too and smiled.

"Please excuse me," he said. "All part of the game. Please, follow me."

Hassan led the way up the long lawn and across a wide terrazzo patio. Hillary was now as taken with the beauty of the grounds as he was overcome with the violence of the falcon's attack moments before. Grass was a rare luxury in the Gulf, usually reserved for only the very rich and even then only in tiny, carefully cultivated plots. The heavy salt air and the blazing sun condemned it to a quick death.

Hillary took in the glittering palace, the precious grounds. He could hear the sounds of women splashing at a swimming pool somewhere nearby. The rest of the compound was also out of sight—the car barn, the servants' quarters, the governmental annex. Hillary had read of them somewhere. And somewhere, too, he knew, the sheik had his own private airfield. Nothing unusual about that, true. Many estates had one. But not many had hangars and landing strips large enough to accommodate the pair of F-16s the sheik was said to keep there on constant alert. Hillary searched for words. What does one say to the richest man in the world?

He gave up trying. "Nice place."

"Thank you," Hassan smiled. "It's quite impractical, really. We have to resod the entire lawn twice every summer, even with the irrigation system. It's frightfully expensive, but it's an extravagance I truly enjoy. It reminds me of my school days in Cambridge. You're a public-school boy, aren't you, Mr. Hillary?"

Hillary nodded, taken aback. "Oxford. Queen's College."

"Ah, yes," the sheik laughed. "Skull and Bones."

"Skull and Bones," Hillary answered. "A long time ago."

The sheik swept a hand toward the house. The gamekeepers, servants, even the four bodyguards, unseen until then, marched up the steps and into the main house. Hillary was alone with the sheik of al-Quaseem.

"Let me make you a drink, Peter. Oh, may I call you Peter?"

Hillary nodded, surprised and somehow frightened by the sheik's hospitality. He knew the people of the Gulf. If they were your enemies, they could kill you without thinking. If they were your friends, they would just as readily die for you. But friends or enemies were not made this quickly, not with the *dhimmis,* the tolerated infidels, the Christians and Westerners of the Gulf. The Arabs had another side, too, that of the gregarious business-man. They could be gracious hosts when they wanted something. But Peter

Hillary could not imagine what the sheik of al-Quaseem could want with him.

"Johnny Walker Black, isn't it?" The sheik poured a stiff scotch on ice. For no apparent reason, Hillary felt a chill in the scorching Gulf afternoon. He suddenly wanted to be somewhere else, even back in Bahrain, at the Diplomat. At least you knew where you stood there, he thought.

The sheik brought the drinks to the table. Hillary noticed Hassan was drinking ice water. Was it religion, modesty, or prudence? Was it unwise to drink liquor in the sheik's presence? It didn't matter. Hillary craved the drink and gratefully accepted.

"We have met before, you know," Hassan said. "At the Gulf Cooperation Council meeting in Kuwait, two years ago."

"I remember. I tried to interview you. You pretended not to speak English."

"And you pretended not to speak Arabic," the sheik smiled. "I knew then you were a most capable man. And, I have since learned, a well-respected and honest man. I often have need of such men. I need one now."

At least now we're getting down to business, Hillary thought. The fawning attention, the flattery—the sheik's manner was not unlike the basket dealers in the *souk*. The fact that Hassan had received him on the patio and not inside, in the *diwan,* where formal negotiations were normally conducted, was not lost on Hillary. And if Hassan thought Hillary as perceptive and sophisticated in the ways of the Gulf as he said, he would have known the mild insult would not go unnoticed. Still, it was not unpleasant to be courted by a man whose personal worth exceeded that of most countries. And, Hillary thought, it was not as if he had other prospects.

"At your service, Your Highness."

"Not so quickly. After you hear my proposal, you may not agree to help me. I must tell you there may be some risk involved."

"Risk? You mean personally or professionally?"

"Both, I am afraid."

Hillary swallowed his drink quickly.

"It doesn't matter. All I had was my career, and that's pretty much shot now."

"Not necessarily," the sheik said casually. "Of course, your report from Bandar Abbas was complete fiction."

Hillary put down his glass and stared at the sheik.

"Yes, it was," he said. "But how did you know that?"

Hassan smiled. "The Americans say money talks, and it's true. But it can also listen. With the fighting so close and so much at stake, I make it my business to stay informed of what is occurring across the Gulf. Surely you know there are too many people involved to keep it a secret much longer. What are you going to do when the truth comes out?"

"I don't know. I'll find something," Hillary shook his head. "But I can't go back to journalism. That's the thing about being a reporter, you know. You have to stay a virgin. It's all right to screw up every now and then. People will forgive you if you were trying to get it straight. But once you deliberately lie to them, you're through. No one will ever believe you again."

The sheik nodded. "The Prophet says the ink of the scholar is more sacred than the blood of the martyr."

"Yes." Hillary stared blankly at the Gulf. "But in this case, they happen to be the same thing."

The sheik walked to the bar and brought Hillary a fresh drink.

"I understand why you did what you did," Hassan said deliberately, "and I commend you for it, although I agree most people would not see it that way. But what if I could offer you a way out? What if I could give you an opportunity to really affect the fighting in Bandar Abbas and save the lives of your friends, and even return to journalism with your reputation intact? What would you say to that?"

Hillary smiled. "I'd say, '*Allah akbar*.'"

"God *is* most great, Peter. Most great indeed."

The Yellow Bite

Ghostrider Flight
Over the Arabian Sea

Scooter Jeffries could never get over the way the *Eisenhower* shrank when wet.

Back in Norfolk, when Carrier Air Wing Seven was preparing to embark aboard *Ike,* when no one outside of the Pentagon had heard of Ready Eagle, the carrier had seemed enormous. There were more than five thousand officers and men on board. The ship had its own hospital, its own jail, its own television station. You could build a good-sized mall on the flight deck and have plenty of room to park cars down below.

As soon as the *Eisenhower* left pier 77, however, it began to shrink. Scooter didn't notice it much at first. The wardrooms got a little smaller; the bulkheads and the hatchways started to close in. Mostly, Jeffries noticed, he was never alone. At work, off duty, eating, sleeping, he saw the same faces, day after day, and wondered if they were as tired of him as he was of them.

It was worst during blue-water ops, when the carrier was too far from a land base for fighters to divert if they were in trouble. Except for the Alert birds, which always went up with tankers, the F-14s were grounded during the Azores stretch. And for Scooter and the rest of the Tomcat pilots, the mighty *Ike* was reduced to the size of a tramp steamer in a Bogart movie, heading for nowhere, it seemed, and in no hurry to get there.

Forced into sudden action on their arrival at Gonzo Station, Battle Group Bravo swung, however ungracefully, into wartime status. For Scooter, this meant the carrier contracted further still. Whole sections of the ship were now closed to him. The few passageways remaining open were clogged with crewmen all trying to get to different places by the same route. The *Eisenhower,* with the exception of flag country, could never be mistaken for a cruise ship in any circumstance. On alert it became what its designers intended— an integrated weapons system, like a tank or a fighter, with precious little room to spare.

But the real disappearing act came when Scooter climbed aboard his Tomcat and launched off a catapult. The five acres of flight deck shrank to the size of a postage stamp when the wheels went up. Just try to find it in the middle of the ocean! Coming home, shot up (again), low on fuel (again), the thing might as well be a porpoise. His instruments said he was right on top of the *Eisenhower,* but all Jeffries could see was the endless emerald carpet of the northern Arabian Sea.

Scooter had expected to join other aircraft in the holding pattern behind the carrier. The rest of the Alpha strike, including his new wingman, were already safely on board the *Eisenhower.* There had been no one at marshal to meet Ghostrider 12 except a lonely KA-6D. It made sense. Only the tanker had enough fuel on board to divert all the way to Mogadishu in case Jeffries didn't make it. With only one carrier, Battle Group Bravo couldn't take a chance on a fouled deck preventing the rest of the aircraft to land. And Ghostrider 12 was an accident waiting to happen.

"How's it hanging back there?"

"No sweat, Scooter." Daffy Brewer scanned the gauges. The Tomcat was still losing fuel. He didn't need the instruments to tell him that. Daffy could see the jet-A streaming behind the F-14 in a long, gray cloud, condensing in the warm, moist air. Brewer made some quick mental calculations. With the gas they had just taken on from the tanker, they *should* be able to make it back to the boat. *If* they could find it. "Ah, you spot *Ike* yet?"

"No joy," Jeffries said with frustration. "The ILS puts it right on the nose, but I'll be damned if—wait a minute! There it is!"

Brewer grabbed the handhold and leaned out to peer around Jeffries in the front seat. All he saw were three tiny specks on the horizon. "You sure that's them?"

"Nope," Jeffries said.

"Be careful. That Russian destroyer that's been shadowing the *Ike* is back here somewhere."

"Look, Daffy, at this point I don't care if it's one of ours or if it belongs to Mikhail's Navy," Brewer said. "If it's big and gray, I'm landing on it."

A quick radio call could confirm that the specks were indeed *Eisenhower* and her close-in escorts, *Valley Forge* and *Copeland*. Brewer almost thumbed the switch to make the transmission, then remembered the new rules dictating radio silence. He could, of course, have declared an in-flight emergency and called anyway. No one would blame him. It was the right thing to do: safe, sane, and prudent. But it was not the Navy way.

Besides, maybe EMCON *was* the best policy. The air wing had been getting shot up pretty badly lately. The Fulcrums had been waiting for them over Bandar Abbas again today, just as they had for the past two weeks. Thanks to the Russian tattletale trailing the battle group, the MiGs knew exactly what the Navy planes were up to as soon as they took off. When the carrier aircraft went in alone, the Fulcrums stayed home and let the Americans soak up ground fire and SAM launches from the Iranians. When the air wing tried to escort resupply missions from Egypt, the MiGs blew through and went for the transports. And when the cargo planes tried to sneak in unescorted, the Fulcrums *and* the Iranians clobbered them. It was obvious the enemy was trying to isolate the Division Ready Force from resupply. So far it was working.

"I got it. It's *Ike!* Got the deck!"

"Got the ball?"

"Not yet. I'm going to do an overhead."

Brewer frowned. The Tomcat had a hole exactly the size of a .50-caliber bullet in the number-one fuel cell right behind him. The tanks were supposed to be self-sealing. Not quite. And there was always the chance that the tank could rupture further. If the spilling fuel got too close to the burning engines, the flames would snake up the underside, touch off what remained of the forty-five hundred pounds of fuel in the tank, and blow Ghostrider 12 into a thousand pieces no one would ever find.

However, an overhead pass would be really cool. And style is all in the fighter business, taking precedence over other minor considerations such as safety, military efficacy, and mere life and death. This was the Last Pass. Overnight, the *Constellation* would rendezvous with Battle Group Bravo on Gonzo Station, and her air wing would take over responsibility for protecting the American paratroopers at Bandar Abbas. After two weeks of getting shot at, shot up, and shot down, Scooter Jeffries did not want to end his tour by boring straight in on the deck and sliding into a net barrier on a bed of foam. No, he wanted to celebrate his survival by recovering in the normal fashion, buzzing the carrier first and then circling around for an arrested landing. As squadron CO, Lt. Comdr. Don Brewer thought it was a stupid move, a reckless risk of a thirty-two-million-dollar aircraft and two highly trained naval aviators just to satisfy a macho urge. As a fighter jock, however, Daffy thought it was a really cool idea.

"Go for it, Scooter. Just take it easy on the pitchout, okay?"

Jeffries eased the throttles and nosed over, trying not to add too much speed in his slow descent from the platform. The Tomcat swooped down from five thousand feet to less than fifteen hundred. Jeffries could clearly see the flat, jagged outline of the *Eisenhower* now, three miles ahead, flanked by the spires and towers of her two escorts. At four hundred knots they were over the carrier quickly and headed out again toward open ocean.

Ordinarily he would have loaded up with G going into the pitchout, but, mindful of Brewer's admonition not to stress the airframe, Scooter settled for an easy swing through 180 degrees. He pulled out well to port of the carrier, almost directly over the USS *Valley Forge*. The boxy gray superstructure of the Aegis cruiser crawled underneath the Tomcat's belly as Jeffries entered the inside downwind leg of the approach.

"AOA?"

Jeffries checked the angle-of-attack indicator at the top left of the forward instrument panel in response to Brewer's inquiry from the landing checklist. He was slightly nose down, just as he was supposed to be: "Delta three."

"Speed?"

"270 knots." Scooter had managed to scrub off considerable airspeed even in the rather mild pitchout by not accelerating into the turn. The central air data computer automatically swept the Tomcat's wings forward to compensate. This, combined with the aircraft's stiff, birdlike landing gear and the way the split tailplanes waggled like tail feathers in the approach, had earned the F-14 the nickname "Turkey" among Navy deck crewmen.

"Weapons safed?"

"Weapons safed. Radar caged in standby."

"Gear down?"

Jeffries reached for the big switch covered with yellow rubber sticking out incongruously from the left side of the high-tech instrument panel. He pulled the release for the arresting hook on the right side.

"Three down and locked. Good hook."

"Slats?"

"Slats set."

They were at the perch, parallel with the *Eisenhower*'s stern. Jeffries swung the F-14 into a slow, descending port turn, the streaming fuel behind them describing a gentle curving smudge a hundred feet above the Arabian Sea. Jeffries could only guess what the men on the LSO platform, clearly visible now as he pulled out on final, thought of the smoking, hulking beast shooting a perfect approach on their carrier. It was like landing a kamikaze.

Even the landing signal officer—that perfectionist bastard—would have to log an underlined "OK" on this trap if Scooter could pull it off.

"I've got the ball."

Jeffries concentrated on the beams of the light landing device, flashing optical cues for the correct glideslope to landing. Yellow lights blinked momentarily; like most carrier pilots, Jeffries had a tendency to come in a trifle high during daylight hours. A slight throttle adjustment and he was in the green and on the beam, a half mile from the *Eisenhower*. In ten seconds it would all be over.

To Scooter and the rest of the Navy's carrier pilots, an arrested landing, even under the best circumstances, was a controlled crash. Aircraft had gotten too fast, too heavy. The margin for error was steadily disappearing, and yet they continued, day in and day out, slamming the monsters on deck in a routine miracle that was, if anything, *harder* than it looked. Navy pilots called it "sex in a car wreck." Trapping aboard an aircraft carrier, they felt, was the toughest trick in aviation and the one thing that forever set naval aviators above the ranks of mere pilots.

The Tomcat crawled in at an angle to the big white wake kicked up by the nuclear-powered carrier. The ship's bow cut a V of rounded waves in the smooth sea. Jeffries knew this was the tricky part. In calm weather, the ship had to make its own wind for takeoff and landing. Hustling around at thirty knots, the disturbed airflow from the carrier's island stirred up a nasty crosswind over the ramp. He flicked his eyes steadily from the ball to the angle-of-attack indicator to the end of the angled deck and back to the ball again.

In the back Daffy braced for the landing. His heart skipped a beat as a red light flashed on the caution panel: fuel pressure! He scanned the gauges. Port engine fuel pressure: zero! Should he tell Jeffries? No. Scooter would know. No need to distract him. There was an ominous rattling and coughing in the port intake. A spike of fear shot up Brewer's spine. Fuel starvation led to compressor stall just as easily as disturbed airflow. Sure enough, two yellow lights and another red flashed on the warning panel, as the turbine behind Brewer's left elbow wound down.

The Tomcat dipped a wing, suddenly. As if connected by a string, all the lights on the ball flashed simultaneously. Waveoff! Daffy could hear the LSO bellowing in his helmet: *Barrier! Barrier! Barrier!* Now that was a stupid call! It was too late now. They were committed. There was no time to rig the netted barrier that would snag the F-14 aboard (and probably destroy most of it in the process). If Ghostrider 12 went around again, it would not come back. Ever.

In the eternity of seconds that followed, Brewer did the following things: He wrapped one hand around the ejection-seat handle (but not tightly, lest, by some miracle, they actually got a trap—the inevitable shock would jerk the handles up and punch both men out). He poised the other hand above the emergency fire-extinguisher system, which he intended to initiate at the first sign of fire. He transmitted a terse, "on final" to the *Ike,* hoping the air boss, if indeed he had been fool enough to actually send men on deck to rig the barricade, would get them out of the way of this potential fireball hurtling at them at a couple hundred miles an hour. And he said a quick, silent prayer for the safety and well-being of his wife and two children. Just in case.

Seconds ago the carrier had seemed a set of neat black rectangles, not as small as it was far away. Now the dark deck swelled and rose to meet Ghostrider 12. It sprouted details—planes, people, gear—all jagged edges, frighteningly close. The ramp and the round-down, trimmed in safety orange for night landings, spread before the aircraft. Too low! "Dwight D. Eisenhower"—Brewer could read the ship's name in black letters spread across the stern. It was the last thing many carrier pilots ever saw.

Somehow, through sheer will, Jeffries managed to right the plane and throw it up on deck. The tailhook struck the ramp hard, sending a shower of sparks across the steel deck until it caught the number-one wire with a sharp click. The wheels slammed down, first the main gear and then the nose wheel. Scooter saw, peripherally in the blur, waves of sailors jumping into the safety nets that lined the flight deck. Instinctively, he reached to run the throttles up; if the hook had not snagged the wire securely, the Tomcat would need every ounce of power remaining to get airborne again lest it dribble off the end of the angled deck and sink forever in the ocean.

"Scooter, no!"

Jeffries snatched the throttles back before they hit Buster. Brewer was right! The afterburners would certainly ignite the fuel, now pouring in pools on the black nonskid surface of the flight deck. The Tomcat would have been blown off the *Eisenhower,* along with every other plane spotted aft of the island. Scooter hit the emergency fuel shutoff handles and spooled down both engines. The wire pulled back with a reassuring tug. Ghostrider 12 was home.

Suddenly the air was filled with a fine white mist. Smoke? Fire? Christ, not now! Jeffries checked the caution lights around the vertical display indicator. Everything seemed normal again. He reached for the canopy release lever, only to find the canopy already opening. A figure in a silver suit and helmet, looking for all the world like an evil robot on the cover of a 1950s science fiction pulp thriller, reached in to grab him.

"Get your hands off me, sailor!" Jeffries shouted. "And quit spraying Halon all over everything. This aircraft isn't on fire, and neither am I!"

The rescue crewman removed his helmet and smiled sheepishly. "Sorry, sir. We didn't want to do it. Admiral's orders."

The "hot suit" disappeared down the side of the fuselage, his place taken by a brown-shirted plane captain.

"Glad to have you home, sir," he said, reaching in to help Jeffries unsnap the hydra of cables, wires, and straps connecting him to the F-14. "We were a little worried for a minute there. I'm supposed to tell you, CAG's waiting to see you guys by the deck hatch. He doesn't look happy."

"CAG never looks happy," Jeffries grunted. He stood up in the seat, swung his left leg over the canopy rail, and felt for the footholds recessed below the red ejection-seat warning triangles. He jumped the last few feet, landing with a thud. The carrier seemed huge once again, a limitless expanse, a little continent. Funny how that worked.

Jeffries looked around for Brewer.

He found him on the catwalk, as always, hands white knuckled on the railing, throwing up into the sea.

It had shocked Scooter at first; the sight of his backseater puking his guts out after every mission did not exactly inspire confidence in the man who, literally, held Jeffries's life in his hands every time they left the ground. But Scooter kept quiet. Brewer was, after all, Ghostrider One, the squadron CO and Jeffries's immediate superior. More important, Daffy had proven himself, as a flyer and as a man, through perhaps the toughest air combat American forces had faced since the Battle of Midway. Scooter knew what Daffy had been through. Because he had gone through exactly the same thing, thirty-six inches before Brewer did.

They had been shot down together. And, although no one anywhere was willing to admit it, that made a special bond between two men. They had faced death together and survived. Together. Many men in the squadron had not been as fortunate. From sunrise, after their ejection, bobbing atop the Persian Gulf in a little yellow raft in the middle of a war, to sundown, when the *Ike*'s ResCAP choppers finally dared venture into the Gulf to pick them up, Scooter and Daffy had had plenty of time to get more closely acquainted.

"What are you looking at, sailor?" Jeffries shouted a little too harshly at a yellow-shirted deckhand staring open mouthed at Brewer. "Haven't you got any work to do? Move it, or I'll put you on report!"

The sailor slunk away toward the flight deck. Jeffries hung back, waited patiently for Brewer to finish, then walked past him quickly.

"CAG wants to see us."

"I heard," Brewer smiled thinly. "Three guesses what it's about."

"I could give a shit," Jeffries answered indifferently. "What can he do to us? Send us to the Persian Gulf?"

Scooter unstrapped his helmet and twisted it from his head. He snatched off his soaking gray skullcap and ran a gloved hand through his wet, matted hair.

"Good-bye to the goddamn Strait of Hormuz!" he said with a mock salute to the north. "Good-bye to the goddamn mystery MiGs! And good-bye to this goddamn war!"

Jeffries's last words were drowned out by the thunder of an EA-6B Prowler roaring off Cat 3. Now that Ghostrider 12 was safely aboard, the *Eisenhower* resumed normal flight operations, with constant antisubmarine, surface search, and BARCAP patrols. But for Scooter and Daffy, as for most of *Ike*'s fighter and attack pilots, the cruise was over. Ready Eagle was on its way to becoming a bad memory.

Cmdr. Mike "Ma" Carridy was waiting at the entrance to the island. As officer in charge of the hundred planes and more than two thousand men that comprised Carrier Air Wing Seven, Carridy was entitled, he thought, to more respect than he received. Universally referred to as "CAG"—a throwback to the days when Navy planes were painted navy blue and had propellers and the Old Man was called commander, air group—Carridy was constantly caught between the aviators, who flew the planes, and the sailors, who manned the ship the planes flew from. Now he had another difficult mission to perform.

"Welcome home, boys." Carridy spat on the deck. "Let's go down to my space and talk."

Jeffries and Brewer followed Carridy into the island, past the sleeping bodies of exhausted young deck workers and the curtain of "cranials"— multicolored, segmented helmets—hanging in the dark, still space. He led them, two steps at a time, through a maze of steep stairways and narrow hatches to the cramped cubicle in which he worked, slept, and worried.

"Have a seat if you can find one." Carridy waved toward the sprawling confusion of papers and flight gear opposite his small desk. "I've got to tell you guys something, but I'm not so sure you'll want to hear it."

"Look, CAG, if it's about the overhead, I can explain..."

Carridy dismissed Jeffries with a wave of his hand.

"I don't give a crap about your little air show, Scooter. It's your butt up there, and you guys can do whatever you want. I've got other things on my mind right now."

"Yeah, but I understand that Meredith..."

"*Admiral* Meredith was not pleased, that's true. He told the captain and the captain told me and I'm telling you. Next time you've got a hole in your plane, come limping in like a true victim," Carridy smiled. "It's good for morale."

"Excuse me, CAG," Brewer interjected. "But if that's not what you wanted to talk about, what is it?"

"This." Carridy rummaged through a desk drawer and brought out a yellow telex form. "You ever see one of these before?"

Scooter shook his head.

"I have," Daffy nodded. "It's a Yellow Bite."

"A what?"

"A Yellow Bite, Lieutenant," Carridy answered. "A priority communication from the Joint Chiefs of Staff."

"Why do they call it a Yellow Bite?" Scooter asked, puzzled.

"Because it's yellow, dumbass," Carridy laughed. "And because it usually takes a bite out of something you don't have enough of to begin with—time, money, or people. The problem with these things is you can't fight them, finesse them, or forget them. The JCS always gets what it wants."

"And what do they want this time?"

"They want you, Daffy," Carridy said. "You and young Steve Canyon here."

"What do they want us for?" Scooter asked timidly.

Cassidy examined the document. "Something called the First Air Regiment."

Scooter and Daffy exchanged a puzzled expression.

"What's that?" Brewer said.

"Beats the hell out of me. I just got this thing yesterday. You're supposed to take the mail plane to Abu Dhabi and then fly commercial into al-Quaseem. That's one of the emirates, I think. God only knows what happens after that."

"What if we don't want to go?"

"That's up to you, Scooter. The Navy can't force you to take a seconded commission. If you'd rather spend the rest of your hitch in a trash hauler, say, humping spare parts back and forth from Somalia to Diego Garcia, that's your decision." Carridy leaned back in his swivel chair and linked his arms behind his head. "But from what I've seen today, son, you strike me as a young man with a lust for adventure. This is your once-in-a-lifetime chance to play Errol Flynn in an F-14. Why don't you think about it a while? Take your time. Take twenty minutes. Exactly. Come back when you've had a shower and smell human again."

Jeffries gave a halfhearted salute and disappeared through the hatch. Brewer rose to join him.

"Daffy, wait a minute, will you?" Carridy said quietly.

Brewer shrugged and sat down again.

"What's on your mind, CAG?"

"I, ah, wasn't being entirely forthright with Scooter there."

Brewer looked at his hands. "I know."

"Well, what the hell? He's young; he's not married; he hasn't got any kids. What has he got to lose? They'll give him another chance to back out once he gets there and finds out what this is all about. I owe you more of an explanation. After all, you have a personal stake in this."

"Why is that?"

"Because whatever this First Air Regiment is, Brick White is behind it." Carridy sighed. "The message came from his office, and he chopped off on it. I'm not sure exactly what he's got in mind, but it seems to me it's some sort of Rough Riders outfit, with Brick playing the part of Teddy Roosevelt. And instead of horses in Cuba, this time it's jets in the Persian Gulf."

Brewer sat back in his chair, stunned.

"I don't get it, CAG. Brick White and I were never exactly buddies. Are you sure he asked for me?"

"No, he didn't, as a matter of fact." Carridy reached in a breast pocket of his flight suit, fished out a pipe and lighter, tamped down the pipe, and lit it. "It's like this, Daffy. I got this message yesterday, as I said. They asked for the CO of a fighter squadron from the *Eisenhower*. My guess is they're looking for someone who's been tangling with these Fulcrums over Iran, somebody who can give them the real skinny on the way they fight, their tactics, and so forth."

"It's a smart move."

"I agree," Carridy said. "It's what I'd do if I were in his place. But seeing as he was behind it, and seeing as what he was really looking for was a pilot—an Air Force puke like White *would* assume that a fighter squadron CO would have to be a pilot and not a backseater like you—I asked Devil Palmer to do it. And he agreed. But..."

Carridy's voice trailed off. He didn't need to complete the sentence. Brewer knew why Palmer wouldn't be joining First Air. Palmer was the commanding officer of VF-142's sister squadron on the *Enterprise,* the Pukin' Dogs of VF-143. *Was.* Just that morning, Palmer and his RIO, caught between Iranian ground fire and three MiGs above them, had flown into the side of Genow Mountain. There were no chutes.

Carridy stared at Brewer, relighting his pipe. "Anyway, knowing how you and Brick White feel about each other, I've been on the horn to Dar al-Harb, which is the airfield they're going to use up there at al-Quaseem. Brick White wasn't around. I got hold of a Major Padgett and offered to take Devil's place myself. Padgett said no; White wouldn't go for that. He was real nice about it, but I'm an attack pilot. That's not good enough. You know how it is."

Brewer nodded. Carridy was the air wing commander, but he was also an A-7 pilot. He flew Corsairs off the *Ike,* taking the same risks as the fighter jocks, with no opportunity to fight back. The MiGs were gunning for the strike pilots; they usually left the Tomcats alone if they could avoid a fight. An underpowered A-7, loaded down with Mk-82s and locked in on a bombing run with threats in every direction, was the worst seat in the war. Carridy must have been good. He was still alive.

But Carridy didn't fly air to air, so his opinion didn't count to those who did. Brewer knew Carridy's frustrations all too well. He had spent his entire career in fighters. But Brewer was a backseater—he had not flown fighters, just flown in them. He was an integral part of the mission and couldn't count the times he had saved his pilot's life with a timely tally on a bogey or a quick radar missile lock. It didn't matter. In the fighter community, if you didn't have your hand on the stick, you were just along for the ride. Brewer didn't agree with that attitude, but he had learned to live with it.

"You know what they say," Daffy said. "You can always tell a fighter pilot, but you can't tell him much. What else do you know about this outfit Brick is putting together?"

"A lot more than I'm supposed to," Carridy grinned. "I got the word from General Coleman, the 82d Airborne CG. He was in here the other day, blood in his eye, giving me hell for not sweeping the skies over the Persian Gulf."

"What did you say?"

"I said what any self-respecting Naval Academy graduate would say: I told him my admiral was an asshole," Carridy laughed. "We got along famously after that. There's apparently no love lost between those two. Coleman's bleeding for his troops. I've got to respect him for that. I know how he feels. He's frustrated. You know Meredith. He's just wondering where his next star is coming from."

"So what did Coleman tell you about First Air?"

Carridy tamped his pipe and stared at the ceiling.

"It's funny, Daffy. I don't get it. I don't know if Brick White is a genius or if he's nuts, but he's assembling the damnedest collection of aircraft you ever saw. I saw the whole thing. Coleman brought me all the message traffic— I guess he was hoping I could help him figure it out, being an airplane guy. At least *he* doesn't think of us attack pukes as human cruise missiles.

"Anyway, Brick's sending out requests everywhere, not just to the American services but to air attachés all over the world. Sometimes he's asking for pilots and planes. Other times he only wants pilots. Or just planes. And sometimes he just flat out asks for money. Lots of it. He wants a half-billion dollars from Japan alone. And you know what? Judging from the replies, it looks like he's going to get it!"

"Brick always was an operator."

"Yeah, so I hear. But at least you used to be able to tell what he was up to, and it always made sense. But this time, I don't know." Carridy shook his head. "You should see the planes he's asking for—everything from fifties fighters to aircraft I didn't even know existed yet. And the pilots! It looks like half of them are in the brig on charges, and the other half are practically running the Air Force. Some of them haven't been near a cockpit in years. Hell, a lot of them don't even speak English! Still..."

Carridy looked to Daffy for an answer. Brewer looked at his hands, lost in thought. Finally, he spoke.

"I don't know, CAG," he said doubtfully. "Look, I don't think I have to prove anything to anybody. If it was anyone else running this operation, I'd be up there in a minute, you know that. But Brick White! I don't know..."

Carridy sighed. "I understand, Daffy. And I don't blame you. You've done more than your share already. Let somebody else carry the ball from here. You've earned a rest."

"Thanks, CAG." Brewer put his hands on his knees and rose to leave.

"Just one more thing." Carridy leaned back in his chair and stared up at the overhead, as if looking for the next words to say. "I don't know how to put this, exactly. I wasn't going to tell you, but since you've decided not to go—and I think that's a wise decision—there's something else you might want to know."

Brewer settled back in the chair. "What is it, CAG?"

"There's...another name associated with the First Air Regiment, Daffy. You won't find it on any of the message traffic. It's definitely not official. General Coleman let it slip while we were talking. It's..." Carridy struggled for a way to say it. "Christ, Daffy, it's Bobby Dragon. He's supposed to be the one who's really running this First Air Regiment."

Brewer made his decision in the blink of an eye.

"Sign me up."

"Come on, Daffy! You can't be serious! Bobby Dragon's dead; everybody knows that. I just told you what I heard because I didn't want you to hear it from somebody else and think I was holding out on you."

"I appreciate that. But you're wrong, CAG. Bobby's alive. I know he is."

"Look, I've heard those stories, too," Carridy said, frustrated. "It's just boat talk; that's all it is. Wishful thinking. Rumor control. Bobby Dragon's name pops up every single time one of these spook operations comes along. Somebody says they saw him at the Blackbird hangar at Mildenhall. Somebody else spots him out in the Aleutians, at that antenna farm on Adak. Hell, just a couple of days ago, my intel guy says he heard Bobby Dragon buzzed an AWACS out at Nellis in a batplane! Can you believe that? Bobby Dragon in a goddamn Wobbly Goblin?"

"Of course I don't believe all that crap," Daffy said. "I've been hearing it for years, and every time I check out one of these stories it turns into smoke. But I do believe Bobby's alive. I think Brick stuck him in that ghost town out in—well, you know what I'm talking about. And right now, I think he can use someone he can trust."

Carridy frowned. "Well, I *don't* believe it. I think Brick White's just putting his name out to see if he can get anyone to bite. He's using everything he can think of to get this First Air thing going. I'll admit, floating the story of a dead man as head of the operation is pretty cynical, even for Brick. But these are tough times. Nobody wants to give up planes and pilots with the world so close to war."

Carridy sighed and leaned back in his leather chair. "Personally, I think Bobby Dragon stayed dead. But it's your hide. And you *were* the last person to see him alive. You should know. If..."

"That's right, CAG," Brewer interjected. "I was there, and I tell you there was nothing wrong with that aircraft. We didn't have a hung Sparrow. We couldn't have—we hosed off all our AIM-7s that morning over Hanoi. Bobby was never tight with missiles. He never liked bringing them home."

"That wasn't in the report," Carridy said soberly.

"There were a lot of things that weren't in the report," Daffy shot back. "What did you expect the Air Force to say? They couldn't very well announce to the world what really happened that day over Hanoi. It would mean telling the truth about what Brick was doing, about Doom and the tiger hunts and about a lot of other things that were better left unsaid. They had too many public-relations problems as it was. They made Bobby Dragon a hero to solve those problems, not create more. If he wanted to go riding off in the sunset, they didn't have any choice but to sell him to the public as some sort of airborne Lone Ranger. Actually, it worked out for the best, from the Air Force's point of view. It certainly tied up all the loose ends. And there's no hero like a dead hero."

A troubled look clouded Carridy's face.

"Look, Daffy, you're a good man, a real asset to the wing, and I don't want to lose you. More than that, I'd hate to see you throw your life away on a crazy scheme like First Air. I don't see how a bunch of cast-off airplanes and renegade pilots are going to stand up to MiGs that have been dicking the best air wing in the U.S. Navy. It's a suicide mission," Carridy said. "Now, don't get me wrong, but somebody's got to look out for your interests here if you're not going to. Somebody's got to ask a couple of tough questions."

"Such as?"

"Such as, *if* Bobby Dragon is alive, and *if* he's running this Flying Tigers outfit out in the Gulf, and *if* he needs you as much as you seem to think he does," Carridy ticked off the *ifs* on his fingers, "then how come he hasn't asked for you?"

Brewer developed a sudden, vital interest in the bleed air valve on the right thigh of his G-suit harness.

"I can't answer that, CAG."

"Okay, you think about it. And while you think that one over, here's another hard one: What makes you think he won't run out again?"

"Because he didn't run out the first time."

Carridy shook his head. "Wait a minute, Daffy. First you tell me Bobby Dragon didn't die like the Air Force said he did, when that hung missile blew up over the South China Sea. Okay. But he never came back. That only leaves one alternative: desertion. I can appreciate your loyalty to Bobby Dragon. I admire it. But I don't buy your story. Desertion is inexcusable, no matter what the reasons. I couldn't fly with a man like that."

Daffy sighed. There was no use trying to explain. Carridy was a good officer and a good commander, but he hadn't been there, and that made all the difference. You had to have been there, in Da Nang in 1972, with Bobby and Brick and the rest of the Heartbreakers, to really understand. You had to have been there with the politicians, in uniform and out, with the North Vietnamese chipping away outside and the South Vietnamese boring from within, with the press everywhere, alternately fawning and castigating. Each contributed its crumb and stick, its own particular piece of dirt to build the towering hive of cynicism. And at the center, worshipped and trapped like an insect queen, was young Bobby Dragon. Who could stand up to that kind of pressure? Who could blame him for what he did?

Everyone, obviously. Especially those who had pushed him into it. It was the easy hypocrisy that so disgusted Brewer, the facile way in which those who had patted Bobby on the back soon began pointing their fingers. Either they had no conscience or no memory or both, Daffy thought bitterly. Eventually, everyone came to agree with Bobby about the war. All were forgiven. Some were made heroes. But Bobby Dragon suffered the martyrdom and damnation that has always befallen the prematurely correct. And despite Daffy's willingness to share the burden, Bobby Dragon had chosen to bear it alone. This time, Brewer swore, they would face it together.

"No one's asking you to fly with him, CAG," Brewer said quietly. "I'll go."

Carridy stared at Daffy and shook his head. He knew it was pointless to try to talk him out of going.

"I just hope you know what you're getting into," Carridy said distantly. "There are worse things in war than dying."

It was only then that Brewer noticed why CAG's space was so crowded. The place was littered with mail, service forms, and personal articles. Brewer recognized the names on some of them: pilots from the *Eisenhower*, killed in action over Bandar Abbas. Carridy was writing letters to their next of kin.

Carridy extended his hand. Brewer shook it and walked out quietly. "You done?"

Daffy looked up to see Scooter standing in the passageway, showered and changed, obviously waiting for Brewer to finish his conversation with CAG.

"Yeah."

"You going?" Scooter asked.

"Yeah," Daffy answered.

"Me, too."

Brewer looked at Jeffries with concern.

"You don't have to go, Scooter. It's not your fight."

"It's not yours either, Skipper. You don't have a monopoly on hero hormones. I've spent too long training you to break in a new backseater. And I won't have you stooging around up there with some new driver who doesn't recognize your finer qualities. You need the best. You deserve it. You need me."

Brewer closed his eyes, obviously touched. Still, he couldn't let Jeffries go, couldn't ask someone else to fight his battles and wrestle with his demons.

"Look, Scooter, it's not like you think up there. There's a lot about the First Air Regiment that you don't know."

"Like what? Like Bobby Dragon is running it?"

Brewer was stunned. "How did you find that out?"

"I know a guy." Scooter smiled. "One of those aides that follows Merrydick around. He was so excited that an actual jet fighter pilot would talk to him that he spilled his guts out to me about the message traffic the admiral's getting about this First Air stuff."

"Wait a minute," Daffy said suspiciously. "You haven't been gone twenty minutes. Where did you talk to him?"

"In the shower. I snuck up to flag country. The guy has a dick this big," Scooter held up a hand with the fingers barely an inch apart. "I knew it all along."

Daffy laughed. "I appreciate your loyalty, Scooter. But I can't let you go along on this one. It's personal."

Brewer started to step down the passageway. Jeffries leaned across it, blocking his way.

"What's the matter?" Scooter asked softly. "I'm not good enough for you? You think you'll have better luck with somebody else driving you around?"

"Of course not." Brewer was stunned. "What makes you say that?"

"Christ, Daffy!" Scooter exploded. "Here I am, Mr. Top Gun graduate, the squadron's weapons and tactics expert, and I haven't even gotten close enough to *wave* at a MiG since that first day. Not only that, every time I bring the bird home it's full of BBs from some raghead on the ground taking potshots at us. I don't have to tell you how I used to wax everybody in the wing during fleet maneuvers. Now, when it counts, I might as well be driving a bus with a big bull's-eye on it. You know how pilots are. They're just eating it up. They say I'm a paper tiger, one of those guys who kicks ass in exercises but just can't pull the trigger in the real world. First Air is my last chance to prove them wrong. And I'm taking it. You can't stop me."

"Look, Scooter, this cruise is over. The wing is headed to Naples and then back to Norfolk. You'll be reassigned," Daffy said. "I know you've put in an application to go back to Miramar as an instructor. I've already written my recommendation. I'm sure CAG will put in a good word for you. With that and your real-war experience here, you're a cinch to get a slot on the Top Gun staff."

"No thanks," Jeffries said flatly. "That doesn't interest me anymore."

"What do you mean? It's all you've been talking about since we left port," Brewer said. "I don't blame you. It's a dream come true. You fly the hottest jets in the world by day, and at night you get more pussy than Frank Sinatra. Don't tell me you're going to give that up. For what? What does First Air have that Top Gun doesn't?"

Scooter looked Brewer straight in the eyes and smiled.

"Real bullets."

Dog and Pony

**Dar al-Harb Air Base
Emirate of al-Quaseem**

The Tornadoes swept down like hawks, their swing wings spreading wide to grab the thick air over Dar al-Harb. They set down in pairs over the long black strip until all six were gathered at the end of the runway. The lumbering Transall followed about a minute behind. It was quite a feat—from Jever, on the foggy North Sea coast of West Germany, to steaming al-Quaseem, on course, on time, and all together.

Brick White stood before the white concrete operations building admiring the airmanship of the *piloten* and *kampfbeobachters* of Jagdbombergeswader 38. He wished he could feel same way about the timing of the German *oberst* who had come all the way from Riyadh, where he was air attaché at the embassy of the Federal Republic of Germany, to ruin Brick's morning.

"You understand, General White, these are difficult times. Our people would be up in arms to learn that their scarce and expensive aircraft, needed so desperately in this period of tension, had gone to support some sort of American business interest in the Persian Gulf."

Brick cursed softly to himself. He thought this was a done deal. Hadn't the president's people personally spoken to the chancellor like they promised? Brick needed these planes. It had been tough enough getting fighters for First Air, with the world so close to war. But he desperately needed precision tactical bombers for his plans, and he couldn't find any anywhere for much the same reasons Kleinst was telling him. Or rather *not* telling him: If First Air didn't work—and most Western governments had big doubts about the scheme— they would need these same aircraft in the nuclear showdown that could very well follow.

Most of the British and West German Tornadoes and nearly all of the American F-111s in England had been assigned nuclear land-line delivery missions as part of the NATO master plan for a general war in Europe. They were off limits. Only Jever, formerly the Tornado conversion base, was free of a nuclear commitment. Brick thought he could get those planes for First Air. Now he could see it wasn't going to be that easy.

"Herr Kleinst, I can't guarantee that if you give me the flight of Tornadoes I need for counterair work, your troubles in Germany will be over," Brick argued. "But I can say that if you *don't* help out with First Air, you'll be closer to war than if you do."

"Of course," Kleinst said diplomatically. "Nevertheless, Bonn has refused your request. Your men may wish to waste your lives, but in times like these the Luftwaffe has no aircraft to spare for such a romantic and foolish enterprise as your First Air Regiment."

The way he said it made Brick want to kick the little colonel across the runway. He held his temper, watching the Tornadoes taxi in a long line across the runway to the ramp in front of where he was standing. Their normal green finish had been replaced with gray-and-tan desert camouflage. Luftwaffe markings had been scrubbed out, with civil registration numbers scrawled in their place.

"Well, maybe this is some sort of desert mirage I'm seeing, but it looks to me like there are..." Brick quickly counted the tall tails of the planes lining up neatly in front of him, "six Tornadoes on my ramp right now. How do you expain that?"

"Yes, well," Kleinst gave out a nervous cough, "although the *Bundestag* is steadfastly opposed to current U.S. policy in the Gulf, we cannot completely turn our backs on our American allies. To do so might cause them to rethink their commitment to NATO. I don't need to tell you what the removal of even part of the American forces would do to the alliance at this critical time. Therefore, in a spirit of cooperation, the West German government has agreed to send eight Tornadoes and their crews to al-Quaseem..."

"That's great!" Brick interrupted. Apparently the White House *had* done some political arm-twisting. "You won't regret it."

"Let me finish!" Kleinst said sharply. "We have agreed to send this detachment to the First Air Regiment *as observers only*. Their orders are to look and learn. Under no circumstances are they to engage in offensive missions. They will attack only if they are themselves attacked. Is this clear?"

It was all too clear to Brick. He had been having similar conversations with representatives of various Free World forces throughout the past week. Every plane that landed at Dar al-Harb seemed to be trailing a mile of string behind it. Brick had done his damnedest to cut those strings; Bobby insisted that no conditions be put on the planes and pilots that made up First Air. If he was going to take the responsibility, he wanted complete control over every aspect of the Regiment. No more micromanagement, no political constraints that the enemy could use to his advantage—they had made that mistake before. Brick agreed completely. But he wondered if Bobby knew how difficult it was to convince governments and generals to surrender multimillion-dollar aircraft and irreplaceable pilots to an unknown entity like First Air.

Brick looked at Kleinst and spat derisively. The saliva steamed instantly on the burning concrete.

"Hell, yes, it's clear. And I'll be just as clear with you," Brick said deliberately. "Fuck off!"

"What?" Kleinst was astonished.

"You heard me! Get the hell off this base and take these lightweights with you!" Brick shouted angrily. "I don't have room on my ramp for tourists. They're taking up space that real men could use."

"I see," Kleinst said quietly, with a curious smile. "Perhaps you would follow me, General?"

"What for?" Brick asked, then realized he was talking to himself. Kleinst walked briskly toward the Transall. Brick shrugged and followed him.

A half-dozen Luftwaffe ordnance specialists quickly unloaded the contents of the cargo plane's hold onto a train of ammunition carts towed by a small green tractor. Kleinst motioned for Brick to examine the load. Brick lifted a tarp, whistled, then looked at another and then another. He couldn't believe it: MW-1 antirunway weapons. Beluga cluster bombs. Cerberus jamming pods and BOZ-101 chaff and flare dispensers.

"This is just the first shipment," Kleinst said softly. "There will be many others."

"I don't understand," Brick said. "These are all counterair munitions. They're for bombing airfields, not shooting down airplanes. I thought you said these guys were supposed to attack only in self-defense."

"I did," Kleinst answered dryly. He looked around to see if anyone was listening and added, "but why wait until the last minute?"

Brick shook with sudden laughter. "All right. I think I understand you."

"I hope you do." Kleinst tugged the tarp back over a crate of cluster bombs. "These men are all volunteers. But you will be held responsible for anything that happens to them."

"Don't worry, Herr Kleinst," Brick said evenly. "I'll make sure your 'observers' get a real close look at the war."

The shadow of a jetliner crossed over them. Brick looked up, checked his watch, swore silently, and waved a hand toward the ops building. An American enlisted man drove up in an open, camouflaged Land Rover. In the back, a Quaseemi bodyguard rode shotgun with an H&K MP5. Brick patted the driver's shoulder. The Land Rover scooted around the building and through a barricaded checkpoint guarded by local troops wearing blue berets. The perimeter was surrounded by double chain-link fences ten feet high topped with razor-studded concertina wire. A German shepherd snarled as they drove past. The dog was tethered to a sign in Arabic with the English translation underneath: "Welcome to Dar al-Harb, Home of the Royal Air Force of the Emirate of al-Quaseem."

Dar al-Harb. House of War. The sheik's great-grandfather, Brick had learned, had staged raids out in the Gulf from the natural harbor at the end of the runway. There was still a lot of pirate in the sheik, but these days he preferred F-16s to *dhows*. The tactical air base, modern in every respect, was built in tandem with the large civilian jetport, Quaseem International. Their parallel runways both ended in the Gulf, on the northern shore of the island.

The Land Rover, amber lights flashing in the yellow sun, crossed the concrete of the airport runway at speed, just missing a gaudy blue-and-silver VC-22 taxiing toward the ramp. Brick pointed toward the white spires and shining glass of the civilian terminal. The driver gunned the engine.

The big plane shook at idle on the ramp, the noonday sun baking its polished fuselage. Tires screaming, the Land Rover weaved its way through a gridlock of transports and arrived just as the aircraft's door opened. A small man in the uniform of an American Army general peered out, perturbed. He seemed to be looking for something as he put a tiny hand against his forehead to shield it from the beaming Gulf sun.

Jumping from the Land Rover, Brick took this as a salute and returned it.

"Good morning, General Forest," he shouted, trying to be heard above the plane's roaring engines. "Welcome to al-Quaseem and Dar al-Harb, home of the First Air Regiment, Inc."

Forest searched the asphalt underneath him with a scowl, finally spotting Brick standing below him, alone on the ramp. A couple of contract maintenance workers wheeled a movable stairway into position against the VC-22, an aircraft identical in most respects to a civilian 727 jetliner save for the fact that it was even more plush and all the passenger seats faced backward. Forest drew himself up to his full height and walked stiffly down the gangway.

"Well, White, I must say I expected more of a welcome than this."

Brick winced and stifled an urge to smile. As national security advisor, Forest was one of Brick's bosses. It would not be good to alienate him. However, Forest was a fool. That was not a heated judgment or a personality difference on Brick's part; it was a fact. Beaufort Forest was a fool. Everyone in Washington knew it. He was a political appointee, chosen by a president jealous and suspicious of the power of past national security advisors and gleefully approved by a Congress and military establishment anxious to have Forest in a position where they could keep an eye on him.

Although it was generally accepted that Brick White was the real military mind at the White House, his personality and his past made it impossible for him to actually assume the post of national security advisor. Instead, Brick worked through Forest to do what had to be done, knowing that, should it ever come to a showdown, the president would not hesitate to back him up. Forest knew it, too. He enjoyed the position and its perks, and while he maintained a high profile, he remained curiously silent when real decisions had to be made.

"We wanted to give you a big reception, General, but you came at a bad time," Brick said. "There's still so much to be done around here. But I'll be glad to show you around."

Brick helped Forest in the Land Rover, climbing in the backseat behind him. The driver slowly threaded his way through the tangle of military transports and chartered civilian airfreighters on the apron at al-Quaseem. There were dozens of them, moving in, unloading, moving out. None of them seemed to stay too long.

"Look at all these heavies," Forest exclaimed. "What are they carrying?"

"Bombs and maps and steaks and computers and toilet seats and about a thousand other things you need to fight a war these days," Brick answered. "You never know how much it takes to keep an air unit like this going until you have to start one up from scratch."

"I couldn't even take a wag at how much this must be costing," Forest said, then added with obvious relish, "Oh, well, that's not my problem. Schatz is the money man. I'll let you guys fight it out."

Brick sighed. Kevin Schatz was a wonderkid, a young man who had made a tremendous amount of money on Wall Street. After the latest round of Pentagon procurement scandals, the president had tapped Schatz as secretary of defense precisely *because* he had no military experience. Schatz had accepted—and made Brick's life doubly miserable.

As liaison between the national security advisor and the secretary of defense, Brick was charged with translating their policies into action. It was a tough job. Neither Forest nor Schatz *had* any discernible policies. The job was made even more difficult by the fact that the two men hated and mistrusted each other. Forest saw Schatz as an outsider, a fast-buck artist on the make.

Schatz saw Forest as a self-important fool, in love with the trappings of office and unmindful of its power and responsibilities. They were both correct.

Somehow, Brick White not only made the situation work but turned it to his advantage. By playing one against the other, he was able to accomplish whatever he chose. When he gave orders, people naturally assumed those orders came from higher authority. Since Schatz and Forest rarely communicated, Brick was able to get his way with either by intimating the other had ordered whatever he wanted to do.

It was a tightrope, but as long as Brick could keep the two men apart he could keep First Air going. And soon the Regiment would have a life of its own, impossible to stop. All it took was combat.

Today, though, was especially difficult—both men were scheduled to arrive at al-Quaseem to "inspect" the First Air Regiment. Neither had any real interest in the operation, but Brick's endeavor in the Persian Gulf had caught the imagination of the Washington crowd. All sorts of people who at first had wanted nothing to do with First Air suddenly sought to seem somehow connected. Brick was happy to hear Hassan was going to hire a front man to do public relations for the Regiment—he had too much to do without baby-sitting political bigshots, and Bobby flatly refused to deal with anyone not directly connected with First Air. If the new man did nothing but stage dog-and-pony shows for the press and government officials, he would be worth whatever the sheik would pay him. But Forest and Schatz were different. Brick had to take care of them personally.

"Why are we stopping?" Forest asked, impatient in the heat.

Brick pointed toward the Gulf, where a C-5 hung in the pattern over the water. Its huge bulk made it seem very close and very close to stalling. The Galaxy was actually still three miles away. The main gear twisted down, flaps clawing for every bit of lift on final.

"There are actually two airports here, General," Brick continued, shouting over the noise of the Galaxy's tortured brakes as it rumbled past with a hiss and a roar. "This is Quaseem International, the commercial side, one of the biggest passenger and freight terminals in the Gulf. It's closed now—all the airliners except the ones we charter have to land in Abu Dhabi or Dubai."

"It doesn't look closed to me," Forest said doubtfully.

"This is all First Air stuff," Brick waved a hand at the parade of transports and commercial charters crowded around the terminal building. "After we get set up, we won't need so many, and this side will be used for the strike aircraft and most of the support planes."

"So where are the fighters?" Forest asked.

"On the other side, General. At Dar al-Harb." Brick whispered in the driver's ear. The Land Rover shot across the runway and through the guarded gates of the air base.

A pair of Harriers rolled by on the taxiway paralleling the road. Their

British roundels were plastered over with the black triangle insignia of First Air. Forest noted with displeasure that First Air pilots, now unburdened by regulations they had chafed under in their own air forces, had taken to personalizing their aircraft with sharks' mouths, nose art, and other garish markings. He made a mental note to remind Brick that military discipline begins with appearance.

"Those are funny-looking TAB-Vs," Forest said, pointing at a hardened aircraft shelter half dug in the desert. Theater air-base–vulnerability shelters, a type of armored igloo that protected tactical aircraft, were common throughout Europe, but Forest had never seen them in this part of the world. The road through Dar al-Harb branched off in many places, each spur leading to a half-dozen pits holding a single aircraft. The roofs, made of reinforced concrete and covered with sand, were level with the ground.

"These are actually better than European TAB-Vs, General," Brick said. "They're open at the front and back, so you can stuff aircraft at either end and the jet blast goes out the other way. And you don't need a tug to get them in and out. If the airfield is bombed, most of the blast will go right out at ground level. It'll shove some sand around, but the planes should be okay. Even if an enemy plane scores a direct hit on the ramp—which I don't think even I could do—none of the shelters is facing the same way."

"What do you mean, if the airfield is bombed?" Forest's voice rose in surprise. "Could the MiGs raid this place?"

"Hard to say, General," Brick said matter of factly. "They're not built for that, but you could hang bombs on a Fulcrum if you wanted to. Any modern aircraft with an inertial navigation system will do a halfway decent job of mud moving. And it's a lot easier to destroy aircraft on the ground than in the air. That's what I'd do if I were in their shoes."

"So what are you going to do about it?" Forest sounded worried.

Brick pointed at a huge hangar situated between the two runways.

"You see that?" he asked. "That's the Zulu shack, now. It used to be a hangar for airliners in for depot-level maintenance. We keep two birds on alert there twenty-four hours a day, fueled and armed."

Forest shuddered. He hadn't considered the fact that First Air could itself be attacked. He didn't want to be the one to tell the president. In fact, he didn't want to stick around much longer at all.

"I think I've seen enough," Forest said abruptly. "This is all quite impressive, but we're running out of time. We need air support over Iran, and we need it now. When do you expect First Air to be operational?"

Brick had expected the question. He had not yet thought of an answer.

"It's hard to say, sir. No one's ever done anything like this before. I still don't have all my pilots and planes, and we've got to work together a lot more before we're going to be a danger to anyone but ourselves."

"You don't have time," Forest said testily. "I've been getting it from every side. The Navy can't last much longer. The chief of naval operations is breathing down my neck to get First Air flying so he can get his ships out of the Gulf. My Army colleagues are wondering whether there'll be any of their people left in Bandar Abbas to rescue by the time you're operational. The Air Force is bitching because you're commandeering all their best planes and pilots. The Navy's squealing even louder for the same reason—they say they don't have any planes left to give you. And the president is on the warpath because we've put so much time, effort, and money behind the Regiment and it has yet to show any results."

"Well, I don't think it's fair to say we haven't shown any results..."

"No?" There was a sudden edge to Forest's voice. "Then tell me—the president's main concern is finding out where the Iranians got the bomb and whether or not they've got any more. What have you done about that?"

"Nothing yet, sir." Brick frowned. "We're hoping that will come later, after we help the guys on the ground break out."

"I see. I'll just tell the president you don't share his priorities," Forest sniffed. "And while I'm there, I'm sure he'll ask me about who it is, exactly, that we're fighting over here. You know what a stickler for details he is. I assume you've uncovered more about this mysterious MiG unit that came out of nowhere to single-handedly stymie the armed forces of the United States of America."

"No, sir, not exactly. But we're working on it."

Forest smiled tightly. He was not happy with the answers he was getting, but he seemed to enjoy putting Brick White on the hot seat.

"Damn it, White, that's not good enough. You tell me you don't know who you're fighting or when you're going to be ready to fight back. And you tell me you're not even *trying* to find out how many—if any—bombs the Iranians have left, which is why we sent you here in the first place. This is unacceptable. What am I going to tell the president?"

Brick wanted to lash out but calmed himself. He had come too far to throw everything away in a rush of anger.

"Tell him the U.S. has had about fifty years to come up with a plan that dealt with the realities of the Middle East, and we've pissed it away," Brick said evenly. "I'm trying to make something work that should take at least five years. And I've got about two weeks to do it. It's not like we've been wasting our time here."

"No one's suggesting that," Forest said. "It's just that we've got to know when we can count on the Regiment. We've got to make plans, White. We've got to fit First Air into our Middle Eastern policy."

"Policy?" Brick asked. "What policy? Every time some crisis with Iran flares up—and it seems to happen every couple of years—the planners and the politicians break out the same maps and say the same thing: 'Look how big it is!' The next thing they say is: 'Look how far away it is!' After that, they're usually content to send in the Navy to cruise courageously up and down international waters. Well, that's not going to work this time. This is it. This is war."

"I don't understand," Forest said. "Why don't you just go with the planes and pilots you've already got and add the rest as they arrive?"

"Sure, we could do that. But we're not going to. We'd just get chewed up like the Navy's doing now. We simply don't have the bodies, let alone planes, to waste." Brick shook his head. "No, we're going to do it right. First Air flies as a unit, or we don't fly at all."

Forest turned red. He began to say something, then stopped. He didn't want to force a showdown with Brick, not now. Forest wasn't about to tell him what the president really said at their brief meeting, that Brick White seemed to be the only American in the world who was actively trying to deal with the situation in Iran. And that it was his job to give Brick anything and anyone he wanted. If push came to shove, Forest had no illusions—he would be out and Brick would be in.

Forest felt Brick's eyes bore into his own. He dropped his gaze and noticed the pin on Brick's lapel, a silver "1" on golden wings.

"Is that a First Air pin?" Forest asked, grateful for the opportunity to change the subject. "You know, you could get a lot of money for that in Washington these days. Everybody in the Pentagon wants one."

Brick felt his temper rising. The tiny speck of gold and silver seemed to be the only thing about the First Air Regiment that really interested Forest. What would it hurt to give him what he wanted and send him on his way?

But no, Brick thought stubbornly, he wasn't going to do it. He wasn't going to cheapen the Regiment before it even got off the ground. The "winged one" stood for something, something a weak dick like Forest could never understand.

Brick decided to give it to Forest straight.

"Sorry, sir. These are for regimental distribution only. There are only two ways to get a First Air pin—fuck one or be one. And you don't fly with us, General." Brick shook his head and smiled. "What would people think?"

The two men sat in silence as the Land Rover drove across the runway back to the terminal at Quaseem International. A 707 in White House colors rolled to a stop on the ramp, the noise from its idling engines preventing further conversation. The passenger door opened. A single figure stood silhouetted in the sun at the top of the stairs.

"Oh, shit!" Brick muttered, looking up.

Forest followed his gaze. "Shit!"

Secretary of Defense Kevin Schatz looked down at the figures in the Land Rover. He had expected to see Brick White. He had not expected to find General Beaufort Forest in al-Quaseem. "Shit," he muttered.

Schatz walked down the stairs, zeroing in on Forest.

"Beau, you old son-of-a-gun!" Schatz said, too pleasantly. "I didn't think you were going to be here. Why didn't you let me know you were coming? We could have flown in together."

Brick watched as the two men shook hands. It was like watching a shark shake fins with a tuna.

"Well, actually, I was just about to take off," Forest said. "I've got some business in Frankfurt to attend to. I'll leave you in General White's capable hands."

"All right, then. Sorry to see you go so soon," Schatz said, with more relief than regret.

Forest turned to Brick. "You've done a bang-up job here, White. Just follow those suggestions I made, and I'm sure First Air will be up and flying in no time."

Suggestions? "Yes, sir, General," Brick said, "and thanks for dropping by."

He saluted Forest and watched him stumble down the ramp, searching for his plane in the heat. In a way, Brick was almost sorry to see him go. Forest was bad enough, but Schatz was actually intelligent, which made it even worse.

"You'll excuse me for not putting in a proper welcome, Mr. Schatz. We didn't expect you until later this afternoon."

"I know," Schatz said smugly. "I always show up earlier than scheduled for inspections. Why give people time to sweep things under the rug?"

Schatz turned and snapped a finger toward the open cabin door. "Let's get right down to business. I've got something here that should really interest you."

An aide, resembling an even younger version of Schatz with his slicked-back hair and red tie, trotted down the aircraft gangway carrying an alligator briefcase. He handed it to Schatz and, looking as if he smelled something foul in the desert air of al-Quaseem, disappeared back into the airplane.

Schatz opened the briefcase on the gangway steps and brought out a thick stack of papers with a light blue cover.

"You know, General, I have to hand it to you. I'll admit, I didn't think too highly of this First Air thing when you first proposed it. In fact, if the president wasn't so keen on the idea I would have killed it right away. Now I realize what a fascinating concept it is. Of course, you're not a money man. You couldn't realize what a gold mine you came up with."

"What are you talking about?" Brick asked uncomfortably.

"Money, General White." Schatz smiled like an alligator. "Lots and lots of money. As secretary of defense, I don't have much direct operational input into plans and so forth, that's true. But all the money for defense goes through my office. And you can't fly airplanes or shoot cannons or do any of the other things you soldiers so like to do without money. Are you with me so far?"

Brick nodded.

"Okay," Schatz continued. "Up to now, First Air has been a tremendous fiscal drain, a net importer of money. Good God, General, do you know how much this thing is costing American taxpayers?"

"Well, let's see...we're paying you a dollar a day for these planes," Brick pretended to add it up in his head. "I don't think we're up to a billion dollars yet, but we're getting close."

"Darn right!" Schatz agreed. "And it'll be more than two billion when you get everything you want. Now, how do you expect us to pay for all this?"

"I don't know. Why can't you do what they've always done to pay for a war?" Brick chuckled humorlessly. "Print more money."

Schatz stared at Brick. It was obvious he didn't think there was anything funny about money.

"I guess you can't be expected to know a great deal about financial matters," Schatz sighed. "But we have in the United States now what is called a balanced budget. The money going out has to equal the money coming in. The First Air Regiment was not included as a line item in the current fiscal budget."

"So?"

"So that means the United States government will realize a net revenue shortfall of more than two billion dollars this year," Schatz said, frustrated. "Doesn't that mean anything to you?"

"Nothing at all, Mr. Schatz. I just fly them. I don't have to pay for them."

"Well, somebody does, General. And you'd better start thinking about where that money's going to come from before it dries up." Schatz fingered the document. "Fortunately for everyone, I've been thinking about it. And I have a plan to get the Regiment off our balance sheet."

He proudly handed over the document to Brick, who browsed through it absently, uncomprehendingly.

"What's this?" he said, puzzled. "It looks like some kind of contract."

"Good!" Schatz said, with an air of patronization. "That's exactly what it is. It makes First Air a corporation and a government contractor."

"You're a little late," Brick said, handing the papers back to Schatz. "We've already incorporated as a limited partnership, down in the Bahamas. The sheik took care of it."

"I'm not talking about some legal maneuver intended to indemnify the United States government or fool the rest of the Gulf into believing First Air is some sort of private enterprise," Schatz said. "I'm talking about a *real* corporation, General. Something you can make money on."

Brick stared in disbelief.

"Look," Schatz continued, leafing rapidly through the pages. "This sets us up on the Big Board as a publicly held corporation. I've already talked to some of my connections at the brokerage houses about capitalization. This is private-sector initiative at its finest! This is definitely the way to go!"

Brick said nothing as Schatz continued his pitch.

"Now, there are performance clauses in the contract—so much per bombing mission, a certain amount for each enemy plane shot down. But who's keeping track of that? We are! We could stand to make some serious money out of this, Brick."

"*We?*"

"Of course," Schatz said, surprised. "You don't think I've gone to all this trouble for nothing, do you? It's only fair. I've already done the hard part. You have no idea what a complicated deal this was to put together. All you have to do is get your people here to go along. It shouldn't be any problem. They'll all come home rich men."

"*If* they come home."

"There's a clause in here about that," Schatz said, searching through the thick document. "The money goes in a pool, and it's split among the, uh...remaining parties."

"Isn't this a conflict of interest, Mr. Schatz?" Brick asked, dazed. "Pardon me for saying so, but I thought you were prohibited from dealing *with* the government if you were *in* the government."

"Not at all," Schatz answered. He seemed to take the question as an insult. "The new ethics laws are designed to allow the government to compete with the private sector for the best executive minds in America. We're no longer penalized for serving our country. As long as I keep my share in a trust until I step down as secretary of defense, I'm allowed to participate in any outside business venture I choose. Of course, you'll have to resign your commission, General. But that's not a problem—you can make all the money you want as president and chief executive officer of FirstAirCo."

Brick was speechless.

"Well, General," Schatz waved the contract proudly, "what do you think?"

"Do you want to know what I think?" Brick hissed. "I think it's the biggest crock of..."

His words were lost in the scream of an ancient Turkish F-4 taking off in full afterburner. As it roared by, the jet wash tore the contract from Schatz's hands and scattered it across the runway in a blue-and-white blizzard. Brick watched as the papers swirled high in the air, dancing in vortexes above the shimmering heat of the asphalt.

Schatz went down on his hands and knees, snatching whatever he could reach. To Brick, the sight of an American secretary of defense crawling after his lost riches on a runway in the Persian Gulf was an epiphany.

Like most Americans, Brick had always thought it natural, even comforting, that the halls of power in Washington were stuffed with rich and powerful men. Surely, with money of their own they were incorruptible, able to act in the nation's best interests. Now, watching Schatz down on all fours trying to salvage the pieces of his scheme, Brick realized: It's just another job to them. Another scam to make a buck.

Brick leaned over Schatz and smiled.

"I think you've got the right idea, Mr. Secretary," he said smoothly. "But you're facing the wrong way. Mecca's just about due west of here."

Schatz scrambled to his feet and shot Brick a black look. "So you think this is funny?"

"No, sir," Brick said evenly. "There's nothing funny about American soldiers being pushed into the sea because their government didn't have any idea what it was doing when it sent them there. And there's nothing funny about a government that will hand over the keys to the treasury to any contractor with a weapon to promote but isn't willing to pay what it takes to protect its own interests when push comes to shove. Funny isn't the word for it. It's pathetic."

"That's enough, General."

"I don't think so," Brick said bitterly. "I'm tired of the way you've been nickel-and-diming this operation to death since the beginning. You know what's really griping you? It's all this money going out, and you can't figure out a way to get a piece of it."

"You don't understand high finance. You don't understand how these things work."

"No, I guess I don't," Brick said with mock humility. "And you know what? I have a feeling the president won't, either. You haven't told him about your bright idea yet, have you?"

"No. I was..."

"I thought so," Brick said. "You were going to use me as a front, weren't you? You were going to stay in the shadows and tell the president it was all my idea and then rake in the bucks while everybody thought *I* was the one trying to take advantage of the situation. What a fucking lizard you are!"

Schatz's face turned as red as his tie. The two men stared at each other. Schatz's assistant scurried down from the airplane and handed the secretary an envelope. A smile spread across Schatz's face as he read the name on the teletype message.

"It's from Admiral Meredith, commander of our task force out in the Arabian Sea," Schatz said smugly. "Are you surprised, General White? At least some military men recognize the benefit of keeping the lines of communication open along the chain of command. The admiral has been quite helpful in keeping me informed of your lack of progress up here."

Brick remained silent, seething as Schatz tore the message open. A slim grin passed across Schatz's face as he read.

"So, General," Schatz said. "We may not need you and your expensive little air force at all. With the arrival of the *Constellation* and her fresh air wing, Admiral Meredith is personally supervising an air offensive that will permanently sweep the skies over Bandar Abbas. What do you say to that?"

Brick stared blankly. The fool! Hadn't Meredith learned anything? Brick felt sorry for the brave men aboard the *Constellation*. If "personally supervising" the air strike meant following Meredith's failed tactics, Brick knew many of the men would not be coming back.

"It's a mistake," Brick said hoarsely. "Call it off."

"I'm afraid I can't do that," Schatz said. "The first wave of aircraft is taking off now. Besides, I wouldn't recall the mission if I could. I think it's about time someone took action around here. We can't wait forever for First Air. By the way, now that the question has been rendered academic by Admiral Meredith's splendid initiative, tell me: When *did* you plan to make the Regiment operational?"

"It's not my decision," Brick said, distracted by the thought of *Connie*'s doomed Alpha strike. "The sheik is running this show. He wants to make sure he's not isolated in the Gulf. Iran has to make the first move. They've got to give him provocation, a legal reason for attacking Bandar Abbas."

"What?" Schatz exploded. "Is that what you've been waiting for? My God! That might never happen! It's a good thing I came here today. Wait until the president hears about this! Wait until I tell him how you've been stringing him along, with no intention of ever *using* these valuable forces you've been collecting!"

"I intend to use them, Mr. Secretary," Brick said steadily. "Someone's going to have to pick up the pieces after Meredith gets through shoving the *Connie*'s air wing through the meat grinder. We're just waiting for Iran to give the sheik a reason."

"Oh," Schatz said sarcastically, "and when is that supposed to happen, if I may ask?"

"Tonight," Brick said. "It's supposed to happen tonight."

Schatz looked at Brick incredulously.

"Hassan's an Arab," Brick smiled and shrugged his shoulders. "Go figure."

Paratov's Cobra

Above the Dasht-e-Lut
Southeastern Iran

Just as Paratov was beginning to think nothing the Americans could do would surprise him, they came up with the biggest surprise of all—predictability.

That the American invasion of Iran began with the tragicomedy of *Ready Eagle* was almost to be expected. Americans, Paratov knew, always fought poorly in the beginning. But you could count on the United States to adapt quickly. They had always proven, in the final analysis, to be a very warlike tribe. You couldn't call them wise, exactly. But they were very, very smart. Americans might start off stupid, but they never got stupider.

Which was exactly why the four diamonds on Paratov's radar so disturbed him. That they were F-14s was beyond dispute. The Tomcats' huge AWG-9 radars scattered hoards of unmistakable electrons indiscriminately through the eastern Zagros. And if that weren't enough, there was the all-too-easily distinguishable infrared signature of their Pratt and Whitney TF30 engines, in full afterburner, no less. The delicate infrared search-and-track sensor, mounted on the MiG-29's nose just forward of the cockpit, swiveled and stared, as if in disbelief, at the hot, juicy targets silhouetted against the cool sky.

What were they doing there, nudging fifty thousand feet and well on the hot side of the mach? Paratov considered closing on the Tomcats—it was not like him to let any target go unmolested—but then decided not to engage. By the time the MiGs turned and climbed, even at maximum speed, the flight of F-14s would be halfway back to Gonzo Station. The Tomcats were invulnerable at their speed and altitude, perhaps. But they were no threat to Paratov's MiGs, either.

A trap, perhaps? Geometry was against them. Still, Paratov did not take chances.

To make for a more perpendicular angle (the better to spoof the Tomcat's Doppler radar), Paratov pulled a slight left turn heading through the Allahbad pass. The eleven Fulcrums behind him made the same adjustment, without, Paratov noted proudly, a word spoken on the radio. The pilots of Squadron 22 were all exceptional aviators. Two weeks of combat with the *Eisenhower*'s air wing had molded them into a formidable fighting unit. As they dragged their shadows across the *Dasht-e-Lut*—Iran's endless and desolate eastern desert—Paratov's MiGs also towed a reputation that was quickly discrediting the myth of Western air superiority.

The word had not yet reached the public or even allied line pilots. But at points all along the Silver Net—at the headquarters of the Tactical Air Command, the Royal Air Force, the *Armee de l'Air,* and the *Heyl Ha'Avir*—there was a growing awareness, a feeling that the axis had swung, that the Soviets were at last not just to be respected but also feared. There were those, mainly USN pilots and proponents, to be sure, who argued that the mauling the *mighty Ike*'s air wing had received at the hands of the MiGs was not due to a fundamental flaw in American weapons and tactics but rather was the fault of a battle group commander ignorant of the realities of modern air combat. Nevertheless, lights burned late in air-staff offices throughout the Western world.

The Tomcats passed directly overhead, streaming four white contrails, as the hydrocarbons in their unburnt fuel formed ice crystals in the frozen sky ten miles above the steaming desert. Their heading put them on a course for Zaranj, but Paratov wasn't worried. Although it was possible to hang bombs on an F-14, the crews received no training in air-to-surface tactics save for a casual, once-a-year refresher course in nuclear-weapons delivery that pilots considered more depressing than educational. At any rate, the speeding Tomcats would not have the gas to reach Zaranj. In fact, unless they turned south soon, Paratov doubted the Navy fighters would have enough fuel to reach their tankers, which were undoubtedly waiting along the coast over the Arabian Sea.

No, Paratov was not concerned about the Tomcats bombing Zaranj. What *did* worry him, though, was what the F-14s were doing on that heading in the first place. Then it hit him. Of course! It was a textbook Phoenix missile attack: a wall of Tomcats, line abreast, wings pinned back for high speed, sweeping the sky before them with their frighteningly capable weapons systems that could track scores of targets simultaneously and knock them down with the huge, sophisticated Phoenix missile from a hundred miles away.

The fighter sweep, called a BARCAP by the U.S. Navy, was intended to pick the MiGs out of the sky as they rose from Zaranj and—so the Americans must have assumed—dutifully climbed to medium altitude and flew predictably in a straight line to Bandar Abbas. There was only one flaw in the plan. Paratov was not cooperating. Typical American arrogance—did they really think he would lead his squadron straight at their F-14s like a pack of drones just because that was where their wonderful weapons worked best? Hadn't two weeks of combat losses taught them anything?

Paratov knew these planes and pilots were fresh to the fight, members of Carrier Air Wing 11 aboard the *Constellation,* sent to relieve the exhausted *Eisenhower* and her air component. But he had expected them to be farther along the learning curve than this. Surely the Navy knew Paratov was aware of the launching and composition of every raid sent against Bandar Abbas. Surely they knew Paratov was not interested in challenging their fighters— it was the strikers and resupply aircraft he was after. And yet the Navy persisted in its ineffectual tactics. Today was a step backward, if anything.

Inflexibility, predictability, the irrational pursuit of failed tactics—it was a classic case of theater-level officers trying to micromanage tactical engagements. Paratov knew the syndrome all too well; it was one reason why he tried to stay so far outside Moscow's orbit. But he had not expected it of the Americans, with their much-professed emphasis on individual battlefield initiative. Paratov smiled grimly—the unknown admiral aboard the American battle group's flagship was a prime candidate for the Order of Lenin. He might even have been comfortable in the service of the czar.

The Fulcrums zoomed down the slot formed by the mountain valleys northeast of Bandar Abbas. Indications of the Tomcats, now well behind Paratov, slowly flickered out on his radar. But the screen did not remain empty. Already there were fleeting indications of the quick-witted APG-65 radar of the Hornets, which formed the second wave behind the F-14s.

The F-18s were performing close-air-support missions for the beleaguered American paratroopers at the airport. The Soviet destroyer tattling on the battle group had reported the Hornets were carrying AIM-9 Sidewinder heat-seeking missiles on their wingtips, which was standard procedure for both air-to-air and air-to-ground missions.

However, the ship had not been able to determine if the F-18s were also toting the larger, radar-guided AIM-7 missiles because the view of the conformal rack for the Sparrows, which was snuggled up against the fuselage, had been blocked by the drop tanks carrying extra fuel for the strikers' long journey up the strait. If the Hornets, notoriously short-legged to begin with, had decided to forgo the weight of the heavy Sparrows in the hot, thick air of the Gulf and to rely on the F-14s for long-range protection, then the MiGs could pick them off at a distance. Although Paratov didn't believe the Hornet pilots would have been so unwise as to voluntarily give up their capability for long-range self-protection, there was a very good chance that they had been ordered to do so in an effort to increase the amount of air-to-ground ordnance they could carry in support of the troops.

Paratov hoped this was the case. The F-18 was a formidable dogfighter, generations ahead of the slow and unwieldy A-6s and A-7s the *Eisenhower* had sent on close-air-support missions. He would rather not mix it up with the Hornets unless he had to.

Paratov churned the stick in a short, sharp barrel roll. It was the signal to attack—transmitting in the clear in a combat zone was prohibited in Squadron 22. No one in the squadron knew what the punishment would be for using the radio. They were too afraid of Paratov to risk finding out.

The Fulcrums boiled out of the valley in pairs, streaming in all directions. Paratov switched his MiG's HO-193 radar on active; the screen was immediately studded with indications of the American planes over Bandar Abbas. He could see them, barely, through the haze, a hornet's nest buzzing over the airport. The Americans broke in all directions—no doubt they, too, were getting indications on their threat-warning equipment of the swarm of Fulcrums that had suddenly appeared from nowhere.

Paratov's radar display, tucked in the upper-right corner of the instrument panel, blossomed in clouds formed by puffs of chaff ejected by the Navy strikers. Some chaff clouds were resolved and eliminated from the screen by the MiG's radar software. Others remained, posted as diamonds on the Fulcrum's clear head-up display. Paratov picked a bogie on the edge of the display, a Hornet just rolling off its bomb run. He turned into the F-18, following as it headed for the beach.

The diamond on Paratov's radar grew spikes as the Hornet, now alerted, sent out frantic signals from its tail-mounted electronic countermeasures antennas in a desperate attempt to jam the Fulcrum's radar. It was too late. The MiG's powerful transmitter burned through the jamming and locked onto the F-18.

A big black-and-white Alamo missile roared from beneath the MiG's right wing. Homing in on reflections from Paratov's radar, the AA-10 followed the Hornet through two kinked turns before its proximity fuse detonated ten feet below the target. The explosion sent white-hot shrapnel through both of the F-18's engines, instantly crippling the American jet. The Hornet flipped over and crashed on the beach in a long, ripping line of flame.

Paratov put the MiG on its tails and gunned the engines. Twisting in a slow roll, he pulled out of the Immelmann on his back, high above Bandar Abbas. Through the top of his canopy, Paratov could see the whole mad scene. The sky above the airport was thick with jets, buzzing like black gnats in a dozen individual and overlapping dogfights. It was impossible to determine who was whom, let alone who was winning. Paratov picked out another straggler, a Hornet hawking the fight from high above. Search...track...lock on...he was just about to fire when the horn went off in his helmet.

Locked on? How? Who? Where? Paratov cranked his neck around, looking for the Hornet that was trying to kill him. He cursed R. A. Belyakov, general designer of the A. I. Mikoyan Design Bureau, for building an airplane with such restricted rearward vision. He cursed the man responsible for the big, heavy helmet that weighed a ton in turns. He cursed himself for having guessed wrong about the Hornets' not carrying radar-guided missiles. And finally, he cursed the unseen American behind him for his courage and tenacity in the face of stupid and impossible orders.

The warning horn blared incessantly in Paratov's helmet. *Why was the American waiting so long?* He pointed the MiG at the sky, then abruptly cut power. The Fulcrum zoomed up, hesitated for a split second, then slid back on its tails. That moment of hesitation was enough to break lock, as the Hornet's radar ceased to detect motion. The noise in Paratov's helmet finally quieted, to his great relief.

He kicked the rudder and flipped the MiG around, straight down. A flash of gray streaked past the canopy. Paratov hauled the plane around and set after the Hornet that had given him such a scare. The energy from the dive and the thrust of the twin Tumansky R-33D engines in afterburner allowed Paratov to overtake the F-18. He could clearly see the Hornet, the subdued dark gray markings of the Stingers of VFA-113, the empty bomb racks and...no Sparrows! So that's why the Navy pilot had not fired—he was bluffing! He had suckered Paratov with a full systems lock just to get the MiG to break.

With anger and admiration, Paratov closed on the Hornet. The American jet flew steadily east, straight and level, apparently unaware that the MiG was fast approaching perfect infrared missile parameters. Paratov was about to launch when the F-18 broke sharply to the left. At the same time, Paratov noticed a flash in one of the three eight-inch curved mirrors mounted on the Fulcrum's canopy bow. He broke right.

The Sidewinder missile flew through the air vacated by the hunter and hunted. The Hornet that launched it, apparently the wingman of the F-18 Paratov had been chasing, was now chasing Paratov. The MiG led the Navy fighter back through the mass dogfight over the airport, hoping some other Fulcrum could get a shot or at least divert the American from his earnest pursuit.

Jets screamed on every side of Paratov at crazy angles, all too wrapped up in their own dramas of mortal combat to be distracted by their leader's plight. The Hornet, with only one missile left, was working the angles, trying to make sure his last shot was a good one. Paratov was working just as hard to deny him a clear target.

They spun and zoomed, wheeled and danced through the sky in an airborne stalemate. The battle, which had begun at high speed and high altitude, wound down to a slow-speed knife fight right on the deck, as the fighters spent their precious energy in high-G turns. Paratov was getting nervous—the F-18 was renowned for its slow-speed maneuverability. The Hornet, it was said, could put its nose on you faster than any aircraft in the world. That was all the advantage needed now—the brilliant seeker in the American's AIM-9 missile would do the rest.

But the Fulcrum had a few tricks of its own. Paratov snatched the long stick back hard and quickly. The MiG's nose rose straight up and then beyond the vertical as the plane briefly flew tail first. The nose then settled back to a more conventional angle, and the Fulcrum resumed normal flight with one important difference—the plane had gone from 250 knots to 60 knots in three seconds.

The maneuver, called "the Cobra," had been first demonstrated by a Soviet pilot in an Su-27 Flanker at the Paris air show. Western experts there had dismissed it as a barnstormer's stunt, of little relevance in combat. And they had doubted the MiG-29 could duplicate the maneuver.

Unfortunately for the Hornet pilot pursuing Paratov, the experts had been wrong on both counts. The F-18 shot out ahead of the MiG like a rocket. Paratov quickly triggered an AA-8 infrared missile. The Aphid flicked out and buried itself in the Hornet's starboard engine. The American plane spit out a huge orange fireball and keeled over to the right.

The pilot ejected just before the plane shattered against a mountainside. The chute opened almost immediately at the low altitude—Paratov had to swerve quickly to avoid hitting the Navy pilot dangling in the shrouds under the gray canopy.

Paratov turned to the northeast and joined the rest of the Fulcrums scurrying up the valley. The Hornets—those that were left—were low on fuel and in no mood for pursuit.

Paratov counted his MiGs. Two missing. He was not sorry. Losses were to be expected. Paratov had told his men the Americans would be tough. He was glad to be rid of those unlucky or unskilled enough not to survive.

Besides, Paratov had every reason to feel satisfied. The first pitched battle between third-generation American and Soviet aircraft had ended in a decisive defeat for the United States. Paratov had shot down two F-18s himself; the other members of the squadron had accounted for four Hornets. Just as important, they had once again prevented the Navy planes from supporting the American troops at Bandar Abbas. Paratov wondered how many more defeats the American people would tolerate before they found an excuse to call the carrier home and leave the fate of the stranded paratroopers in the hands of the First Air Regiment.

First Air! Paratov felt a rush of elation. If his disfigured face could smile, he would have smiled. Everything was going perfectly, exactly as planned.

Illyushin had admonished him for thinking too big; if the colonel general of aviation had known the true proportions of the plan, he would have indeed thought Paratov mad. He, an obscure pilot languishing on the frontier, had moved armies on both sides of the line, had tipped the balance of world power, and had begun the long-awaited redrawing of the map along lines more pleasing to the Kremlin.

Oh, Uncle, Paratov thought, *if you only knew.* To move the world was secondary; the reshaping and upheavals were only means to an end. His end. Paratov could see it coming together at last. It would happen. He would have his revenge.

Paratov pulled straight up. The column of MiGs—*his instruments!*—passed underneath through the brown valley. He snapped the Fulcrum into a tight, joyous victory roll. When all emotion had been burned from his face, Paratov had, perhaps subconsciously, come to use flying as a means of self-expression. The trailing loop of smoke and the white, screwing vortexes, the boom of the mighty engines and the wind whistling across the wings—it all came together in a complex symphony and a simple song, a Wagnerian opera with a recurring theme, one common message that vibrated through man and machine now as it had for years: *Bring me Bobby Dragon!*

The Gulf

Sammarah
Emirate of al-Quaseem

Bobby Dragon stood alone beneath the moon and stars of Arabia. Nothing moved along the shoreline. There was no wind. There were no waves. The ancient darkness of the Persian Gulf was so empty it hurt his eyes as he searched across the curving earth for his next war.

It was impossible to see. The Strait of Hormuz was at least a half-dozen horizons away from where he stood, on the northern coastline of al-Quaseem. It was a twenty-minute fast-jet ride to Bandar Abbas and the fighting, a trip Bobby knew he would be taking soon. Just how soon was what he had come to Sammarah to find out.

Sammarah! Was there ever such a place? He turned his back to the Gulf and blinked in the sudden brightness of the endless neon. The hotels and casinos and bars and restaurants and on and on; it stretched for miles across the tiny island. Sailors on the Gulf said you could see the lights of the Sammarah strip from a hundred miles away, a glowing monument to sin and fast money, fittingly wide but not deep, burning defiantly in the land of the Prophet.

Sammarah. A beacon to businessmen tired of the ways of Islam but not its money. A siren beckoning Muhammad's faithful onto the shoals of reckless Western ways. A lighthouse for those throughout the Gulf and the world who lacked patience but not ambition or greed. Unfathomable fortunes were won and lost every night on the backs of cards, on the wheels and tables, in the quiet lounges and noisy beds of Sammarah.

Bobby struggled toward the lights, his feet sinking in the heavy sand. It was tough going until he reached the blue tile sidewalk that ran the length of Sammarah's Gulf shore. He passed the *Continental* and the *Gulf Ibis,* the *Meridian* and the *Lycee Arabein.* He passed men folded into white dinner jackets, women pinched with jewelry. Ramadan and the scorching months that followed normally marked the off season in Sammarah. Tonight, however, the wide boardwalk was chilly and packed, as was every hotel, restaurant, and bar on the island.

From every mecca of the Godless West, from New York, Washington, London, Tokyo, and Paris, they came to Sammarah. It was a new crowd in name only. The celebrated rich. The influential curious. Pilgrims who followed the vortex of sex, fame, love, money, power, and violence as it whirled around the earth, seeking energy and sparking it. It hummed these days in Sammarah. War was attractive.

The lights of the *Lido* danced and shimmered in the fountains out front; huge splashes of neon orange and yellow caught in the silver spurts of the waterspouts. Long black cars droned slowly around the driveway in a constant circle. To Bobby, the rich, coming and going, looked just like their limousines—shiny, similar, underpowered, and overbuilt. Too much chrome.

He stepped up the marble stairs of the casino, scanning the funhouse facade of brass and glass, trying to discern the actual entrance from the false reflections. Following a young woman in a white evening gown through the real door, Bobby encountered another obstacle—the imposing figure, in sweltering red velvet, of the *Lido*'s imperial doorman.

"May I help you, *monsieur?*" the doorman said, in a tone that perfectly conveyed the man's real sentiment: that it would be a frosty day in Arabia when he would help this tramp any way but out of sight of the deserving rich who actually belonged in a place like the *Lido*.

Bobby shuffled uncomfortably. "I want to go in."

"I am sure you do." The Arab doorman showed no teeth in his condescending smile. "However, I think you might be happier in some of the establishments further along the boardwalk. If you will—*W'allah!*"

The doorman reeled back in pain, struck with the flat of a walkie-talkie wielded by a huge, stern-looking Arab who had appeared as if from nowhere.

"Ibn kalb!" the man shouted. The doorman shrank with fright. If he objected to being beaten and called a son of a dog, he dared not show it. His assailant wore sunglasses, a dark business suit, and, on his lapel, a small green pin in the shape of a quarter moon—the badge of the *Gahtell,* elite security guards in personal service to the sheik of al-Quaseem.

"Forgive me, *ja sayyidy,"* the doorman said, almost pleading. "I did not know this man was under your protection. We have orders to keep the mercenary pilots out of the *Lido.* They have no money, you see, and they dress like ragmen. If you..."

Dismissing the doorman, the guard turned to Bobby. "Colonel Dragon? You will come with me, please."

Bobby, dazed, followed the man's bulk back down the stairs to a long black Mercedes limousine waiting at the curb. Another *Gahtell* guard loitered at the fender. A mirrored window in the rear rolled down silently, revealing a bemused Peter Hillary.

"So you *are* alive." Hillary smiled.

"So far," Bobby said, stunned. "What the hell are you doing here, Hillary?"

"The same thing you are. Hop in, I'll give you a lift."

"No thanks." Bobby regarded Hillary with a wary eye. There was something about Peter Hillary dressed in a formal white dinner jacket that inspired mistrust. "You look like you're going to church. Or maybe to court."

"Actually, it's a little of both." Hillary cast a disparaging eye at Bobby's clothes. "Come on, he's waiting. And you'll never get in the front door of this place dressed like that."

Bobby considered his appearance in the reflective glass of the driver's window. Everything had happened too fast to worry about luggage. Bobby, at any rate, owned nothing. There was no dress code in Dreamland, where he had spent the recent years, days and nights, in Nomex and khaki and the restless company of machines. Bobby, then, dressed as normally as he could for his journey back in the world: white t-shirt, blue jeans, and desert boots.

To guard against the night chill of the Gulf, he wore a new leather A-2 flight jacket, a welcoming gift from Brick. Sewn on the right sleeve was a triangular patch featuring the "winged one," the symbol of the First Air Regiment. On the left sleeve, according to military custom, was the insignia of the unit in which he had last seen combat, the 585th Tactical Fighter Squadron. God knows where Brick had come up with a Heartbreakers patch so long after Vietnam, but it had never looked better—the big, blue circle with the silver silhouette of a Phantom slashing through a blood-red heart.

Riding on the epaulets were a pair of shining new eagles—not stylized, like the eagles of an American colonel, but golden eagles, wings flapping, talons stretched. Bobby felt uncomfortable beneath their actual and symbolic weight. It was a tangible reminder of a reality that he was still struggling to accept—that there was indeed a private air force called the First Air Regiment, Inc. And that he, Bobby Dragon, was its regimental colonel.

The *Gahtell* man opened the limo door. Bobby shrugged and climbed in. Hillary pressed a button, and the big Mercedes rolled away from the *Lido* and motored slowly down the Sammarah strip.

Bobby ran his hands across the leather-and-walnut interior of the limo. "I'd heard you'd given up journalism for pimping. Is that where you got this ride?"

Hillary tried not to take the bait. "Oh, I'm still a journalist. I'm just doing a little public-relations work for the sheik, that's all."

"That's not what I hear," Bobby said darkly. "You screwed the pooch in Bandar Abbas, and now your press buddies won't talk to you. You're lucky the sheik needed a gofer."

"I just can't win with you chaps, can I?" Hillary said angrily. "I suppose you're still upset about *The Reluctant Dragon.*"

Bobby looked out the window at the neon playground of Sammarah and sighed. Da Nang seemed a lifetime ago.

"No, Hillary, your book was accurate, as far as it went. But you had the wrong perspective. You wrote it from the ground. Things look a lot different from the air. Take the tiger hunts, for example."

"You mean Brick White's fighter sweeps over North Vietnam?"

"You could call them that," Bobby drawled. "Or you could also call them suicide runs, glory hunts for Brick, using his wingmen for bait. Just two Phantoms, screaming over Route Pack Six at low altitude, so close together they looked like one plane on the radar screens. The idea was to make the North Vietnamese controllers think we were a single, unarmed reconnaissance aircraft. The MiGs always went for stragglers and singletons. Otherwise, they'd just stay home and let their SAMs and guns do the dirty work. The tiger hunts were Brick's scheme to get the MiGs to come up and fight it out like men."

"That was all in the book," Hillary said defensively. "And I still don't see anything wrong with it. On the contrary, I think that Brick White should get credit for his imaginative ruses. He seemed to be the only pilot in the U.S. Air Force who actually wanted to win the war."

"Yeah, well, like I said, it's all perspective," Bobby said bitterly. "From the ground it might have made sense. But when you were screaming over downtown Hanoi, trying to keep all your body parts in the correct position, it was difficult to see any tactical necessity for the tiger hunts. But that's not the point—so many things we did in Vietnam were ultimately pointless. The thing that got me was *how* he did it. He'd usually take the most junior pilot in the squadron along. That way, if the guy got smoked, it could be chalked up to inexperience. And nuggets generally didn't put up too much of a squawk. Hell, they probably thought that was the way it was supposed to be."

"Again, I fail to see how this made General White an evil man," Hillary said. "It's a commander's burden to decide who must fight and die. If anything, it's to White's credit that he went on those missions himself instead of merely sending his men out alone. I would think..."

"You just don't get it, do you?" Bobby turned to Hillary and stared. "Okay, let me spell it out for you. You know about rules of engagement. You have them in every war, but in Vietnam they were real nutcrackers. You couldn't bomb certain villages, for instance, even if you were taking fire from an antiaircraft gun parked right in the middle of it. Or maybe you could— the rules changed almost every day. Nobody could keep track."

"I can understand your frustrations," Hillary said, "but what does that have to do with the tiger hunts?"

"Just this: If we had a hundred rules about what we could attack on the ground, there was only one rule about what we could shoot down in the air—we had to see it. There were some unrestricted weapons-free zones, but in almost every case where it counted we had to visually identify the target before we threw a missile at it. The rules of engagement were designed to keep us from dicking our own planes or starting a larger war. I could understand that."

"But you didn't agree?"

"*You* said I didn't agree, Hillary," Bobby laughed. "Nobody asked me if I agreed or not. Those were the rules. But the problem was, the F-4 was an interceptor, not a dogfighter. It was built around a huge radar and its radar missiles. That was the one thing we had that the MiGs didn't. They could turn circles around us, but if we could pick them off with Sparrows before they got to the merge, their maneuverability wouldn't make any difference."

"And the rules took that away from you."

"That's right. The ROE took away our beyond-visual-range capability and made us jump into the furball with the Gomers. Now, to really appreciate this distinction, you'd have to have hassled around with a MiG-17 or a -21, at low speed, low altitude, and low expectations, in a beast like the F-4. And I didn't see you up there with the Blue Bandits."

"Oh, come on, Bobby, aren't you being a bit unfair?" Hillary protested. "I never pretended to be anything other than a journalist. And you weren't the only one who had to fight with one hand tied behind your back. All the other American servicemen in Vietnam found a way to work around the rules."

"Oh, we found a way," Bobby answered. "We came up with a tactic called 'eyeball shooter.' Since we flew in four-ships back then, with a welded wingman—a wingman who stuck on your six no matter what—we'd send a pair of Phantoms up ahead in zone-five afterburner to check out the bogies. The eyeballs would rocket through the formation and scream, 'MiGs! MiGs!'— as if we didn't know already. Then the shooters would lock them up on the radar and hose off a couple of Sparrows. Even if the missiles didn't guide correctly—which was true most of the time—it made the MiGs break off, spoiled their attack so we could set something up. Eyeball shooter wasn't the perfect solution to the ROE problem, but it was the only one we had."

"I still don't see how this makes Brick a bad man," Hillary said, puzzled. "He didn't make up the rules of engagement. And he wasn't the only one who flew the eyeball-shooter maneuver, either."

"No," Bobby answered. "But eyeball shooter was a dangerous enough gambit with a four-ship of experienced crews. Sending a rookie out ahead, all alone, was..."

"Murder?" Hillary suggested.

"It's always hard to call anything murder in the middle of a war, especially in a wonderland of morality like Vietnam." Bobby frowned. "Still, there was a feeling in the squadron that what Brick was doing wasn't right. Maybe he could justify it militarily, or politically, but fighter pilots have their own sense of right and wrong. And the tiger hunts were wrong. It wasn't that we didn't want to kill MiGs. But the Heartbreakers took a lot more pride in making sure our wingmen came home with us. That didn't seem to bother Brick much. When I got there, he had shot down four MiGs. But he had lost three wingmen."

"And you were next," Hillary said.

"Well, I was the junior man, so I got the nod," Bobby agreed. "But I got lucky. I survived. In fact, I managed to shoot down or chase away the MiGs before Brick got there, which didn't exactly endear me to him. It took him a year to get his MiGs. I got four in about six weeks."

"And then came Doom," Hillary said softly.

"Yes. Then came Doom."

Hillary turned away and watched the glittering hotels slide past the limo's windows. It was a writer's worst nightmare. *The Reluctant Dragon* was his best book, certainly his most popular. And now he was learning that it was fundamentally flawed. Oh, the facts were correct. But it was a book about Vietnam, and facts were a very small part of the book. And the war.

"I've always wondered—was that his real name?" Hillary asked. "Certainly that was merely a *nomme de guerre.*"

"You mean Doom?" Bobby said. "Yeah. We never knew his real name. Intel could always get the dope on the rest of their aces, but not him. We just called him Colonel Doom, in honor of the Da Nang Officer's Open Mess, which is where the subject usually came up. The guy flew shit hot—thirteen kills. Most of the North Vietnamese fighter jocks were very cautious, by-the-book pilots—they just followed the vectors their controllers gave them, and if they didn't get the drop on you they'd head straight back to the barn. Doom was something else. He flew like Brick wanted to fly. And Brick wanted Doom more than he wanted anything else in the world. It got to be an obsession."

"But you killed Doom," Hillary said. "The day after Christmas 1972. It was the middle of the Linebacker II raids..."

"Christ, Hillary, give it a rest!" Bobby broke in. "This isn't one of your lectures. I was there, remember? I had a great seat for the last big show of the war. Everybody was up that day. I mean *everybody,* from B-52s to Birddogs. You can't imagine what it was like. There were jets everywhere."

Bobby closed his eyes. He could see it so clearly, even now, that moment frozen in time—dozens of men locked in earnest, frantic combat in the sky. He had that peculiar talent for three-dimensional memory; fellow pilots were always amazed at Bobby's ability to remember everything—speed, altitude, heading, relative position—at every moment in every dogfight. His reputation was such that in mock dogfights, where lying was preferable to admitting defeat, Bobby's word was always taken as the final authority. Other fighter pilots envied him for it. After so many nights waking up alone, sweating, reliving some desperate fight from a time long gone, Bobby often wondered if his precision of memory was not, in fact, a curse.

"Brick had somehow got us the assignment to CAP the airfield at Kep, which was where Doom flew out of, about fifty miles northwest of Hanoi. We got downtown just as Doom was turning around to start his run back in. I had my hands full trying to thread my way through a tangle of Navy strikers and MiG-17s over the river. When I looked up, Brick was gone." Bobby shook his head. "All I saw were two little red dots on the horizon. He lit the burners and took off without me. He didn't even tell me he was engaging, which is something you never do to your wingman. Never!"

"Wait a minute," Hillary cut in. "I thought you said you were the one who had to go on ahead and flush out the MiGs for Brick on the tiger hunts."

"Usually I was," Bobby said. "But I guess he had gotten tired of me shooting them down before he got there. Or maybe the temptation was too great. If Brick managed to get Doom, not only would he beat me in the 'ace race'—God, I hated that term!—but he would have done it by shooting down the Yellow Baron himself. Now *that* would have a been a story for all you reporters hanging around Da Nang."

"Not as big a story as the one we eventually wrote that day," Hillary pointed out.

"True," Bobby admitted. "And it's a good thing Brick wasn't around to read it. I had to fight my way out of the furball; since I didn't have a wingman, I drew MiGs like a magnet. I didn't have time to hassle with them—I just threw missiles everywhere, every Sparrow I had. I didn't have a lock on anything, but the MiG drivers didn't know that—they split off like the Blue Angels and I lit out after Brick. By the time I got there he was going down. I don't know what happened."

"You haven't asked Brick about it?"

"You don't ask fighter pilots about stuff like that, especially a guy like Brick," Bobby said. "His Phantom was falling out of the sky in a big, black corkscrew of smoke over the mountains. There was only one chute. I learned later his backseater didn't make it."

"And you were sure Doom shot him down?"

"Oh, yeah," Bobby said. "North Vietnam's a pretty small place in a big plane. All the action was in about a thirty-mile radius of Hanoi and Haiphong. I was in burner for about a minute—that put me halfway to China. There was nobody else up there but me and Brick and Doom. I looked up and saw this Fishbed pitching up to slice back into the flight, a gray MiG-21 with a black tail—Doom's plane. One Atoll missing. You didn't have to be a genius to figure out what had happened. So I shot him down."

"Just that quickly?" Hillary asked, surprised.

"Just like that," Bobby sighed. "I wish I could sit here and wave my hands around and tell you how I gave him the old high-speed low yo-yo and all that fighter pilot poop, but the fact is, it was an easy kill. That's what air-to-air combat is really like. It's not like training. This five-minute dogfight crap is okay for Top Gun, but in real life it doesn't last five seconds. Nine times out of ten they never see what hit them. That was the way it was with Doom. He was silhouetted against the sky at my twelve o'clock. I had a Sidewinder cooled up—I never flew without something uncaged. The growl almost hurt my ears—good tone, perfect parameters. The missile flew off my wing and went right up his tailpipe. The MiG exploded in a fireball and went into a shallow dive, still burning. I was going to follow it down, but my backseater, Daffy Brewer, reminded me that we'd better be getting back to Da Nang or get ready to swim home."

Hillary felt ill. The story Bobby was telling him was nothing like the story he wrote. Hillary's version had been reconstructed from interviews with controllers, public-affairs officers, and other pilots, most of whom, it was now obvious, had told Hillary a great deal more than they actually knew. But what was he to do? It was too good a story to pass up, even if none of the principals involved had been around to interview. Only Daffy Brewer had made it back to Da Nang, Hillary reminded himself. And Brewer had refused to talk.

"The shit really started to hit the fan when I was making the approach back to Da Nang," Bobby continued. "Our controllers must have told Seventh Air Force what happened, because as I was coming in on final, this weenie in the tower wanted me to do a victory roll! Can you imagine? I tell him no; he tells me he's a general; I tell him I've got radio problems and can't hear him, and we land straight in. That's that, right? Wrong. There's about a hundred reporters waiting on the ramp, screaming, yelling, cameras pointing. I stop the bird, shut down, and pop the canopy—they're all over me! *How does it feel to be an ace? What was it like to shoot down the Yellow Baron?* Crap like that."

"Look, Bobby, that was our job!"

"Yeah, I know, but..." Bobby paused to gather his thoughts. It was the first time he had really talked about what happened that day. Part of the reason was because the memories were so painful, true. But the main cause for his silence was that, unless you did what he did—unless you flew fighters in *that* war—it was impossible to comprehend why he had done what he had done.

But now he had a new war, and a new unit. And, whether Bobby liked it or not, Hillary was part of First Air. You had to deal straight with the members of your unit. They had to know the facts. You never knew when your life might depend on them.

"Linebacker II was still going on," Bobby said deliberately. "It would go on for another week, the most important air battle of the war. American pilots were fighting and dying at that very moment. Most important, my wingman had just gotten smoked. Fool though he may have been, Brick was my responsibility. And now he was going to spend the rest of the war in the Hanoi Hilton—if the bastards didn't murder him first. And these reporters—the same jerks who, twenty-four hours earlier, were telling America that we were locking laser-guided bombs on helpless babies and cuddly puppies—were now waving and smiling like I was Miss America."

Hillary shuddered. He had been there and had indeed been embarrassed about the behavior of his colleagues in the press. For most of the reporters, Vietnam had been a temporary assignment, a stepping-stone. Many considered it a vacation. Few realized that war had its own rules of behavior, its own sense of proper taste and good manners. Away from authority and under pressure to deliver, with no real experience in combat reporting, some journalists crossed the line—and made life miserable for Hillary and the few others who made their living covering the dying.

"It was too much," Bobby continued. "The whole thing—the reporters, the brass band, the banners. I realized right then that we were going to lose that war. I had had my doubts all along, but that's when it really hit me. The only question was whether I was going to get killed before or after we lost it. You know, you ask a lot from a fighter pilot, or any soldier, for that matter. You're asking him to die for something he believes in. Well, what struck me at that moment was that nobody outside the cockpit—you guys in the press, the big brass, even Brick—believed in freedom for South Vietnam. Everybody was in it for themselves, for fame and power and money and everything that was the opposite of sacrifice. And I was the biggest fool of all, because I actually believed. They loved guys like me. We were so easy to use. They used fifty-five thousand of us before it was all over. And I swore, then and there, they weren't going to use me up."

"Did Brewer know what you had planned?" Hillary asked. "Did you talk about it before you landed?"

"No. Daffy didn't know anything about it," Bobby said. "I'm sure he's pissed about that, but I didn't want to tell him what I was going to do because he would have tried to talk me out of it. Daffy was a good guy, but he could be a real old lady at times. So I waited until he climbed out of the pit, and as soon as he hit the ground, I closed the canopy, hit the burner, and just took off."

Just took off. It sounded so simple. But Hillary knew differently. When Bobby left Da Nang for the second time that day, he took what remained of the heart of the American air effort in Vietnam. The Air Force had tried vainly to put the best face on it, making up a cover story that no one really believed, most of all Hillary. And they thrust a reluctant Daffy Brewer into the spotlight in Bobby's place. But for American fighter pilots in Vietnam, their constant struggle between self-sacrifice and self-preservation was over. Their finest had flown away. It was never the same after that.

They rode the rest of the way in silence. The car swung behind the *Lido* and drove underneath to a private garage. The *Gahtell* guard opened the door and led Bobby and Hillary down an ornate hallway of relentless red—red carpeting, red velvet on the walls, red chandeliers on a red ceiling. The crowds that packed the *Lido* were left behind—this was obviously a path reserved for royalty.

Bobby was now amazed at his own naivete in ever thinking he could just stroll into the *Lido* and walk right up to the sheik of al-Quaseem. The hotel was infested with security personnel, in uniform and out, walking dogs, talking on radios, making their rounds, all armed with the short, brutal weapons usually reserved for American drug criminals. Even if Bobby had somehow managed to get past the guards, he thought, there was no way he could have navigated the maze of fire stairs and back hallways through which the *Gahtell* officer was leading him.

The guard stopped before a pair of fire doors marked "Stage Entrance" and said a few words in Arabic into the walkie-talkie. After receiving a short, incomprehensible, but apparently satisfactory reply, he unlatched the door. Bright white light sliced through the opening. Bobby and Hillary walked inside. And into another world.

The broad stage, covered with six inches of white sand, was dominated by an elaborate tent of black goatskin. It looked like an elaborate Broadway production of an Arabian Nights musical. Artificial date trees shielded the high tent from the glare of white-and-yellow klieg lights, their plastic fronds rustled gently by the slow turning of large wind machines tucked in the wings. The breeze carried the scent of cinnabar and marjoram and something decidedly less pleasant—Bobby looked further downstage and saw a pen containing a few nervous goats, a bored donkey, and a pair of bemused camels chewing absently on dried millet.

The scene was made all the more bizarre by what lay beyond. In the casino, separated from the theater only by red usher's ropes, high rollers in tuxedos and sequined gowns gambled away thousands on every card and spin. Within the ropes, however, on every seat and clogging the aisles, tribesmen squatted in white *dishdashas* or leaned absently in sloppy Western dress, smoking and staring silently at the stage.

"What is this place?" Bobby whispered to Hillary.

"This is the court of *Shari'a*," Hillary explained. "Disputes are settled here according to the laws of Islam."

"Why do they have to build a desert in the middle of a gambling casino when there's plenty of real desert right outside?"

"A long time ago," Hillary said, "before there were buildings or proper roads on the island, the *Shari'a* was held on the Gulf shore, on this very spot, on the first night of every full moon. When they built Sammarah, they also built a great amphitheater in the desert, specifically for the *Shari'a*. But, come the first full moon, no one appeared. They came instead to this place, the same place they had been coming for generations. The fact that this hotel now occupied that spot made no difference. There was only one thing to do— if you could not bring the people to *Shari'a,* then you had to bring *Shari'a* to the people. So the court was moved indoors, to this theater. Once a month, they take down whatever show is playing here at the *Lido* and build this false oasis."

A tall figure emerged from the tent wearing a flowing *thaub* of black and gold with a ceremonial *Khanjar* dagger tucked in the waist sash. All eyes followed as he walked across the carpet of sand to where Bobby stood, still taking in the fantastic scene of an artificial oasis built in the middle of a five-star hotel in the middle of a real oasis.

"Ah, Mr. Hillary, I see you have found our wayward warrior. Welcome to al-Quaseem, Colonel Dragon."

The man did not introduce himself. There was no need. Everyone on the island knew Sheik Hassan. If Western visitors had somehow missed His Shining Presence on television, or in magazines, they could hardly fail to notice it upon their arrival. In the airport, on the buildings of Quaseem City, on television, and on posters in the streets, the face of Sheik Hassan beamed down beatifically on his island kingdom. Though Muslim law frowned upon realistic art, Hassan, with his odd gray eyes, gray-flecked beard, and black robe, strived to project a decidedly religious image in the ubiquitous portraits. It was this face, stern yet temperate, that he showed to Bobby Dragon.

The sheik swept a hand toward the tent. Hillary and Bobby began to move forward. The *Gahtell* guard stopped Hillary with a gentle hand on his chest.

"You will excuse us, Mr. Hillary," Hassan said smoothly. "Colonel Dragon and I need a moment to get acquainted."

Hillary watched, humiliated, as the two men shuffled softly across the sand.

"I am very glad you're here, Colonel," Hassan said. "I was beginning to think you were not coming. Why did you send my men away when they offered to take you here?"

"No offense, but I don't get into strange cars with strange men in strange countries," Bobby said. "Not these days."

"You are wise," Hassan nodded. "These are troubled times. But you put us in a rather peculiar position. Luckily, Mr. Hillary offered to escort you here. Otherwise, I am afraid you would have been late."

"Late?" Bobby asked, puzzled. "Late for what?"

"My assassination," the sheik replied matter of factly.

Bobby's jaw dropped. "What do you mean?"

Hassan smiled. "All in good time, Colonel."

A Quaseemi security guard in a light blue dress uniform opened the rear flap of the tent. Bobby followed Hassan inside. The interior was bare, except for an ornate black-and-gold rug spread across the sand. The front of the tent was open, revealing the throng crowding around a solitary figure in black sitting on a chair at the edge of the stage. Hassan sat down cross legged on the rug, motioning for Bobby to do the same.

The sheik stared downstage as the argument there rose in pitch. A small, fat tribesman in a dirty white headdress and a yellow, Western-style golf shirt pleaded his case in a high, shrill voice. The *Khadi* listened, leaning back, his hand on his chin. Finally he had heard enough. The judge waved a hand for silence, then spoke one word.

Bobby didn't need to know Arabic to understand what was said. The accused man became even more agitated. He directed his appeal to Hassan now, imploring him with loud, pitiful arguments. The *Khadi,* too, turned to Hassan and spoke calmly, a short, reasoned speech that ended with a question.

"This man is charged with robbery," the sheik explained to Bobby in a low voice. "What he has stolen is of little consequence—a radio and some tires, this time—but this is not his first conviction. He has already confessed, in any case."

Hassan drew the dagger from his waist sash and tapped his left forearm lightly with the gleaming blade. *"In sha-allah!"*

The man's screams were drowned out by the roar of the crowd. Two guards in black grabbed the criminal and tugged him to an ornamental fountain in front of the stage where a huge Arab, also in black, stood waiting with a two-handed Arabian cutlass. He bowed slightly to the *Khadi* and to Hassan, then deeper, due west to Mecca. Bobby saw the blade swing high and flash. The clear water in the blue pool ran red. The man, silent now in his shock, was thrown to a doctor who wrapped the bleeding stump in white gauze.

Bobby caught his breath and tried to stay calm. "I had no idea it would be so..."

"Savage?" Hassan smiled grimly. "Yes, and not to my taste. Often I am tempted to follow the example of the other Gulf rulers, who remain in their offices and merely sign documents approving the decisions of *Shari'a*. But that would only cause delay and distance me from my people. In my opinion, a man who cannot bear to watch his sentence carried out is not fit to judge."

"But is it necessary to create such a...spectacle?" Bobby asked. "Most of these people don't seem to have any business here. It looks to me like they just came to watch the mutilation."

"You have to understand, Colonel Dragon. This is not a democracy," the sheik said, explaining but not apologizing. "It is easy to have a democracy with educated people. The people here—not the merchants and the politicians who depend on my money, but the common people, the people who make revolutions—are not so sophisticated. They require a show."

It became suddenly clear to Bobby what Hassan was doing at *Shari'a*. He was politicking. In a very short time, aircraft based in his country and under his nominal control would attack Iran, a nation most of the people in the auditorium—and the country—still looked to for spiritual guidance. These people could not be bought. They could only be led if Hassan could convince them that he was leading them on the correct path, the way of the Prophet. With the ayatollah gone and a dozen unworthy mullahs fighting for his place, the sheik was seizing the chance to assume spiritual as well as political power in the Gulf.

Bobby looked at Hassan, sizing him up. Brick had said the sheik was a smooth operator. It was a neat trick for the wealthiest man on earth, the man who had built Sammarah and introduced sin on a Western scale to the land of the Prophet, to pass himself off as a quasi-religious figure.

Brick had also said Hassan wanted Iran. Well, it was up for grabs now. The cloak of Islam would be quite useful in controlling his population in the coming war. If Hassan was to rule Iran, however, it would be absolutely vital. And the sheik was positioning himself as Iran's perfect savior—a civil servant to those Iranians anxious to throw off the constraints of a religious dictatorship and a devout follower of Muhammad to those who still felt the nation should be guided according to strict Islamic principles. As for the West, America and Europe would be, no doubt, more than willing to turn Iran over to a tough but trustworthy Arab, their only ally in the perfidious Gulf, if and when Iran was conquered—that is, should there be enough left of it after the fighting to turn over to anyone. And after the day's events, that outcome was growing ever more remote.

"I was coming to see you anyway. We have to talk," Bobby said to the sheik. "You know, the Navy got creamed today."

Hassan, who had been studying the crowd, looked up, distracted. "I beg your pardon?"

"The Navy strikers. From the *Constellation*," Bobby explained. "It wasn't their fault. Planning that bad always starts from the top."

"Hmm," the sheik murmured.

"They're not going to have anything left if this keeps up. We'd better start thinking about getting this First Air thing up and running. We've got a lot of work to do and not much time to do it in," Bobby pressed. "When do you think we'll become operational?"

"Soon," Hassan said vaguely. "When it is time."

Bobby felt his temper rising. "Look, I've got to know. I've got to start making plans. Tomorrow I'm going to brief a hangar full of pilots who, right now, know more about the First Air Regiment than I do. And the first thing they're going to ask me is when the balloon goes up. What should I tell them?"

"Americans like photographs," Hassan said enigmatically. "The artists of Islam prefer the mosaic. Thousands of tiny pieces of stone, arranged bit by bit, with foresight, skill, and patience, will reveal a larger truth."

"Okay, I'm an American. Show me a picture," Bobby spat. "I don't..."

Hassan held up a hand and smiled. "Forgive me, Colonel. I do not mean to be circumspect. It is only that in this part of the world, where loyalty can very often mean loyalty until death, friendships are not made quickly. All will be revealed, I assure you. But for now, let us take some time to get to know one another, eh?"

"I'm sorry if I offended you," Bobby said, confused and angry. "But I don't have time to be polite. And I didn't come three thousand miles for a job interview, either. Brick said you asked for me. I guess he was just setting me up. My mistake. Sorry. Have a nice war."

Bobby rose stiffly to his feet and drew back the tent slit. The Quaseemi sentry stood, unmoving, blocking the way.

"My apologies, Colonel," Hassan said tiredly. "General White was correct. I did agree to the formation of the Regiment only on the condition that you lead it. Now, if..."

"Why?" Bobby turned to stare at the sheik.

"Pardon?"

"Why did you ask for me?" Bobby repeated. "The Air Force has hundreds of officers—without my, ah, colorful history—who could command a unit like First Air. And they'd jump through whatever hoops you pointed at, just for a chance to run it."

"Come now, Colonel," Hassan clucked. "You do yourself a disservice. There is only one Bobby Dragon. You cannot be unaware of your reputation as a warrior. Even my son Faisal, who is quite an accomplished jet pilot himself, fairly worships you."

"Well, I'm glad your boy feels that..."

"Faisal is not a boy," Hassan said, annoyed. "The West, and especially the Western press, is obsessed with age as a measure of ability. In this part of the world we judge a man by what he does, not how old he is. When I was Faisal's age, I ruled al-Quaseem. Alexander ruled the world. And you conquered the sky."

"I don't know about that. The truth is, I didn't know what I was doing."

"Precisely my point. Youth can accomplish anything because it doesn't yet know what is impossible."

"I was just trying to survive up there," Bobby said. "But you're right— as soon as I started thinking, things went right to hell."

"And that is the life to which you are in such a hurry to return?" Hassan asked. "Please, Colonel, sit down. Indulge me. We may have gotten off to a poor start, but I think you will find we have much in common."

"Like what?"

"A desire for peace. A love of aviation." The sheik's eyes narrowed as he added, "A commitment to those men we lead in battle."

Bobby stared at Hassan. The sheik held all the cards, and he knew how to play them. Bobby shrugged and sat.

"I do not question your courage or your talent, Colonel. But it is important that we get to know each other, understand one another. Soon the world will learn of First Air and your part in it. Before that happens, I have to have an answer for every question that will surely be asked. And right now, the only important question is, are you ready to fight?"

"Do you think I'm a coward?" Bobby asked. "If I ran out once, I might run out again. Is that what you think?"

"I have no feelings one way or the other," Hassan said calmly. "But then, I have a certain understanding about the West and about air warfare that my people do not share. I am afraid if you pled your case to the *Khadi,* he would certainly condemn you for desertion."

"Oh?" Bobby asked, amused. "And what's the punishment for that?"

"They cut off your testicles."

Bobby crossed his legs. Hassan smiled.

"Please, do not worry. After tonight, my people will recognize your bravery and your loyalty."

"What do you mean? What's going to happen tonight?" Bobby asked.

Then he remembered. "That's right. You said you were to be assassinated."

"Do not worry. Hopefully, if Allah wishes, they will not succeed," Hassan laughed. It was then that Bobby noticed the flat lines of the Kevlar vest underneath the sheik's flowing robe. Dozens of security men lining the stage would, no doubt, help Allah come to the right decision. Hassan may have been a man of faith, but he was apparently all too aware that he was also a man of flesh and blood.

Bobby eyed the audience nervously. "Have you got any idea who would want to assassinate you?"

"Of course. A man named Seyed Farokhi."

Bobby shook his head. "Never heard of him."

"He will be very famous tomorrow, I assure you," Hassan said, resolutely. "Tomorrow his head will be on a pole at the crossroads of Quaseem City."

"I don't understand. If you know who's going to try to kill you, why are you here? Why don't you go arrest this guy? Don't you know where he is?"

"Certainly," the sheik replied. "He is no more than five kilometers from here, at the dormitory of the Amir Hassan Institute of Marine Biology, studying for his upcoming examinations."

"You've lost me completely," Bobby admitted. "The whole thing sounds screwy to me."

"On the contrary, Colonel, it makes perfect sense. You asked before why I picked you to lead the First Air Regiment. Very well, I will tell you. It is because you can ensure the support of almost every group involved. To the other pilots, you are a hero, a brilliant aviator and tactician. To the press— and think of them what you will, no one wins a modern war without their support—you are an interesting story, a sympathetic figure. And, although we both know First Air enjoys the sponsorship of the United States through General White, we cannot afford to let the Regiment be pictured as a tool of the Americans. No offense, Colonel, but your past record ensures at least a neutral response from even those nations openly hostile to America."

Bobby frowned. He didn't like to admit it, but what the sheik said made sense. "Go on."

"What is missing is a reason for al-Quaseem to go to war with Iran. There are many in this country who oppose the American invasion, despite the Baghdad bomb. While we can certainly justify First Air as a means to protect the country during these troubled times, we need a much stronger reason to execute offensive missions against Iran. Farokhi will give us that reason tonight."

"Then this guy's an Iranian?"

Hassan nodded. "He is a student at the institute. Oddly enough, there are many Iranian students here, just as there are at the University of Petroleum and Minerals in Saudi Arabia and even in your country. He is also the leader of something called the People's Revolutionary Islamic Council. In the past, student groups of this sort received their direction from Tehran and were useful only for limited action. Now, however, with the situation so confused in Iran, they have apparently decided to follow their own course of action. Fortunately, these groups are easily penetrated, and we have learned they plan to attack tonight."

"And you're going to just sit here and wait for them to shoot at you?"

"At us, Colonel," the sheik said tranquilly. "It is a necessary part of the plan. I have confidence in my security forces."

Bobby looked up at the sheik, smiling in his ceremonial *ghuta*, surrounded by his faux Bedu paradise, the perfect picture of a sixth-century monarch caught in the twentieth century's last war.

"With all due respect, I think you're crazy," Bobby said. "You're not the first insane ruler in the world, but you're the first one who's asked me to ride along on a target drone with him, which makes it my business. And I say no thanks. I'm a fighter pilot, not Rambo. I don't think I'd be much help to you here. I'd feel a lot more bulletproof if I had an F-15 wrapped around me, so if you don't mind, I think I'll head on over to the base and strap one on."

Bobby unfolded his legs and stood stiffly.

"If you wish," Hassan said, disappointed. "But it would serve as a great symbol to my people if you were to be standing at my right hand during this danger."

"Bull's-eyes are great symbols, too," Bobby said. "No, I'd..."

A faint slap shook the canvas at the rear of the tent. A tiny hole punctured the fabric. Bobby examined the tear, not two inches from his head, then threw himself down on the sand-covered stage. Two more holes, and then a great ripping fusillade shredded the goatskin wall. The tent collapsed. Bobby, staying low, worked himself out from under the wreckage to see Hassan being led off the stage inside a phalanx of *Gahtell* men. The men were firing back into the audience, most of whom had had the presence of mind to crawl underneath the seats at the sound of the first shot.

Uniformed soldiers ran in from the wings. Bobby was caught in the middle of a ferocious cross fire. Shots kicked up small geysers of sand all around him. The bullets were getting closer. Suddenly, he felt himself being lifted by his armpits and half-shoved, half-carried from the stage. Bobby looked back to see the same giant *Gahtell* guard who had escorted him inside the *Lido*. The man pushed Bobby up the aisle, firing back with his free hand.

The casino was in chaos. Any class, social, and economic differences that divided the people on both sides of the velvet ropes had disintegrated with the first round. Quaseemi tribesmen and jet-setters alike fought for the exits, dived under furniture, or cowered against the wall. The lowest common denominator of human self-preservation had taken over. The place smelled like panic.

Bobby, running stooped over behind the enormous security guard, felt his feet hit level ground, a sign they had cleared the slightly sloped aisle of the auditorium and entered the casino area. The man spun and grunted, pointing toward a lighted exit sign behind the roulette wheel. Bobby nodded his understanding and his thanks. The man leaned forward. Bobby caught him, almost toppling under the bulk. His arms went around the guard as a reflex. His fingers felt something warm, sticky.

Bobby stepped back in revulsion. The giant collapsed on the floor, face down. The back of his head was…gone. Just gone. Nauseous and horrified, Bobby sprinted for the exit. Bullets pattered all around him. He was suddenly aware of the sounds of gunfire, the sharp booms of shotguns, the shattering of automatic weapons, and the pops of handguns. The exit seemed a hundred miles away.

Suddenly he was there, through the door and running down a long hallway. He went through a kitchen of some sort, down another long hallway, and then found himself outside the *Lido*.

Bobby kept running, down the stairs, past the fountain, over the boardwalk. He ran until there was nowhere else to run. The Persian Gulf spread before him like a moat around the mad kingdom of al-Quaseem.

He turned back to Sammarah, shocked that everything seemed normal. The only signs of the slaughter going on inside were the shrinking lights of the sheik's motorcade and, off in the distance, the faint wailings of police and ambulance vehicles.

Bobby wheezed and shook, exhausted with relief and the giddiness that comes from surviving. *Have to…calm down,* he told himself. *Have to…get myself together.* He was surprised to find his hands were shaking. True, he had faced death countless times before, but that was in the air. His battles there were savage and violent, but…*neater.* Fighter pilots called it the morality of altitude. There were no civilians in enemy cockpits and certainly no women and children. The bogies were all volunteers, just asking for it. From that distinction—the clean kill—rose the myth of air combat as the last bastion of chivalry.

On air-to-ground missions it got messier. Surely there had been innocents underneath a few of the scores of bombs he had scattered over North Vietnam. Well, that was war. It was infinitely easier to kill if you never saw the victims. Bobby felt a flush of sudden pity for the grunts he had thoughtlessly derided as part of his stylistic and moral obligation of being a fighter pilot. It was all too easy to understand them now that a stranger had died in his arms. God help the poor bastards; no wonder anyone who saw any real fighting in Vietnam never got over it.

The haze that had hung in the air through the day and most of the evening had lifted. Bobby turned his eyes to the sky. The black shadow that completed the moon shone faintly against the deep blue of the night above the Persian Gulf. Misty air circled it with a silver ring of condensation that seemed to belong to the moon itself and not the humid atmosphere. A canopy of white stars spread beyond, the closer ones blinking blue.

The warm water of the Gulf tide rushed along the beach, slapping on the white sand. The real shoreline underneath was gray mud streaked with salt. This sand, oddly enough, had been trucked in from the Empty Quarter of Saudi Arabia, the only true desert in the Arabian peninsula, a sea of sand and shifting dunes thousands of miles across. The real land of the Gulf, Bobby had learned, was desert as well, but not nearly as romantic. Blown dust. There was little white sand. Gravel, mostly, and brown, sandy dirt. Just nothing, really. Nothing floating on oil.

Tiny specks of dull light glowed from the tidewater reef offshore, bio-luminescence of marine life on its way to becoming coral. Flicks of moonlight danced on the tiny waves. White jellyfish bobbed on the surface—the Gulf was thick with them. A tanker, distant in the channel, appeared as a perfect tiny triangle of red and yellow lights on the horizon.

The whole scene was beautiful, unreal. Dangerous. The conquered moon, the sky most peaceful. A HAWK missile, so far away its shattering noise was just a rumble, split the night sky like a shooting star. Should he wish? What do you wish for when you wish on a missile?

Behind him were the elite, playing in the artificial lights of Sammarah like there was no tomorrow, unaware of the *Lido* massacre. Across the water people were living and dying in the dark. It was like this everywhere in this part of the world, the vast distance between what was and what seemed to be, horror disguised as beauty, conquest as liberation, war as peace. Like most outsiders, Bobby could not seem to grasp this land or its people, who oscillated from sophisticated grace to biblical savagery, who seemed to hold treachery and honor equally high, who played the role of the victor and victim simultaneously.

Without meaning to, Bobby thought, the West had struck the perfect word to describe the distance between truth and untruth, perception and reality, East and West, when they called this land the Gulf.

The Thin Green Line

Bandar Abbas International Airport
Southern Iran

G o!"

At Casey's signal, six men jumped from the sandbagged barricade at the main terminal, running in a low crouch across the ramp at Bandar Abbas International. They flattened at the edge of the runway, M16s pointed at the hangar directly opposite.

Still behind the barricade, Maj. Steve Casey squinted into the sunrise, searching the east side of the runway one last time. He would have preferred to stage the raid at sundown, when the glaring sun would have interfered with the aim of enemy soldiers rather than his own, or, better yet, under the cover of darkness. Casey figured this operation broke at least four of the seven rules of tactical movement the drill sergeants at Fort Benning had pounded into his head back in basic. But after days of studying the snipers' routine, it was apparent the Iranians had fallen into a pattern with a curious lack of activity at sunrise. A surprise assault at dawn stood a good chance of catching the snipers during a watch change.

171

Casey hoped so. He would rather not have to attack at all. He certainly couldn't spare any more casualties. But the men were clamoring for action. After having their nights shattered for so long by snipers and mortar fire, they wanted to strike back, to silence the Iranian strongpoint on the hangar.

"Okay, Randolph. Keep an eye on that rooftop. If anybody moves, open up. And try not to hit any of us, okay?"

The machine gunner nodded and cocked the M60. Casey jogged out to the edge of the runway and moved his free arm back and forth quickly, as if throwing a softball underhanded. The men picked themselves up and followed him in a sprint across the dirt divider between the ramp and the runway.

God, it was hot, Casey thought. Hot already, even at dawn. The hangar shimmered like a mirage in the orange light. Sweat steamed in his eyes and burned when he blinked. His M16, carried in countless recent battles but never fired, felt heavy and slick in his hands. Pretty soon the metal parts would be too hot to touch. Only the Americans would fight a war in Iran during the summer, he thought. Even at the height of the Gulf war, the combatants had observed an undeclared truce during the fiery months of Ramadan, the scorcher, lest troops fall from heat exhaustion and tank crews cook inside their metal ovens.

Casey was halfway across the runway when the machine gun opened up. The squad threw themselves in all directions. At the head of the pack, Casey found himself on the wrong side of the runway. He dove face down in a shallow trench, suddenly struck with deep gratitude for the unknown engineer—an American, probably—who had the foresight to dig a drainage ditch along a runway in one of the driest parts of the world.

He raised his head slowly, expecting to see tracers from the Iranian positions. Instead he saw a man in the ragged uniform of an Iranian Guardsman slumped over the corrugated steel air-conditioning duct that served as cover for the enemy machine-gun position on the hangar. Two other Iranians were running across the hangar to a ladder on the side of the building.

Casey stood up: "Okay, Airborne! Let's go!"

The rest of the squad picked themselves up and sprinted across the runway. They all knew now what had happened. The machine gun they had heard was friendly fire, Randolph's M60 back at the barricade, firing at the Iranians on the hangar. They had caught the snipers by surprise!

Casey reached the hangar first, covering the last hundred yards on pure adrenaline. His legs felt like rubber. The helmet and flak vest, made of lightweight Kevlar, weighed on him like the steel armor of a medieval knight. He was exhausted and scared and grateful to be so—those were the emotions of the living, the surviving. Casey motioned for a couple of troopers to follow him to a fire ladder on the side of the hangar.

A blast of dirt kicked up an inch from his heel. Another shot picked paint off the gray maintenance building behind him. Casey heard a burst at his side and looked up to see an Iranian soldier falling from the ladder, landing at his feet.

"Good shot, Willis," Casey said, almost as a reflex. The trooper who had just saved his life slung his M16 gingerly over his shoulder and started up the ladder.

"Stay here, sir," Willis said. "Doc and I'll check this out."

Casey didn't argue. He looked at the dead Iranian soldier, not much more than a boy. The sight of a corpse didn't shake him. He had seen too many of his own troops dead and wounded since the start of the nightmare that was Ready Eagle. And the trauma of his own barely avoided encounter with death faded quickly. After all, he had been shot at plenty of times lately. He never got over it, but he had gotten used to it.

Still, there was something about the dead youth that profoundly affected Maj. Steve Casey. He looked at the teenager, dressed in a Guardsman's khaki uniform shirt and blue jeans with American sneakers. Casey reached down and pulled at something in the Iranian's hand. The corpse would not let go. Casey had to bend down to examine it further. It was a string of colored beads.

Pops of gunfire from the rooftop interrupted his thoughts. Casey stepped back, raised his assault rifle, and took aim at a figure on the edge of the roof.

"Don't shoot, sir. It's me, Willis." The sergeant leaned over the roof's edge and waved his free arm back and forth. "It's all clear up here. Two dead. Nobody left. Doc and me are both okay. We caught them napping!"

Casey nodded, forcing a smile. He looked at the dead man's hand again. Casey didn't need to count all the beads to know there were ninety-nine there— one for each of the ninety-nine names of Allah. They had not caught the enemy napping. They had caught him praying.

"Hey, Major! Better come up here quick, sir!"

Casey's reverie was broken by the shout from the top of the hangar. He clambered up the ladder. Willis was standing very still, facing the southwest. Casey walked over to meet him, his heavy jump boots pounding out echos on the metal roof.

"What is it, Sergeant?"

"Shh!" Willis held a finger to his lips. "Listen."

In the desert, you can not only see for miles; you can hear for miles. And Casey heard tanks.

"Tracks?" he asked. Willis nodded. "Where?"

"I can't see them, sir. I think they're behind that little hill there, coming up from the city."

The airport road curved gently around the small rise of gravel and dirt before connecting to the main highway that ran into Bandar Abbas to the southwest. The hill was covered with huge, round oil-storage tanks. Beyond them, Casey could clearly see the low hovel of the town's outskirts, much of it burned or smoldering. The newer buildings at the city center shimmered in the far west.

Since the invasion, the Division Ready Force had encountered no trouble from Bandar Abbas proper. Most people had left, scattered to the valley towns of the north, and west to Bandar-e Lengeh. The small recce patrols Casey had sent out at night returned with tales of a city shattered by hunger and violence, of confusion and gunfire in the darkness, as the different factions battled one another for control.

In all, the people of Bandar Abbas seemed too busy with their own problems to worry about the Americans at the airport. Casey had tried to fuel their fears by projecting an impression of a force much larger than the one he actually commanded. So far it had worked, much to Casey's relief. Had word of the true nature of the tiny invasion force leaked out, there was more than enough firepower in Bandar Abbas to sweep the Americans into the sea.

The news of an advance on the airport from the city was therefore quite disturbing. And tanks! Most of all, paratroopers feared tanks. The 82d could hold its own against other infantry. But heavy weapons were something else again. If the Iranians had tanks, the Americans were in serious trouble.

Suddenly, behind him, Casey heard nine rounds fire in quick succession, the sound of an AK-47 in full auto. He hit the deck, pressing his cheek against the scorching metal of the hangar roof. Willis was already prone, lifting his M16 to fire.

"Hey, relax, Sarge!" Doc said, waving the AK-47 over his head. "War's over!"

"You dumbass!" Willis shouted. "I should have shot you."

"What are you so sore about?" Doc sounded hurt. "You should be happy. Everybody's gone. All the ragheads bugged out. We won!"

"Like hell we did," Willis said. He rose slowly to his feet, favoring his right shoulder. "Can't you hear that? There are tanks coming."

"Oh, shit!" Doc caught the unmistakable grind and whine of low-geared diesel engines faintly in the distance.

"Corporal, where did you get that weapon?" Casey demanded.

"I took it off that camel jock at the foot of the ladder," Doc said defensively. "The one that tried to hose you, sir."

"Have you seen any more bodies?"

"No. Just that one and the other two that were up here. But there's no one else around. We looked everywhere. They all deserted when we finally stood up to them. I knew they would. They're ragheads. They're chickenshit! If we'd only..."

"Corporal, listen to me very carefully," Casey said sternly. "Did you or any of the other men find any more weapons?"

"No, sir, just this one here," Doc said. "Why?"

"I knew it!" Casey snapped. "Sergeant Willis, gather up all the men on this side of the runway and hustle back to the terminal. On the double!"

"Yes, sir!" Willis wondered what Casey considered so urgent—the tanks were still a good distance away. He was about to ask Casey what was up, then reconsidered. In the past two weeks Willis, like the rest of the surviving members of the Division Ready Force, had come to depend on Casey's quick and sure judgment. It had kept them alive, and that was good enough for Willis. He ran past Doc and disappeared down the ladder.

Casey stared at Doc. "Have you got a car, soldier?"

As paratroopers, the 82d arrived without transportation and usually depended on captured or "commandeered" vehicles for mobility. Some of Casey's men had taken the opportunity to liberate expensive luxury cars whose owners had suffered the misfortune of being at the airport when the invasion began. Casey knew if anyone could be counted on to take advantage of an unofficial license to steal, it would be Doc Hallday.

"Sure, Major, I've got a ride. A real nice one. Out in the parking lot."

"Get it and meet me back here. On the double!"

"Yes, sir!" Doc smiled, glad to be back in Casey's good graces. He trotted off toward the ladder.

Casey stood alone on the hangar and scanned the horizon. To the northwest lay two large brown mountains. Like most desert terrain features, they looked smaller and closer than they actually were—the nearest, Genow Mountain, was more than ten miles away and rose from the flat coastland to a sudden height of nearly eight thousand feet. To the east there was more desert, interrupted by brief green patches around a seasonal marsh river, dry this time of year. Casey expected no trouble from either direction and turned his gaze to the west.

From his vantage point he could see the entire airport. Burned-out cars and the remains of shattered helicopters littered the parking lot. The wreckage of the 737 still blocked the runway. All were scenes of battles. Casey's band fought only when they had to, keeping the Iranians from getting close enough to discover the secret of their pitiful numbers. Far below him, Casey saw Willis leading the raiding party back across the ramp to the terminal. He stopped and shouted up at Casey, "Coming, Major?"

Casey nodded at Willis. He took one last look. As if on cue, a half-dozen tanks lumbered into view, grinding dust and gravel beneath their tracks. Casey raised his binoculars, counting five, no, six M60s, and a number of M113 armored personnel carriers. American made, left over from ancient times when the United States and Iran were allies. He spotted a number of soldiers on foot; it would take the Iranians a good fifteen minutes to get into attack position. A Revolutionary Guards officer climbed on top of an armored personnel carrier and trained his binoculars on the hangar. And on Casey.

"Oh, shit!" Casey lunged for the ladder and half-climbed, half-fell to the pavement below. Sprinting across the aircraft apron, he was almost run down by a shiny black BMW 720i. The door on the passenger's side flew open. Casey threw himself in.

"Drive!"

Doc looked puzzled. "Where to?"

"It doesn't matter," Casey panted. "Just get the hell away from here!"

Doc shoved the car in gear and screeched off across the runway toward the main terminal building. Casey leaned across the seat, staring out the back window. Could he have been wrong?

No. The hangar exploded in a shower of sparks. Other buildings along the far side of the runway erupted in flames, crumpling one after another in a systematic series of demolitions. The entire east end of the airport was an inferno of twisted metal.

"Jesus, Major!" Doc looked back at the burning buildings. "Did you do that?"

"No," Casey sighed, slumping back in the seat. "The Iranians did. It was a trap. They wanted to sucker us over to that side of the runway and blow it up. And us along with it."

Casey stared straight ahead. His hands were shaking; he couldn't let a soldier see that. He reach for his M16, to grab the barrel, as he always did, and noticed he had left the weapon on the hangar roof. Casey grabbed the sides of his binoculars instead, squeezing indentations in the protective rubber cover.

"Well, it doesn't matter," Doc said with admiration. "You outsmarted them, like you always do. I don't know how you do it, Major. But we won. They're gone, and we're still here."

"Oh, they haven't left," Casey said. "Those guys coming up the road are the same diehards we've been fighting for the past two weeks. I'm sure of it. They were slowly being cut off, and they knew it. So they sneaked out during the night, leaving the three on top of the hangar as a covering force to convince us they were still around."

Doc frowned. "Jeez, what does it take to get these ragheads to give up? And where did those tanks come from?"

"Who knows?" Casey shrugged. "They're here; that's what matters. They're probably stragglers from some of the armored units that left the Iraqi border when the bomb went off. They're coming here to mop up. They probably think we were all killed when they set off the charges in the hangar."

Casey motioned toward the terminal. Doc swung the car in an arc on the runway.

"We probably should have been wasted. How did you know it was a trap?"

"I got suspicious when everybody left at once. These guys don't desert. They'll die first, like the ones they left behind on the hangar. Besides," Casey smiled, "they took their guns with them. No deserter does that. The first thing they ditch is their weapon."

"But how did you know the hangar was wired? Sergeant Willis told us to look, but we didn't find anything."

"You probably never would, no matter how hard you searched. But I got suspicious when I saw the Iranian column stop halfway here. It looked like they were waiting for something to happen. I asked myself what that could be," Casey glanced at the burning buildings, now pumping black smoke into the clear sky, "and this was it."

Doc brought the BMW to a sharp stop at the terminal gate. Casey put his hand on the door lever, looked at Doc, and frowned. "Where's your radio?"

"Sir?"

"Your *radio*, Corporal. You *are* an RTO, aren't you? You were this morning."

"Yes, sir," Doc said, flushed. He didn't want to be in Casey's doghouse again. "It's in the trunk, sir."

"What's it doing there? You're supposed to wear it whenever you're on duty."

"I know, sir, but we haven't been using it much lately. On account of the batteries. You know," Doc said nervously. "Besides, there's no one else to talk to. There's just the Navy, and they've quit listening."

"Damn it, soldier!" Casey was as angry as Doc had ever seen him. "If we live through this, I'm going to kill you. Now let's break out that radio, on the double!"

"Yes, sir!" Doc jumped out of the car and ran back to the trunk. "I'll get it!"

Doc opened the trunk. It was all still there. He grabbed the portable radio. The stubby, black rubber-coated antenna snagged on the side of the compartment. Doc wrestled with it, groaning when he heard Casey's door slam and his footsteps approaching.

Casey looked in the trunk and whistled. "Well, what do we have here?"

Bored, restless, and a long way from home, Doc had taken up a hobby popular among soldiers throughout history: looting. The trunk was crammed with guns, radios, watches, portable stereos, wallets, jewelry—anything that might be considered valuable.

Casey rummaged through the trunk. His eyes fell on a pair of curious copper squares. He pulled them up by the metal chain and dangled them in front of Doc.

"What the hell is this?"

"Dog tags, sir," Doc said nervously.

"I can see that, soldier. They're not ours, and they don't look Iranian. Where did they come from?"

"Willis and I took them off a dead MiG pilot. You remember the one that got hosed by that HAWK the first day we were here? He came down on that hill on the way into town. He punched out, but he must have been too low. There wasn't much left of him when we found him—just these."

Casey examined the dog tags, rubbing off some of the dried blood to look at the name.

"'Carlos Rivera,'" Casey read quizzically. "Doesn't sound like an Afghan to me. What else have you got?"

There were some expensive jewelry in the trunk and quite a lot of money, mostly Iranian currency, more or less worthless now, with a surprising amount of German, Saudi, and even American cash. Casey couldn't begin to estimate the worth of Doc's stash. Refugees fleeing their homeland always took their most valuable possessions.

"All right, soldier, listen up. I want you to drive this car around back to the parking lot. I want you to park it there, lock it up, and give me the keys. And there'd better not be anything missing, either. Anything. We didn't come here to steal, not cars or anything else. You got that, Corporal?"

"Yes, sir," Doc gulped. "I wasn't going to keep it, Major, honest. Besides, it's not like anyone's coming back for it. If I don't get it, someone else..."

"Skip it!" Casey's eyes caught a flat satchel at the bottom of the trunk, charred but still intact. The crest stenciled on the side interested Casey the most: the peacock seal of the Emirate of al-Quaseem.

"Do you know what this is, Corporal?"

"No, sir. I found it in the wreckage of that airliner on the runway. It was just about the only thing left."

"It's a diplomatic pouch," Casey explained. "They're built not to burn."

Casey tried to open it, but the pouch was sealed, the zipper fused by the heat. He took his K-bar from his jump boot and sliced a gash across the end. There were some papers inside that looked to Casey like some sort of briefing, written in Arabic, with some words, obviously untranslatable, spelled out in English. Casey didn't know who sent it or who was meant to receive it but something told him it was an important document.

"Baluchistan," Casey mused, staring at the report. "Where the hell is Baluchistan?"

"Hey, Major!" shouted a voice behind him. "Sergeant Willis is looking for you. Says we need to get on the stick. Tanks will be here soon!"

Casey tried to stuff the papers and the dog tags in the thigh pocket of his BDUs. There was already something there—Hillary's book on Bobby Dragon. He'd never gotten around to rereading it.

"Doc, get on the horn to Red Crown. Tell them to bring everything they got. Tell them..." Casey smiled, "tell them there's a couple dozen tanks and about twenty APCs. They'd better bring Mavericks and Rockeyes, and they'd better come quick. I'll meet you in the parking lot by the barricade."

He stalked off toward the terminal building, stopping near a soldier manning the machine gun covering the runway.

"Nice going, Sergeant Randolph," Casey gestured at the hangar. "You saved our ass back there. Did everybody get back all right?"

"Far as I know, sir. Willis is inside counting noses. He's waiting for you." Randolph squinted into the sun, rising now above the burning buildings. "What was that all about over there?"

"Martyrs, Sergeant," Casey said. "That's what this whole damn war's about. Only I'm not volunteering."

Randolph drew back the bolt on his M60 and smiled. "Neither am I, Major."

Casey slapped him on the back and entered the shade of the terminal building. After two weeks of habitation and confrontation, the men of the 82d had managed to erase most traces of civilization from Bandar Abbas International Airport. All couches and chairs had been moved away from the windows and into the hallway. Every pane of glass had been shattered and swept away, replaced with chain-link fencing taken from the parking lot to keep out grenades. Doorknobs and crawl-space ventilators had been marked with orange fluorescent spray paint. There were sandbags everywhere. Sand was the only thing the soldiers seemed to have in adequate supply, and they put it to good use, stuffing it in plastic bags from the airport gift shop.

The fighting had also taken its toll on the terminal building. The east side, facing the runway, was pockmarked from small-arms fire, the west side scarred with shrapnel from mortar rounds that had impacted in the parking lot. Epithets, directed at everyone from the dead ayatollah to the unfortunately all-too-alive Adm. Sam Meredith, had been scrawled boldly on every flat surface. Casey had objected to the graffiti at first on the grounds that the sight might appear unprofessional to the other units that were bound to relieve them soon. As time went on and it became more apparent that the Division Ready Force was isolated and might never be reinforced, Casey gave up trying to keep the walls clean. It helped the men occupy time and keep their spirits up. Besides, Casey had other things on his mind than good housekeeping—like trying to keep his men alive.

The men had changed, too. Army regs had gone out the window, along with the glass panes (which could scar gunners like shrapnel in the superheated

winds of an antitank missile launch). Most soldiers wore the canvas camouflage covers for their helmets inside out; the dark overall khaki effect was
not perfect, but it stood out less against the uniform beige and concrete of
the airport buildings than did the speckled desert-pattern colors on the other
side. Some dispensed with the cover altogether, giving the helmet the effect
of a dark gray armored baseball cap.

The BDU blouses, touted by designers as warm in the winter and cool
in the summer, had proven just the opposite, although no known fabric could
hope to cool the hundred-degree-plus temperatures of summer in the Gulf.
Most troops wore only undershirts underneath their flak vests, with rank and
name written shakily in camo stick on the sleeves. And on their ALICE
harnesses the majority carried only grenades, a canteen, and ammunition clips,
taped back to back, Israeli style, for quick reloading. Rations, clean socks,
and headphone stereos were stashed in rucksacks at the terminal. The men
knew they weren't going anywhere soon.

Changes on the inside were less readily apparent though no less dramatic.
The troops that had fallen on Bandar Abbas were young and raw, well trained,
but not experienced. Two weeks of sniping, patrols, and firefights had turned
them into cold killers. The ones who were left were stoic, businesslike, and
smart enough to realize their only hope for survival lay in mutual support,
in killing anyone who tried to kill any one of them. An outsider would see
it as bravery, even heroism. Perhaps it was.

Casey caught up with Willis at the entrance to the parking lot, now sealed
with sandbags and wire.

"We don't have much time, Sergeant. They'll be here in about ten
minutes. Are we set?"

"As ready as we'll ever be, Major. But..." Willis shook his head. He
didn't need to tell Casey what the odds were. The Iranians had more men
and ammunition. And they had tanks. At last count, the Division Ready Force
could muster only 127 men on the line, not counting the sick and wounded.

"What about the Dragons?"

The Dragon was a portable antitank missile system. Ineffective against
the compound armor of contemporary tanks and extremely dangerous if
mishandled, the Dragon was due to be replaced by a more modern, user-
friendly system. But it was a familiar story—the new weapon was delayed
with developmental problems. Unlike most other Army units, the 82d had
no other antiarmor weapons system except for light antitank weapons. LAW
rockets were the soldiers' personal, portable bazookas, but they lacked range
and punch. When the Ready Eagle orders came down for the 82d, Dragons
were all they had.

"We've got five Dragons operational and about seven reloads," Willis
said. "I put a team on each corner on the parking lot side. That way they

can support each other. The blast will go out the window behind them, and they'll have a better chance at a flank shot. I sent another team to the control tower."

"Good idea," Casey agreed. "They can shoot down at the thinner armor on top, and maybe the tanks won't be able to elevate their main guns high enough to shoot at them."

"Not unless they shoot from long range. I told our guys not to open fire until the tanks are actually in the parking lot."

Casey nodded. "Just make sure they're on the second level of the tower, not right at the top. We don't want to make it too obvious."

"That's what I told them."

"Where did you put the other two Dragons?"

"One's dug in at the end of the runway. I don't expect any trouble from there, but if they come through the fence, we won't have time to move one up. Let's call it a reserve. The other one's..." Willis hesitated. "The other Dragon's at the Alamo, sir."

Casey frowned. The first night after they landed he had ordered the troops to construct an antivehicle barrier between the road and the parking lot. With pickaxes and shovels, they built a sheer wall of broken concrete and sand five feet high. The wall and corresponding ditch would not keep out a determined tank attack—it was intended to stop car bombs, not armored fighting vehicles—but it would slow them down and expose their weak bottom armor to attack.

In order to get into position to attack from that angle, as well as to prevent attempts by enemy infantry to breach the barrier, the troops later dug a long slit trench in the dead space a hundred meters behind the wall. Casey had considered the possibility of an armored attack remote, but to keep the soldiers occupied during lull periods he ordered the trench's gradual improvement. As time went on, the position, with its intricate gridwork of sandbags, wire, and fake mine fields, took on the appearance of a desert fortress. Troopers called it the Alamo, because, in the words of one of the proud soldiers who worked on its construction, "We'd never get out of here alive, but we'd take a lot of them with us."

Casey had no doubts that the men in the Alamo were prepared, though not necessarily willing, to die there, if Willis so directed. In the days since the start of the invasion, the soldiers had come to rely on Willis, to trust his judgment and courage. Casey had come to depend upon him as well. Only six officers had survived the hellish airdrop into Bandar Abbas. Three had been wounded in the fighting afterward. In addition to Casey, only two officers remained: a young lieutenant of unquestioned courage and questionable judgment and an aging Psy Ops captain whose part in the original Ready Eagle plans had been to seize the radio station and play Hall and Oates tapes to a bemused civilian population. Neither officer was of much use to a force fighting to stay alive.

Sgt. William Willis had stepped in to take up the slack. Casey had taken little notice of him at Bragg. Willis's dossier said he was a good soldier, solid, if lacking initiative. But war has a way of bringing out character in some and of cheapening others. It brought out the best in Willis. Or perhaps it had been there all along; the peacetime Army, in its pursuit of the all-around citizen soldier, tended to overlook the natural warrior.

At any rate, Willis was a leader at a time when Casey desperately needed one. He was truly brave but not stupid, a careful soldier, and a master of small-unit tactics. His personal courage was beyond question: A shoulder injury he sustained while parachuting in must have been excruciatingly painful, but Willis never complained, although many soldiers had been medevacked to the *Saipan* with lesser injuries. Willis *did* complain often about his bad luck of winding up in the middle of the action, but Casey knew it was not luck, bad or otherwise, that placed Sergeant Willis at the front of the thin green line.

"You're right, Sergeant," Casey said. "That's a good place for a Dragon. Just make sure they hit them quick, though. You're getting awful close to minimum range. Who're you putting in charge at the Alamo?"

Willis stared at the unlit lights on the airport ceiling. "I thought I'd go out there, sir. That is, if it's all right with you."

Casey looked at Willis. Both men knew what that meant. Ordinarily, Casey would not have risked a man like Willis in an untenable position like the Alamo. But stakes were high. And the truth was, Willis was needed there. Tough as it was to go, it was even tougher ordering a man to go to his likely death. Willis knew that. So did Casey. But that was command. And Willis, consistent with his career soldier's conviction of never volunteering, needed to be ordered to go. Casey owed him that much.

"All right, Sergeant. You'd better move out; we don't have much time."

"Yes, sir." Willis shouldered his weapon painfully and moved toward the barricaded entrance.

Casey watched Willis climb over the barricade. He had wanted to shake his hand, to say some words of encouragement. But that would have been an insult to a soldier's dignity. Besides, Casey thought, he might even see Willis again.

"He's a good guy, Major."

Casey turned to see Doc, who, after finishing his last reluctant drive, had entered the terminal through the parking lot.

"Airborne. All the way," Casey said.

The radio buzzed in Doc's ear. "It's Red Crown, Major. You'd better talk to them. They won't listen to me."

Casey grabbed the headset. "This is Gator 8...Yes...What?...That's not acceptable...Look, I've got tanks about to crawl all over my people in about five minutes. I can't wait...No!...I don't care what the admiral says. He's supposed to work for General Coleman, not the other way around...Hey, sailor, I don't have time to argue with you! I've got a real-world situation here...Yes! CBUs and PGMs and pretty damn quick, or there won't be anything left for your precious Eagle One to support, you copy?...All right, yes...Gator 8 out."

Casey tossed the headset back to Doc. "Damn squids."

There was a muffled whump in the distance, then a whistling like that of a distant train. The tank round sailed over the terminal and impacted on the runway behind it.

"They're heeere!" Doc giggled.

"This way," Casey shouted. "Stick with me, no matter what. And keep that channel open!"

Casey paced the length of the hallway, reviewing his troops on the eve of battle. Before past actions, he had had to remind his men about basic points of soldiercraft—don't get skylined, fire around cover rather than over it, that sort of thing. A few words, kind or gruff, were sometimes needed. Lately, however, Casey had only to show himself. It seemed to have a rallying effect on the troops. However, it unnerved Casey no end.

"Hold your fire, everyone!" he shouted. "Let them get close. Remember, they think they blew us up, along with half the airport. I want them to keep thinking that. Sergeant Willis is in the Alamo. Don't shoot until he does."

Sandbags stacked ten feet tall blocked the view from the terminal entrance. Casey looked through one of the irregular holes cut through the barricade. A second tank shell fell in the parking lot, chewing up pavement without hitting any of the American positions. Casey saw nothing. His troops were there but were too well hidden.

The whump and whine of another tank round sent troopers scurrying to the barricade and flattening in the hallway. Casey, squatting behind a pile of sandbags, looked up to see Doc staring at the parking lot in horror.

"What's the matter with you, soldier?" Casey shouted. He pulled at Doc's sleeve, but the man stood straight up, staring out. Casey winced at the shell's impact, the crash of metal and pattering of small fragments revealing the shot had hit something besides asphalt.

Casey pulled himself up to see what had caught Doc's mournful attention. The BMW was on its side, in flames, destroyed by a direct, if lucky, hit. Jewelry glittered on the pavement surrounding the burning car. Money floated in the air, settling in flutters across the parking lot. Doc stood still, as if in shock, watching his fortune blow away in the smoke. A gash across his cheek began to run red.

"Snap out of it, Corporal," Casey shouted. "You're hurt!"

"Am I?" Doc said, dreamily. He reached up and felt the wetness on his face. His fingers were bright crimson. "Well, look at that!"

A sparkle behind Doc caught Casey's eye. He dug into the sandbag and pulled out a diamond wedding ring.

"This is what hit you." He shook the ring at Doc. "It should have killed you."

"You're right, Major," Doc said softly, in a strange voice. He took the ring from Casey and dropped it in a pocket of his BDUs. "It should have killed me."

Casey turned away, disturbed and disgusted, but somehow feeling pity for Doc and his lost fortune. He couldn't worry about that now. The battle would soon begin in earnest. Already, Casey could hear the throb of the Iranian tanks approaching the barrier. A puff of gray smoke appeared over the antivehicle ditch—the kind of smoke the exhaust of an M60 makes when it attempts to climb over a high obstacle.

Casey reached for his new rifle. The barrel of a 105-mm L-5 tank gun poked vertically over the barrier. He saw treads chewing at the broken concrete, then the hull, and finally the turret. The tank hung precariously on top of the barrier, then fell forward heavily into the parking lot. The turret swiveled right to left, its commander scanning the American positions.

Casey knew what would happen next. Obviously under orders from the lead tank, the snouts of two other M60s appeared over the barricade.

"Now!" Casey said softly.

Willis was thinking the same thing. A Dragon sizzled from the bunker of the Alamo, burying itself in the side of the lead tank. The missile might have trouble defeating modern composite armor, but the Dragon had no problems dealing with ancient technology like the M60. The explosion caved in the hull and knocked the turret from its mounting; no one on board could have survived.

At the same time a volley of LAW rockets snaked out from the Alamo. The tank on the right was hit between the turret and hull. Hydraulic fluid, called "cherry juice" by American crews, burst into flame. The commander's hatch popped open. A man on fire jumped out, staggered a few steps across the parking lot, and lay down to die. No one else escaped.

The crew of the left tank was more fortunate. That M60 took a hit from a light antitank weapon in its starboard track just as it was cresting the barricade. The tread flew off, and the tank wobbled in a furious, tractionless spin before sliding down the embankment on the Iranian side.

Small arms began popping off all around Casey. The patter of return fire rippled in the sandbags as Iranian soldiers shot at the terminal from behind the antivehicle ditch. Sweeping bursts from a machine gun inside the Alamo raked the top of the barrier. The Iranians ducked behind the broken concrete, then rose again, concentrating their fire on the troops manning the bunker.

It was a stalemate, which was all Casey had hoped for given the circumstances. He looked to the sky. He saw no Navy planes. He had not expected to. But at least there were no MiGs. If the Fulcrums chose this moment to attack, the Division Ready Force could not hold.

Above the pattering of small-arms fire and the moaning of the wounded on both sides, Casey heard a new sound, a high, ominous screeching. He peeked around the barricade. A line of red bandannas, the mark of the true Iranian *Salah al-Din,* appeared above the antivehicle ditch. In twos and threes, they rose over the broken concrete. Furious automatic-weapons fire from the Alamo cut them down like wheat, but there were always more to take their place. Soon the entire length of the wall was a solid mass of red and khaki.

Casey had been afraid of this since the beginning. Human-wave attacks, throwbacks to World War I and the Battle of the Somme, had been Iran's most effective tactic in the Gulf war. They had turned the tide at Khoramshaar and again at Basra. The cost had been tremendous, but a nation that valued martyrdom above all else was more than willing to pay the price.

Human-wave assaults were easy to counter if you had enough men and ammunition. Casey didn't. He desperately needed artillery. He had none. Air support would do it. He had no air support. Casey watched the Iranians, still screaming their battle cry of Islam, pouring over the wall and vowed that, no matter what happened, he would not be taken prisoner.

Suddenly the wall erupted in flame. The heat burned Casey's face as explosions warped the atmosphere and sucked the air from the stifling midsummer day. The line of Guardsmen atop the wall fell back, on fire. No others appeared to take their places. Randolph came running from the rear entrance with a message relayed by hand signals from the tower.

"It's over, Major," he said. "They're running."

Casey nodded, still wondering, like the Iranians, what had hit them. "This time, maybe. Tell the men to hold their fire and stay in their positions. It's not over yet."

Randolph saluted and left to pass the word. Casey loaded a fresh clip in his M16, not realizing he hadn't fired a round from the old one. Suddenly tired, he planted the butt of his assault rifle against the terminal floor and boosted himself to his feet. He moved out in a sprint across the parking lot, sliding like a baseball player in the sand floor of the Alamo.

"Safe!" Willis shouted, with the giddiness of a survivor. "How is everybody back at the terminal?"

"So far, so good," Casey answered. "Doc took a hit when they blew up his Beamer. I think it's shock more than anything else."

"Serves him right," Willis answered. "We're okay up here. One of the machine gunners took a round in the hand, but it doesn't look that bad. Next time it'll be worse."

Casey nodded somberly. "That's what I think, too. They got a good look at us, and they won't come charging in like wild Indians again. We're not as dead as they thought we were. By the way, what was that stuff on the wall? It looked like a damn flamethrower."

"Eagle cocktail," Willis smiled. "It's a little something I learned from our friends in the 101st. You take a plastic bag and fill it with fuel—napalm is best, but we didn't have any, so we used sand soaked in gasoline. You tape a thermite grenade to it, plus a couple of smoke charges, and run a wire from the pins back to where you are. You pull the pins, the thermite grenade ignites the fuel, and—presto—instant inferno. It's not much good for anything but scaring the hell out of people."

"Well, it sure as hell did a number on those guys this time, Sergeant. Good thinking."

Willis cocked his head toward the Iranians and asked, "What do you figure they'll try next?"

"I don't know," Casey answered. "I'd try smoke or gas or something besides coming in head on, but they probably don't have any or they would have used it this time. Or I'd wait until nightfall, but there's no moon and I doubt they have any night-vision equipment left, either. What would you do if you were out there?"

Willis walked outside the bunker into the open trench. Casey followed.

"See that little hill over there, Major?" Willis pointed to the tank farm between the airport and the city. "That's where they all ran to. If I were them, I'd put one of those tanks up on the other side. That way they could use indirect fire to shoot down into the parking lot and keep us busy. Our Dragons couldn't hit them with that hill in the way."

A single M60 rumbled in the distance. Casey watched its treads throwing dirt as it crawled to a point just past the summit of the hill.

"So far you're batting a thousand, Sergeant. Go on."

"Then I'd take another tank and blow a couple of holes in the wall from a long way off. I'd send an APC full of riflemen up near the wall to hose down the Alamo with RPGs and machine guns to keep our heads down, and then let the tank bust through and clean up whatever's left."

"It's a good plan," Casey said. "I wish we were on the other side. What can we do to stop it?"

Willis rubbed his chin. "We need to move right up against the wall with some automatic weapons and some antitank stuff and hit them before they get that far."

"All right, let's do it."

Willis went down the line, ordering various fire teams to move out and take up positions along the barricade. He stepped out of the bunker and walked forward with Casey.

"What did you hear from the Navy, sir?"

"Same old story," Casey said. "Meredith's dragging his feet. Deck spotting, turnaround time—you know the drill."

"Well, after the way those Navy planes got their ass kicked yesterday, I don't suppose he's anxious to send them up here again."

Casey did not say the obvious—that without air support, the Division Ready Force had no hope of surviving much longer. The Navy had proved itself either unwilling or unable to give them the support they needed. Casey found himself pinning his hopes on another air unit, a curious organization mentioned briefly by General Coleman during their recent radio exchanges. Casey knew nothing about the First Air Regiment except that his life, and those of his men, would soon be in its hands.

The soldiers reached the wall and began setting up their weapons.

"There's something about this that bothers me," Casey said.

"What's that, sir?"

"If you were so good at predicting their moves, they must have somebody on the other side who can guess what we're going to do to counter it."

"I guess so. Yeah."

"So put yourself in their place, Sergeant. What would you do to keep us from taking a position along the wall?"

"That's easy, Major," Willis said. "I'd leave behind a couple of men and position them as snipers, and when—oh, shit!"

Willis grabbed for Casey, trying to pull him down to the pavement. It was too late.

Getting shot was not at all like Casey had thought it would be. And like all soldiers, he had thought about it often, especially lately. He had imagined it would be a piercing sensation. It was more like getting hit with something, a baseball bat maybe. It felt like he was hit in the thigh with a baseball bat.

He sat down very carefully, growing less aware of the dimming noise and fading sight of his troops, suddenly fighting again. Everyone was fighting, and Casey realized, vaguely and happily, he would not have to fight again, or tell people what to do, or kill anyone, or be shot again, for that matter, because he had been shot once and that was enough. It was more than enough.

It was quite pleasant, actually. The searing orange sun faded to a faint yellow. The heat, too, left suddenly, and he was at last cool. So, for the first time in two weeks or two decades, Casey closed his eyes and drifted off into peaceful sleep.

Tales of the Sierra Hotel

Dar al-Harb Air Base
Emirate of al-Quaseem

The blue step-van screeched to a halt in a shower of gravel and profanity. The driver, a Quaseemi contract worker, leaned back and shouted cheerfully, "Here you damn go!"

Daffy Brewer rose from the bench, gathered his helmet bag, and stumbled to the front of the van. He stared through the window at a featureless white building set in the courtyard of a modern businessmen's motel.

"This doesn't look like the BOQ to me," he said to the driver, doubtfully. "What is this place?"

"What place does it the hell look like?"

Brewer took a closer look. Freshly turned earth and parked construction vehicles established the fact that it had been recently built. A handpainted sign over the door read "The Sammarah Hotel." Other than that, Daffy hadn't a clue as to where he was being dropped off.

"It doesn't the hell look like anything."

"It is bar! To drink!" the driver exclaimed. He looked skeptically at Brewer's civilian clothes, afraid he had made a mistake. "You are fighting pilots, no? For the Regiment?"

Daffy nodded.

"Okay. That is what fighting pilots like your damn selfs do. You drink!"

Brewer shook his head. "It's been a long trip. Maybe we should..."

"I don't know about you, pard, but I think this joker's got the right idea. I could go for a long, cool one right now."

Scooter Jeffries lifted his bags and made his way to the front of the van.

"But Scooter, we just got here. Don't you think we should report to somebody?"

"I am. I'm reporting to Colonel Budweiser." He turned to the driver. "Thanks for the lift, Sheik. Here's a new English phrase for you: 'Blow me hard, Air Force weak dick.' Got it?"

"Blow me hard, Air Force weak dick," the driver repeated solemnly.

"Good!" Scooter said heartily. "It's a term of respect. They really like it when you call them that. It works with Marine pilots, too."

"Thank you very, very much. I will damn remember," the driver said gratefully. He pushed the door open. "Out you go now! Have a night day!"

The two men tumbled out of the van, which sped off back toward al-Quaseem International. Standing by the side of the service road next to the runway at high noon, one fact of his new life hit Daffy Brewer immediately: It was hot.

The joke aboard the *Eisenhower* was that the weather forecast for al-Quaseem and vicinity remained remarkably constant: "Clear to partly hellish."

Brewer hadn't appreciated the humor until he stepped out of the cool van and into the 104-degree heat and stifling humidity of summer in the Persian Gulf. He had flown and fought over the area many times but, being a modern warrior, had gone to battle in a civilized, air-conditioned manner, from the Ghostriders' ready room to the cockpit of his F-14 and back to the *Ike*. He had known the temperature and relative humidity, of course, from the briefings and had dutifully dialed the numbers into the Tomcat's computers. But he had had no real concept of how hot the Gulf could get. Until now.

The twenty-foot walk seemed like a twenty-mile hike in the heat. Brewer set his bags down and reached for the entrance. As he touched the handle, the door flew open. A Royal Navy pilot sailed out backward from inside, followed closely by a Marine Harrier jock. The two rolled together in the dust, swearing and fighting.

Scooter stepped over the struggling men and joined Daffy, who was peering inside, astonished.

"Shit hot!" Jeffries exclaimed. "This is more like it."

Daffy didn't say anything. There was nothing to say. As far as he was concerned, he was home. He had never been to this place before, but he was home.

Everything about it was familiar. It was much too cold in the summer and, Daffy knew, if there was anything resembling a winter in al-Quaseem, it would be too hot then, too. And too dark. Too noisy too often, with occasional crushing silences. Blue smoke hanging in every corner, the smell of cigarettes mixed with stale beer and popcorn—it was all too perfect. Brewer began to have more respect for the people running the First Air Regiment, Inc. Somehow, right in the middle of the Persian Gulf, not far from where the Prophet walked, they had built a Mecca for jet jockeys, the ultimate fighter bar.

"Hey, Navy, heads up."

A green beer bottle sailed end over end across the bar. Jeffries ducked. Brewer snagged it one handed, bringing cheers from a clutch of pilots in the corner.

Daffy smiled, nodded, opened the bottle and gulped. San Miguel, the official beer of the tactical air community; "Filipino vino," one of the few positive legacies of Vietnam. You could drink it like water. Twenty minutes later, it would hit you like rot whiskey. A painless death. That was all they had asked for back then.

His eyes swept the place. One huge room, divided into sections by pools of light. A group of A-10 pilots slumped over the bar, already seriously drunk in the middle of the afternoon. Another group—all Phantom crews, judging from their patches, but in a variety of uniforms—carried on a loud, raucous conversation in several languages at a large table. A huddle of newly arrived Luftwaffe Tornado crews, still in their bright orange overwater flying gear, stood nervously by the fireplace, in which colored cellophane crackled noisily and brightly but without heat. Crowded around the pool table, a couple of American F-15 pilots were teaching the finer points of Crud to four Mirage jocks. The French pilots, who had learned how to play just five minutes earlier, were already arguing over the rules of the game.

"Some place, huh?"

Brewer turned to see a smiling Navy commander with prematurely gray hair and a five-thousand-hour Tomcat patch leaning over a table piled high with empty beer bottles.

"Good to see another Turkey driver," he said, noticing the Tomcat patch on Daffy's helmet bag. "When did you get in?"

"Just now. I'm Daffy Brewer."

"Blade Wilkinson." The man reached over to shake hands, knocking several beer bottles to the floor with a clang. He dismissed the broken bottles with a belch and a wave. "Don't worry about that shit. They've got people who come by and clean it up."

Daffy nodded and scanned the scene. "Hell of a place."

"Sure is," Wilkinson agreed. "I've been at Johnny's Place in Naples when the fleet was in. I even rode the rocket at Cubi Point. But I've never seen anything like this. Truly outstanding."

A wedge of light shot through the dark, smoky bar like a laser. The two pilots Brewer had seen in an apparent death struggle outside walked back arm in arm, the best of friends.

"That happen often?" Brewer said, nodding toward the pilots.

"What, the fighting?" Wilkinson shrugged. "All the time. I tell you, this should be a hell of a unit if there's anything left of it by the time we get around to fighting anybody else. You can't blame the guys—they're just bored."

"Bored?" It didn't seem like an appropriate emotion to Brewer, given the place and the time.

"As in calcified." Wilkinson took another swig. "Oh, I forgot, you just got here. I was one of the first. Every day it's the same damn thing. Twice a day, once in the morning and once in the afternoon, we all line up, take off, and chase each other up and down the Gulf. The attack pukes do the same thing, except they go over to the other side of the island and do some major dirt beating before they come back. Not that I'm complaining. The flying's good—no Mickey Mouse NATOPS rules for First Air, no, sir. Anything goes. These guys are real men. They'd rather die than look bad. And they're good, too. I've learned more about air combat in two weeks here than I've learned in ten years in the Navy. I like to think I've taught a few lessons, too."

"Sounds great," Brewer said. "So what's the problem?"

"When you land," Wilkinson said, tipping over a beer bottle, "you're here. It's a small enough island as it is, and the sheik apparently doesn't want us to see any more of it than we have to."

"The sheik?"

"Hassan. Mr. Big Bucks. He built this whole goddamn bar for us practically overnight after a couple of us threatened to go over to Sammarah and associate with real people."

"But the sign over the door says this place is *in* Sammarah. The Sammarah Hotel."

"It is now," Wilkinson agreed. "Last week it was called the Airport Inn. A bunch of guys from the Regiment are staying here under contract. You can forget about checking in at the BOQ, by the way—Dar al-Harb's got a lot more folks than it was built to handle since First Air moved in, and it's getting worse. The motel's not bad, but there's nothing to do when you're not flying. So we got together and drew up a petition calling attention to a serious lack of aircrew debriefing fluid in our daily diet. As you know, fighter jocks require a minimum of three beers a day, or else we turn into airline pilots. The next day the name was changed, and the bar was open."

"I don't get it," Daffy said, puzzled. "Why did they have to change the name of the hotel just to serve drinks?"

"It was either that or change the location," Wilkinson explained. "See, this is a Muslim country. We're talking Bedsheet City here. Abu Dhabi might as well be Tijuana compared to al-Quaseem. The whole place is dry except for Sammarah, which is why it's so isolated. Hassan doesn't even want his own people going in there except to take foreigners' money. So overnight he just extended the boundaries of Sammarah across the creek and around this hotel."

"Can he do that?"

"He's the sheik. He can do whatever he wants. And apparently he does, from some of the stories I've heard." Wilkinson raised a beer bottle in a mock toast. "So welcome to the Sierra Hotel, swabbie. You're looking at one of the most exclusive resorts on the planet. People are dying to get in."

Daffy smiled. It was inevitable that the name of a fighter bar built in a place called the "Sammarah Hotel" would be instantly changed to the "Sierra Hotel." The two words denoted the letters *S* and *H* in the phonetic alphabet of aviation. And those letters stood for "shit hot," the fighter pilot's supreme compliment.

Wilkinson shifted uncomfortably. One aspect of the military that came in handy in bars was that you could tell a lot about a man just by looking at the patches on his flight suit. If nothing else, you could always look down and pick up a name you had lost somewhere back at the fifth or sixth beer, a benefit not to be underestimated. The trouble was, Daffy—or Duffy, or Fluffy, or whatever the hell his name was—wasn't wearing a flight suit.

"So, uh, hoss," Wilkinson slurred, "where did you guys come from?"

"The *Ike*," Brewer answered. "By way of Italy. That's the Navy for you. Admiral Meredith wouldn't cut us orders to take the COD bird here, so we had to sail a couple thousand miles through the Suez to Naples and then fly commercial back here."

"Meredith's a dildo," Wilkinson said agreeably. His face clouded over with a new, serious expression. "The *Eisenhower,* huh? Whew, that's tough duty."

Daffy nodded. "It wasn't as bad as what the guys on *Constellation* are going through now, though. I hear the admiral has taken personal control over air ops for Task Force Bravo."

"Meredith doesn't have personal control over his own bowels," Wilkinson belched. "He was a nervous little shit at Annapolis, and he's even worse now. And you can tell him that for me. I joined this outlaw air force here just to get away from limp dicks like him."

As Wilkinson lifted another San Miguel, Brewer noticed his shining Naval Academy ring. It was a symbol of sacrifice now; Daffy wasn't sure if it was just Meredith or if the feeling went higher up the chain of command, but, from the difficulty he and Jeffries had getting off the ship and getting to al-Quaseem, it was obvious the Navy was less than thrilled about First Air. Wilkinson would have a tough time picking up his career when—if—he left the Regiment. The word may have come down from the commander in chief for full cooperation, but in the real world the Navy—and probably all the services, for that matter—jealously hoarded its pilots and prerogatives behind a phalanx of slow paperwork and prompt professional intimidation. Daffy had gotten the full treatment from the admiral's aide before he left. Daffy had told him to go to hell.

Brewer scanned the room. Most pilots had settled into groups, but a few stood alone at the bar, apparently shunned by the rest.

"Who are those guys?"

"Let's see..." Wilkinson squinted through the darkness and his own growing alcoholic haze. "The one on the end is the sheik's kid."

Daffy stared at the tall, dark-haired youth leaning casually against the bar in a tan Quaseemi flight suit. "Prince Faisal?"

"Yeah. We just call him Sonny. He's an F-16 jock, and he's pretty damn good, too, although it's hard to tell if he'd be any help in combat. I've seen a lot of hot hands freeze up over the Gulf of Sidra. The trouble is, he's so young—I've got shirts older than he is."

"Why isn't anyone talking to him?"

"Human nature, I guess," Wilkinson shrugged. "Every fighter pilot likes to think he's the ace of the base, and it's real difficult to maintain that fantasy when you're standing next to a guy who's younger, richer, better looking, and a hotter stick than you could even *pretend* to be."

"So I guess he must be pretty full of himself."

"Sonny?" Wilkinson asked. "No, he's a sweet kid. Pretty down to earth, too, for a guy who's going to become the richest man in the world someday. That's the real problem, though—nobody wants to be seen kissing up to the boss's son. This isn't that kind of outfit."

"And who's that one?" Brewer pointed at a tiny Japanese F-15 pilot in a huge cowboy hat.

"That's Minya Mashuta," Wilkinson laughed. "We wanted to call him Godzilla, but he's just too damn small, so we named him after Godzilla's kid instead. He's an Ego driver. Flies a lot bigger than he looks. Doesn't speak much English, so he comes in here every night and just props up the bar. He did solve a big problem for us, though."

"What was that?"

"The playlist."

Brewer nodded. He knew at once what Wilkinson was talking about. At every fighter bar he'd ever been in—and Daffy had been in most—the central argument did not concern tactics or politics but rather what records to play on the squadron jukebox. It seemed to be split into two camps: the older pilots, who considered country-and-western music the pinnacle of Western art, and the younger jocks, with seriously contemporary haircuts and an unshakable belief that every country ballad ever written was, in fact, the *same damn song*.

"How did you handle it?"

"We did it the Air Force way," Wilkinson smiled. "We turned the matter over to a committee that knew absolutely nothing about the problem at hand. In this case, Minya—our one-man musical selection committee—solved the problem with the exercise of three simple criteria: Was it honest music? Was it sexist, with an annoying, driving beat? Were any synthesizers used in the arrangement? If the answers were yes, yes, and no, the song found a place on the First Air Top Forty."

Brewer smiled. The jukebox was blaring "Dixie Chicken." Half the pilots in the bar were singing along. Mashuta beamed as if he were performing the song himself.

Daffy's eyes fell on the last loner at the bar, a slight man in glasses and a regulation Air Force major's uniform.

"Who's that?"

"I think his name is Padgett. Some kind of intel guy. Not rated, though," Wilkinson added, as if that effectively ended the discussion. Typical pilot, Brewer thought. If you didn't fly, you didn't count.

"Intelligence, huh?" Brewer remarked. He suddenly remembered why he had been asked to join the Regiment. Well, *he* hadn't been asked, he reminded himself, but even so, he was ready to make his contribution. "I think I'll head over there and talk to this intel guy for a little bit. They want me to give them the lowdown on MiG tactics over Bandar Abbas."

"Suit yourself," Wilkinson said, though his tone expressed a different message: *Don't say I didn't warn you of your impending social doom if you insist on speaking to a staff weenie in the presence of real men and fighter pilots!* Wilkinson took one more drink, closed his eyes, and fell backward, chair and all, neatly and in slow motion, passing out in true fighter-jock style.

Brewer looked around. No one noticed. He stepped carefully over Wilkinson's inert, snoring body and walked to the bar. Padgett was hunched over a Coke, deep in thought over a crossword puzzle. Just like an intel nerd, Daffy thought, then looked again—the crossword puzzle was in Russian.

"Major Padgett?" Brewer said, extending his hand. "I'm Don Brewer. From the *Ike*."

Padgett looked up from the puzzle, his eyes blinking in surprise behind thick glasses. He shook Brewer's hand.

"Happy to meet you. We've been expecting you. Well, not *you*, necessarily, but someone from the *Eisenhower;* we weren't sure who," Padgett said, flustered. "Sorry to hear about Commander Palmer."

"Devil was a good guy," Brewer said, solemnly. "We lost a lot of good guys off the boat. Say, Major Padgett, I..."

"Call me Krypto."

Brewer was taken aback, then nodded. "Oh, I get it. It's a nickname. Crypto, like the secret codes, huh?"

"No, like the dog."

"Dog?" Daffy said, puzzled.

"Superboy's dog. When I was little, I used to read comic books. Superboy was one of my favorites. He had a dog that came with him from Krypton. Superboy grew up to be Superman. But nobody knows what happened to the dog. I always wondered."

"I see," Daffy said, transfixed. He waited for an answer. It didn't come. "Well?"

"Well, what?"

"What happened to the damn dog?" Daffy demanded.

"Nobody knows. I tried to figure it out. I read all the comics. I even wrote to the comic-book company. They never answered my letters. But it bugged me. I mean, the dog was super, like Superboy, right? He was invulnerable. Nothing could kill him, so he must still be alive. I talked to my friends about it so much they started calling me Krypto. I'm like that. Once I get something in my mind, I can't get it out. I guess that's why I got into intelligence."

"Did it ever occur to you that the question didn't have an answer?" Daffy asked curiously. "That nobody even thought about the dog or cared what happened to it?"

"No," Padgett said firmly. "Every question has an answer. You just have to keep looking until you find it."

Daffy smiled. You couldn't help but like a guy like Padgett. He hoped that Krypto the Superdog would somehow, someday, fly in from wherever he had been hiding and lick Padgett's face.

"Well, I can't help you with that, but maybe I can answer some questions about those Russians over Bandar Abbas."

"Excuse me, Commander," Padgett said, "but they're not Russian."

Daffy's eyes widened. "Well excuse *me,* Major, but I've been fighting the bastards for two weeks. I got a pretty good look at them, and I can assure you, those are Soviet planes!"

"Oh, I'm sure of that," Padgett agreed. "But those aren't necessarily Russians flying them."

"Then who the hell are we fighting?"

"The MiGs belong to an outfit called Squadron 22. It's nominally an Afghan Republic Air Force training squadron, but..."

"Wait a minute!" Daffy interrupted. "I've heard this line from the intelligence guys on the *Ike,* and I didn't believe them either. Those guys can't be Afghan students. Hell, if they had pilots like that, they wouldn't have lost the war."

"Diplomatically speaking, they *are* Afghan students. They've covered all the legal bases and, technically, it's no different than American 'advisors' fighting in Central and South America in 'self-defense,'" Padgett said. "But, in a real-world sense, you're right. The Afghan thing is just a cover. Those MiG pilots you've been fighting are not Afghans. Well, maybe a couple of them are, but the rest are Czech, East German, Polish, North Vietnamese— you name it. It's a sort of all-star team put together by a Soviet colonel named Paratov."

"Why?"

"I beg your pardon?"

"Why are they there? Why are they fighting?"

"That, Commander, is the big question." Padgett shook his head. "I don't have any big answers yet, just a lot of little ones. If it's any consolation, the Russians—the *real* Russians, the ones in Moscow—seem as baffled by this Squadron 22 as we are. If we..."

"Hey, Daffy, is this a great place or what?" Scooter rushed up from the back of the bar and tugged Brewer off his stool. "Come on—there's a couple of guys you've got to meet."

Daffy smiled at Krypto and shrugged. "Duty calls. Look, we'll drop by your office once we get settled, and you can debrief us on what the bogies are up to over Bandar Abbas. Okay?"

Krypto nodded and smiled weakly. Brewer staggered after Jeffries, amazed at the young man's energy. Then again, this was Scooter's first real, operational fighter-jock party. Although the two had held each other up through plenty of squadron blowouts before, those were nothing compared with this. These guys were professionals. And they were fighter pilots at war, always among your most serious party monsters, Daffy knew from experience. There was nothing like nearby death to make life seem sweet and joyous.

Brewer in tow, Jeffries pushed his way through a crowd of pilots ringing one of the pool tables. All eyes were on two men, a tall, starkly handsome pilot in shorts and a Hawaiian shirt, and a short, stocky man wearing dark glasses and an old, leather World War I vintage aviator's helmet.

"...doesn't matter. It's all electrons," the tall man was saying to the rapturously attentive crowd. He took a cue ball and placed it in the center of the pool table. "Okay, let's say this is a neutrino. Cutest of the particles."

"I dunno, Don," the shorter man interjected doubtfully. "They sound like a breakfast cereal to me. I'm kind of partial to gravatinos, myself. Photinos are cool, too, except that they don't exist."

"But that's what's so cool about them, Wally," Don argued. "Anyway, all of these hummers may or may not be quarks. You might know them as leptons."

The expressions on the pilots' faces betrayed the fact that none of them had the slightest idea what the man was talking about. Particle physics was not a frequent topic of conversation in fighter bars. Don continued.

"As you know, it takes three quarks to make a photon or neutron. Or maybe not—they're still working on *that* one. But we do know the future of electronic warfare lies in these WIMPS."

"Wimps?" ventured a pilot in the crowd.

"Weakly Interactive Massive Particles," Don explained tiredly, as if talking to a child. "Jeez, don't they teach you guys anything in E-school anymore? We're talking about the basic building blocks of all matter, here. The Velveeta of the universe! The grand unification theory! The problem of everything!"

The faces in the crowd stared back blankly but amused.

"Okay, now, if you accept the theory of quantum fluctuation—which I do, with some reservations—even when you have nothing, there is something going on. So let's say..." Don looked up from the pool table and saw Daffy in the crowd.

"All right, class dismissed," Don said abruptly. "I want to interview a special guest in the audience tonight."

He reached out and grabbed Brewer's elbow. The crowd melted to the corners of the bar.

"Hey, Wally!" Don cried out. "You know who this is? This is Daffy Brewer!"

Don pumped Daffy's hand. Wally did the same.

"Okay, you know who I am," Brewer said, confused. "Now, who are you?"

"Are you kidding, Daffy?" Scooter interjected. "Everybody knows these guys. These are the Weasel brothers!"

"The who?"

Daffy had heard of the Weasel brothers, of course. Everyone had. But he didn't know they actually existed. They were not, so the story went, actual brothers but a former aircrew of an F-105 "Wild Weasel" electronic warfare aircraft in Vietnam. Wild Weasels used themselves as bait, daring the surface-to-air missile operators to lock onto them so they could fix the threat's position with their sophisticated sensors and destroy it.

As such, Wild Weasel pilots and their backseat "Bears" were a different breed. Their courage was unquestioned—nearly every Weasel outfit in Southeast Asia proudly displayed a trophy, a pair of steel ball bearings in a leather pouch nailed to a wooden plaque, given to them by some other unit whose flight they had protected and whose lives they had no doubt saved. But they were also, by nature, a little nuts. And the Weasel brothers were the nuttiest of all.

According to the bar tale, Don and Wally Weasel (their real last names had long since been sacrificed to secrecy and a good story) returned from Vietnam not a little maladjusted, but with a burning fascination for electronic warfare. And, as it turned out, they were absolute world-class geniuses at it, which was not surprising, since their technical expertise and academic background were why the Air Force had "volunteered" the unlikely pair for such duty in the first place.

But not even the Air Force was prepared for the electronic marvels that emerged from the Weasel brothers' desert laboratory. Electronic countermeasure pods; high-speed antiradiation missiles; loitering, radar-jamming drones— just about every recent American advance in electronic warfare, though manufactured by defense contractors under license, started out as a gleam in Don's and Wally's eyes at the Custerdome, the Weasel brothers' research facility/playhouse in Dreamland. The Air Force kept them isolated and made them happy, giving them whatever they wanted as long as they kept turning out miracles. Their reputation had grown so pervasive and respected that American pilots referred to any advanced and useful electronic gizmo as a "Custerdome job," whether or not the Weasels had had anything to do with it—because they usually had.

"Oh, come on, Daffy. You've heard of the Weasel brothers!" Scooter was saying. "These are the guys who sent off to the East German fighter base at Gross-Doln for an autographed picture of a MiG-31."

"Hey, we were *curious,*" Don said defensively.

"Yeah, we had a bet," Wally added.

"These are the guys who threatened to put a Tacit Rainbow antiradiation missile through the transmitter of the Las Vegas cable TV company if they ever played *Porky's II: The Next Day* again."

Don shrugged. "It worked, didn't it?"

"The way I look at it," Wally said drily, "we performed a much-needed public service."

"These are the guys who were testing the new AN/ALQ-200 radar jammer," Scooter giggled, "and opened up every electronic garage door from Indian Springs to Lake Tahoe."

"Well, that one got away from us, granted," Don admitted.

"We're working on one now that will open up *Russian* garage doors," Wally added. "So as soon as they get garages and doors, we'll be ready with the American answer."

Brewer laughed dizzily. Everything was happening so fast. So the Weasel brothers *did* exist. And they were as crazy as everyone said, maybe more so. Daffy was glad to hear it and, in a way, not so surprised. No one could make up stories like that.

"So what are you guys doing here?" Daffy asked. "What made you want to join up with First Air?"

"Bobby asked us," Don replied.

"Bobby? Bobby Dragon?"

"Yeah," Don looked uncomfortable. "We're buds, man. He lives out where we do."

"You were his backseater, weren't you?" Wally asked suspiciously. "He's talked about you. You act like you didn't know Bobby was running this show. Didn't he ask you to come?"

Brewer and Jeffries looked at each other.

"Of course he did," Daffy lied. "It's just that he's trying to keep a low profile, that's all."

"That's Bobby!" Don grinned. "Mr. Personality. Sometimes I think the reason we get along so well is that he's an even bigger asshole than we are."

"He comes over to the Custerdome all the time," Wally said. "Doesn't say a word, hardly. He just comes over and eats pizza and plays with our toys."

"Tell him about the Cannonball," Scooter interjected. "Wait'll you hear this, Daffy."

"Ah, the Carob Cannonball," Don sighed. "That's *really* why we're here."

"We used to call it Custerdome One," Wally said. "Back when it was black all over. Now it's desert camouflage, brown and tan. Looks like a Mars bar. That's why we call it the Carob Cannonball."

"Call what?" Daffy asked. "What is it?"

"It's like an AWACS, an EF-111, Compass Call, Rivet Joint, and AB-CCC all rolled into one C-130 airframe," Scooter said excitedly. "It's really neat."

"What? What are you talking about?"

"It's like this, Daffy," Don explained. "Bobby says First Air is really hurting for electronic countermeasures platforms. The problem is they cost large dollars and there aren't that many of them around, so nobody seems to want to give them up. But you can't cross the street these days without ECM support. You need to jam their radars and their radios. You need to have a radar airborne to direct your own fighters. And you've got to have somebody forward to direct your air-to-mud effort, if only to act as a radio relay to the guys in the weeds. You follow me so far?"

Daffy nodded.

"Now there are two theories of electronic warfare," Don continued. "Theirs and ours. You can have six different airborne platforms and a couple dozen average guys sucking up gas, leaking electrons, and just generally getting in everyone's way. That's the Air Force's theory. Or you can have one platform and two exceptionally sharp individuals named us."

"That's our theory," Wally explained. "You can tell because it's the correct one."

"Now, wait a minute." Daffy shook his head. "Are you telling me you can do all those things with just one airplane?"

"Sure," Don said. "The Carob Cannonball. It's an airborn command-and-control center for coordinating air-to-air and air-to-ground missions that also detects, transmits, and jams any frequency along the electromagnetic spectrum."

"It also makes great coffee," Wally added.

"Shit!"

"See, I told you he wouldn't believe it!" Scooter crowed.

"Well, you've got to admit it's a little hard to swallow," Daffy said. "How does it work? Where do you get the power for something like that?"

"We don't need a lot of power," Don explained. "We're not the damn Air Force. We don't need to stand off a hundred miles away and eat doughnuts while we're sanitizing the subcontinent. We go in with the strike package and blow a corridor in and out, one plane wide. You don't need big electrons for that. You just need smart ones."

"You can't outpower the Russians anyway," Wally said. "Their electrons are bigger than ours. They've got electrons the size of basketballs, I swear."

"And we don't have room on board for enlisted trolls or big flying Lazy Boy recliners for generals to park their butts in," Don added. "We built it that way on purpose. Pilots zooming around with their hair on fire and each eyeball pointing a different direction don't like to hear a bunch of crap from either end of the chain of command. So we just do our thing and send them what they need by data link. The whole thing is hooked up to one big computer, which is constantly pumping out information to our guys while it automatically detects and jams the bad guys. If they want any more threat dope, they can just call us up and ask for it."

"This I got to see," Daffy said. "Is it here? What does it look like?"

"The Cannonball?" Don replied. "It's over at Al-Quaseem International, in the Pan Am maintenance hangar. But I wouldn't go looking for it, not unless you like getting shot at. If the Air Force knew we brought the Cannonball into a place like al-Quaseem they'd have a hissy. There isn't much to see, anyway. It looks like a regular C-130, except it's got an E-2C radome stuck up on top and all kinds of weird bulges and antennas sticking out all over the fuselage."

"So if this thing is so wonderful," Daffy asked, "how come the Navy or the Air Force hasn't bought a bunch of them?

"Because there's only this one," Don answered. "It's an experimental job. We've been working on this thing off and on for about ten years. Every now and then the Air Force will saw off a piece of it and give it to one of their pet contractors. They'll run it through their money amplifiers and get it out in the field. But the Cannonball is really just a test bed, a work in progress."

"Besides, nobody knows how to work it but us," Wally added. "There aren't any operations manuals. Hell, there isn't even any writing on most of the instrument panels. It's more like a musical instrument than an airplane. There's some stuff in there, even I don't know what it does."

"Let me get this straight. This is a one-of-a-kind airplane, an irreplaceable prototype. It's never been tested in combat..." Daffy stopped when he saw Don and Wally exchange a meaningful look. "Has it?"

"Uh, let's just say we take vacations like anyone else," Don said mysteriously. "And we have rather eclectic tastes."

"They just promised us we'd see the world," Wally allowed, looking at the ceiling. "Nobody said anything about *landing*."

"Still, you've got to admit it's going to be pretty damn exciting stooging around the coast of Iran in a C-130," Daffy pressed the point. "Hell, Scooter and I were there in an F-14, and it's just dumb luck, really, that we're standing here today. What makes you think you're not going to...uh..."

Brewer hesitated. Fighter pilots never used the words *kill* and *death* in conversation. Any expression denoting crashing or getting shot, except as it applied to the unfortunate enemy, was considered bad taste. Don knew what he was getting at and saved him the trouble.

"Because Bobby promised us, that's why. He said they'd have to get through him to get to us, and that's good enough for me. You know what he's like in the air," Don said. "I mean, I'm a damn good pilot, all right? But this guy's a jet monster. I've never seen anything like it. If they get him, then nobody's safe, I mean it. We might as well buy it here as back in Nevada."

"Besides, I'm kind of anxious to see Bandar Abbas," Wally drawled. "I hear it's a major party town over there."

Daffy looked at Scooter and laughed. Well, these were the Weasel brothers. And they *were* nuts. Still, Brewer could detect a note of capability and determination under their humor. Daffy could tell professionalism when he saw it. He was glad the Weasels were here.

He was also elated to know he had been right about Bobby, that he was alive and in al-Quaseem. Although he had known it all along. He didn't know how he knew it, but he knew.

Daffy took a swig of beer. Things were indeed looking up. He had endured his last days aboard the *Eisenhower* in an atmosphere of desperation and fatalism. It was good to hear laughter again and optimism. But then again, he reminded himself, these pilots had not fought the MiGs over Bandar Abbas. He had.

"So what do you think?"

"That's a tough question, Daffy. We could be here all night," Don laughed. "What do I think about what?"

"About all this, about First Air. You're a smart guy. What do you think are our chances?"

Don turned serious. "I'm not a fortune-teller. And I'm not a spook. I'm a flying physicist. I can only express myself in those terms. And if I had to hazard a guess, I'd say what we've got here is a singularity."

"A what?" Scooter interjected.

"A singularity," Wally explained. "A point beyond the event horizon at which matter is infinitely dense. The laws of mathematics can't deal with infinite numbers, so that means nobody knows what the hell's going on in there. It drove *Einstein* nuts."

"So you think it's not going to work?" Daffy asked. "You think First Air is going to fail?"

"I didn't say that," Don answered. "I just said there's no way to predict what's going to happen. Nothing like this has ever happened before. The best plans, planes, and pilots on both sides of the line are being sucked into a black hole called Bandar Abbas. There's going to be a big bang there soon, pardner. And I want to be there when it happens. It's my duty as a scientist."

"Dead bug! Dead bug!"

Brewer hit the floor at the first shout, landing next to Scooter. Soon the entire Regiment was crawling across the carpet, victims of a stupid children's game that had been a favorite in fighter bars since the time of the Red Baron. When someone yelled, "Dead bug," you hit the floor. No one knew why. No one asked; you just did it. The last pilot standing had to buy the next round.

In this case, it was an Egyptian Phantom jock, who was apparently unaware of the rules. Tough luck—the crowd rushed the bar while the friends of the unfortunate F-4 pilot explained the rules of the game to him.

Daffy found himself next to a small group at the end of the bar. None of their uniforms matched, but they were all Hornet pilots; he could see that by the patches. Only one was American. The others were Spanish, Canadian, Swiss, Australian—Brewer didn't realize the United States had sold F-18s to so many countries.

A big triangular patch above the right breast pocket of a Canadian pilot's black flight suit caught Brewer's eye. It looked newer than the rest of the insignia, a dark background with a silver numeral 1 superimposed on a pair of gold wings.

Brewer tapped the patch with the neck of his beer bottle. "What's that?"

"Our new regimental insignia, eh?" The man's name tag identified him as Capt. Gerry "Hoser" Francis from the 419 Squadron at Cold Lake, Alberta. "How do you like it? We just got them in a couple of days ago."

Daffy stared at the patch, trying to make out the writing on the bottom: *"Facite Magnopere Aut Iti Domun."*

"I'm afraid my Latin is a little rusty," he said. "What does that mean?"

"Uh oh, now you asked for it," Francis smiled. He put two fingers in his mouth and whistled across the bar. "Hey, Dagger!"

A young man in a Dutch flight suit and shoulder-length blond hair separated himself from a gaggle of F-16 pilots and sauntered over to Daffy's group, beer in hand.

"When he's not flying Falcons for 323 Squadron at Leeuwarden or cheating at darts, Darrel Amundsen here is our resident expert on Imperial Latin."

"I was curious about this motto here," Daffy said, pointing to the patch.

The Dutch pilot's eyes brightened.

"Oh, it's very simple, you see? It can't be translated literally, oh, no. The closest I could get was 'Go forth in splendor or return to your hearth.' If you translated it literally, it would say, 'Take a big shit and go jump in the fire.'"

The crowd at the bar roared with laughter. Daffy looked confused.

"Translated what? What does it mean?"

"It's the First Air motto," Francis said proudly. "We all voted on it. It means *'Go big or go home.'*"

Incident in the Arabian Sea

**Gonzo Station
North Arabian Sea**

Whatever it takes.

That's what Adm. Sam Meredith had told the skipper of the USS *Copeland*. Now the little frigate had a sixteen-foot gash in her starboard side, and two sailors were dead. Two American sailors, at any rate. Who knew how many Russians had been killed when *Copeland* collided with the Soviet destroyer?

Meredith reflected on his order with brief remorse. It was the right thing to do, he decided. It had to be done. This was war. People get hurt. Better a couple of sailors now than dozens of pilots over the Gulf, with their valuable and increasingly scarce aircraft. And without those aircraft, the men on the beach, and their mission, would quickly become just a grim chapter in American military history. And he would be blamed.

By the time the SH-60B touched down on the wide fantail of the USS *Missouri,* Meredith had regained his confidence. Visiting the stricken frigate, if only from the air, had been a correct decision, too, he thought. It showed compassion. True, he had been visibly shaken by the sight of the bleeding wounded and the two draped bodies being winched into hovering helos. They were, after all, the first of the many casualties of the war Meredith had actually seen, albeit from a shaky distance. But, the admiral reasoned, that would only make him more human in the eyes of his men.

Before leaving the helicopter, he paused to pat the crewman in the left seat on the back.

"Good flying, son," Meredith said. "Don't worry. We'll get out of this all right."

He did not see, as he stepped on deck, the man turn to the crewman in the right seat—who was, as in all helicopters, the actual pilot—and jerk his hand up and down, laughing.

Meredith strode across the aft deck of the *Missouri*, buoyed once again by its immense presence, its aura of invincibility. Here was a ship fit to command! Task Force Bravo's other ships, though modern and in many ways more capable, seemed small and harmless in comparison, their armament concealed below deck or hidden in a superstructure that more resembled a condominium than a man-of-war. Even the carrier, huge as it was, was flat and featureless; without its aircraft, it was nothing more than a floating parking lot. But the battleship, with its tremendous sixteen-inch main batteries and decks bristling with guns and missiles of every caliber and description—this was a warship! Meredith stepped briskly across the dark golden teak deck, congratulating himself again for choosing to transfer his flag here.

They were waiting for him on the flag bridge.

"How is it, Admiral?" Capt. David Moyne, the *Missouri*'s skipper sounded worried.

"*Copeland* will be all right," Meredith answered. "Damage control did a great job putting the fire out. There's a big hole, but it's above the waterline. She'll still sail."

"I was asking about the crew, sir," Moyne said softly.

"Oh, they're fine." Meredith sounded annoyed. "We've got more important things to worry about than a couple of banged-up sailors. Are we ready to launch?"

"Whenever you give the word, sir." Lt. Cmdr. Malcolm Hirsch, Meredith's chief of staff, continued staring at the horizon through his binoculars.

"Then let's go," Meredith said. "This time we'll catch them with their pants down."

"Uh, sir, you'd better take a look at this first."

Meredith snatched the glasses from Hirsch and looked east, across the beryl blue waters of the north Arabian Sea.

"It can't be!" Meredith shouted. "That ship is dead! I saw it myself. Twenty minutes ago she was dead in the water!"

Still, Meredith could see with his own eyes that the *Stoiky* was not dead.

Far from it. Not only was the Soviet destroyer moving well under her own power, her radar antennas were nodding and circling again—more bad news for Task Force Bravo.

"Goddamn it!" Meredith exclaimed. "What does it take? That ship was on fire less than twenty minutes ago. She had a hole in her bow you could drive a truck through."

"Still does, Admiral." Moyne stared at the distant ship through gyro-stabilized binoculars. "But it doesn't seem to have slowed her down too much. Pretty fair damage-control work for a bunch of Russians."

Meredith dismissed Moyne's comments with a wave. "Hirsch, what's the situation aboard *Connie?*"

"Still ready to launch whenever you give the word, sir."

"Not yet. Tell them to stand by." Meredith watched the Soviet destroyer gain ground on the slow-moving *Missouri.* "We're not launching until we shake this tail. I don't want another damn turkey shoot over Bandar Abbas."

One of the best attributes of the aircraft carrier is its ability to stage air attacks, without warning, from, tactically speaking, an almost infinite variety of locations. The Soviets had taken that advantage away by assigning *Stoiky* to tail the battle group. With its exceptional speed and powerful radar, the new *Sovremmeny*-class destroyer shadowed the *Constellation,* reporting the aircraft carrier's launches and recoveries to controllers at Zaranj.

The advance warning allowed Paratov's MiGs to conserve fuel and pounce on the incoming Navy strike aircraft in carefully planned ambushes. Not only were the Fulcrums preventing the 82d Airborne's small Division Ready Force from breaking out of the airport, they were also slowly grinding down *Constellation*'s air wing, just as they had done to the *Eisenhower,* forcing its early retirement back into the Mediterranean. The strategy helped the Fulcrum pilots intimidate, demoralize, and ultimately shoot down many Navy aircraft over the Persian Gulf. Too many, Meredith thought. It was time to even the odds.

But if the situation was critical in the Gulf, it was just as tense all around the world. Global commitments and maintenance schedules left only one other carrier—the USS *Ranger*—available for duty in the battle for Iran. And despite a Herculean effort on the part of the air wing and crew to get her ready to sail, *Ranger* could not possibly arrive on station for ten days. For Meredith, that might as well be ten years. At the current loss rate, he would have no attack aircraft or fighters on the flight deck by the end of the week.

Meredith could not allow that to happen, not on his watch. There were opportunities in war for ambitious men. So far, no strong personality had emerged, no one name that would be forever tied to the action in the Arabian Sea. Meredith wanted to be that man. It wasn't imperative that he be heroic, Meredith thought. The important thing was to not screw up.

His reverie was broken by the sudden and unwelcome arrival on the bridge of Gen. Curtis Coleman. In the two weeks since the start of Meredith's Arabian nightmare, the 82d Airborne's commander had been almost as tough an adversary as the Soviet MiGs and warships. Whatever he did, Meredith thought bitterly, it was not enough for Coleman. The general recognized the sacrifices the pilots of the *Constellation* were making in the air, just as he had appreciated those of the now-departed *Eisenhower*. And he saluted the courage of the *Saipan*'s helicopter crews, who fought their way in every night to deliver what supplies they could to the beleaguered troopers in Bandar Abbas.

But it was not enough. The relatively small number of Navy planes could never hope to improve the situation, only to stabilize it, at best. And the resupply barely sustained the troops. What worried Coleman most, however, was what would happen if Task Force Bravo pulled out, a maneuver he sensed Meredith was just looking for an excuse to execute.

"I hear there's been trouble," Coleman barked. He nodded curtly to Moyne and Hirsch, but his tone to Meredith was barely civil.

"Nothing you need be concerned about, General." Meredith's voice was just as cold. "It's a Navy matter."

"From what I've seen so far, Navy matters are too important to be left up to the Navy," Coleman snapped.

"And what's that supposed to mean?"

"It means, Admiral, that you've got your priorities backward. Your mission is to protect my men, not your ships."

"My mission is whatever I say it is," Meredith shot back. "Until the Joint Chiefs get around to putting one of us in charge, we're going to have to work together. Now I can't tell you what to do, General. I wish to God I could, but I can't. But you can't order me around, either. I'll dispose of my forces as I see fit."

"Dispose is the correct word, all right. You've been throwing them away in dribs and drabs for two weeks. And what have you got to show for it? Nothing. Meanwhile, my men are being picked off one by one at Bandar Abbas International. Another couple of weeks and neither one of us will have any forces worth fighting over."

Red faced, Meredith stalked to the other side of the flag bridge. The two weeks of fighting had taken their toll. Meredith felt weak, dizzy. His knees shook. His nerves were ragged, raw. This assignment, so late in his career, had seemed at first a godsend. Now it was becoming a curse. What was he doing wrong? There were no rules for a situation like this. It wasn't in the book. He could feel the eyes of the other naval officers on his back. I have to stay calm, he thought. I have to look like I'm in control.

"All right, General, what would you have me do? *If* you were in charge."

Coleman rubbed his chin, thinking. "For starters, I'd turn this battlewagon around, take the carrier and the Marines and this whole damn armada, sail up into the Gulf, and blow the hell out of everything on the wrong side of the runway at Bandar Abbas."

Meredith let out a brittle laugh. "That just shows how much you know about naval operations. The MiGs would be all over the *Missouri* in ten seconds. And if there was anything left after that, every Iranian gunboat, aircraft, and cruise-missile crew would be waiting to pick our bones. No, that's not an option."

"Well, it's a hell of a lot better than sitting out here on our ass in the middle of nowhere, slowly bleeding to death."

Meredith swallowed. He glanced at Moyne and Kirsch, who looked discreetly away. What Coleman had just proposed was blasphemy to any Navy man. It was axiomatic that carrier ops be conducted well outside the range of enemy land-based airpower. Did Coleman really think Meredith would take the *Constellation* and the rest of Task Force Bravo away from the relative safety of open water into the shallow, dangerous bottleneck of the Strait of Hormuz?

"That's out of the question, General," Meredith spat. "We're not going near the Gulf until we get complete air superiority."

"That's how you get air superiority," Coleman said flatly. "You fight for it. Hell, by the time your planes get all the way to Bandar Abbas from here, they're already almost out of fuel."

"He's right, Admiral," Moyne interjected. "As it is, we can only sortie as many planes as we have tankers for. The *Eisenhower* left her KA-6s with us, but that's still not enough to mount a real Alpha strike."

"Keep out of this, Captain Moyne," Meredith said sternly. "I'm not sailing north of the Tropic of Cancer, and that's that."

"Then you might as well go home," Coleman said. "You're not doing anybody any good out here."

"That's your opinion, General. Fortunately, I don't take orders from you. My orders, such as they are, are to provide air support for the troops at Bandar Abbas until General White gets his little air force going. Although God knows when that will be. Why don't you fly over to al-Quaseem and give *him* one of your inspirational chats?"

"Brick White is working as fast as he can," Coleman said. "It's going to take a while to get the First Air Regiment operational. The planes are still coming in. The pilots need time to learn to work together. You've got to give him the benefit of the doubt."

"The hell I do. He told me I'd only have to hold out for a couple of weeks. Well, I have. It's been two weeks now, and that flying circus of his hasn't flown mission one. Meanwhile, we've been getting mauled over Bandar Abbas every day. It seems to me your confidence is a bit misplaced, General."

Meredith turned quickly and strode to the bridge brow, where Moyne and Hirsch were studying the approaching *Stoiky.*

"Gentlemen, we cannot let that vessel get any closer to the *Constellation,*" Meredith said. "Any suggestions?"

"How about a Harpoon across the bow?" Hirsch offered. "That would sure get their attention."

Moyne frowned. "They're too close. That's just about minimum range for a Harpoon. There's a good chance it would skip right over *Stoiky* and lock onto the support ships."

Meredith stared through the binoculars. Sure enough, there was the task force's replenishment group, bringing up the rear: the oiler *Freedom Gas Star; Harris Titan,* a bulk loader; and the containership *S. L. Baker.* The Navy auxiliary supply ships, which started the cruise, had long since exhausted their supplies and returned to Diego Garcia and Mombasa for more.

The group's three dedicated underway replenishment ships, *Kiska, Concord,* and *Canestio,* now forward with the main body of the task force, had been forced to reload from the chartered civilian vessels, none of which had the speed to keep up with the fleet or the ability to directly off-load supplies when they got there. Resupply had been a constant headache for Meredith. Who could have foreseen the amount of fuel, ammunition, and supplies it would take to keep even a modest force sailing in combat these days?

"How about a Standard, then? I think the *Copeland* is in good enough shape now to hose one off," Hirsch suggested.

"Isn't that a surface-to-air missile?" Coleman asked.

"Yes, sir," Hirsch answered. "But we've used them to take out Iranian gunboats before. As long as you can put the fire-control radar on the target, the missile doesn't care if it's a slow-flying airplane or a fast-moving ship. It'll kill it just the same."

"I don't think that would stop them," Moyne said. "We could beam them with the fire-control director, but *Sovremmenys* have a pretty sophisticated electronic warfare suite. Unless they saw a missile in the air and got a paint from the Standard's own terminal guidance radar, they'd know it was a bluff."

"Captain Moyne," Meredith sounded exasperated, "I've heard just about enough from you on the subject of what we *can't* do. Why don't you try to think of something positive that will scare this ship off our tail?"

"I've got an idea."

The men turned to look at Coleman, staring out at the *Missouri*'s bow. "I was just noticing these big damn guns here. Why don't you use them?"

Meredith thought for a moment, then beamed.

"As much as I hate to admit it, that's a splendid thought, General," he said. Then, staring at Moyne, Meredith added, "I'm surprised the captain of this vessel didn't think of that."

"Begging your pardon, sir," Moyne said. "I wonder if that's such a good idea."

"Oh, come now, Captain," Meredith said smoothly. "I'm sure if I were conning the *Stoiky* and a few sixteen-inch shells crossed my bow, I might decide to change course."

"That's just it, sir," Captain Moyne said nervously. "I'm not sure we can get close enough."

"What?" Coleman interjected. "That little book you gave me said those guns can fire a shell that weighs more than a Volkswagen over thirty miles!"

"It's not the range, General," Moyne said. "It's a question of accuracy. The shells are propelled by powder charges stored in silk bags. Some of those charges date back to World War II."

Meredith knew that, of course. The main guns aboard the *Missouri*'s sister ship *New Jersey* had proven wildly inaccurate in Lebanon for just that reason. And the volatile charges had been at least partly responsible for the tragedy aboard *Iowa,* when its forward battery exploded. Still, Coleman wanted action. At this point anything was preferable to another needling by Coleman.

"So what do you suggest?" Meredith demanded. "Do you think we should just sit here while that ship warns the MiGs my planes are taking off? Captain Moyne, I want you to train Battery A five hundred yards ahead of that Russian ship!"

"But Admiral Meredith..."

"Now, Captain!" Meredith thundered. "That's an order!"

"Aye, aye, sir." Moyne reluctantly picked up a sound-powered telephone and murmured the command. A long buzz could be heard faintly from the other end of the line.

"I know, mister," Moyne said sadly into the phone, "but that's an order."

Moyne hung up the line and looked at Meredith with anger and resignation.

"It will take a couple of minutes, Admiral. They're loading the charges now."

Meredith grunted, turning back to watch the *Stoiky* through the binoculars. He had been getting nothing but static since the whole affair began, he thought. First from Brick White and Curtis Coleman and now from his own officers. By God, he wouldn't stand for it. He'd make *Stoiky* turn back. A sixteen-inch shell across the bow would change the Russian captain's mind. Then circumstances would turn in his favor. Then he'd begin to get the respect he deserved.

A siren blast echoed throughout the ship. The huge bulk of the *Missouri*'s forward turret skewed slowly abeam. Sailors, already in battle dress for general quarters, leaned out to see the big guns fire. The first of the three barrels shuddered, spewing yellow fire and gray acrid gunsmoke. The big ship dipped sideways in recoil.

The first shot landed well ahead of the *Stoiky,* splashing into the Arabian Sea a mile and a half ahead of the Russian destroyer. *Stoiky* kept coming.

"Damn it, Captain, that's not even close!" Meredith said. "What did you tell your gunner's mates?"

"We have to play it safe, Admiral. We're just getting the range."

Meredith grunted. The siren blared again. The middle gun barrel erupted. By now the whole ship smelled of cordite. The shot hit the water a mile ahead of the *Stoiky,* closer than the first. But not close enough for Sam Meredith.

"Give me that phone, Captain!" Meredith grabbed the receiver from Moyne. "Fire Control, this is Flag. I want you to put a round one hundred feet in front of that ship, and I want you to do it now! Is that clear?"

Meredith slammed down the phone.

"By God, Captain, if you don't have the guts to do it, I will."

"It's not a question of bravery, Admiral," Moyne said defiantly. "It's a question of physics. I can guarantee an accuracy of a half mile, no more. I respectfully request that you rescind that order, sir."

"And I respectfully request that you get the hell off this bridge, if you can't obey orders, Captain!" Meredith bellowed.

"Maybe he's right, Meredith," Coleman said softly. "It's his ship. He ought to know what she's capable of. Maybe we're taking too much of a chance here. We just want to scare them away, not start World War III."

"Please, General, this is none of your affair," Meredith said angrily. "I'm not going to tell you again—what happens on board this ship is none of your business."

"Here we go!" Hirsch shouted.

The siren buzzed again. The last tube recoiled, spitting thunder and lightning out over the Arabian Sea. Every man on board could see the flight of the huge shell as it bolted from the barrel and arced across the sea. And hit the *Stoiky* directly amidships.

The Soviet destroyer rose in a geyser of fire and water. The explosion broke the back of the lightly armored warship. The two pieces tilted upward and then bubbled underwater. In thirty seconds, the *Stoiky,* and the three hundred Russian officers and men on board, had ceased to exist.

"Holy shit!" Hirsch gasped.

There was a still silence on the bridge as the four men watched the bubbles float to the surface where, moments before, a Soviet warship had sailed. There were no signs of survivors.

"Orders, Admiral?" Hirsch said nervously.

"How could this happen?" Meredith whispered. "How could I have let this happen?"

"Uh, sir, if we're going to do something, we'd better do it soon," Hirsch repeated. "Don't you think so? Sir?"

Meredith continued to stare at the patch of sea where *Stoiky* had gone down with all hands.

"Commander Hirsch, we'd better get those planes up," Moyne said firmly. "That ship may have gotten off word she was under fire before we hit her. I don't know what the Soviets will do now, but the *Connie* will be a sitting duck unless she clears the flight deck."

Hirsch lifted the sound-powered telephone.

"With your permission, Admiral?" Hirsch looked at Meredith, who was still staring blankly out to sea.

"Forget it, Commander. He's out to lunch," Coleman growled. "Captain Moyne's right. Go ahead and make the call."

Hirsch looked about the bridge nervously. "Why don't we wait just one more minute? Let's give Admiral Meredith time to crystalize his thoughts."

"We don't have another minute, Commander," Coleman barked. "If you ask me, he's already crystalized. Look at him!"

Meredith stared, frozen in the heat. His wide eyes reflected only the blue of the now-empty sea.

"Look, Hirsch," Coleman barked, "I'm the only two-banger within a thousand miles of here, so what I say goes. Is that clear?"

"You can't..."

"That's the way it is, Commander. Somebody's got to take charge. Now, Captain Moyne, you're the expert. What would you do now?"

Moyne glanced at Hirsch, then Meredith. "The first thing I'd do is launch the Alpha strike off the *Connie*."

"To where?"

"It doesn't matter. Just get them off the deck and in the air. Have them hold an orbit around the task force while we see what the Russians are going to do. If the *Connie* gets hit with those bombed-up planes still on deck, we'll lose half the air wing and maybe even the ship itself."

"Sounds right to me," Coleman agreed. He gestured to Hirsch. "Call them up, Commander. Launch those birds!"

Hirsch hesitated for a moment. He realized it would be senseless to protest. He put the call through.

"What next, Captain?"

"We're at general quarters, now," Moyne said. "I'd put the task force on battle stations."

Coleman nodded. "Do it."

Moyne ducked into the gangway and whispered a command to his executive officer. Coleman walked over to Meredith and put a hand on his shoulder.

"Maybe you should go below now, Sam. Get some rest," he said gently. "We'll come get you if anything starts to happen. You can't do it all yourself, you know."

Meredith looked at Coleman, smiling weakly. There were tears in his eyes. In the sharp shadow of the bridge overhead, precious darkness on the bright ship, Coleman took out a handkerchief from his BDUs and wiped tears from the admiral's eyes. It wouldn't do to have the men see their commander this way.

Coleman motioned for Hirsch. "Commander, I want you to escort Admiral Meredith to his quarters. I don't know how it happened, but he seems to have been blinded by the flash of the explosion. I'm sure he'll be all right soon, so let's keep this to ourselves, okay?"

Hirsch led Meredith by the arm through the hatch. Coleman gestured for Moyne to join him outside in the privacy of the bridge brow.

"Captain Moyne, I think you're smart enough to know we're in deep shit now. I don't know a damn thing about boats, but I know how to give orders. So I'm going to have to take your word on tactics. But I'm in charge. Is that clear?"

"Yes, sir."

"Good. Now, the first thing we ought to do is send a helo over where that Russian ship sunk and look for survivors. I don't think we'll find any, but if we're going to try to convince the Soviets we didn't mean to hit their ship, we need to at least make it look like we're sorry."

"I've already given that order, General."

Coleman looked at Moyne with new respect, then annoyance. "Good thinking, Captain. But don't do any more thinking without asking me first."

"Aye, aye, sir."

"Okay. Now—do you think that ship sent any messages before she went down?"

Moyne frowned. "Hard to say. My exec tells me *Stoiky* sent a message after the collision, saying she was hit and there were casualties but that the damage was under control and the ship was moving under its own power."

"And who was that message sent to?"

"The *Kirov*. That's the flagship of SovIndRon, the Soviet Indian Ocean Squadron."

"And where is she?"

"With the rest of the group, anchored somewhere between us and Socotra. About two hundred miles to the southwest."

"And how many of them are there?"

"Besides *Kirov*, there's another *Sovremmeny*-class destroyer, the *Bolvoy*, and a couple of *Udaloy*-class subchasers, *Marshal Shaposhnikov* and

Admiral Tributs. They've got a tanker and a bulk carrier with them. Oh, and there's an aircraft carrier, too, the *Baku.*"

Coleman slammed his fist down down on the bulkhead.

"Christ, Captain, why didn't you tell me that sooner? That changes everything. I didn't even know the Russians *had* aircraft carriers."

"Don't worry, General, they're not supercarriers like ours. They're antisubmarine ships, really. Helicopter carriers. *Baku* only carries about a dozen planes, and those are Forgers—Russian Harriers. We call them 'VTODs'—vertical takeoff and die. They haven't got the gas or the guts to come out here and get us."

"So what are we worried about?" Coleman asked. "And don't tell me the Navy isn't worried. Meredith just about pissed in his pants when we hit that ship."

"*Kirov,*" Moyne said nervously. "She's a real bear, General. Big. Fast. It's a nuclear-powered battle cruiser. We don't have anything like it."

"But it's two hundred miles away."

Moyne shook his head. "It's got those new cruise missiles. SS-19s."

"And they could hit us from way out there?"

"Absolutely. Easily," Moyne said softly. His face brightened suddenly. "*If* they had the right data."

Moyne shot past Coleman and scurried down the ladder, two steps at a time. Coleman followed, shouting, "Wait a minute! Where are you going?"

"CIC," Moyne shouted over his shoulder. "Come on, General, we don't have much time!"

Moyne stopped five decks down, before a door barred by a Marine guard.

"This is the combat information center, General. It's where we fight the ship."

The guard saluted and moved aside. Moyne hurried in and stepped quickly across the darkened space to talk with an officer near a plotting table. Coleman paused to let his eyes adjust to the dim glow of the blue battle lamps. The room was lined with faint green, sweeping radar screens, and computer displays. Sailors stared into them intently, talking softly and constantly, but never to each other, always to someone on the distant end of a headset.

On a large sheet of gridded glass in the center, a seaman plotted the positions of the ships that made up Task Force Bravo. Coleman noticed the grease pencil mark that was the *Missouri,* closely followed by the three support ships and the crippled *Copeland.* To the north lay the *Constellation,* surrounded by a cluster of warships—the cruiser *Valley Forge* and the frigates *Gary* and *Trippe.* Four more ships—the cruiser *Biddle* and the destroyers *Charles Adams, Berkeley,* and *Paul F. Foster*—formed a protective ring around the task force.

There were other marks on the grid: alphanumerics for the call signs of aircraft from *Constellation*'s air wing, a handful of which were always on patrol. A spot marked "SSN 699," Coleman knew, was the nuclear attack submarine *Jacksonville* prowling well ahead of the task force. Less precise and more ominous were the dashed red lines of submarine data leading to a dot marked "Charlie II," with "gone?" scribbled cryptically underneath. This meant a Soviet attack sub might or might not be in the inner ring of the layered defense, a fox among the chickens. Even Coleman knew that was not good.

"We're in luck, General," Moyne said, striding across the CIC with a computer printout in his hand. "The last pass was twenty minutes ago."

"Last pass?"

"The Russian intel satellite," Moyne explained. "Cruise missiles need precise targeting data. *Kirov* usually gets its target information from an installation on shore, or from a Bear D reconnaissance aircraft. But there aren't any Russian intel stations near here. The closest one is Ras Karma, on Socotra. That's why we've been cruising this far east. And the *Connie*'s fighters have been doing a good job chasing the Bears out of the box. So the Soviets have had to launch a special COSMOS just to keep an eye on us. That satellite orbited past here just after the *Stoiky* blew up. It won't be back for another hour and a half."

"So the *Kirov* can't fire any missiles without the satellite?"

"Oh, yes, sir, she can," Moyne said. "They just wouldn't have accurate data. They'd have to dial in the numbers of our last known position and hope that when the missiles enter their terminal guidance phase, the seekers lock onto something important."

Coleman stared at the plan position indicator, studying the position of ships on the grid. His face clouded over in sudden rage and concern.

"Turn this boat around!" Coleman bellowed.

"Sir, there's no need to..."

"That's an order, Captain! And tell some of those destroyers to get back here, on the double!"

"Aye, aye, sir." Moyne nodded to an astonished radio operator, who could not help overhearing the loud exchange.

"Captain Moyne, how fast do those missiles go?"

"The SS-N-19 is high subsonic, General. About four hundred knots. They pick up speed when they drop down to wavetop level during the terminal phase."

Coleman made some quick mental calculations. "That doesn't give us much time."

"General, you don't think..."

"Why not?" Coleman interjected. "Look, I don't know a damn thing about Russian ships, but I know Russians. And if I just had one of *my* destroyers sunk, I sure as hell wouldn't sit around waiting for some satellite. I'd want to kill something, and I wouldn't be too particular about what it was. Ready, fire, aim! That's the smart thing to do. Even if you didn't hit anything, you'd put the other guy on the defensive."

"But they wouldn't do that, General. Cruise missiles have no conscience. Once they lock onto something, that's it. There's no turning back." Moyne shook his head. "I just don't think the Soviets would risk firing missiles at an American task force."

"We just sank one of their goddamn ships, for Christ's sake!" Coleman shouted. "What do you expect them to do? Give us the Order of Lenin? We started it! They've got to do something!"

"Maybe so, but I still don't think..."

"Excuse me, sir." After leaving Meredith's quarters, Hirsch had followed the two men into the CIC, where he had been quietly monitoring task force communications. "I think you ought to take a look at this."

Coleman and Moyne stepped up to the bank of radar displays. Moyne peered into the first screen and barked a laugh of relief.

"You're paranoid, Commander. Those are our own planes. This track here is the E-2C that the *Connie* just launched."

"I know, Captain. That's the short-range scan," Hirsch said. He flicked a switch below the display. "This one goes out to two hundred miles. Take a look."

Moyne and Coleman stared incredulously as a cloud of bright green dots slowly appeared at the bottom of the screen.

"Jesus Christ!" Moyne shouted. "I don't believe it!"

"Believe it, Captain," Coleman said. "That sure looks like trouble to me. The question is, what do we do about it?"

Hirsch chewed on a fingernail. "We can get some of them, probably. Maybe even most of them. But we're in a bad spot. Everything's pointing the wrong way."

That same thought had occurred to Coleman when he first saw the grid. Most of the fleet's firepower had been positioned in the direction the task force was heading, true to doctrine but at odds with tactical reality. The whole group of ships traveled in a wide, constant circle known as a modified location, or ModLoc. In this case, the ModLoc was known as Gonzo Station. And the part of the circle Task Force Bravo was heading in pointed due north. The missiles, however, were approaching from the southwest.

Coleman rapped the screen with his West Point ring. "Where's this picture coming from?"

"*Valley Forge*," Moyne answered. "They're coordinating air defense for the whole task force."

"Why them and not us?"

"*Valley Forge* is a *Ticonderoga*-class cruiser, General," Hirsch explained. "They've got the new Aegis system. The whole ship is built for air defense."

"And they can see out that far?"

"Technically, yes. Their theoretical radar horizon is 230 miles. But as far as fire control goes, you don't really begin discriminating targets until about fifty miles, or even less."

"So that gives us—what?—about thirty minutes or so to shoot down these missiles?"

"About that, yes," Moyne said, impressed with Coleman's rapid calculations.

A petty officer wearing a headset whispered into Moyne's ear. "Excuse me, General," Moyne said. "Captain Suarez wants to talk with you. It's urgent."

"Who's he?"

"Skipper of the *Valley Forge,* General," Moyne answered. "He's looking at this, too. I'll bet he wants permission to fire."

"Good man!" Coleman clapped his hands together. "You talk to him, Captain. Tell him I said hit those missiles with everything he's got!"

Coleman turned to Hirsch, peering into the radar display. "Where's the *Connie* now?"

"Bugging out," Hirsch pointed to a blip at the top of the screen. "The TAO says she got most of the strike airborne, but her number-two catapult is down, and the forward deck is fouled. An A-6 lost pneumatic gear pressure and ran into the starboard jet blast defector. It's sitting nose down, blocking the way. They're trying to tow it off, but it's going to take some time. A lot of the strikers are still on deck, loaded and ready to go."

"God almighty!" Coleman exclaimed. "Listen, you'd better call up the air boss on the *Constellation* and tell him to shove that son of a bitch overboard. Don't even worry about recovering it. We don't have time to waste."

"Aye, aye, sir," Hirsch said.

Coleman took a deep breath. Watching other men talk on telephones— it was a hell of a way to wage war.

Moyne put his hand over the mouthpiece and shouted across the CIC to Coleman.

"The missiles are about a hundred miles away. Suarez has diverted a couple of Tomcats from the *Connie* to intercept them before they get within range." Moyne turned to Hirsch. "Have they got Phoenix?"

"No," Hirsch said sadly. "They're reconfiguring a couple of birds now with AIM-54s, but there's no way they're going to be up in time."

The F-14s had been fragged to escort the strike package originally planned to attack Bandar Abbas and as such carried only short-range heat seekers and Sparrow radar-guided missiles. The heavy Phoenix missiles, designed to shoot down attacking planes and missiles from a hundred miles away, were of little use in the tight, confused confines of the Persian Gulf, where Meredith's rules of engagement severely restricted their use. They were therefore left behind on an Alpha strike, replaced with pods carrying much-needed fuel. There was no time to change armaments and still get the Tomcats airborne.

"Have you got an estimated time of intercept?" Coleman asked.

Moyne checked the big twenty-four-hour clock on the wall. "About five minutes. If they..."

The headset buzzed in his ear. Moyne waved Coleman over, pointing frantically at the radar display. The blips representing the Soviet missiles, now frighteningly close, were joined by two other dots. Coleman hoped they were the Tomcats from the *Connie.*

"Yes, Bob, I see them," Moyne said in the headset. "What? Damn it! Well, at least that's better than nothing. No, you'd better call them off. I don't want to take a chance of hitting them with our own missiles. Okay, we'll start now. Keep me posted."

Moyne handed the headset back to the operator and motioned for the *Missouri*'s executive officer. The two men spoke briefly, heatedly. Moyne's exec whirled away and headed quickly for the electronic warfare station. Moyne joined Coleman and Hirsch at the radar plot.

"What was that all about?" Coleman asked. "He didn't seemed too thrilled about it, whatever it was."

"Banzai jamming," Moyne explained. "We're going to pretend we're an aircraft carrier. The SQQ-32 is going to generate a radar picture of the *Constellation* with us right in the middle. Hopefully we'll soak up all the missiles before they get to the *Connie.*"

"Is that, uh, wise, Captain?" Hirsch asked nervously. "I'm not thinking of myself now, but this *is* the flagship, the center of command, and if..."

"Look, we don't have a choice, okay?" Moyne shot back. "If the *Constellation* gets caught with those planes on deck she'll go up like a skyrocket. *Missouri*'s the only ship big enough to radiate a signal that can draw those birds away from her."

"I know, sir, but..."

"Don't worry, Commander. This ship'll take it. She's got more than a foot of armor at the waterline. This relic took plenty of kamikazes in the Pacific, and she's still fighting."

"I hope you're right, Captain," Coleman said.

"I hope I am, too," Moyne said. "Because there's no other way. The Tomcats could only knock down one of those missiles in their first pass. I can't risk them trying again. *Valley Forge* is going to start letting missiles fly any minute now. I don't want them shooting down our own guys."

"Captain Moyne!" A voice shouted across the CIC. "*Valley Forge* reports first missile away."

"Christ!" Coleman exclaimed. "Look, Captain, I'm an old soldier. It makes me nervous sitting down here in the middle of a battle. They seem to have everything under control here—isn't there someplace we can go where we can see what's going on?"

Moyne smiled tightly. "Sure, General. We'll go up to the flag bridge. They've got pretty much the same communications equipment up there that we do down here."

Moyne led the way through the hatch and up the ladder. The light hurt Coleman's eyes, and the air was heavy and hot after the air-conditioned coolness of the CIC. But he was glad to be back in the real world.

A siren blast in the distance signaled another shot from the *Valley Forge*. A gray missile shot straight up from beneath the cruiser's foredeck, trailing a white plume of smoke.

"Jeez, you know, I had no idea those things got out so fast. It looks like a damn bottle rocket going off," Coleman said absently.

"Good news, General!" Hirsch had already picked up one of the sound-powered telephones connected to the CIC. "The *Valley Forge* picked off one of the missiles. Counting the one the Tomcats splashed, that means only two left."

"Only four missiles?" Coleman said with relief. "I would think a monster like *Kirov* could fire more than that."

"They've got twenty launchers, General, and they're laid in vertically, so in theory they should be able to salvo all of them at once," Moyne explained. "But we've never seen them launch more than four at a time. It's probably got something to do with a limited number of fire-control channels."

"I'm not complaining, Captain. We need every break we can get. When are they going to get here?"

"Any minute now," Moyne said. He thought for a minute, then added nervously, "You know, General, these could be *nuclear* missiles. The Russians use the same airframe for both conventionally armed and nuclear missiles."

"Don't worry, son, they're not shooting nukes," Coleman said reassuringly. "The Soviets don't work like that. They're not nearly as reckless as..."

The horizon lit up in a bright flame followed by a mushroom of thick, black smoke. A roar of noise rolled across the sea and shook the mighty *Missouri*.

"What the hell was that?" Coleman demanded.

"I don't know," Moyne said, troubled. "It looks like one of the support ships took a hit."

Hirsch bounded across the flag bridge. "Did you see that?" he exclaimed. "The *Baker* just evaporated!"

"That explains it, General," Moyne said. "The *S. L. Baker* is—or was—

a civilian containership chartered to haul munitions for the task force. She was loaded with rockets and missiles and shells for the ships. No wonder she went up like that."

"Oh, good," Coleman sighed. Then, noticing the astonished look on the other men's faces, he added. "Well, not good. It's a tragedy. But at least I was right about the Russians. I thought for a minute, though, the way that ship blew up, they *were* using nuclear weapons."

The men stared silently at the smoke on the horizon. The two other support ships closed in on the *Baker,* which was going down fast.

"There *might* be some survivors," Moyne said, although his tone of voice suggested rescuers would find nothing left of the thirty crew members on board.

"That leaves just one left," Hirsch said breathlessly.

"And there it is!" Moyne shouted. He pointed off the stern to starboard. Coleman strained his eyes and finally made it out. The missile was surprisingly large and getting larger as it closed in on the *Missouri.* The big ship swung to starboard, trying to bring both Phalanx guns on that side to bear.

Whump! The chaff launchers directly below pumped a shower of blinking tinsel into the air. The lumbering battleship struggled to move its huge bulk out from under the cloud of chaff in case the missile took the bait and went for the decoy instead of the prize. Shouts rang across the deck as lookouts spotted the missile. Like demented robots, the white-domed Phalanx mounts sprang to sudden life, nodding and swiveling. The forward Phalanx sniffed its prey first, winding up into a roar. The second quickly joined in, spewing a stream of 20-mm shells made from depleted uranium at a rate of three thousand rounds per minute.

The Phalanx cannons swept the sea, searching for the missile. The streams crossed about a hundred feet from the ship, where they shut down automatically to prevent their fire from hitting the *Missouri* itself. The Soviet missile roared over the battleship's stern, unharmed and unerring in its flight.

"Shit!" Moyne shouted. "We missed."

"Well at least it missed us," Hirsch said, relieved.

"It's heading for the *Constellation!*" Coleman pointed off to port. "Look!"

The missile zoomed on, fire bursting from its twin engines, the four wings neatly lined up on the flat top of the aircraft carrier, like cross hairs on a gun sight.

"We've got to bring it down!" Moyne yelled above the roar. "If it hits the *Connie* with all those planes on deck..."

His words were lost in a deafening clatter, as the Phalanx batteries on the port side opened up automatically. The missile was caught in a beam of yellow tracers. A burst from the forward mount snapped a wing. The missile cartwheeled and broke up, scattering pieces across the sea. The Phalanx batteries wound down. A silence settled over the *Missouri;* then a cheer rose from the sixteen hundred officers and men on board.

Coleman snapped his cap on the brow, smiling. Hirsch beamed. Moyne clicked on the intercom: "Combat, this is Flag. Any more missiles incoming?"

"Negative." The exec's voice on the intercom sounded relieved. "All screens are clear."

"Whew, that was a close one!" Hirsch sighed.

Coleman stared out to sea. It could have been a hell of a lot worse. As it stood, they were about even. One frigate damaged plus one support ship sunk equaled one dead destroyer in the mathematics of war. The equation balanced. Everybody lost; nobody won. They could stop now.

He admired the gently rolling ocean with relief. The screech of alarms and detonations had ceased. Salt spray wafted away the irritating smell of cordite. Halfway between the *Missouri* and the *Constellation* the sea bubbled in white foam. A deep blue missile rose from the ocean and streaked in a low trajectory straight for the carrier.

"Vampire!" screeched the intercom. "Missile in the air."

"Where did *that* come from?" Coleman shouted. Then he suddenly remembered the *Charlie II*–class submarine marked "gone?" on the plotting board. Clearly, the Soviet sub was far from gone and had used the diversion from the *Kirov* to press its attack. It was a well-thought-out operation, with no communication between the battle cruiser and the attack sub. No doubt the plan was worked out well in advance for just such a contingency.

There was nothing anyone could do. The missile shot straight at the *Connie* in a low arc, embedding itself in the carrier's fantail. The red blossom of the missile's warhead quickly set off secondary fires and explosions of aircraft fuel cells igniting and munitions cooking off on the crowded deck. From ten miles away Coleman could see the billowing tower of black smoke.

"*Constellation* reports a general emergency," Hirsch said, looking up from the sound-powered telephone. "Fire out of control. They can't even get in there to clear the deck with a tug. They're going to have to let it burn itself out."

"Is it going to sink?" Coleman asked Moyne.

"No. *Constellation* should stay afloat. The carrier's got an armored flight deck built to take hits from major-caliber bombs. But she's not going to be much help from now on. What good's an aircraft carrier without aircraft?"

"You don't think there's going to be anything left?"

"No, sir," Moyne said. "Not after this. That fire's going to spread from plane to plane. In an Alpha strike, all available aircraft are loaded up and spotted on deck. It's just a question of time."

"What about the planes in the air?" Hirsch asked.

"They're going to have to divert, that's for sure," Moyne said. "Although

I don't know where to. They've only got enough fuel to reach Oman, and the sultan won't let them land there. They'll have to ditch, I guess. This is why Meredith pushed so hard for another carrier, General. You need the flexibility of cross-deck operations out here in the middle of nowhere."

"Tell them to head for al-Quaseem," Coleman said firmly.

"Excuse me, General, but do you think that's wise?" Hirsch said tentatively. "According to Admiral Meredith, Brick White is trying to distance himself from the U.S. I would think the last thing Sheik Hassan wants is to give the impression he's letting American warplanes stage out of there for raids on Iran."

"Have you got any better ideas, Commander?" Moyne shot back. "Don't forget, the *Constellation*'s rescue choppers went up in flames with the rest of the aircraft on deck. If those pilots ditch in the middle of this shark-infested water, you'll never get to them in time."

"Don't worry. I'm sure the sheik will let them land at Dar al-Harb. I just don't know if he'll let them take off again," Coleman said. "We've got bigger problems than that right now. We need to get in touch with somebody higher up and stop this thing before it gets any further."

"You're right, General," Moyne said. "But it's the middle of the night in Washington. The CNO is asleep."

"I wasn't talking about some damn sailor," Coleman said. "Get me Brick White on the horn."

"Begging your pardon, General," Hirsch said nervously. "But shouldn't we try to contact someone higher up, someone in Washington? After all, General White is..."

"Brick White can talk to the president directly, and that's what we need now," Coleman thundered.

Hirsch nodded dully and picked up the line.

"Excuse me, General," Moyne said. "But the battle group needs orders. What should we do now?"

"Nothing."

"Nothing?"

"Yes, Captain," Coleman sighed. "If time weighs heavy on your hands, you can help the survivors, try to put the fire out on the *Connie,* and maybe sink that goddamn submarine. But unless the Soviets attack again—and I think that poor bastard of a Russian captain on the *Kirov* is as confused as we are at this point—I don't want you making any offensive moves. Is that clear?"

"But, sir, we can't..."

"Now you listen to me, son," Coleman said angrily. "This is the real thing. Us against them. Direct combat between Soviet and American forces. So far, it's a draw. We started it. Let's not compound the error, or the next missiles they send over *will* be armed with nuclear warheads."

"But can't we even send over a P-3 and get targeting data?" Moyne pleaded. "We ought to at least..."

"Don't do anything!" Coleman bellowed. "Do you understand? It was an accident. Let's make it look like that. Call up Naples and tell them what happened. Use one of those codes the Russians have broken—I'm sure there are plenty to choose from. Keep your ships on alert and headed north. Keep your guard up. But don't make any hostile moves."

"Yes, sir."

Hirsch handed the receiver to Coleman. "It's General White, sir."

Coleman grabbed the receiver and leaned against the bridge railing, collecting his thoughts. The towering spire of smoke from the *Constellation* rose behind him; across the horizon, the *Missouri*'s helicopters buzzed over the patch of ocean that had swallowed the ammunition ship. He hoped Brick White could get to the president in time. He hoped the president could work out some sort of a deal with the Kremlin to prevent future fighting. But whatever the outcome, Coleman knew, Brick's troubles were just beginning. There was no way the crippled *Connie* could support the American soldiers at Bandar Abbas. It was all up to First Air now.

Coleman lifted the receiver. "General White? I'm afraid I've got some bad news..."

The Source

**Quaseem City
Emirate of al-Quaseem**

Top of the world. Why not?

At twenty-two stories, the Khalij Trust would go unnoticed in most major cities. But, as Peter Hillary had come to realize, things were never what they seemed in this part of the world. Like the city over which it towered, the Khalij Trust building was new and prosperous and no bigger than it needed to be. Ostentation was for those without.

Hillary was no longer without. New hope, new job, a new life. He stared out the wall of windows facing the Gulf and tried to determine whether his sudden good fortune resulted from Karma earned or owed. That notion had no place in Islam, of course, where men were bound to follow the will of God as actors in a play, a tragedy.

He had no use for either notion or for any other religion. As an educated man, Hillary could see no discernible evidence of a storybook God in the heavens and wondered, if there were such an entity, why it would bestow

225

on man reason to prove in a thousand ways God didn't and couldn't exist. As a war correspondent, he had seen firsthand the power and ravages of religion, which he considered the single most destabilizing force in the world.

Still, Hillary was happily troubled. In God's absence, he was hard pressed to explain the recent fortuitous turn of events. Less than two weeks before, he had been washed up, wiped out, shooting toward the rapids of alcoholic ruin. Now he was suddenly rich and powerful. Revenge and forgiveness were his to dispense. Hillary had seen power at work. He knew it was good to have. But he had never dreamed he would someday be on the other side, to have reporters, with their stubbornly maintained arrogance—easily transparent as envy, now—coming to interview him. *Him:* Peter Hillary, managing director, First Air Regiment, Incorporated.

Hands clasped behind him, the broad shoulders of his new Jermyn Street suit square with the world, Hillary gazed through the wide windows at the clutch of modern skyscrapers that formed Quaseem City. The buildings lowered and faded into the *dhow* port at the end of the creek that divided the upper island. To the northeast, the perpetual lights of Sammarah glowed their brilliant, sinful signals. And to the northwest, tiny planes, soundless bits of darkness in the blue sky, floated in from the Gulf to the black strips of Dar al-Harb and Quaseem International.

Hillary had waited long enough. He strode to his desk and pushed a button.

"As hum mawjood?"

"Na'am, sayyid." Hillary's secretary came through clearly on the intercom.

"Zayn," Hillary said. *"Shukran."*

Hillary knew the press had arrived and had been, in fact, stationed in the board room well before the scheduled start of the news conference, which was twenty minutes ago. But Hillary also knew power expected time as a token of respect. A life spent waiting for the powerful had taught him how the game was played. Twenty minutes should be enough to get their attention, he thought. That much could be politely explained away as *bukra,* the slippage of schedules and the lack of urgency so common in the Gulf. Any more than that, though, might convey a lack of organization, and that would not be good. Reporters would tolerate just about anything but poor organization.

Hillary stepped inside the private elevator, falling from the heavens to the waiting press. The office suite, which Hassan used rarely, had been built with the sheik's particular needs in mind. For security reasons, the elevator opened directly into the board room. It also lent a *deus ex machina* quality to Hassan's persona when he interrupted directors' meetings of the Khalij Trust with his sudden appearance. Hillary hoped to make a similar dramatic entrance today.

When the doors opened again, Hillary thought he had gone too far, thought the elevator had bypassed the ground floor and gone straight on to hell. Electronic strobes flashed in his face. The relentless beams of television lights lasered bright squares into his retinas. Even the heavy-duty air-conditioning system of the Khalij Trust could not keep pace with the hundreds of journalists packed in the room and the hall outside with their heated impatience and burning equipment. Hillary had wanted to arouse their curiosity. He had certainly done that; now he was almost sorry he had.

Bodyguards pushed the most persistent away. Hotel security men finally managed to clear enough room for Hillary to reach the podium. He held up a hand for order.

"Ladies and gentlemen, please. Quiet. I have a brief statement to read, and then I will be happy to answer all your questions. Please. Sit down."

Those few who had seats reluctantly sat. Most, however, remained standing, slouching against the walls or standing in the doorway. The video cameras continued to hum under the relentless glow of their artificial lights. Flashguns exploded intermittently like supernovas, accompanied by the impertinent whir of motor drives. Hillary had known the press for a pack of wolves, indeed, had run with them at their head. Now he was the wounded ox, the straggling cattle, their target. It was not a pleasant feeling, and he felt suddenly ashamed for much of his past.

Then he recovered. *This is different,* Hillary reminded himself. *This is the biggest story in the world, and they've got to come through me to get it.*

"At approximately 0600 this morning," Hillary began reading,

the USS *Missouri,* flagship of the U.S. Navy's Task Force Bravo, was conducting a routine weapons test in the northern Arabian Sea when the Soviet destroyer *Stoiky* appeared in the exercise area. The ship had already provoked a collision with the American frigate *Copeland* approximately thirty minutes earlier. Ignoring several warnings from the battleship's crew to stay clear, the Soviet destroyer was accidentally hit by a sixteen-inch shell from the *Missouri*'s main battery, with a serious loss of life.

The Russians responded with a salvo of antiship missiles launched from the battle cruiser *Kirov,* flagship of the Soviet Indian Ocean Squadron. Although the task force was able to defend itself against most of the missiles, one round hit and sank the chartered containership *S. L. Baker,* which was ferrying ammunition from Diego Garcia to the underway replenishment ships. The freighter went down with all hands.

A Soviet attack submarine then initiated an unprovoked attack on the USS *Constellation,* launching a missile that struck the aircraft carrier's flight deck. The explosion set off a fire that is only now coming under control. The bulk of the carrier's air wing was on the flight deck at the time, preparing for a scheduled air strike on Bandar Abbas this morning in support of the 82d Airborne's Division Ready Force. Most of the aircraft suffered class-three damage. The *Constellation* was rendered effectively out of action and will remain so for an indefinite length of time.

At this point in the incident, both sides contacted their respective national command authorities for guidance. An agreement has been worked out between Moscow and Washington. All American and Soviet naval combatants have been immediately ordered out of the Persian Gulf, the Arabian Sea, and the Indian Ocean north of the Tropic of Capricorn.

The press murmured softly to one another. They all knew what this meant—no more naval air cover for the American soldiers in Iran. Hillary gestured for quiet and continued reading from the statement.

At this moment, the Division Ready Force is under attack by elements of an Iranian armored division. The American peacekeepers—who have been welcomed by the Iranian people after their government's murder of the Islamic martyrs of Baghdad—are now isolated, cut off from the tactical, logistic, and medical aid that had been, up to now, abundantly supplied by the U.S. Navy.

Hillary paused. He looked up, straight at the reporters. Though he had memorized exactly what he was about to say, he wanted to give the effect of reporting spontaneously, from the heart. It was a technique that had always worked with him.

Less than forty-eight hours ago, Sheik Rashid Bin Ahmed al-Hassani, our beloved and most holy leader, survived an assassination attempt by the People's Revolutionary Islamic Council at the court of *Shari'a*. This cowardly and reactionary group of jackals has been brought to swift justice under the sacred law of Islam they sought to profane. However, many were injured and five innocent people were killed, including three members of the *Gahtell*, whose bravery and resourcefulness were instrumental in foiling the malevolent attack.

By the massacre of hundreds of thousands of the faithful in Iraq and by their sponsorship of this recent terrorism here in al-Quaseem, the government of Iran has revealed *itself* as the *Iblis,* the Great Satan of the sacred Koran.

Throughout history, when self-proclaimed holy men have strayed from the ways of Islam, Muhammad has chosen a champion, a *caliph,* to lead his people back to the path of the Prophet. Today, Sheik Hassan al-Quaseem formally assumes the title of *Amir al-Mu'minim,* commander of the faithful, to lead the true believers everywhere on a holy *jihad* that will rid the world of those who would blaspheme the name of Islam for their own dark purpose.

In this, Sheik Hassan wants to make clear he does not declare war on Iran itself but on those leaders who, in their worldly greed and jealousy, have perverted the promise of a truly Islamic state. Indeed, this is a war *for* the Iranian people, and Sheik Hassan welcomes the assistance of the faithful there who have been deceived and tyrannized by the false *mullahs* in Tehran. In this, he joins the people of the United States, a country that—despite its occasional excesses and lapses of judgment—boasts a proud record of sacrifice in the name of freedom and religious tolerance.

Hillary looked back at his notes.

That concludes my prepared statement. Now you all have the press release. That should answer most of your questions. I regret that I cannot respond to your numerous requests for personal interviews at this time. However, if there's anything further you'd like to know, please feel free to ask now.

The board room erupted again in tumult as reporters shouted out a din of simultaneous questions. Hillary picked out a familiar face in the crowd and pointed at a man in the front row.

"One at a time, please," Hillary said. "And I'm sure no one would mind if I start the news briefing with an old friend and colleague, Mr. Dennis Nelson of the *London Times.* And take it easy on me, please, Dennis. I'm new at this job."

The crowd laughed. Hillary knew humor would work to get them on his side. It had always worked on him. Nelson rose, eying Hillary with skepticism.

"All right, Peter, I'll make it easy for you," Nelson said, in a way that made it clear to Hillary he had no such intention. "My question is a simple one. What's the real story behind this First Air Regiment nonsense?"

The room grew silent, save for the reflex action of the news machinery.

Confrontation! Nothing played better. Lights flashed. Cameras clicked. Hillary smiled.

"I'm not sure I know what you mean, Dennis. Didn't you get a copy of the news release?"

Nelson nodded.

"Then I'm surprised," Hillary joked. "You're in print media, not television. You should still be able to read."

The crowd roared with laughter. Nelson's face turned red.

"Of course I read it. We all read it. But that can't be all there is to it."

"I'm afraid it is, Dennis," Hillary said patronizingly. "First Air isn't nearly as sinister as you chaps are making it out to be. It's a precaution, pure and simple. What with everything that's going on in the Gulf these days, Sheik Hassan is just calling in some extra help to protect his assets, that's all."

"I don't think so," Nelson said stubbornly. "I wouldn't call the cream of the Western tactical air community and dozens of front-line fighters 'extra help.' There's something else going on up at Dar al-Harb."

Hillary laughed. "Well, if there is, I wish you'd let me in on it. Have you been up at the air base, then?"

"No," Nelson admitted. "Nobody has. They won't let us near the place. You know that."

"But that hasn't kept you from filing stories, though, has it?"

Nelson ignored the insult. "Is the Regiment operational?"

Hillary paused. "Yes."

There was a gasp from those few in the room who recognized the significance of the term operational—First Air had completed training and working-up drills. It was now capable of carrying out missions.

"Is the Regiment going take part in Hassan's *jihad*? Is it going to bomb Iran?"

"If we had any plans to do so, I certainly wouldn't stand up here and tell you," Hillary smiled.

"That's not a denial! That's not a..."

Nelson's voice was lost in hoots and hisses from the impatient crowd. This was supposed to be a press conference, not a one-on-one between Hillary and Dennis Nelson. Hillary was relieved to hear the muttering and not-so-subtle calls for Nelson to sit down. He knew that Nelson, a careful and experienced foreign correspondent, would be his toughest critic. He had no intention of giving him anything to go on. By drawing out Nelson's questions, stalling for time, Hillary counted on the press to silence Nelson for him. And they were living up to his low expectations.

Hillary looked away. He was not proud of what he had done. Just two weeks before, in Bahrain, he had sat with Nelson at the bar of the Diplomat and complained about the shallowness and arrogance of television journalists. Nelson had stood by him to the last, after most reporters had ceased acknowledging Hillary's existence. And now Hillary had cut him, one of his own.

But that was the past. Hillary now saw the world from a different perspective, one that had no use for the prying eyes of dedicated investigative journalists. He needed the power of the electronic media and welcomed its reluctance to dig beneath the obvious, to accept whatever package was offered, as long as it was attractively wrapped. Truth be told, from what Hillary really knew about the First Air Regiment—and it was not much, certainly not nearly as much as he implied he knew—it could not stand up to the sort of scrutiny Nelson was capable of. But it made for wonderful images. So truth was out, and television was in.

He nodded to the next questioner, an anchorman from one of the American television networks. The man was dressed in a two-piece khaki outfit covered with pockets. Hillary had seen that look before on countless "war correspondents" in Vietnam who, in their two-week working holiday to "see what this war was all about," had rarely left the confines of their Saigon hotels.

"Mr. Hillary, I'm Troy Damon," he said smoothly. "As you know, I consider what you're doing so important I insisted on coming to al-Quaseem to get the story firsthand."

Hillary wanted to say, *"We can see that, you bloody fool,"* but said, instead, "Thank you, Mr. Damon. We appreciate the attention of such a well-known and respected journalist."

"You're welcome," Damon beamed. There was still a part of Hillary that shuddered at the obvious false flattery. But Damon represented forty million viewers nightly, a fact that would certainly help Hillary get over his ill feeling.

"Mr. Hillary, I *did* read the press release..." the anchor smiled at the smoldering Nelson while the crowd tittered, "but I'm afraid there are some points that are still unclear to me. Who exactly is in charge of this new air force?"

Hillary smiled and tried to hide his delight at the poorly phrased nature of what Damon obviously thought was a tough, pointed question.

"The First Air Regiment is not an air force in the strict sense," Hillary said. "It is, in fact, a private corporation chartered to provide security for al-Quaseem and its interests in the Gulf. While many pilots and aircraft that make up the Regiment may be seconded from the air forces and navies of various Free World countries, First Air is itself not a military unit representing any nation or group of nations or political beliefs. It is here to stop trouble, not start it. In that sense, it is more like a fire brigade than a police squad."

Hillary paused. Television digested news in thirty-second bites, and the line about First Air being a "fire brigade," he knew, was a good one. He didn't want to risk stepping on it and making for a difficult edit.

"In this case," Hillary continued, "the Regiment is under the operational command of the government of al-Quaseem. Day-to-day orders are given by Air Marshal Sultan Abdul Faisal Hassan, His Excellency, the crown prince of al-Quaseem."

This set the crowd buzzing. Sheik Hassan was good copy but somewhat inaccessible. His son, however, was a different story. Rich, charming, and desperately good looking, Prince Faisal was as familiar a sight on magazine covers as he was at the gambling tables and clubs of Sammarah. Men liked him, women loved him, and yet the notion of the fate of the Free World riding on his young shoulders was startling, unsettling, and, to the crowd, quite unbelievable.

"He's just a kid!" shouted a reporter. The crowd murmured its assent. Hillary was prepared for this. He held up his hand for silence.

"Prince Faisal is not a 'kid,' I assure you," Hillary said smoothly. "True, he is only twenty-five years old, but he has been trained for leadership since birth. Educated at Brown University and Cambridge, well traveled and experienced in the ways of the world, His Excellency is mature beyond his years."

This brought snickers from some reporters, including the few women in the crowd. What Faisal knew, he hadn't learned at Cambridge. Not unless the dons had all been replaced by debauched English rock stars.

"As far as his military qualifications are concerned," Hillary continued, "Prince Faisal's record is exemplary. After exchange tours with the Royal Air Force and the U.S. Air Force, he assumed command of the Royal Air Force of al-Quaseem last year. With more than five hundred hours in the F-16, His Excellency has led a team of Quaseemi pilots to fine showings in a number of multinational bombing and fighter competitions."

"Wait a minute!" shouted a reporter. "I heard Brick White was in charge."

"Yeah!" yelled another. "And what about Bobby Dragon? Somebody said he has something to do with all this!"

The crowd's interest picked up. *Bobby Dragon!* There was a story! The rumors had been flying in hotel lobbies and bars since the press invaded al-Quaseem a few days before. Those too young to remember—which included quite a few television reporters—were quickly filled in on the story. It had everything: drama, death, mystery. It might even be true.

"Gen. William White..." Hillary shouted to be heard above the din. "General White was indeed instrumental in the formation of the First Air Regiment and remains as air adjutant and advisor."

That didn't satisfy the crowd. Hillary knew it wouldn't. Even he was unclear about the part Brick White played in First Air. He had not seen Brick since Vietnam. For all Hillary knew, Brick wasn't even on the island. Not that Hillary was anxious to meet him again—the two men had never been on the best of terms. Strange that coincidence had brought them together after all the years, but he was not about to help it along. His brief meeting with Bobby in Sammarah was enough to let Hillary know those wounds that the Heartbreakers had suffered at the hands of Hillary and his kind had not healed over the long years.

"What about Bobby Dragon?" a voice in the crowd insisted.

"I cannot go into operational details at this open briefing," Hillary said with affected tiredness. "I'm sure you will understand why. The names of the pilots who make up the First Air Regiment must remain secret for security reasons."

Protest swelled from the crowd. Hillary could clearly hear one name repeated in the din. He leaned closer to the microphone.

"As far as Bobby Dragon goes..." The crowd hushed quickly. "I will neither confirm nor deny his affiliation with First Air. I must, however, remind you that the United States Department of Defense still lists Lt. Robert Dragon as missing in action since December 26, 1972."

The name Bobby Dragon buzzed and rippled through the board room. It was the sound of the colonial animal that was the press making up its mind. Hillary wondered if he had done the right thing. His directions from Sheik Hassan had been vague: Get the Western media on our side, he had said. Make them feel good about First Air. Keep their interest with good pictures but keep them too far away to get the facts. The sheik knew enough about the Western press to recognize its ultimate, if arbitrary, power. Hassan also knew it could be manipulated, but only from the inside out, from someone who knew the correct buttons to push and strings to pull.

"This is all rather ghoulish speculation," Hillary attempted to change the subject. "Let's get on with the next question, shall we?"

He pointed to a young woman, a correspondent for CNN.

"Mr. Hillary, it's difficult to know exactly what's going on over at Bandar Abbas, but all indications point to a difficult position for the American forces, quite at odds with your eyewitness report," she said. "Can you explain the reasons for this discrepancy?"

There it was. The challenge. Hillary knew it would come to that. He was prepared. Once again he admired Hassan's insight and perception. The sheik's offer to Hillary was the best thing that could have happened, the only thing that could have saved Hillary's reputation, his life. Still, he knew, though he had all the cards, he had to play them correctly.

"I won't comment on my story from Bandar Abbas."

"You aren't retracting the story?" the reporter asked. "Are you saying what you wrote was true?"

"I won't comment on it."

Flashguns blew in Hillary's face. He tried to remain calm. He was almost there. He knew what the reporters were thinking. He would have thought the same thing himself. He was one of their own not too long ago, and although they were quite alone in this estimation, reporters considered themselves creatures of virtue, driven by a restless worship of truth. Facts *were* for sale, but at a very high price indeed. To twist the truth and thereby banish himself from their ranks—a fate reporters thought preferable only to lethal injection—Hillary must have had a very good reason.

Hillary had heard the stories: that the whole thing was planned from the beginning. That he had written the false story just to buy time to set up a mercenary air force in al-Quaseem. That Hillary secretly worked for MI-5, or any number of spooky American organizations.

Actually, it was all true. Or it could be made to look that way. And from his former life as a journalist, Hillary knew that was just as good. As long as he never said so himself, the press would jump the short hurdles of coincidence and intimation he laid out for them. That they were actually running the course backward was of no concern; it was, after all, a circular track in the shape of a halo—salvation and a new life for Peter Hillary.

The reporter pressed the point: "Did Sheik Hassan offer you the directorship of First Air before or after your visit to Bandar Abbas?"

"Really, I'm quite surprised and insulted at your insinuation," Hillary said with mock anger. "I organized this briefing in good faith, and how am I repaid? I read wild stories about some sort of flying mafia out to destroy Iran. And as if that wasn't enough, you as much as call me an agent in the pay of some Western government. I really must leave now. I have too much to do to waste my time listening to such idle speculation."

Hillary turned and headed for the elevator. Reporters and cameramen rushed toward him, only to be held back by security officers and Hillary's new bodyguards. The doors closed. Hillary smiled as the elevator took him back to heaven.

The Heartbreakers' Ball

Al-Quaseem International
Emirate of al-Quaseem

Morning sunlight filled the circular ventilating shaft cut in the east end of the otherwise dark and cavernous hangar. The whirring blades of the cooling fan chopped the light into bright pulses that impacted the makeshift stage like tracer bullets. The shuttering light lent an ethereal, mysterious quality to the figure of a man standing alone on stage, straight and still. The effect of the strobing sunlight was unwelcome and certainly unplanned; no stagecraft was needed to make the reemergence of Bobby Dragon a dramatic event.

Bobby stood, caught in the light, as the pilots' stares washed over him like the flickering sunbeams. He could almost feel their gaze; he could certainly hear the murmurings. Since his arrival, Bobby's presence in al-Quaseem had been an open secret, but few had seen him in the flesh. In the yellow morning and blue twilight he flew alone, cutting curves in the desert air to keep his edge. In between, he stayed locked in the ops shack with Brick

White and Krypto Padgett planning...something. What? That was what the men of First Air had gathered to find out.

The Regiment entered through the side door of the closed hangar in twos and threes, grown men in baseball caps and techno-rococo watches that would embarrass a Japanese schoolboy. Those few who were not scheduled to fly were dressed in street clothes, the garish, all-too-casual look of off-duty combat pilots, completely inappropriate for al-Quaseem or any other civilized country, for that matter. Most, however, wore flight suits, one-piece coveralls made of pockets and Nomex. Bobby gazed as the auditorium filled up with the greens, grays, blacks, and tans of the uniforms issued by the various air forces whose pilots made up the First Air Regiment. He shook his head. *How can they expect to fly together?* he wondered. *They don't even dress alike.*

The men settled into rows of folding chairs set up in front of the stage. Bobby was pleased to see they arranged themselves according to types of aircraft rather than nationality. Two weeks together, days of flying and nights of drinking, had assembled them into the flying machine that was First Air. The heat of battle would provide the final weld that pulled the machine together. Or the fire that would cause that machine to crash and burn.

"All right, listen up!" Bobby called. "My name is Bobby Dragon. I am the director of operations for the First Air Regiment. I have been given the honorary rank of colonel in the Royal Air Force of al-Quaseem for the duration of this assignment. So have you. Congratulations, men—you're all colonels now!"

There were laughter and some cheering. It was a good way to break the ice; even Bobby smiled. Brick had devised an elaborate scheme to determine the hierarchy of pilots in the Regiment, based on their rank in their respective air services, flight time, relative importance of home country, and so on—Bobby threw it out. It was exactly the type of elitism that destroys elite units, he said. There was no need for a rigid chain of command if everyone was capable. And if they were not capable, they didn't belong in First Air. There were, of course, operational roles to be cast—flight leader, mission commander, that sort of thing. And who would decide that? Bobby would. End of discussion. Brick agreed.

"Now, I'm sure you all know what's been going on in the Gulf the past couple of days. It's bad, and it's getting worse. The Navy has bugged out. The paratroopers have had their hands full with tanks. And here's a flash you might not have heard about—there are more tanks heading their way."

The pilots whispered quietly to one another in a dozen languages. They all realized the Division Ready Force could not withstand another armor attack.

"So it's come to this. At this moment, the First Air Regiment is the only real Free World military power in the Gulf, the only thing keeping the Russians in Russia and the MiGs and the Iranians from sweeping the American invasion force into the sea. If you've ever wanted to make a difference, if you've ever dreamed of a big destiny, to be part of history—well, now's your chance." Bobby paused for emphasis and added, "It's time to go big or go home. And we're not going home. We fly this afternoon."

There was a hush. Suddenly, the hangar reverberated with cheering. Many pilots had thought the Regiment was only a political artifice to show the Soviets a solid Western front. Others believed that First Air was real enough but that by the time the Regiment was ready for combat, the crisis in the Gulf would be settled, one way or another. The news that they were about to fly a mission electrified the pilots, who erupted with excitement and relief.

"This is what we came here for!" Bobby shouted over the din. "This is what we've been working toward. It shouldn't come as a shock to anyone. It's a little earlier than I'd hoped, but we asked the Navy for two weeks at a minimum, and it turns out that's exactly what we got. If there's anybody here who doesn't feel 100 percent confident in his ability to fly the mission, then, for God's sake, get out now and do us both a favor."

Bobby scanned the pilots. As expected, none of them moved. He walked to the back of the stage and snapped on an overhead projector.

"This is Operation Private Lightning," he said. "If it starts sounding familiar to you, it's because you've been practicing it for the past two weeks without knowing it. I hope the bad guys are as bored as you are with these late afternoon hops and think today's just another drill. You've only been rehearsing your little part. This is the big picture."

Bobby placed a transparency on the projector. The Gulf coast of Iran around the Strait of Hormuz appeared in stark black and white behind him.

"The objective of Private Lightning is simple," he said matter of factly. "We're going to blow the hell out of everything on the Iranian coast from the fifty-sixth meridian, inclusive. Make a lot of noise, lots of smoke. The idea is to create pacifists, to convince the Iranians that heroes are an endangered species. I want them to think every airplane in the world is over Bandar Abbas personally looking for them. We can do it. We've just got to make the most of our resources and not screw up."

Bobby pointed at a spot along the coast.

The area we're concerned about is a twenty-mile stretch of beach from the Iranian naval base to Bandar Abbas International. That's just about all that's out there for hundreds of miles—if you control Bandar Abbas, you control the Strait of Hormuz and pretty much all of the Iranian Gulf coast from Bandar-e Lengeh to Charh Bahar.

There aren't that many roads in that part of the country, let alone ports and airfields. And there's a serious mountain range and parts of two deserts between the Gulf and the rest of Iran. If we can neutralize the resistance along this stretch, we can bring in the rest of the 82d along with everything else we need to accomplish the mission. If we can't, then we've failed, and every American soldier in Iran is going to die. It's that simple.

Bobby paused to let that sink in.

Our primary mission today is to relieve the pressure on the Division Ready Force at Bandar Abbas International. It's going to be a bit sticky, because the bad guys are practically right across the street from the friendlies. Also, we don't want to tear up the runway because the 82d wants to use it when we're through with it. So that means nothing heavier than cluster bombs for the strikers at the airport. And you Hog drivers better check your guns, because you'll definitely be needing them.

"Now, I've been on the horn to a Sergeant Willis over at Bandar Abbas," Bobby smiled grimly. "Yes, Operation Ready Eagle, the American invasion of Iran, is now under the command of an enlisted man. That's how much the situation has deteriorated there. I don't know what happened to all their officers, and I didn't ask. Sergeant Willis tells me he'd much rather risk getting fragged by friendly fire than the near-certainty of being chewed up by Iranian tanks, but it's not a yes-or-no question. If you watch what you're doing out there and get in close enough, chances are no one will get hurt except the guilty parties.

"That's the big picture," Bobby said. "We'll get into tactics a little later. But now, a detailed look at threats and targets. I'm going to turn the briefing over to our regimental S-2, Krypto Padgett."

Padgett sat up nervously from a folding chair in the front row and walked quickly to the stage. Unfolding his hated glasses, he began reading from notes.

"I'm Dick Padgett, First Air intelligence officer, seconded from the U.S. Air Force," he said in a small voice. "You'll have to forgive my manner. In the spook business they give you free karate lessons, but, needless to say, they don't teach public speaking."

No one laughed at Krypto's joke, so carefully rehearsed. He flushed, buried his nose in his notes, and pressed on.

I'm afraid there's not a lot of hard information about the MiGs. They are nominally an Afghan Republic Air Force conversion unit—Training Squadron 22—but there are very few students there. And since no Afghan pilots have ever flown the MiG-29 operationally, I'd have to assume the unit is more or less a subterfuge, a way to keep a front-line Soviet fighter presence while maintaining the pretense of a complete withdrawal from Afghanistan, for the sake of world public opinion.

Squadron 22 flies the latest version of the Fulcrum A, with the enlarged horizontal stabilizers and software update for the fire-control system. They are Soviet-made models, not export versions. The unit apparently has more aircraft than it needs, so combat losses and maintenance problems haven't affected their operations.

We'll go into their tactics in detail later in the briefing. Right now, let's just say they are a very, very tough nut to crack—I got the word from a couple of new First Air aviators from the *Ike,* who have been fighting the Fulcrums for the past couple of weeks.

The MiG drivers are all good pilots, individually, all sound aviators. But what makes them so formidable is that they work together very well. They've got excellent flight discipline. They cover each other's six and they stick tight. It's very rare you get a clean shot at one without having a couple of others moving in on you. They use the Stairstep, they use the Box and the Pincers, they come in together, and they separate together. They've been flying as a unit for a long time, and it shows. So be careful. Just assume there's always somebody lining up on you, even though you can't see him. Because chances are there is.

The air defenses at Bandar Abbas are tough. There aren't that many, maybe, but these guys are good. After the Navy started going after the SAM sites, the Iranians began moving them around just about every day. The trip-A also moves constantly, and there's a lot of it, so watch out for guns wherever you are.

Padgett placed an overlay on the map of the coastline.

These are the major locations for Iranian HAWK batteries. Like I said, they move around a lot, but they come back to these spots frequently. At least, this is where they were yesterday. Don't ask me how I know, just take my word for it. So we're just going to nominate every known site and strike it. If you get there and there's nobody home at your target, call me up—I'll be on the net, call sign K-Ball—and I'll give you another one. There are plenty of targets to go around.

Padgett drew out a folding pointer and pinpointed spots on the map.

We're pretty sure they've got a HAWK site up on Genow Mountain. It was there a couple of days ago, and the Navy didn't touch it. There's only one way to get up the mountain from the ground, a road—just a trail, actually—along the north slope. It's difficult to get a jeep up on the mountain, let alone a SAM battery, so they probably won't move it unless they have to.
  Another favorite HAWK site—right here.

Padgett tapped a spot on the coast road at the west end of Naval Air Station Bandar Abbas.

There's a cannery there, and they site the missiles in a paved storage area between the plant and the end of the runway, right on the beach. That way they can cover the port, the air station, and a good ways out into the Gulf. They may have moved the battery, but probably not very far—it's too good a position to pass up.

"Other HAWK sites? Here, here, and here," Padgett slapped the map. The pilots began to grumble worriedly. "Hey, don't blame me! If they would have asked, I could have told them arms for hostages was a bad idea—there's no such thing as an Iranian moderate."

Padgett went back to the map.

HAWK sites have been spotted at the naval base, here, at the east end of Bandar Abbas, here, and over here, at this little village at the foot of the mountain, called Tazeyan. Now, I'm not saying there are SAM batteries at each of these locations. They only have so many missiles. I'm just saying that when they've moved their sites around, these are some places where they've shown up. If it's any help, my guess is that there are really only two HAWK batteries active, one at the cannery and one on the mountaintop, but you just never know. Keep your eyes out and watch the cuts on your RHAW gear.
  As far as targets go, there's nothing particularly hardened, which is good. Remember, we plan to use most of these facilities

once we scare everybody away, so try not to bust a runway or sink a ship in a harbor. Starting from west to east, there's a new naval base over here.

Padgett pointed to the left side of the map.

There are some guns on the ground, but your main threats are the weapons systems on the ships themselves. Fortunately, most of Iran's modern ships are up north or at the bottom of the Gulf, but these little patrol boats can shoot some nasty short-range SAMs, and they've all got decent gun systems. Those boats are your main targets—try to get them at the docks and don't let them out in open water.

Padgett's pointer moved up the coast to the commercial port of Bandar Abbas.

This is the new port, a vitally important target. It's the only place you can dock ships big enough to carry tanks and construction material and the rest of the heavy equipment the U.S. will have to get ashore if it's going to make the invasion go. Every other port is too shallow for deep-draft ships, but this one has been dredged out for supertankers. Fortunately, since it's a commercial port and out of the range of Iraqi air strikes, the Iranians haven't made any moves to fortify it. You might see some guns there, but no heavy stuff.

Padgett shifted to an inlet at the center of the map.

Now over here are three targets so close together they might as well be considered the same one. There's the probable HAWK site at the cannery—we've already discussed that—the old port, and the naval air station. The air base is a real prize. It's got a runway long enough for most C-130s and C-141s, and it's untouched. There were some P-3s based there, but in the panic after the bomb they disappeared. I understand one of the Iranian Orion pilots loaded up his family and flew to Syria right before the 82d landed. If that's true, he's probably the smartest Iranian who ever lived.

The old port is virtually useless for our purposes. It's shallow and fouled. Nothing can get in or out of there but *dhows* and fishing boats and the occasional coastal freighter. Until the new port was completed a few years ago, big bulk carriers had to heave-to a mile or so offshore and transfer their cargo to smaller ships. There are some gunboats based there now—those Swedish Bogenhammer speedboats with the big engines that the Navy hates so much. They stage their missions from the abandoned oil platforms in the Gulf, but this is their home base. As far as I'm concerned, that's as good a reason as any to make a statement here. Just blow the hell out of it.

East of that, there's the city of Bandar Abbas itself. It's of little significance, militarily, and it's already in pretty bad shape. The Iranians have been fighting each other there for a couple of weeks, and the city center is in ruins. Most everyone who could leave already has. There are mainly just old people and children and women left there now. I think we should leave it alone. If you start taking hits from somewhere in the city, then go ahead and return fire—this isn't Vietnam, and we don't want to make those mistakes again. But my guess is that most people there have had enough of war for a lifetime and just want to be left alone.

At the east end of the city, about a mile out of town, the coast road forks. One branch dead-ends at the inlet to this little seasonal river, which is dry now.

Padgett pointed to a blue line on the map.

The other branch swings north to the airport and runs between these two mountains to a tunnel about twenty klicks up the road. My guess is that by the time we get there, you'll find the Iranian tanks somewhere along this road between the city and the airport. If something happens and they get delayed, we should still be able to spot them, seeing as we're hitting targets all up and down the coast. Just keep your eyes peeled, and if you see any tracks, call in and report them.

Padgett folded his pointer and snapped off the overhead projector. "That's all I have, gentlemen. Any questions?" Padgett looked for hands in the audience and saw instead only faces deep in thought. "All right, then. Good luck today, men. Be careful."

Bobby stepped back to the stage. He paused to take a deep breath. This was the hard part. This was the point in the briefing where he was supposed to give a little pep talk, exuding confidence and sending his killers cheerfully on their way with a sense of sport and invulnerability. Brick White was a master at it, but it was all new to Bobby, and he was shaking inside. Today he would lead the Regiment into a wilderness that had killed many good pilots, men in some ways better prepared than the ones whose faces he was staring into now. He saw his concern mirrored in their eyes. *How can I protect these men?* Bobby thought. *How can I tell them they will all return safely when we all know no one can promise that?*

"All right, time hack," Bobby said, with as much authority as he could muster. He had always wondered why every ops officer continued, in these digital days, to begin his summation with a mindless check of the time. Now he knew. It settled you down—most people adrift in uncommon surroundings grasp for the familiar. It was necessary, after all. But mostly, it was because time was the one thing in the entire briefing that everyone knew was absolutely true.

"It'll be exactly seventeen after, Zulu, on my mark. Ready? Fifty-eight, fifty-nine, hack!"

Like every other pilot, Bobby pushed the button down at the signal and then realized he was the one man in the Regiment who didn't need to. *What to say next?* Words of inspiration would come later, if he could think of any. He decided to begin with what he knew best: tactics.

We'll discuss specifics like TOTs, IPs, and ROE at the Warlords' meeting when we break up into individual flight briefings. Right now, though, let's go through an overview of the entire mission.

We're going to step about 1700. The strike is planned for right around sundown, for a number of reasons. First, because of the extremely high humidity this time of year, there's a thick haze, especially around sunrise and sundown. The haze reaches up to five to ten thousand feet and gets particularly dense along the coastline. That means you strikers fragged for missions right on the Gulf might not be able to see your targets until you're right on top of them. But then again, the gunners on the ground won't be able to see you, either.

Another good reason for a later afternoon attack is that Muslims are obligated to pray at sunset, and we might catch them out of position. I feel kind of bad about this, but taking advantage of national religious habits has become sort of a tradition in surprise air strikes. The Japanese attacked Pearl Harbor on Sunday—in December, no less—and the Yom Kippur strikes show that this is a useful tactic, if not particularly forthright.

But the best reason for going at sunset is that if we come in from the west, the sun will be right in the eyes of the MiG drivers and the ground gunners. Again, this seems like a small thing, but you guys know what I mean—it's hard as hell to pick out a fighter coming out of the sun, and with it so bright over here you get lazy and you don't even want to look. Remember, the guns on the ground are just as big a threat as the SAMs and the MiGs. They can ruin your whole day, and you'll find those folks just about anywhere. Plus, the angle of the sun will give us good contrast for electro-optically guided systems like Maverick and Pave Tack. It just makes sense.

I'll go in first with Breaker flight. The Cannonball will be right behind us, with the Tornadoes orbiting out over the Gulf. There'll be another flight of F-15s right behind, locked onto us so we don't get hosed by our own people. We're going to head straight into Bandar Abbas from over the coast, line abreast, a four-ship wall of Eagles at around flight level three hundred or so. That ought to get their attention.

We'll sweep the area from the city to the northwest, all the way up to the Shamil pass. If we don't run into any MiGs by then, we'll swing around by the coast, come back to the city, and do it again. The Eagles behind us will do the same, followed by a couple of flights of Tomcats. The idea is to set up a series of fighter sweeps at intervals of about thirty miles, close enough for mutual support but far enough away that we can keep track of who the good and bad guys are.

Now, the biggest advantage the F-15s and F-14s have are their long-range missiles. The biggest drawback is that rules of engagement usually prevent us from using those missiles at long range. This plan lets the fighters shoot at anybody they can lock onto. I'm not going to stick my neck out in this twin-tailed tennis court they call the F-15 and fight like I'm in a little F-5 or something. I'm going to use everything I've got. At these odds, I have to. I'm going to use my BVR missiles at beyond visual range, the way God and Raytheon intended, and if some poor sucker gets a Fox Two in the snot locker because he wasn't following the program, then tough shit.

This touched off a cheer among the air-to-air pilots in the back of the auditorium. Here, at last, they felt, was an operations officer who understood how they operated.

Hopefully, the Cannonball will be able to sniff out where the HAWK batteries are and who's on the air and call in the Tornadoes before they get a lock on us, but don't count on it. Protect yourself out there. Remember, these are American missiles, HAWKs, and they're tough to beat. We've got the codes, now, thanks to our pen pals in the *Heyl Ha'Avir,* but that just gets you started. Don't forget, the break for the HAWK is up, not down, and it only works once, so get it right the first time. I expect a skyful of SAMs today, but the good news is that that should be it. Lucky for us, they shot most of their missiles at the Navy over the last couple of weeks. And if it's any consolation, the HAWKs are shooting at the MiGs, too. Welcome to the Wild West.

You heard Krypto Padgett talk about the MiGs, and they are good. The Fulcrum is by far the best fighter the Soviets have come up with since the MiG-21. I know—I've flown it. And their pilots are no hamburgers either. But they're not invincible. You can take them one on one. I know you can.

Bobby said seriously, "I've seen your records. You're the best of the best. It can be done, and you can do it."

He paused to let his words sink in. Coming from Bobby Dragon, a compliment like that meant a lot to the pilots. Bobby searched their faces to see if it had had the effect he intended. It did. He continued:

The trick to beating these guys is playing your game and not theirs. Try to split them off. Fight in the vertical rather than the horizontal. Try to pick them off before the merge and don't try to turn with them. Never, *never* stay in the furball. Just blow on through, then separate. I don't care if you're in an F-16 and think you can get behind them with one of those square turns you're so fond of. They'll always outnumber us, and like Krypto said, they are very good at coordinating their attacks. We're not fighting individuals out there as much as a system. And if we're going to come out alive today—much less win—we're going to have to break down that system first.

One good way to unravel the furball is to shoot down as many MiGs as you can before the merge. That's easier said than done— the Fulcrum has a pretty good BVR capability itself. Their look-down, shoot-down mode isn't all it's cracked up to be, but on the other hand, we're fighting over water and sand here most of the time, so there's not a lot of surface clutter to lose yourself against.

Once you get to the mountains you can probably hide. My advice to you strikers is to ingress at an oblique angle—say, through the

Shur Valley or over the rocks at Tang Dalan—as low and as fast as you can, instead of just coming in over the city straight from the Gulf. That will give you some surface features to hide behind and maybe enough offset to blank out the Fulcrum's radar with a zero-Doppler turn. It's worth a try, anyway. At any rate, stay as low as you can as long as you're feet dry. Our rules of engagement say we can kill anything above flight level one hundred without even looking, so staying low will help keep you safe from our fighters as well as theirs.

The Navy planes were cruising into Bandar Abbas at medium altitude, trying to conserve fuel. It must have looked pretty impressive, but they got hosed hard for their trouble. Everybody could see them, and if the Iranian HAWKs didn't get them, the MiGs did. So remember, strikers—the ground is your friend. Split the sand and shave the rocks. Fifty feet and the speed o' heat and you should be okay out there today.

You Phantom drivers, remember to keep your speed up, especially on the way in. I know you'll be pigging around out there today, loaded up with iron, being so close to the ground and it so hot. So be sure to nail your initial point far in advance so you won't have to turn until you come off the target. And after you do your ground pounding, drop everything and head for the Gulf. Don't stop for anything, and for Christ's sake don't go back to reattack the target. If you don't shack it today you can try again tomorrow. Unloaded and in burner you can stay with the Fulcrum at low altitude, but if you try to turn with him you're MiG chow. Guaranteed.

I've noticed some of you air-to-sand specialists carrying Sidewinders on the outboard pylons in addition to iron bombs. That's a good idea, but don't go overboard. That's why we've got fighters. We're there to protect you. Don't screw it up by chasing after MiGs and missing your target. That just means you'll have to go back tomorrow and hit it again. We can kill every MiG from here to Moscow, but if you don't nail your targets, the mission has failed and those guys on the ground are just a little closer to buying the farm. Remember, strikers, you're the reason we're out there. Nothing would please us more than to have the MiGs go home without us having to duke it out with them. Either way, we win.

You guys in the Tornadoes. Same thing. Don't slow down for anything. You've got it a little tougher in that you might have to reattack your targets several times, especially if they shut off their radars so the Cannonball can't get a fix on them. That's fine— if they're not radiating, they're out of business, and you've done your job just as effectively as if you'd pounded them in the sand. A hard kill is always a good thing, but not if you have to die to get it. Just make sure you never enter the target area the same way twice. Listen to the Cannonball and try to coordinate your attacks so they can't pick you off one at a time.

That goes for you Hog drivers, too. We're counting on the A-10s to keep the bad guys' heads down at the airport. Once you get around Bandar Abbas International, your biggest threat is going to be guns, not missiles and MiGs. There are an awful lot of automatic weapons on the other side of the airport road. We want you Hog drivers to set up a weave so that at least one of you is hosing their side all the time. If nothing else, you'll scare the crap out of them. One of the Cobra pilots from the *Saipan* says they might have some heavier stuff over there, too, either 20-mm Vulcans or maybe Shilkas captured from the Iraqis. If you see it, nail it, and don't stop shooting until it does. It's vital that we take out any AAA at the airport.

Bobby paused. His throat was dry. It seemed like he had been talking for hours. He looked at his watch. He had been speaking for five minutes. He searched his mind desperately for a big ending. Everything he had planned to say sounded glib or corny now that he was staring into the faces of the men—his men—who would soon be facing death under his command. Then it came to him: Stuff the Knute Rockne crap. He would tell the truth.

"That's all I've got," Bobby said.

But before we break up and head back to Dar al-Harb for the Warlords' meeting, I just want to say how proud I am of you guys and what you've accomplished in the past two weeks. They said it couldn't be done, and we did it. First Air is up and flying. And fighting. And it's thanks to your hard work.

It's going to be tough out there today, no doubt about it. I know you would have liked to have more time to train together. So would I. But we're not asking you to do anything you haven't done thousands of times before, back with your own units. We're just asking you to do it with new people. We're asking you to trust each other. Because that's what First Air is all about. If we can't fly together, we'll die together. We've got to trust in ourselves, in our wingmen, in the Regiment.

I know we haven't been together for very long, but I want to press home the fact that we are a unit, a single team. When we get out there today, I don't want you to think of yourself as a Navy pilot or an A-10 driver or a Frenchman, or whatever. Because however you may see yourself, whatever other group you belong to, today you are, first and foremost, a member of the First Air Regiment. The greatest group of fighter pilots in the world. I know it. You know it. Now let's go out there and prove it to the world.

Good luck, men. And good hunting.

The briefing ended with a cheer and the scraping of folding chairs echoing through the hangar. Bobby was relieved to find the pilots too engrossed in their own thoughts to try to engage him in conversation. The men filed out to board buses that would ferry them to Dar al-Harb. Bobby walked quickly through a door on the opposite side of the hangar.

"What's your hurry, hoss?"

Bobby blinked in the glare of the sunlight outside. He turned to see Daffy Brewer, in a Navy flight suit, leaning against the side of the hangar, smoking.

"So you never did kick the habit, did you?" Bobby asked.

"No, I never did," Brewer smiled, and flicked the cigarette on the concrete ramp. "After what we went through, I thought I'd never live long enough for it to make any difference."

Silence settled as they stared at one another. There was too much to say for words. Neither acted surprised to wind up at this remote spot together after so many years. A good crew—pilot and back seater—grew to become one in combat. They had been a good crew, once, and they could still seem to read each other's thoughts. Right now, Daffy was thinking about unfinished business, Bobby knew. He knew because he was thinking the same thing.

"You seen Brick yet?" Bobby asked, finally.

"No, not yet," Brewer said. "I just missed him on the *Eisenhower*. He was jawing with Meredith while Scooter and I were floating in a raft out in the Gulf."

"What do you think he's going to say when he finds out you're here?"

"Who knows?" Daffy shrugged. "What the hell, maybe he's mellowed. Maybe he's ready to let bygones be bygones. He rehabilitated you, didn't he?"

"That was different. He needs me," Bobby said. "Besides, I didn't steal his thunder."

"Hey, it wasn't my fault," Daffy protested. "What was I supposed to do? It was the Air Force's idea to give backseaters credit for kills, just like pilots. I had nothing to do with it."

"Well, you know how much Brick wanted to be an ace. That was the reason behind the tiger hunts in the first place. And you know how he felt about weapons system operators. That's why Brick kept changing his wizzos.

He didn't want backseaters to get any credit. If he could, he would have flown without them."

"That would have been fine with us," Brewer said bitterly. "Nobody liked flying with him anyway. If you're going to get shot at, it's only natural to want some say in the cockpit. But half the time Brick flew with the intercom switched off. If he had listened to Buzz Holman, he wouldn't have gotten shot down. And Holman would be alive today. Buzz was just a kid, but he was smart. He wouldn't have gone charging in like that."

Bobby stared across the runway and sighed.

"We were all kids back then, Daffy. Brick could have had the pope in the backseat that day, and he wouldn't have listened to him."

"I wish to God that Brick had listened to somebody," Daffy said sadly. "I wish none of it had ever happened."

"Hey, what are you complaining about?" Bobby asked with mock cheerfulness. "You're an ace. You're a hero. You're the man who shot down Colonel Doom, the terror of North Vietnam."

"I'm going to let that slide, Bobby. I don't deserve that, and you know it. The Air Force had to have a hero. The press was waiting at Da Nang. Washington needed to salvage something good out of the situation. Holman was dead. So was Brick, as far as we knew. You bugged out. I was the only one left. A hero by default."

"You can't tell me you didn't enjoy it."

"No, I didn't," Brewer said angrily. "It was the worst time of my life. The more fuss the Air Force made over me, the more the jocks gave me the cold shoulder. They thought I was some sort of social climber. They thought wizzos should stay in their place."

"Well, what did you expect?" Bobby asked. "A medal?"

"Oh, I got a medal, Bobby. I got lots of medals—one of each," Brewer said. "But I never asked for them. I didn't want them. I just wanted to be left alone. And they wouldn't let me alone."

"Is that why you joined the Navy?"

"Yeah. It was either that or get out."

"I would think the Navy'd be happy to get someone like you."

"You'd think so, wouldn't you?" Daffy sounded almost bitter. "The Navy's a strange world. They take care of their own. The trouble was, I wasn't one of their own. I had to get my congressman to get me in. Can you believe that, Bobby? My *congressman!* To get me *into* the goddamn Navy! Even at that, they took away my time in grade. I was a captain in the Air Force. I started my Navy career as the world's oldest ensign. But, because I was an all-jet ace, a decorated war hero, and such an exemplary naval aviator, I soon worked my way up to my present exalted status—the world's oldest lieutenant commander."

"So why did you do it?" Bobby asked. "Why didn't you just get out when your hitch was up?"

"This may be difficult for you hotshot pilots to understand, but I couldn't leave the service. I love to fly."

"Oh, I understand, Daffy. Believe me. I've kind of got the same problem myself," Bobby laughed softly. "Where else are you going to get people to pay you to fly thirty-million-dollar jet fighters? There's just one problem, though. Every now and then you have to go out and kill somebody."

"It comes with the territory, pal," Brewer said firmly. "I thought we settled that one back at Da Nang."

"I thought we did, too. But I guess not. It keeps coming up." Bobby tried to change the subject. "So, how's this new guy you're flying with?"

"Scooter? He's okay. Good hands, aggressive. But he's young. He could use some judgment."

"That's all right, Daffy. I'm sure you'll beat some sense into him. You did it to me."

"No, I didn't have to teach you anything," Brewer said wistfully. "You're a natural fighter pilot. That part of the legend is true. Scooter's good, but he's no Bobby Dragon."

"Good for him," Bobby said with a touch of irony. "Still, I'm surprised Brick invited you guys, considering this Scooter is so young and knowing the grudge he's got against you."

"He didn't invite us," Brewer smiled. "We sort of invited ourselves. Brick asked for one of the fighter squadron COs from the *Ike*. And you know Brick—backseaters are invisible to him. It never occurred to him an RIO would be in command. Hell, he probably forgot there's two seats in an F-14. Anyway, Scooter came along because he's been fighting MiGs over Bandar Abbas for two weeks now, and he hasn't bagged one yet. He's pissed. Now maybe that's not a good reason to hang your ass out on the line, but you've done more dangerous things for reasons that made even less sense. And don't tell me you haven't, because I was there, remember?"

"Well, at least he's still alive after all the Navy has been through down here," Bobby agreed. "That makes him good enough for the Regiment. But why did you join up?"

Brewer fixed Bobby with a hard gaze.

"I'm here," he said, "because you're here."

Bobby nodded. "That's what I was afraid of."

"What's the matter?" Daffy sounded hurt. "I thought you'd be pleased. It wasn't easy getting here, you know. First there was that thing with Brick. And then Meredith held up our orders. If you..."

"Look, it was me, okay?" Bobby exploded. "Not Brick. I was the one that told Krypto to dismiss your application. And when you decided to come anyway, I was the one who told Brick to slow down your orders. What, did you think I'd be *surprised* when you showed up? You don't think I knew what you were up to, where to find you? Hell, Daffy, I've spent the last two weeks up to my ass in personnel files from every fast-jet-rated Air Force, Navy, Marine, and NATO pilot there is. It's been hard *avoiding* you."

"You've done a damn good job of it so far," Brewer spat. "I'm sorry I'm not good enough for your little air force."

"It's not that, Daffy," Bobby said plaintively. "You know it's not that. You're one of the finest aviators I ever met."

"Oh, come on, Bobby. I get the picture. You don't have to blow smoke up my..."

"No, it's true. All that crap people said about me—the flying part, I mean—they had it all wrong. We were a team. We were the best."

"We can still be a team."

"No." Bobby turned away. "Can't you see? All these other guys, they volunteered. They heard about the Regiment, and they made up their own minds. With you it's different. It's personal. You came to help me out. And I appreciate it, but I don't need it, and I don't want it. I don't want to be responsible for anybody but myself. I can't handle it. Not now."

Brewer fished in his flight suit for another cigarette. You weren't supposed to smoke around the hangar. *What are they going to do—send us to the Persian Gulf?* Scooter had said that. Daffy listened to the match scrape in the silence. The gray smoke curled into the yellow sky.

"I've heard that song before, Bobby," Daffy said softly. "It's not your fault. They drill that crap into you in fighter school. *I'm in control. I can handle it.* You're not supposed to talk about what's bothering you. God forbid you should ask for anybody's help, even your backseater's. Then one day it gets to be too much, and you just fly away."

"I don't know what you're talking about," Bobby said, shortly.

"Oh, yes, you do." Brewer stared at the ground, then looked up. "Bobby, what happened?"

Bobby knew exactly what Daffy meant—that last mission over North Vietnam. "Oh, hell, Daffy, you know what happened. You were there."

"I was there, but I'm not sure I know what went on. As far as I could tell, it was a pretty good mission. Sure, Brick got smoked, but it was his own stupid fault. And we got Doom. That's what everybody wanted."

"That's just it!" Bobby's voice rose, broken. "That's what everybody wanted. But not me. That's not what I wanted. What kind of war is that? If you know who you're killing, it's not war anymore. It's murder."

"That's what war is, Bobby," Brewer said evenly. "You knew that when you signed up."

"No, it wasn't supposed to be like that. I joined to fly. And I'd fight for my country if I had to. But I didn't expect to help Brick assassinate people just to make a name for himself."

Brewer shook his head. "You didn't know what you wanted. You were just a kid."

"I'm not a kid anymore. But I still don't know what I want. What the hell am I doing here? Not too long ago, I didn't even know where al-Quaseem was. Now I'm supposed to be willing to die for it. Worse, I'm going to lead other men into battle who might have to die for it. Why?"

"Because that's what you do best, Bobby," Daffy said earnestly. "That's who you are. You're a fucking samurai, a warrior with honor. You may not realize it. You may not *want* to realize it, but I knew from the first time I flew with you that you were the best damn fighter pilot in the world, probably the best who ever lived."

"But I don't want to do it!"

"Hell, no, you don't want to do it," Brewer agreed. "But you have to. Ask any writer if they like to write. They hate it. It drives them crazy, but they're worse off if they can't. It's the same way with doctors, lawyers, executives—every leader from Caesar to Hitler to Brick White bitches about the awesome responsibility of power. Yet they'll die before they give it up. You've got a gift, Bobby. But it didn't come free. It never does."

"Some gift," Bobby said bitterly. "I'd give anything to get rid of it."

"And there isn't a pilot on this base who wouldn't give anything to have it. But it doesn't work that way. You can't transfer it. You have to do what you can do best."

"Kill people?" Bobby snorted.

"Yes," Brewer answered. "And save people. Protect them. Look, Bobby, I could give you a dozen good, sound political and moral reasons why we're here. Right now, it so happens we're the only thing standing between the world and World War III. You said so yourself at the briefing. I don't care if you believe it or not; it's a fact. But I know you, Bobby. I know you better than anybody here, Brick included. This John Wayne act you put on today is good. Real good. It's the right way to play it. But it's not you. It's not the Bobby Dragon I know."

"You don't think I could change in twenty years?" Bobby said defensively.

Brewer smiled. "Not really. Not that much. People never really change. Look at Brick—I bet he's still the same."

"So what are you saying? Are you afraid I'm going to cut out again?" Bobby asked. "You're not the only one that thought has occurred to, you know."

"No, nothing like that. I'm just saying that you're under a lot of pressure now. There's a lot riding on your shoulders. I know you have doubts. Everybody has doubts. But when you want to talk to somebody, do me a favor and come talk to me, okay?"

Bobby looked at Brewer and smiled. "Okay."

"And if you're looking for a reason for being here, there's a whole regiment's worth of them back at the bar who think riding on your wing makes them bulletproof. They're not here to fight and die for al-Quaseem or the United States of America. They're certainly not here because of Brick White, no matter what he thinks. They're here for the same reason I am. They came for you. Because you're the only man in the world who can make this thing work."

Brewer stood up straight and looked across the runway to the Gulf, north to Bandar Abbas, unseen across the distant horizon. He thought about the men trapped there, about the Russians in Tehran, about the Iranians left in their shattered country, about his family and home.

"And it needs to work, Bobby," he added softly, almost to himself. "It's got to."

Air War—Iran

Dar al-Harb Air Base
Emirate of al-Quaseem

Flight bags in hand, Brick White and Krypto Padgett stood outside the crew door of the brown-and-tan C-130 and stared suspiciously at the freshly painted nose art. Across a drawing that looked to Brick like a big malted-milk ball with a lit fuse sticking out the top, someone had stenciled: "The Carob Cannonball—Persian Excursion."

"I don't know about this," Brick muttered to Padgett. "I don't like the idea of going to war in a trash hauler."

Don Weasel popped his head out the hatchway and smiled. "Thanks for your vote of confidence," he said sarcastically. "You won't regret it."

Don disappeared back up into the cockpit, leaving Brick and Krypto to hustle their bags up the steep crew ladder. Truth be told, Don didn't like having Brick on board any more than Brick liked being there. Padgett was okay. The Weasels had grown used to toting various intel types—"guest spooks," they called them—on operational missions. They were a great source of information and amusement to Don and Wally on long trips over hostile territory.

Brick was another thing entirely, the Hated Brass, an antibody on the Cannonball. The Weasels had left the Air Force to leave people like Brick behind, people who thought they had the answers and would risk your life to prove themselves correct. In the past, Don and Wally had simply refused to fly with anyone above the rank of light colonel. The Weasels were civilians. The Air Force had to comply.

Now they weren't civilians anymore, Don thought. They were members of the First Air Regiment, whatever that was. Although the job offered several attractive perks—free drinks, good pay, and no dress code—it also had some overtones that were beginning to smell faintly military. Brick was one of them.

Bobby had had to personally intervene to get Brick and Krypto on board. This was a tense situation. Brick was the Regiment's link to the National Command Authority. The Cannonball, with its cosmic communications and sensor package, was the perfect place for Brick to monitor the battle while keeping in touch with friendly forces around the world. It made too much sense for Don to disagree, especially since Bobby had presented the request as a personal favor. Brick wasn't that crazy about it, either, but Bobby knew that, given the choice between riding the Cannonball or listening to the action on the radio at Dar al-Harb, he would come around. Brick wasn't the type to sit through an air battle on the ground. He would rather have gone into combat with his hand on the stick, but the Cannonball was better than nothing.

Or was it? Brick and Padgett struggled up into the plane and blinked in the sudden change from the laserlike Gulf sun to the cool, black insides of the Cannonball. Red LEDs and pastel computer screens punctuated the darkness, winking and flashing along the length of the big plane. Carrera swivel chairs in black leather faced consoles of knobs, switches, and keyboards, none of them labeled with a clue as to their function.

"Hey, neat!" Krypto was impressed.

"Neat?" Brick said derisively. "I feel like a hog looking at a wristwatch."

"Hello, campers! Welcome aboard the fun ship *Cannonball*."

The two turned to see Wally emerging from the darkness aft, towing an umbilical trail of wires and plugs. He wore a headset with a microphone attachment and had some sort of flat LCD computer display strapped to his right thigh.

"Why are you wearing that crap? Are we going to Mars?"

"Not this trip, General," Wally laughed. The lights from the control panel glinted off his thick glasses, giving him the demented look of a mad scientist. "This time we're going to war."

The whine and flutter of the number-four turboprop starting up signaled the beginning of Operation Private Lightning. Wally pointed to a couple of seats installed especially for the occasion. "You first-timers better strap in. It's going to be quite a ride—Six Flags Over Ragland."

Krypto settled into one of the contour seats. Brick turned abruptly and headed toward the cockpit. "Hey, General, come back here," Wally called out. "Don never lets anyone..."

Brick slid through the blackout curtain and climbed the steep steps into the cabin. Don, wearing a "Jetsons" t-shirt and Bermuda shorts, was busy preflighting the bird when he noticed Brick. He leaned back from the pilot's seat and scowled.

"Hey! Get out of here! Daddy's working."

"Look, I hate flying when I'm not flying," Brick said, flustered. "You know what I mean."

Don shook his head. "Sorry, General. I know what you mean. But this isn't the Air Force. This is my plane. You can't order me to let you fly up here. Besides, I've already got a copilot."

Brick peered over the apparently empty seat and saw a life-size cardboard cutout of Elle Macpherson folded into the copilot's station.

"Where'd you get that?"

"I liberated her from a book convention in Vegas," Don said proudly. "Best damn copilot I ever had. Never says a word."

"I'm not ordering you to do anything. I'm asking you," Brick said humbly. "Please, can I ride up here with you? At least during takeoff."

"Well, since you said the magic word, I guess it's okay. Just this once, though. Next time we attack Iran, you pay full fare like everybody else."

Brick lifted the cardboard figure from the chair and prepared to sit down.

"Hey, take it easy, will you!" Don called out. "That's the woman I love. Put her in the flight engineer's seat. I know she's overqualified, but Elle won't mind. She's a wonderful person, inside as well as out."

Brick carefully folded the cutout into the jumpseat set back between the two pilot seats. He looked around the cockpit and whistled softly.

"I've been in a lot of Hercs, but I've never seen anything like this. I don't recognize a damn thing."

Don smiled. "Fly-by-wire. All digital. We've got two or three computers on board, and they get together and vote on how to fly the airplane."

"And you never fly with a copilot? Or a flight engineer?"

"Besides Elle?" Don shook his head. "Nope. Don't need 'em. Don't want 'em. It's like driving to Florida with your mother. You're a pilot. You know what I'm talking about. The only thing worse than having a copilot is *being* a copilot. And as for flight engineers—there's a union job if I ever saw one! There's nothing a poorly trained enlisted goob-a-tron can do that my computers can't do better and faster. And computers don't sit back there six inches from your ear and yak about football and credit problems while you're busy trying to violate someone's sovereign airspace."

Don performed the preflight drill with uncharacteristic precision, comparing the positions of various knobs and switches against the checklists popping up on two small computer screens cut into the instrument panel. He reached down and moved all four throttles slowly forward. The big C-130 rolled down the taxiway and spun onto the main strip.

"Quaseem Tower, Air France 280, charter air service, flight plan filed to Lahore, India, requests clearance for takeoff," Don said into his headset microphone. "*Merci*. Good day."

Without waiting for an answer, Don shoved the throttles to the firewall. The Hercules jumped off the brakes and pulled itself quickly into a steep climb.

"Reengined," Don shouted over the shrieking turboprops. "This is the only trash hauler in the world that can fly up to its own velocity vector."

He leveled out at six thousand feet and set a course to intersect the 1.5-degree east track, an airway commonly used by commercial aircraft that would take them across the Strait of Hormuz over Qeshm Island and slightly east of Bandar Abbas.

"What was that all about back there?" Brick asked. "About Air France?"

"Wally's idea," Don answered. "We're going to try to sneak up on them by pretending we're an airliner. So get French. I hope you brought your beret."

"Do you think that's going to fool anybody?"

"It fooled them yesterday."

Brick's jaw dropped. "You guys have already been to Bandar Abbas?"

"Oh, yeah. Several times," Don answered nonchalantly. "Wally's been collecting autographs from their air-search and fire-control radars. He's got the whole set of electronic signatures now."

"And they didn't fire at you?"

"Oh, no—they threw all kinds of crap up at us. Didn't touch the old Cannonball, though. Wally had the shields up. Tasteful jamming all up and down the electromagnetic spectrum."

"What about the MiGs?"

"We only saw a couple. Bobby chased 'em away. Surrounded them with one airplane."

Brick swallowed. The stories were true; the Weasels did have balls of steel. Flying an unarmed transport over the barrel in Bandar Abbas was not for the faint of heart. And Bobby, flying escort, alone. Well, he never lacked for guts, no matter what people said. So that's what he was doing on those early morning hops!

"Well, if I've got to go to war in a C-130, it's good to know I've picked one that's nice and bulletproof," Brick said with a sigh of relief.

"Don't count on it, General. We won't be doing any global jamming on this mission. If we put out those kinds of sparks today, we'd jam ourselves and every other aircraft over the strait, including friendlies. We'd melt every radar in the Regiment into lava lamps. And nobody'd be able to talk to anybody else, either," Don explained. "Sorry—your fifty-ton stealth fighter has turned back into a pumpkin. We're operating on animal cunning alone today."

The jagged outline of Qeshm Island slid into view, segmented by the multiple panes of the Herc's greenhouse canopy. Bandar Abbas was just over the horizon.

Krypto's head appeared between the blackout curtains.

"Better get back here, General. Things are starting to happen."

Brick sighed and reluctantly unstrapped from the copilot's seat. He paused at the top of the crew stairs.

"Thanks for the ride," he said to Don. "This is a real nice ship."

"Don't mention it," Don answered. He added, gruffly, "You can come up here again later on. That is, if you want to."

Brick smiled. It was quite a compliment. "Thanks. I will."

Brick stumbled into the cabin, unaccustomed to the darkness. It was freezing. Two dim forms moved in the center of the fuselage, silhouetted against a background of computer screens and colored lights.

"We've got one, General," Krypto called out.

"One what?"

"HAWK site, radiating," Wally said. He pointed to a computer- generated map of the coastline on one of the flickering CRTs. "This puppy, right here. Oh, he's a sly devil! Wouldn't have found him except for your superspook Krypto here. They're down in the cannery, all right, but they've moved to the parking lot. He pops up about every fifteen seconds on dummy load. Normally, we couldn't pick that up, but this program sniffs the side lobes and freezes the image."

"I've got no idea what you're talking about," Brick said. "But if that's an active SAM site, I say let's strike it."

"Me too," Wally nodded. He turned to Krypto. "Who've we got to do the honors?"

Krypto studied his clipboard.

"Adler flight," he answered. "German guys. Tornadoes."

The three Luftwaffe Tornadoes shot over the Strait of Hormuz in a tight arrowhead flung straight at the cannery.

Two interdictor versions of the European strike fighter flew on the wings, bright in their new desert camouflage against the serious blue of the Persian Gulf. Adler 82, one of the new Tornado ECR variants, formed the tip of the arrow. Nicknamed "Weasel-Schnitzels" in German service, the electronic combat and reconnaissance Tornadoes were designed to joust with surface-to-air missile batteries and radar-directed guns. That was Adler flight's assignment today, the first combat mission flown by German forces since 1945.

In the rear seat of Adler 82, Capt. Ranier Hass sat back and enjoyed the ride. Only a Luftwaffe *kampfbeobachter* could enjoy skimming mere feet above the Persian Gulf on the way to war. It was generally accepted among NATO jocks that pilots of the new German Air Force were certifiably insane. Here was a typical Luftwaffe mission in West Germany: Take off from your base whenever you feel like it; scream across the countryside co-altitude with the Mercedes (GAF *piloten* worried about hitting power lines on the way *up*); bounce whomever you can, whenever you can, including the odd airliner, each other, and kites; run out of fuel; and dead-stick into the nearest airfield, drink a lot of beer, and then go up and do it again.

Pilots of the other NATO air forces never mentioned this odd behavior for five good reasons. One: It was their country and they could do what they wanted. Two: It wouldn't do any good anyway. Three: The Luftwaffe formed the heart of NATO airpower in central Europe (the boss of 4ATAF was a German general). Four: However haphazard, dangerous, and close to the edge the Germans flew, they would be that much more prepared for wartime operations, which would, if anything, be even more chaotic. And five: The Germans would think the other pilots were just jealous, which they were.

While fighter jocks from other countries gloried in First Air's lack of Mickey Mouse rules, the Luftwaffe crews tried hard to abide what they considered the Regiment's compulsive concern for safety. Chocks, for instance. German pilots had rarely seen wheel chocks before. One Tornado jock had even complained to a bemused crowd at the Sierra Hotel that the chocks were actually a detriment to safety, since he often had to thrust up to full military power to get over them.

So, screaming over the Strait of Hormuz was not a big thing to KBO Hass, although, if there were waves in the Persian Gulf, Adler 82 would have been swamped. (Luftwaffe systems check: Am I alive? Are the wings still attached? Is this a great day, or what?) The round, amber moving map display between the two square CRTs showed the coast and the cannery coming up fast. Hass had already handed off the coordinates of the HAWK site—beamed from the Cannonball—to the HARM missile under the Tornado's wing. The pilot would punch it off. Hass sat back to watch the show.

The high-speed radiation missile was the fighter pilot's revenge on antiaircraft forces for excessive laundry bills going all the way back to the Vietnam War. It was said that HARM would fly relentlessly toward its target, even if the battery's radar was switched off. The American makers of the AGM-88 were more than a little vague about exactly how the antiradiation missile continued so inexorably in the absence of radiation—it locked onto "certain parameters of operation," so they said. But as the Navy pilots who used the missile so successfully in the Operation *Eldorado Canyon* raid on Libya had discovered, the secret to HARM was hate. It was the first missile in history designed with a home-on-animosity feature. HARM hated everything about surface-to-air missiles, hated their dumb, nodding radars, their stupid, square control vans, their obnoxious radio towers spouting inane chatter and data-link languages no real American could pronounce. A skinny little robot with the soul of a kamikaze, HARM would gladly destroy itself if it meant one less SAM site in the world.

The two Tornadoes on Hass's wings pulled off in opposite directions. His pilot unleashed the HARM, which shot off in a rocket of white smoke, climbed a little bit, sniffed, gritted its teeth, and buried itself in the radar dish of the HAWK site. At the moment of impact, the other two Tornadoes reappeared over the cannery, heading straight for each other. Two friendly jets screaming over a battlefield on a reciprocal course would have been called an accident in any other air force; in the Luftwaffe it was called a *Knobelsdorff*, a type of coordinated attack done with great skill and precision that minimized the aircrafts' exposure to ground defenses.

One Tornado dropped a pair of Beluga cluster bombs from its wings. The other pumped out thousands of submunitions from the MW-1 bomblet dispenser on its belly. Within seconds, what had been an operational surface-to-air missile site was turned into a pile of smoking trash.

Adler 82 spun back over the Gulf to regroup with the rest of the flight and orbit while waiting for further assignments. In the turn, Hass caught the flash of a wing, high over the mountains to the northeast. At that moment, the unidentified intruder lit up its radar. No, *their* radars—there were six, so far, on Hass's right screen. MiGs. Fulcrums. This was beginning to get interesting.

"Bogies!" Wally shouted. "I've got half a dozen MiG-29s over Kalmord Mountain. There may be more down in the rocks that we can't process."

Krypto studied the display, with its computer-generated Fulcrum silhouettes inching toward Bandar Abbas. "Where's Bobby?"

"Right there." Wally pointed to the black outlines of four F-15s, just appearing on the CRT.

"Well, this is it," Krypto said. "Bobby said it would come to this. I just hope they have better luck with the MiGs than those poor Navy pilots did."

Brick pulled his chair closer to the screen. "This I've got to see."

Lt. Rowdy Engram had been known as a hot stick in Bitburg, which was saying something. The 36th Tactical Fighter Wing was, arguably, the premiere air-to-air unit in West Germany, perhaps in all of Europe. So he was not just a pilot, or a fighter pilot, or an F-15 fighter pilot, or an F-15 fighter pilot at Bitburg: He was there at the zenith, the very tippy-top, his supremacy secured in countless toothless victories in mock combat with his Bitburg mates. They were the best of the best. And he had beaten them. What did that make him?

A very sad young man, as it turned out. He had joined First Air, pumped up and puffed out, figuring the Regiment needed him and that he might teach them a thing or two. But it was Rowdy Engram who got the education, an accelerated course in jet combat. In practice engagements with his new unit, Engram, in the language of his profession, got his knickers ripped. He got hosed, dicked, morted, removed, got his doors blown in and his shorts shot off. Defeated.

That was lesson number one: There were other worlds where they flew fighters, and they flew them shit hot. Lesson number two was that he wasn't so bad after all, that the guys in the Regiment just had a few tricks he hadn't seen before. After a while he began winning again, and he happily anticipated the end of the war so he could try out his new moves on his old friends in Bitburg. Then Engram had a midair collision with lesson number three: You can't beat Bobby.

Rowdy had, of course, heard the legend of Bobby Dragon many times before coming to al-Quaseem. You couldn't get away from it: *Bobby Dragon did this, he did that; you're good, son, but Bobby Dragon was better. I remember*...Nuts! How Engram had despised that ghost! Sometimes he had wished Bobby Dragon *was* alive, so he could get him in his sights and shoot down that fairy tale once and for all. But that was it. You couldn't fight a legend, a mythic figure whose proportions probably grew with each retelling. But even at his best, how good could this guy have been? After all, he flew in the old days, when pilots still wore parachutes on their butts, and seven Gs was a lot of Gs. Dragon fought in *Vietnam,* for Christ's sake. How long ago was that? Rowdy Engram wasn't even born during the hottest years of the air war over Southeast Asia. He was three when Bobby Dragon shot down Doom. Engram was sick and tired of hearing Vietnam War stories—*ancient history!* And most of all he was sick of hearing about the Greatest Fighter Pilot Who Ever Lived.

Then he met him. Engram had learned of Bobby's resurrection upon his arrival at Dar al-Harb and immediately set out to track him down. A week later, Rowdy spotted him on the flight line at sunrise. He didn't look ten feet tall. He didn't have phased-array radar dishes for eyeballs. He looked like a thousand other old men (old, to a twenty-three-year-old, being extremely relative) that Engram had beaten a thousand other times. He was Rowdymeat, which is what he told Bobby when he challenged him to a duel in the skies.

To Bobby, it had been just another rerun in a long series of Glenn Ford movies in which he had played the starring role in so many fighter bars all over the world—the new punks wouldn't let the retired gunslinger retire. Bobby had given up arguing a long time ago, and you couldn't decline. The easiest thing to do was to just take the little cowpoke upstairs and kick his ass.

Which he did. Rowdy had never seen anything like Bobby Dragon in the air. Come to think of it, he never saw Bobby Dragon in the air, not that day, not much. Every now and then he'd see a wing spinning on the horizon, or the flash of a canopy a few feet from the ground, or up in the stratosphere, or someplace, anyplace normal fighters weren't supposed to be. But Bobby had seen him. He had seen lots of Rowdy Engram, and he had been happy to share the gun camera video with the young hotshot once they had landed at Dar al-Harb. Engram figured he had been "shot down" at least fifteen times before Bobby had mercifully switched off the television monitor.

And then he had Done It. The combat might have been simulated, but the crashing and burning of Rowdy Engram's soul was real enough. His personality, his identity, his entire sense of self was wrapped around the stick of his F-15. Rowdy had beaten the best of the best, and Bobby had beaten *him*. Badly. So what did that make Engram? Worthless. He was about to slink out the door, off the base, and out of the country when Bobby had said, "I need a wingman. You're the best Eagle driver we've got. You want the job?"

Fishers of men! Did he want the job? To sit at the feet of the master? To fly on the wing of the enlightened one? Which way was hell, Bobby? You first! I got your six!

And so Rowdy Engram found himself here, thirty thousand feet over Iran, for real. It was the brownest country he had ever seen, full of surface-to-air missiles and guys in rayon disco shirts who just hated Americans. Bobby Dragon—*Bobby Dragon!*—was off his left wing, about a mile away. On the other side were two other Eagles, driven by a guy from First Fighter at Langley and some PACAF puke from Kadena. Out...there...were real MiGs with real missiles. Engram screwed his butt down in the seat and checked his straps. This, by God, was it!

The wall of Eagles moved along. Engram forced himself to calm down, went through the checklist, armed everything up, gazed at the radar; the evil squares were still thirty miles away, plenty of time, so just—*what was that?* A huge missile shot out from underneath Bobby's plane, a big white Sparrow trailing a plume of dirty gray smoke. What the hell was he doing? You could see that thing for miles! He couldn't have a lock-on, not with an AIM-7 versus rocks at thirty miles, despite what the book said. Was he crazy?

No, not at all. Rowdy realized that when he looked back at his radar screen. The little green rectangles representing the MiGs were scattering all over the scope, their carefully coordinated attack plan shot to hell by a clever bluff. The Sparrow had a dummy load. It wasn't aimed at anything more specific than a mountain range, but the Fulcrums didn't know that. And it had certainly gotten their attention. It was every MiG for himself, now. That was Bobby's plan—divide and defeat in detail. Pretty good plan.

Bobby had a thing about talking on the radio. He didn't do it. It was a sound tactical policy in these days of sophisticated jamming, but it took a while to get used to. *Just follow my wing,* Bobby had said in their few practice sessions together. Fat chance—Rowdy had bent his airplane up in some major bat turns trying to keep up with Bobby only to find out, once they had landed, that Bobby had rarely exceeded 7.5 Gs. How the hell did he do what he did?

At a wing dip from Bobby, the other two Eagles peeled off to take the MiGs to the west. Bobby slid his F-15 over gently and…disappeared! Engram was frantic. Where did he go? He flipped over into a split-S and caught sight of Bobby again, scurrying low alongside Poshi Mountain. Bobby had his flaps up, his speed brake swung out like a door—Christ! *He had his landing gear down!*

What the hell? Rowdy had been told you never fight slow in an Eagle. Supersonic was the best policy, and anything under 350 knots, shoot, you might as well take the bus. And here was the great Bobby Dragon—and no one knew as well as Rowdy Engram just how great that was—crawling along a mountainside.

Rowdy never saw the MiG. He just followed the trail of Bobby's Sidewinder and—boom!—there it was! It hadn't been on the radar. It had been slinking down in the rocks, away from the fight, hoping, apparently, to circle back and sneak up on somebody. It was now quite visible, burning up in a pile atop an Iranian mountain.

Rowdy throttled back, popped the brake, and extended the flaps. He'd be damned if he was going to drop the gear, but he was gradually slowing down to match his wingman's snail's pace when Bobby cleaned up his Eagle, lit the afterburner, lifted the nose, and zoomed straight up like a Saturn V. Engram watched Bobby getting smaller with a sigh, then followed him up into the stratosphere.

There was another dot up there, another MiG. Bobby locked him up, hosed off a Sparrow—perfect parameters—another kill. The Fulcrum disintegrated in a gentlemanly fashion, with parts spitting out of a wrecked engine and the plane flipping over into a flat spin.

Bobby pulled up into level flight again. They flew straight and level for about thirty seconds, which made Rowdy nervous. It was another thing you were never supposed to do. Suddenly, Bobby's plane flipped up on a wing and spun 180 degrees. It was so quick—it wasn't a turn, it was a thought. Engram tried to do the same thing in the same way. When he woke up, the G meter was pegged somewhere around twelve. Wow! If you did that enough, you'd pull the wings off. On the other hand, Rowdy thought, what should he care? He'd be dead by then.

He spotted Bobby a mile away, apparently rehearsing for an air-show demonstration with a Fulcrum over the Sarzeh Valley. At least, that's what it looked like. Bobby was so close. The M61 Gatling cannon in the Eagle's wing root coughed thin gray smoke. The MiG he had suckered in plummeted to the ground as Bobby pulled up. Where did it end?

They worked their way east like that, ducking and shooting. For Rowdy, it had ceased to be a battle and had turned into a seminar. It was not a series of disconnected dogfights but rather one long, fluid attack. Each engagement flowed into another, the way a pool hustler always sets himself up for the next shot, confident he'll make this one. That was Bobby's greatest gift—to see the unseen, to predict the unpredictable, to take the whole dome of blue sky and shake it, like one of those Christmas paperweights with the fake snow suspended in water, until everything settled and he—but only he—could see the scene clearly.

After a while they ran out of MiGs. Rowdy thought for sure Bobby would extend to the west and help out the other Eagles in the sweep. But no—this was First Air. They could handle it. You didn't offer help until someone asked. And no one was asking.

They flew up to the desert, then peeled off over the Gulf. The F-14 sweep was forming up now, and they had to clear the area or risk getting picked off themselves by one of the Tomcats' magic missiles.

"That was some good flying back there." Now, safely over the Gulf, Bobby didn't mind using the radio.

Rowdy winced. Well, humility was a quality only bad fighter pilots were good at, after all.

"Yeah," Engram said. "You really dicked 'em."

"I was talking about you, Rowdy," Bobby said. "Nobody's ever stayed on my wing like that before."

Oh, take me! Rowdy was ready. For he had heard, in the compressed tones of truth squeezed through the Have Quick UHF Band radio, his master's voice and had received his blessings.

*   *   *

"I had always heard he was good," Krypto said, watching the Eagles slide off the bottom of the CRT. "But I've never seen anything like that before."

"Bobby's the best," Wally said. "There's nobody like him. Nobody."

Brick lifted himself from his chair and walked stiffly toward the cockpit.

"Did I say something wrong?" Wally asked.

"I think we both did," Krypto frowned. "Brick was a fighter pilot once. And a pretty good one, from what I understand. But good in an ordinary way. Not like Bobby."

"I copy that," Wally said. "I've seen it plenty of times myself. These guys fly fighters and they're on top of the world. Then they retire, and all they've got left is a big watch and an attitude."

Krypto glanced up at the screen, which showed a gaggle of F-4s coming in from the west. "What's that?"

Wally checked the clipboard and a clock and smiled. "Showtime."

Bubba Windham's initial impression of Iran was that it would be a great place to open a barbecue. He didn't know where the idea came from—perhaps it was because the brown-and-yellow mountains flashing by the F-4's wingtips reminded him so much of his home in west Texas—but it struck him so funny he laughed loud enough for Thumper Combs to hear in the backseat.

Combs looked up, annoyed. Hurtling through the Konji Valley, with missiles sizzling above and antiaircraft guns arcing ahead, did not seem to him like an appropriate spot for levity. But he had gotten used to Windham's personality in their years of flying together, first in Korat, in Thailand, then at Hahn, West Germany. When the 50th Tactical Fighter Wing got rid of their F-4s, they also said *adios* to Windham and Combs. The two had tolerated the Air Force, but they loved the F-4 and followed it into the Reserves in Texas. Now, the 924th Tactical Fighter Group was transitioning to the hated F-16. So Windham and Combs transitioned themselves to the only outfit in the world that seemed to love the venerable Phantom as much as they did: the First Air Regiment, Incorporated.

"Okay, we're coming up on the initial point," Combs said, checking the map in the rear seat against the waypoints of the inertial navigation system. "The valley doglegs to the left. The pass should be straight ahead after that."

Windham's bit helmet nodded in agreement. That was another thing that ticked Combs off—why couldn't he just use the intercom? After all, he kept the line open when he hummed, no matter how many times Combs asked him to knock if off.

The Phantom shot through two low rocky hills, the last of the highlands. The valley floor spread out beneath them. Most of the coast was in smoke and flames. The village of Gachin rolled underneath them. Bandar Abbas lay dead ahead.

"That's our IP up there," Combs said. "By the smokestacks."

"I see it," Windham grunted. Thick columns of black smoke rose from the cannery. "Those Tornadoes really shacked it. Makes you wonder how those Krauts lost the war."

Combs was too busy setting up the WRCS to respond. "The computer's all set."

"Screw the computer," Windham replied. "I'm not taking a chance on it going into idiot mode halfway through the pitch-up."

"But it's working fine, Bubba! Let's not go through this again. I checked it out just before…"

Windham, in reply, lit the afterburners of the two monster J-79 engines. Combs was thrown back in his seat. The aircraft passed over the coast west of the cannery, Rhino 41's initial point. Combs strained to look behind him. The rest of Rhino flight, eight F-4s in all, followed up the valley to the rear, mere black smoky dots in the gray haze. The Phantoms farthest ahead began splitting off to line up on their bomb runs. The attack on the old port was designed so that the F-4s would dive in from all directions within a very short period of time, to surprise the defenders and force them to split their fire.

Combs hoped it would work. The F-4 pilots had decided that, however dangerous the guns on the ground might be, the SAM and MiG threat over Bandar Abbas would be the most formidable. Bobby Dragon's admonition to stay below ten thousand feet or risk being attacked by their own fighters had clinched it—Rhino flight would use the pop-up tactic rather than the usual circle and run-in dive-bombing maneuver. The pop-up, used extensively throughout much of the Vietnam War, placed a great burden on the pilot, who had to put the aircraft in a precise place in space and at a highly defined speed and dive angle to deliver ordnance effectively. Combs had wanted to use the weapons release computer set, which would give Windham visual steering cues to the target and, if so programmed, automatically pickle the bomb load.

But Windham, like many F-4 air-to-ground specialists, had grown to distrust the WRCS. Although Windham's F-4E sported the "improved" DMAS version—instantly dubbed the "dumbass" by skeptical WSOs—the Phantom's computerized bombing system was generations behind the "cosmic" bomb sights installed in more modern fighters. Even when it worked correctly, which was less and less frequently as it aged, the WRCS had never been famous for its accuracy. With precision-guided munitions, such as laser and electro-optically directed bombs and rockets, it didn't matter. But to drop "dumb"—that is, unguided—bombs, you needed smart airplanes. And Windham felt the F-4 was not smart enough to be trusted on this run. The rap on the WRCS was that it dropped bombs more accurately than average pilots but not nearly as well as a jock who knew what he was doing. And no fighter pilot would admit to being average.

Combs saw the spit of land jutting off from the naval air station, their pull-up point, and braced himself as Windham threw the Phantom into a five-G vertical climb. It was just like Windham, Rhino flight's warlord, to pick the toughest approach for himself so the others could come in at safer angles. And it was just like him, Combs thought, to do it without even asking his backseater. Luckily, most of the guns had been suppressed by the Tornadoes' attack on the cannery moments before. But he could still see streaks of light sliding around the sky, searching for Rhino 41 as it roared through the haze.

At the apex of the pitch-up, Windham swung the F-4 upside down and tucked it to the left. Rolling out, wings level in a forty-five-degree angle pointing straight at the port of Bandar Abbas, he checked the Mil setting, 149 for a stick of slicks dropped from seven thousand feet at 450 knots. He checked the fire-control system—it was in air-to-ground mode, direct. He selected all stations, released simultaneously with nose and tail fusing. Hit or miss, no one was going to go back and attack the same target more than once today.

In the back, Combs fought the negative Gs lifting him out of the seat and searched the sky for MiGs. As the speed pushed 450, Windham noticed the pipper moving beyond their target, a fuel storage tank at the end of the small peninsula. He pushed the stick forward, "bunting" the aircraft more upright and pushing the hose down.

"For Christ's sake, punch them off and let's get out of here!" Combs screamed from the backseat. "You're pressing!"

Windham smiled and pickled the bomb load. In years of flying with Combs, he had come to rely on his backseater as the perfect weapons release computer. Just when Combs shouted they had gone too far, Windham knew, they had reached the perfect release point.

A dozen five-hundred-pound bombs fell from the wings and centerline of the F-4 and tumbled into the center of the storage tank. The direct hit burst the tank and ignited the fuel inside, spilling fire in all directions.

Windham pulled out a hundred feet off the ground, trading the negative Gs for positive ones. Pressed down in the seat, Combs swiveled to look back as the F-4 zoomed out over the Gulf and headed for home. Another direct hit. How did Windham do it without the computer?

"How'd we do?" Windham asked.

"A little long, but we nailed it," Combs answered.

"Pussies hit short," Windham said. "Tigers hit long."

Over the intercom, Combs could hear him humming.

"Everything is a joke to you," Brick said, disgusted. He had retreated to the cockpit to get away from the technoplayground of the Cannonball's dim belly, to return to the sun and the sky and the fellowship of a fellow pilot. But he had discovered that although Don Weasel flew airplanes, that was about all they had in common. "You guys never take anything seriously, do you?"

"In all seriousness," Don said, "no. What's the point?"

"This is real war, goddamn it! People are getting killed!"

"They're not going to be any less dead if I suddenly start acting like the chairman of the armed services committee. War's no place for somebody who can't take a joke. A bullet doesn't know if I'm laughing at it. As far as I know, there are no such things as language-guided bombs and speech-seeking missiles, although Wally's working on something along those lines."

"But people's lives are depending on you! You have to pay attention. You have to get serious."

"Ah, but those aren't exactly the same thing, are they? For example, you're a real serious guy, right? I mean, look in the dictionary under 'buzz crusher' and there's your picture. Yet you're not paying attention. If you were, you'd see that HAWK missile at two o'clock low."

Brick looked out the window. Sure enough, there it was—a white missile with black fins, streaking across the sky. "Jesus! Better break, now!"

Don laughed softly and held a steady course. "See? You weren't paying *attention!* Even now, you're so serious, so into it, that it's actually *interfering* with your job, which is to keep your ass alive and flying. Fortunately for you, I remember all the things that you forgot in your blood lust and battle fever."

"Like what?" Brick asked, still eyeing the missile warily as it flashed out over the Gulf.

"Like anytime you can see the fins, it's not pointing at you. Or that the HAWK starts its terminal guidance on the way down, not up. Or that Wally's back there in the tube with enough transcendent Western technology to make that missile sit up and beg, if he wants to. And Wally's *always* paying attention."

"You think you're pretty smart, don't you?" Brick said, embarrassed that he had lost his composure in front of another pilot. "If you're so tough, how come you're not flying fighters instead of this...*science fair!*"

"Careful now, General. Don't be making fun of the Cannonball." Don patted the instrument panel affectionately. "The truth is, you don't have to fly fighters to be a fighter pilot. It's an attitude. You still consider yourself a fighter jock—you dress like one, you talk like one, you affect that blend of nihilism, irresponsibility, and Old Spice that truly dumb women find so attractive. But how long has it been since you actually piloted a front-line fighter?"

"I don't see what..."

"Look, I'm not going to sit here and lecture you about what makes, or doesn't make, a person a fighter pilot," Don cut in. "There's no talking to you. You're obstinate and unreasonable. Everybody else could disappear from the planet and you'd never miss them, except for the fact that there'd be no one around to tell you how great you were. You're an asshole! That makes you a fighter pilot in my book."

Brick laughed softly. "You're an asshole, too."

"Thank you," Don said. "That's the nicest thing you've said to me."

They broke the coast in burner, four Falcons in echelon, Faisal first. The war boiled around them. Two F-4s flashed past the flight, scattering a stick of bombs that splashed concentric rings of shock waves in the puddle of thick air below. The tiny suns of dozens of infrared decoy flares burned brightly in the haze, like a twilight constellation. A million slivers of silver chaff shimmered in the air, clouding the radar screens of the ground-based defenders. There were jets everywhere, chasing other jets, being chased, all gray, all blurred in the hanging dust, friendly or enemy, who knew? Faisal flew on.

Speed is life. Those were words to live by in the fighter business. Faisal was a friend of speed. Everything he did, he did fast. The old could drag their feet and smell the flowers. But the young, with their whole lives ahead, pegged the needle. The world was so big. Why wait?

The F-16's maximum speed is said to be around Mach 2. Dropped from the stratosphere and stripped of everything including paint, perhaps. But hauling iron a hundred feet above the desert in the heat of an Iranian summer, 550 knots was pushing it. The others struggled to keep up, desperately trying to keep the orange glow of Faisal's afterburner in sight through the smoke and dust at low altitude. The story in the Regiment was that the boy was born in burner. He'd rather run out of gas than knots.

The First Air pilots were beginning to feel guilty about not hating Faisal. Contempt and envy are virtually interchangeable emotions, and certainly Sonny was someone to be envied. Impossibly rich, hopelessly good looking, bright, easygoing—where did it end? Was he arrogant? No. Then he must be a grape. Think again. The guy flew shit hot.

There was much resentment in the Regiment, naturally, when Hillary had announced that the crown prince of al-Quaseem was to be First Air's nominal commander. Faisal said it only once, but he said it clearly: That was a political abstraction, a bow to the politics of the Gulf. He was proud to fly with First Air, Faisal said, proud to follow Bobby Dragon like every other pilot in the Regiment. He took the slights and the kidding, and soon enough everyone else knew he meant it. And they quickly realized that, Hassan's son or not, Faisal had the hands to make it in First Air on his own.

Still, it was something of a shock when Sonny volunteered to take out the toughest target in Private Lightning. No one doubted they would have gone up against the HAWK site on Genow Mountain if so ordered. But asking for it? If they stared in their own eyes in the morning, shaver in hand, and asked themselves if they would have the guts to *volunteer*, well, the answer would be no. Of course not. Fighter pilots, especially experienced hands like First Air fliers, survived by knowing their limits and not lying to themselves.

It has been said pets and their owners look alike, but that's nothing compared with the resemblance pilots have to their planes. Whether they choose the aircraft that fits their personality or gradually grow to take on the characteristics of the planes they fly is a philosophical question that probably has no answer. The fact is, fighter pilots are, as a rule, loud and agitated, fast movers, and a trifle dangerous, if only to themselves. Transport pilots are full and friendly, always willing to lend a hand. Recce pilots are at once curious and furtive.

The analogy could be taken further according to type. There's a reason F-15 pilots, as much larger than life as their aircraft, are known as "ego drivers." Tomcat pilots tend to keep people at a distance. Hornet jocks can never decide whether they want to be air-to-air or air-to-ground specialists and exhibit a certain type of airborne schizophrenia.

But no plane and pilot were as perfectly matched in temperament as Faisal and his Falcon. There were other aircraft better at various missions than the F-16, but there was no other plane that could do so many things so well. The F-16 was so quick and so smart that it seemed to humble other planes without effort. So it was with Faisal, a kind of idiot savant of aviation. If he had any idea how good he was, how special, he would cease to be so. His eyes and hands, the whole plane, were one system. He never thought about what he did in the air. He never had to think. That was his secret.

A minute after going feet dry, Falcon flight crossed the Tarzayam road. Genow Mountain rose like a single solid rock before them, the peak towering a mile above the haze. Faisal pulled back in a slow climb, the others following. A geyser of white smoke erupted from the mountaintop. If Faisal thought the HAWK was meant for him he didn't show it, continuing his ascent to give the television seeker in the Maverick's nose a better look at its target.

Sonny's gloved hands flicked across the throttle and the stick, pushing the buttons and switches that studded both black columns. It was every bit as difficult as playing a musical instrument. Each operation—missile arming, target acquisition and lock, electronic countermeasures and countercounter-measures—was like a musical phrase. Faisal performed the intricate operations like a concert virtuoso, without the self-consciousness and internal commentary that plague the amateur athlete or performer.

The mountaintop shuddered wildly in the video picture that had replaced the radar grid in the Falcon's single multifunction display. The picture came from the Maverick's own seeker. The missile, like the rest of the plane, including Faisal, was being shoved around by the thick and uncertain air the

F-16 was pushing through. Faisal saw the sudden rectangle, the flickering image of the HAWK battery's control van. He punched a button and the image froze. The Maverick would remember that scene, would pursue it until it destroyed the radar van, and itself, in a blaze ignited by the 130 pounds of TNT on board.

The Maverick blasted from underneath the starboard wing in a rush of orange-and-yellow smoke. The missile rose briefly for a better look, then nosed over and headed straight for the mountain summit. At Mach 2 and close to minimum range, it didn't take long for the Maverick to impact. Direct hit. The radar homing and warning light in the F-16's cockpit blinked out and ceased its annoying tone as the control van blew apart in a hundred flaming pieces.

Faisal flew through the debris, barely clearing the mountainside. The rest of Falcon flight followed, littering the HAWK site with Rockeye cluster bombs that decimated the launchers and remote radars.

Faisal spun right and swung about. There was no need for a second pass. The HAWK site had been put out of business permanently by a precision attack. Faisal didn't even notice the HAWK meant for him, now unguided, falling stupidly a thousand feet behind him.

"I give up," Brick said. "Why is war like a Zen version of a Gilbert and Sullivan play?"

"Because it is!" Don Weasel answered triumphantly.

"I don't get it."

"You're not supposed to get it, General," Don said. "It's a Zen riddle. It doesn't have a point. That's the point—it's pointless."

"Oh," Brick said. He truly did not understand what Don was talking about. Then it hit him—he wasn't supposed to! *That* was the point.

"I don't understand," Brick said proudly.

"Congratulations, General," Don beamed. "You're getting there!"

Brick shrugged and went back to studying the Cannonball's cockpit. He had figured out most of it, but there was one piece of gear that still had him baffled.

"What's this?" Brick rapped a finger against a small computer monitor mounted above the instrument panel. Duct tape and exposed wiring betrayed the fact that it was obviously a recent addition.

"Ah! A perfect example of the Zen of war," Don said. "That's the Atomic Dog!"

"The what?"

"The sniffer. One of Wally's inventions. It was Bobby's idea, actually, but Wally put it together. You know, people around here tend to forget about it, but one of the reasons we invaded Iran in the first place was to find out if the Rag Men had any more nuclear weapons."

"And that's what this thing does?"

"Yeah," Don answered. "You see, nuclear weapons, no matter how well made, give off stray electrons that don't look like anything else. And anything the Iranians can screw together is probably pretty damn leaky. So Wally came up with the Atomic Dog. There's a pod out on the wing that sniffs it out, and the data comes up here."

Brick looked at the monitor with sudden interest. "So, have you found anything?"

Don shook his head. "Not a damn thing, General. And we've walked the Dog up and down the strait for about a week, solid."

"Are you sure it works?"

"Wally doesn't make anything that doesn't work," Don said. "But come to think of it, we were beginning to have our doubts the other day."

"What do you mean?"

"It was the damnedest thing, General." Don scratched his head. "We were coming back into Dar al-Harb, after searching over Bandar Abbas all morning and coming up with zip. Suddenly, the Dog goes nuts! It actually barks, you know. It's got a synthesizer chip in it, and..."

"Where was this?" Brick broke in.

"What? Where the alarm went off?" Don asked, puzzled. "Over the west end of al-Quaseem. Near the sheik's palace, as a matter of fact. That's how we knew it was a false alarm."

"So what do you think caused it?"

"Beats me," Don said. "The sheik's got an airstrip at the palace, you know. Maybe one of those weird English radars he's got there set it off, although Wally swears that wouldn't do it. We were going to go around again to check it out, but Wally picked up a full system lock-on from one of the HAWK batteries near the palace, and we kind of got the message we weren't wanted. We come in to Dar al-Harb a different way now."

Brick stared out the window, lost in thought.

"Ladies and gentlemen, presenting the U.S. Navy Flight Demonstration Team, the world-famous Blue Angels!"

Oh, how fondly Lt. Dots Harper, former Blue Angel number five, remembered those words. It all came back to him now—flying every day above hundreds of thousands of fawning, ignorant fans (the best kind for a fighter pilot), nights of steak dinners and sometimes better stuff (Harper was a bachelor, as if that made any difference). True, you didn't get shot at, not like here, although there were many times Harper had been grateful the opposing solo pilot's gun had been removed from his Hornet, especially after Harper cut it too close on the occasional knife-edge pass. And at least he didn't have to wear that stupid blue-and-gold double-knit jumpsuit anymore. (*Thank God* for that—there's something supremely tasteless about a flight suit that a fighter pilot had to be ordered to wear.) But, other than that, Harper would have to say he preferred the Blues to combat. Air shows were more exciting.

You couldn't say it was boredom, exactly. Only the most world-weary and affected would consider zooming around a hostile country in a Mach 2 jet, shooting at people, and having them shoot back, a boring way to spend an afternoon. Still, Harper couldn't help feeling he had been here before, done this a thousand times, in simulators, in exercises, on paper, in his head, at the movies.

Perhaps the Navy had done Harper a disservice by exposing the lieutenant, in his relatively brief career, to a lifetime of simulated combat flying. He was a fast mover, a talented pilot with choice connections; (his father, an admiral, had been one of those astronauts who had never quite made it to the top of the rocket). Harper had mapped out his career and had, so far, gotten everything he wanted—the right planes, the right squadrons, the right boats. The Blue Angels were just another stop, another ticket punched on the way to the pinnacle.

And so was First Air. Harper had signed up the minute he had heard about the Regiment, seizing the opportunity to fill the ultimate air square on that personnel form that followed him around. Now he was having second thoughts. The Navy was not thrilled with the Regiment. They had, in fact, taken Harper's plane back. He was now flying a Hornet from the luckless *Constellation,* one of the many planes that Sheik Hassan had seized and interned after their emergency landing at Dar al-Harb in the wake of the naval clash with the Soviets in the Arabian Sea that disabled the carrier.

Harper was beginning to wonder if he would have a plane when he returned to the Navy. Or a career, for that matter. He regretted the day he had joined the Regiment. If the Navy wasn't going to appreciate it, what was the point? He certainly didn't need the combat experience. True, Top Gun and Red Flag and the dozens of carrier and fleet exercises in which he had flown were bloodless, but the flying and the landing and the dogfighting were real enough. And with a large chunk of his professional life riding on each one, the stakes had been high indeed.

Now here, in combat for real, Harper felt let down. Where were the threats? There were airfields scratched out in the Nevada desert more heavily defended than Naval Air Station Bandar Abbas. The airstrip was deserted, its defenses consisting of a sole patriot with a .50-caliber machine gun, quickly frightened away with a stick of Rockeyes scattered across his position.

Harper realized First Air had no way of truly knowing what they would find at NAS Bandar Abbas. And he recognized its importance in American plans to solidify their tenuous hold on southern Iran, if possible. It was a vital target, and it deserved to be capped, to chase away any Iranians on the ground and protect it from the MiGs. Harper also knew the F/A-18 was the perfect choice for the task, since it could perform air-to-air and air-to-ground missions equally well.

Still, it frustrated Harper to cut constant circles above the airfield while the rest of First Air was up to its intakes in action. He monitored the chatter on the various comm networks like a young boy listening to a baseball-game broadcast on the radio from some distant, glittering city. In his orbit, Harper could even see some of the real fighting—pillars of smoke on the coast, bursts of flak over the city chasing tiny specks that were his new rivals and comrades.

Absently, he considered punching on the radio to ask if anyone needed help. Harper quickly dismissed the idea. Volunteering for one mission while you were in the middle of another would be considered the height of overachievement, even for a Blue Angel. But if it...

"Stinger, break right!"

By reflex, Harper snatched the stick to starboard and pulled hard. The horizon rolled sideways through the canopy bow—land, then sea—as the Hornet pulled a maximum-performance break turn through 180 degrees. Harper caught a glimpse of a small gray pole heading toward the mountains on a reciprocal course.

Harper panted from the Gs and the panic. Where was the bandit? Where was his wingman? Why wasn't he dead? The missile must have gone ballistic. No missiles work all the time, especially Soviet missiles, and thank God for that! The Hornet drilled through the sky, straight and level. *A stupid thing to do!* Harper shoved the aircraft into a long reversal, keeping his energy up. He rolled into a slow belly check. Hanging upside down, he saw a small gray fighter cartwheeling in flames over the coast. Christ, was that his wingman?

"Stinger, come to thirty."

No. Harper saw another gray Hornet hanging in the haze two miles to the right. He cranked the throttles and joined up. As he flew closer, Harper noticed the other F-18 was missing one of its Sidewinder missiles. It was clear now what had happened—his wingman had smoked the Fulcrum that had nearly killed him.

Humbled and ashamed, Harper suddenly realized he did not know the name of the man who had saved his life. All he knew was that he was a Spanish pilot, from *Escuadron 211* in Moron. Harper had assumed the man was accepted into First Air simply to fill the ranks—F-18s had been hard to come by, and the Spanish pilot had brought his own Hornet from the *Ejercito del Aire*. Like most Americans, Harper could not conceive of anyone else in the world flying up to the standards of the U.S. services. Now, he realized, if it weren't for the skill of this anonymous Spaniard—what *was* his name?—Harper would be dead. And, it pained him to admit, if his wingman had depended upon Harper to watch his six, *he* would be dead.

Damn! Who could have known that real combat would be such a poor simulation of all those exercises Harper had flown through so flawlessly? They had given him only confidence, it turned out, not experience. Harper had flown against the best and beaten them, and that made him complacent. The MiG driver had come barreling in head on and hooked around Harper like he was a nugget on his first tour. If you tried that at Top Gun, you'd get your ears pinned back, guaranteed. It was a rookie mistake. But this wasn't Top Gun, and Harper, not looking for the obvious bandit, had not seen him. His wingman, an "inferior" pilot, had, thank God.

Harper screwed his butt into the seat and got his eyes out of the cockpit. This wasn't Top Gun. This was real. He was a long way from NAS Miramar. In fact, longitudinally and latitudinally speaking, he was almost exactly on the other side of the world. If you drilled a hole straight down from Bandar Abbas, drilled it deep enough, all the way through the earth, you would probably wind up in San Diego.

And Harper almost had. He resolved to be more careful.

In the hold of the cold Cannonball, Krypto and Wally stared at a computer screen thick with the black shapes of airplanes. It looked like it was covered with flies.

"Well, everybody's committed and nobody's called in," Krypto said. "What do we do now?"

"Wait," Wally said. "Everything's on automatic here. Just sit back and watch the show."

The big C-130 banked slightly, completing one leg of its racetrack orbit. The E-3 AWACS had a tendency to go off the air during turns. If the Cannonball had a similar weakness, Krypto didn't notice it. There was no interruption in the operation of the swinging radar dome above or in the workings of the various transmitters tacked along the fuselage. Every so often, one or another of the wall of computer consoles would blink to life, chatter to itself, and then go back to sleep. Everything was normal-normal.

Krypto peered through the round porthole cut in the fuselage just forward of the cabin head. He saw the whole coast of Iran along the Strait of Hormuz. Yet he saw nothing, just a big ball of dust and smoke. If Krypto's eyes were sensitive to the entire electromagnetic spectrum, however, he would see an entirely different picture: beams of radars of every frequency, some jagged and pulsed, some streaming like searchlights. He'd see shafts of lasers and infrared beams, long streams of voices and data strung along the sky at high frequencies. And he'd see, at the center of the unseen activity, the mighty Cannonball, minding its own business.

Krypto wobbled back to Wally, sitting in front of the CRT, following the fight in full color. It *was* the best seat in the house.

"Uh-oh," Wally said ominously.

"What is it?" Krypto jumped. "What's wrong? Are the MiGs coming out to get us?"

"Worse than that," Wally said. "We've run out of popcorn."

The A-10 is notoriously slow. It is, in fact, say its critics, the only combat aircraft liable to suffer bird strikes from any direction. The aircraft's manufacturers inexplicably nicknamed the ungainly A-10 the "Thunderbolt II"; everyone else took one look at it and called it the "Warthog."

But then again, the A-10 was not designed to zoom around in the stratosphere engaging in supersonic jousts. It was built for one mission— close air support—to mix it up with tanks and guns down in the weeds in support of friendly ground troops. Grateful grunts did not regard the A-10 as a particularly slow airplane. They saw it as a fast tank. And that's exactly what the paratroopers at Bandar Abbas needed at the moment. A *very* fast tank.

"Can you see me?"

Major Glen "Rattler" Reese put the Warthog up on one wing and peered out the big canopy. He swooped down over the highway and peeled off by the terminal. It looked deserted. Swinging around over the runway, Reese spotted a patch of red at the summit of a small hill across from the parking lot.

"Okay, Gator, I've got you."

The A-10 zoomed over the hill a hundred feet off the ground, close enough for Reese to clearly see the red marker panel and two men—a radio operator kneeling in the dirt beside the wrecked TACAN transmitter and a tall black soldier holding the headset, staring up at Reese as he flew by.

Willis's voice was clear over the VHF radio and surprisingly calm, considering what the Division Ready Force had been through—and what they were up against now. "I'm kind of new at this, Rattler. What do you need to know?"

"Ah, how many tanks did you see, and where are they?"

"I saw three, but I know there's a lot more than that," Willis answered. "I can hear their engines. They were just heading out here when you flew over. They got scared, I guess, and headed back to town. I think they're hiding around that first group of buildings, right at the edge of the city. Can you see it?"

"Roger, Gator, I'll go take a look."

Reese swung out of his orbit and followed the narrow black highway south, peeling off before he reached the city's outskirts. If you stayed low, the east end of Bandar Abbas was supposed to be a "low-threat environment." Reese knew there was no such thing, even though the A-10 was built to take hits. Ten percent of the Warthog's considerable weight was devoted to armor, including a titanium "bathtub" surrounding the pilot, said to be able to withstand hits up to 37 mm. Designers claimed the A-10 could lose one engine, half a tail, two-thirds of a wing, and still fly.

Reese had no desire to test any of those claims in combat. He knew the A-10's greatest assets for survivability were the Mark I eyeball and the head-mounted computer. Reese resolved to be as careful as he could and still accomplish the mission. He soon discovered those two goals were mutually exclusive.

Circling around, the A-10 cut back over the city and zoomed in low above the main highway. Reese spotted an M60 idling in front of a gas station. He saw another tank across the street, surrounded by M113 armored personnel carriers. Then he saw another tank, then another, then another. Reese counted twelve before he stopped counting and broke out of the city.

"Ah, Gator, we've got problems. There's a lot more here than we first thought. I'm going to get some help."

"Roger, Rattler. Hurry back, will you?"

Reese could hear the tension now in Willis's voice. He knew what the soldier was thinking. After so many disappointments, the 82d's men in Bandar Abbas had grown accustomed to being abandoned.

"Don't worry, Gator, we'll be back," Reese said reassuringly. "This is First Air. We don't run out on anybody."

Turning back over the coastline, Reese chuckled to himself. He was surprised, though pleased, that he had thought to add the line about the Regiment. It was a real Steve Canyon thing to say, all right, not quite his style. But he meant it. There was something about First Air that inspired confidence.

Unlike most First Air pilots, the A-10 drivers were all from the same unit, the 501st Tactical Fighter Squadron. They were based at RAF Bentwaters in England but spent much of their time detached to their forward operating location in Sembach, West Germany.

Things had gotten tough for Warthog drivers in Europe. Government authorities had severely restricted low-level flying in West Germany in the wake of noise complaints and a distressing number of aircraft accidents. It was all very disconcerting for A-10 pilots, who had fully expected to limbo their way across central Europe in the event of war. And now, the Air Force claimed the Warthog was becoming obsolete, that flying low and slow was suicidal in the face of modern Soviet air defenses. Plans to replace the A-10 with green F-16s were the final insult—Reese and a half dozen of his fellow mud-movers from the 501st were among the first to sign on with the First Air Regiment, where the awkward Warthog was welcomed and appreciated.

Reese joined the rest of Rattler flight, spinning slow circles over the east end of Qeshm Island. He had gone ahead to scope out the situation before bringing in the others—contrary to what the rest of the Air Force thought, Warthog drivers did not relish wandering aimlessly over the battlefield trolling for targets. They preferred getting exact target designations from forward air controllers and zooming in. Better still would be a complete forward air-control party with a laser designator that could direct the A-10s and their smart weapons with pinpoint accuracy.

Willis was not a trained FAC and had no laser, but he was on the ground and he was a steady soldier, which was about all that Reese could hope for under the circumstances. Although his inexperience in working with fast movers was a decided drawback, Willis didn't sound like the kind of man who would let you down. And Reese resolved that First Air would not let Willis down, either.

Reese decided to call in reinforcements before he led the rest of the A-10s into battle over Bandar Abbas. There might not be time later, and there was always the possibility it would be a one-way trip.

"Ah, Cannonball, Rattler. We got a situation here. Looks like a rein-forced tank company at the east end of Rag City about two klicks from the airport. I count at least a dozen tracks, probably more, Mike-Sixties and Alpha Poppa Charlies. You might want to send somebody down here to back us up."

Click-click.

That was it? Reese waited to hear more from the command post, but it never came. Just the two punches of the radio transmission key, signifying that Cannonball had gotten the call and understood. That was the way to do it, of course, the professional way. After all, what more was there to be said? But Reese had gotten so used to chatter while flying with the Air Force, the babbling of controllers and the meddling of commanders, that true radio discipline came as a shock. He liked it. He just wasn't used to it.

"Copy, Cannonball. Rattler flight rolling in hot."

Reese led the rest of the A-10s over the coast east of the airport and set up a slow orbit above the pipeline that eventually ended in the refinery at Minab. He was about to press the transmit button to brief the rest of the flight when his earphones erupted with static and gunfire.

"Ah, better get over here, Rattler." Willis's voice was plaintive and preoccupied. "They're rolling in."

"Okay, Gator, here we come." Reese winged over to the right and headed down the airport road. "Follow me, Rattler. Double diamond formation. Guns only this pass—the bad guys are too close to the good guys."

They caught the first wave out in the open, the lead tank already in the parking lot. Reese hoped Willis had meant what he said when he told Bobby Dragon not to worry about working too close. There wasn't much choice, in any case.

"Keep your head down, Gator. We're coming in."

Reese flew the first tank he saw into the pipper and pulled the trigger. The massive seven-barrel Gatling cannon in the Warthog's hose whirred to life. The GAU-8, more than twenty feet long and weighing two tons, spewed 30-mm shells the size of milk bottles at a rate of over four thousand rounds per minute. In reality, however, only short bursts were possible before the barrels overheated and the eight tons of recoil generated by the firing slowed the already sluggish Warthog into a shuddering stall.

A short burst was all that was needed. Asphalt around the tank churned up in chunks. A power pole by the side of the road jerked up and fell over, sawed neatly in half by a single shell. The tank erupted in white smoke and yellow flames, a result of the pyrophoric effect of shells made of depleted uranium penetrating the steel armor.

Reese pulled off to the left, followed by the rest of the Rattlers. The wreckage of ruined Iranian tanks littered the road. But as Reese swept over the edge of the city on the way to the Gulf, he could see many more—apparently undaunted and thinking the A-10s were heading for home—lumbering out from side streets and heading for the airport.

"Outstanding, Rattler," Willis's voice came over the radio. "We'd almost forgotten what real close air support looked like down here. I'm afraid the bad guys have more tanks than brains, though. They're coming in again. Any chance for an encore?"

"You got it, Gator. We'll be dropping Rockeyes this time, so get your people down."

The flight of A-10s swooped around again, lining up for a cluster bomb attack that would scatter small bomblets over the east end of the city. Reese hoped it would also scatter the Iranians. The A-10 could fly forever, but there was no point in flying without bombs or bullets. In his head, Reese tallied the growing number of targets he had seen and divided it by the dwindling ordnance Rattler flight had remaining. In his heart, for the sake of Willis and the rest of the trapped troopers, Reese hoped Cannonball had gotten the message.

"Let's do it the hard way first," Brick said, standing over Wally with his hands on his hips. "We can always do it the easy way later on."

"You really want to ask for volunteers, General?" Krypto asked. "You can always order them in."

"We may have to," Brick said. "But let's try asking. Volunteering is what First Air is all about."

He nodded at Wally, who keyed the microphone and started spouting like a disc jockey. "Okay, fans, this is K-Ball, Cannonball Radio for Bandar Abbas and the entire greater region of hell. Here's a public-service announcement from your friends at First Air: We need a few sharp individuals to call us now and volunteer to relieve that nagging, aching pressure of excess Iranians at the airport. So if you're a real man and you've got a couple of extra Slicks, Rockeyes, Mavericks, or any surplus ordnance you'd be embarrassed to drag back to Dar al-Harb, just give us a call here at K-Ball and say, 'Yes, I want to be a hero.' Operators are standing by."

"Do you think they got that?" Krypto asked.

"Oh, I'm sure they got it," Brick growled. "I'm not sure they understood it. Why can't you guys just speak English like normal people? They didn't..."

"Shh!" Wally pointed to the speaker.

"K-Ball, Falcon flight." It was Faisal and his F-16s. "I volunteer."

"Well, that's a relief," Brick sighed. "We only need..."

The speaker crackled to life again. "Cannonball, this is Rhino." Bubba Windham and his F-4s. "We're in."

Before Brick could say anything else, another call came: "Cannonball, Stinger flight." The Hornets over NAS Bandar Abbas. "Things are kinda quiet here, and we're in the mood to attack a really big airport, so we're heading over."

It went on like that. Viper flight (more F-16s led by Dagger Amundsen). Magnet flight (Marine and RAF Harriers). Frogger flight (a bunch of French Mirage pilots who hadn't understood what Wally had said but liked the sound of it and volunteered for whatever it was). Limey (a couple of ancient British Buccaneers). Croc (a lone Australian F-111C, whose two-man crew were nicknamed, of course, "Kanga" and "Roo"). Demo (a composite flight put together of solitary aging aircraft no one else knew what to do with—an A-4 from New Zealand, an F-5 from Thailand, an F-1 from Japan, and an AMX from Brazil).

Soon, just about every attack pilot in the Regiment had called in, volunteering to go up against the tanks at the airport. The Division Ready Force's problems were over. Wally, however, now had a problem of his own— how to organize this parade of airpower so they didn't run into one another in their haste to be heroes. He got back on the microphone and started setting things up.

Krypto turned to Brick. "See, General? Ask and you shall receive."

Brick shook his head. "Now it's official. Everybody's insane but me."

No one was happier to hear about the rescue of the American paratroopers than Scooter Jeffries. Not that he cared one way or the other about what happened on the ground—he was a fighter pilot, and it was beneath him. But the gaggle of friendly aircraft gathering above the airport was sure to attract MiGs like a bear to honey.

And Scooter was loaded for bear. No Phoenix missiles this trip, no gas tanks, none of that crap. His F-14 was dripping with Sparrows and Sidewinders, real grab-'em-by-the-nuts-and-shoot-'em-in-the-face missiles. He was locked and loaded, primed to unwind. Bobby and the Eagles had broken up the MiGs' first attack. Now, Scooter could see on his radar, the Fulcrums were forming up another wave.

Good. Let them come. Scooter was ready. He would fight the battle he wanted to fight, not some admiral's chairborne fantasies. He had the upper hand, wingmen he could count on, a sky full of friendlies behind him, and no one in front but those bastards that had given him hell for two weeks. Today, by God, Jeffries would get his MiG.

"Ah, Scooter?"

"Yeah, Daffy. What is it? Have you got a vector?" Jeffries had, until then, thought an itchy trigger finger was a figment of the Hollywood imagination. He was *ready*.

"Sort of." In the backseat, Daffy peered into his displays, which were more detailed than the radar screen in the front seat. He wanted to get this right. He didn't want to disappoint Jeffries. He knew how much a victory meant to him.

But there was no denying it. The MiGs were turning around, heading for home. Daffy made some quick, rough calculations. At the speed they were traveling, and considering the amount of fuel they probably had remaining, there was no way the MiGs were coming back. Not without landing and refueling, and by that time he and Scooter and the rest of Kitty flight would be back in the barn themselves.

"I, ah, hate to break this to you, Scooter, but the MiGs are disengaging. They're separating back to Zaranj."

"No!" Jeffries slammed a fist of Nomex into the instrument panel. "They can't do this to me!"

"Sorry, buddy," Daffy said. "Maybe next time."

"Next time," Scooter repeated sourly. "This is starting to get on my nerves, Daffy. I swear, the only way I'm going to get a MiG is to join the Soviet Air Force."

"What did he say?"

Wally rewound the digital sampler and replayed the transmission. "It sounds like '*proval*' to me, General."

"What the hell does that mean?" Brick asked.

"It's the Russian word for harvest," Krypto explained. "But I don't know what it means."

"Whatever it was, those MiGs sure turned tail and ran when they heard it," Brick said. "They didn't get out of burner until they got back to Zaranj."

"Where did it come from?" Krypto asked Wally.

Wally typed some words rapidly in a computer and whistled. "*Zorky 14.*"

"That's one of their nuclear-alert satellites, isn't it?" Krypto asked.

Wally nodded. "It's a communications relay bird. The Russians threw a bunch up there a couple of years ago, figuring they'd probably never get a chance to launch them when they really needed them. But they're usually not active. I've never heard of the Soviets using a Zorky before."

"Well, whatever it was, it just saved us the trouble of shooting them down, that's all." Brick rubbed his hands together. "Jesus, what a day! What a unit! I've never seen anything like it. The paratroopers say there's nothing left on the other side of the airport road but burning tanks. All the Iranian ground threats have been neutralized. We chased the MiGs away. Who would have guessed that it would all be over in just one day?"

Krypto looked at the screens, once black with threats and targets, now wiped clear by the First Air Regiment. They had done a job, all right, Brick was right about that. But Krypto wasn't so sure about the other thing.

"I don't know, General," he said to Brick. "I don't think it's over. In fact, I've got a feeling that it's just beginning."

Under the Red Star

Moscow
Union of Soviet Socialist Republics

I s this the man?"

Illyushin nodded sadly. "Yes, comrade Marshal."

Feodor Kiroshenko, Soviet minister of defense, stared with contempt at the man standing stiffly before him. Kiroshenko's considerable girth and wolfish expression gave the appearance that he not only would like to but *could* bite off Paratov's head and swallow it whole.

"Colonel Paratov, perhaps you would like to exchange uniforms with me," he began, in a voice not as playful as it sounded. "As you have taken it upon yourself to exercise prerogatives normally reserved for marshals of the Soviet Union, why not wear the insignia that accompanies the rank?"

"No, thank you, sir," Paratov said quietly. "It would not fit."

There was no expression on Paratov's ravaged face. Kiroshenko, however, could sense insubordination when he heard it. His massive frame shook with rage.

"You are correct, Colonel!" he bellowed. "It is too big for you. In every way."

Kiroshenko spun and fixed his eyes on Illyushin.

"And you, comrade, Colonel General!" Kiroshenko barked. "You have always had your eyes on this office, eh? Well, take a good look at it! This is the last you will see of the Kremlin for a good long while."

Illyushin took in the marshal's suite with a pang of envy and regret. He admired the thick green carpet, the high ceilings, the Finnish furniture—not Danish, as in the chairman's suite, he noticed, but any sort of foreign furniture was a sign of status in the Soviet power structure. Most of all, he craved the wide window overlooking the courtyard. This was the good side of the building.

It was not so much the office itself that pained Illyushin, but what it represented—to be inside, to run with the *nachalstro,* the Kremlin's movers and shakers. His track to the top had been derailed on a hot, dirty beach thousands of miles from Moscow. A lifetime of service to the state had gone down in flames along with Paratov's MiGs in the air battle above Bandar Abbas.

"Comrade Marshal, I meant no..."

"Save your voice, Colonel General!" Kiroshenko barked. "Perhaps you can talk your way out of the noose. Perhaps your friends in the Politburo will intervene on your behalf and get you a new office. One in the country, eh? Far in the country. Kazakestan, perhaps. There is always an opening for a man of your influence at the Ninth Spassky Department Camp. Fresh air, hard work—it does wonders for one's appearance, I am told. After a while, even your friends will not recognize you!"

Kiroshenko shook with laughter. Illyushin looked at Paratov, who continued to stare ahead, impassively. For once, Illyushin envied Paratov's damaged face for its unchanging features. Throughout the long, hellish night and day they had been together, on the Candid military airliner from Zaranj to Vnukova II, the VIP airport outside Moscow, through the city to the Kremlin in the armored Zil limousine, up the armory stairs to Kiroshenko's chamber, Paratov had said little and shown even less. Illyushin tried to tell himself Paratov's courage was only the resignation of a beaten man facing certain death. Paratov knew, surely, that he would be killed. As for himself...

"None of that matters at the moment," Kiroshenko sniffed. "The fate of two insubordinate minor military officers is of little consequence compared with the challenge we face in the Persian Gulf. The question remains—what do we do now?"

Illyushin was accustomed to thinking deeply but not quickly. He saw no immediate way to salvage his plan. How was he to know Paratov's fighters would be recalled in the middle of the fight? For all he knew, the ancient marshals were hatching a plot of their own. He needed time to scheme out all the alternatives. On the spot he could come up with only one card to play.

"May I speak, comrade Marshal?" Illyushin ventured.

"Speak? Why of course!" Kiroshenko said with exaggerated expansiveness. "By all means, speak your mind, comrade Colonel General. You should never be afraid to talk to your minister. If you had poured out your pitiful heart to me before this, told me all you knew when there was time to stop it, perhaps you would not be here today. But better late than never. Go ahead. Talk."

Illyushin shifted uncomfortably. "Why should we do anything? Why not let things stand as they are? Condemn Paratov for the renegade he is. Execute him publicly. Tell the world we had no prior knowledge of his plans and actions, which is true. The Americans will understand. They have had similar situations before and have expected us to believe their men were acting alone."

Kiroshenko's expression of shock melted to mean contempt.

"Do you see the worm?" Kiroshenko turned to Paratov, jerking a huge hand in Illyushin's direction. "Do you see what loyalty means in this viper's pit? I cannot count the times he has accosted me in the hallways to recount your latest exploit on the frontier. He spoke of you as a father speaks proudly of his son, always willing to take the credit while he kept you safely hidden in some godforsaken wilderness. But that was different. All was glory then. Now, the first time you fail, he is ready to offer your hide in exchange for his own."

Paratov remained still. If he was angry or frightened, he didn't show it. He never did.

"Get out of here," Kiroshenko hissed at Illyushin. "Get out now, before I throw you out that window you so admire."

Illyushin could feel the panic rising from his belly up his spine. The back of his head pounded. He had expected Kiroshenko to take the easy way out, as he always had before. Illyushin was accustomed to presenting his *fait accompli* to the marshal in the form of a decision, albeit one already made. Kiroshenko had never failed to play the game before. Now, when it counted most, when Illyushin's very life depended upon Kiroshenko's languid temperament, the ancient marshal had turned into a dragon. Illyushin could feel the fire.

"But, comrade Marshal, I did not..." Illyushin backed away, terrified. "Where will I go? What will I do?"

"I do not care," Kiroshenko said tiredly. "It would be too kind to have you arrested now. I want you to think about it, think about what you have done, to me, to your country. If you have any sense of honor left, you will kill yourself and save the state the trouble."

Illyushin turned quickly to leave and bumped into the impassive Paratov.

"Please, Mischa, I was just talking," Illyushin said plaintively. "I was not seriously suggesting that you be executed. I was only..."

Paratov spat. The saliva dripped from the side of Illyushin's face on to the glittering display of medals and ribbons on his chest. Illyushin stared, unbelieving, then turned and walked stiffly out the door.

His head reeling, heart pounding, Illyushin staggered down the gray hallway, half aware of discreet stares from the offices as he passed. *Kiroshenko's men,* Illyushin thought. *Mustn't let them see me like this.*

He stumbled into the men's room, giving silent thanks there was no one watching as he tried to pull himself together. Illyushin had never been comfortable in confrontations and entered into arguments only when he was sure he would win. He had an uncanny knack for manipulation and a shrewd knowledge of human nature, but it did not function in real time. He needed time to think.

His eyes skittered across the room, all porcelain and green tin. It was considerably more than what most members of the Soviet Union made do with, but it was still a place for nobodies. He regretted he had never seen the bathroom, the *private* bathroom, in Kiroshenko's office. Too late now.

Kiroshenko. He was the primary threat. Illyushin forced himself to think, to sort out what Kiroshenko must know from what he could not know. Illyushin's role in establishing the MiG base at Zaranj and installing Paratov at its head was common knowledge, but that could still be explained as a tactical decision well within the scope of the deputy commander of the Soviet Air Force. As for Kiroshenko's personal attack, Illyushin knew the marshal had never cared for him, as the defense minister disliked any military man with ties to the chairman. Illyushin was surprised at the depth of Kiroshenko's dislike for him, but that personal indulgence on the marshal's part could be used against him if and when Illyushin presented his case to the chairman. *Do you see, comrade First Secretary?* Illyushin heard himself saying, *The minister insults you when he insults your friends.*

Illyushin tore through his memory, searching for any clues that Kiroshenko had somehow stumbled onto the larger plan. To his great relief, he found none. There had been no mention of Carlos Rivera, no indication of concern outside Squadron 22. The most convincing evidence was the fact that he was free. If Kiroshenko had any notion of what really lay beneath recent events in the Persian Gulf, Illyushin knew, he would have already been swinging from a rope in the basement of the Lubiyanka.

And what was Paratov now telling Kiroshenko? Paratov was crazy; Illyushin could see that now. Since the accident he had become a creature without morals, a robot programmed for only one mission. But Illyushin thought he could count on Paratov's silence. It was no longer a question of loyalty, he thought, as he dabbed at the spittle on his tunic with a wad of rough Russian tissue. It had been an unpleasant scene, but, in the long run, Illyushin was glad it had happened. Once the news floated around the Armory halls, no one would ever link his name and Paratov's again.

Paratov would not talk, because Paratov was convinced that Illyushin's plan was his own, that he was using the colonel general, when in reality the opposite was true. Surely, Illyushin thought, Paratov must know that anything he said would only incriminate himself. And he was in too deep not to go through with it now. Paratov was no doubt insane, but he was not a fool.

So what *was* going on in the mind of the minister of defense? If he was genuinely upset with Paratov's alleged mutiny, why had Kiroshenko waited until this moment to call him on the carpet? After all, Squadron 22 had been in action for two weeks now. Was it because Paratov's MiGs had failed to turn back First Air's assault on Bandar Abbas? But whose fault was that? Only the Soviet defense minister was authorized to issue the *proval* signal.

Illyushin suddenly saw it all so clearly. Yes, it was all right. The pieces of his plan were still intact. His first instincts had been correct, as usual. The Kremlin's dinosaurs *were* planning a revolt. That was fine. If anything, whatever clumsy plot Kiroshenko might set moving would only serve to accelerate Illyushin's own designs by distracting the chairman from looking too closely at the colonel general's role in the Iranian crisis. With the military and the party at each other's throats, who would notice an obscure Air Force officer whose only crime was loyalty to the misguided son of a dead comrade?

In the past, other officers who had interfered with his plans—those who had lived—had marveled at Illyushin's luck, at his ability to land on his feet. They had even complained, jealously and only half jokingly, that the colonel general must have a crystal ball, some mystic power that allowed him to see the future.

Illyushin smiled. He could not predict the future. His power was far greater. He could make the future happen.

Kiroshenko watched Illyushin leave with a crooked smile.

"Good riddance," he said. "I could never stomach that bastard anyway. Always sucking up to people, spreading gossip, and concocting his little plots. When we were in control he swaggered like a Cossack, all blood and iron. But when this new chairman came to power, I swear to you, you could see Illyushin sprouting the wings of a dove right before your eyes. Bah! Let him stew. We can deal with him later. Now it is time for the men to talk."

Kiroshenko pulled himself from his chair with great effort, waddling to a sideboard to pour vodka from a crystal decanter. He pointed the glass at Paratov in the manner of a question. Paratov shook his head. Kiroshenko smiled.

"I wish I had a face like yours," he said admiringly. "Then no one would know what I was thinking, and I would always have people at a disadvantage. Now, for instance—you can read me like a book. Yet I have no idea what is going on in your head."

"Oh, I think you do," Paratov said briskly.

"You are angry with me, eh?" Kiroshenko laughed. "That is good. I could not trust a commander who is not angry when one of his men is killed."

"Many of my men were killed, sir," Paratov said bitterly.

"Don't worry, Colonel," Kiroshenko settled himself heavily back into his chair. "You will have more men. Many more men. As many as you need."

Paratov looked at Kiroshenko curiously. His anger got the best of his curiosity. "That is not the point, sir. We were doing quite well with what we had. These mercenaries were better than we thought, true. Much better flyers than their Navy pilots we had been fighting. But we were holding our own. It was my understanding that the *proval* signal was to be used only in the event of a nuclear war. Why did you order us to withdraw so abruptly— right in the middle of our attack?"

"I sent the signal because it was the only way I could be sure you would abort your mission. Your attack was unnecessary," Kiroshenko said. "It was necessary only that you *be* attacked."

"I am afraid I do not understand, comrade Marshal."

"Oh, you understand, Colonel," Kiroshenko replied. "You might have been able to sell that fool Illyushin on this nonsense about Baluchistan, although personally I do not think he believed it any more than I do. But he was willing to swallow your fantasy because he saw, as do I, the greater opportunity beyond."

"Sir, Baluchistan is..."

"Spare me your fables, Colonel," Kiroshenko sighed. "I am not a child. Whatever reasons you had for your insubordination are of interest only to yourself and the board of inquiry at your court-martial. I need something considerably more substantial to sell the Politburo. Blood will do."

"I am prepared for what punishment you deem necessary," Paratov said firmly. "However, may I remind the marshal that it is he who took away our victory yesterday at Bandar Abbas?"

Kiroshenko stared at Paratov, then burst into laughter. "Oh, you are naive! Is it possible that you really believed your own story? Could you have presented us with the perfect plan, the opportunity we have been searching for, without even knowing? I am not talking about *your* blood, Colonel. I meant the lives of your hero pilots. The ones who died yesterday."

Paratov shifted stiffly. "Comrade Marshal, it has been a long journey. I am tired and confused and, I will admit, not a little frightened. Please have me killed like a soldier and be done with it."

"I will do with you whatever I see fit and whenever I see fit," Kiroshenko said darkly. Then he softened. "In the meantime, Colonel, please sit down. I have a story of my own to tell you. That is, unless you are in too great a hurry to be executed."

Paratov slumped gratefully into an oxblood leather chair across from the marshal's huge oak desk.

"Everything is in place," Kiroshenko said conspiratorially. "Most of the people who matter here are from the old school. They feel as we do."

"Oh, comrade Marshal?" Paratov was tired and perplexed. "And what do we feel?"

"You really want me to say it, do you?" Kiroshenko said with a mixture of anger and admiration. "You want *me* to step across the line with you and put both our heads in the noose? You really should have stayed in Moscow, Colonel. You play the game very well."

"I really have no idea what you are talking about, sir."

"Very well, Colonel Paratov. You win. I will spell it out for you." Kiroshenko leaned forward and bore into Paratov's eyes. "The chairman is leading this nation to ruin. Under the guise of political and economic reform, he is giving away all we have fought for and died for since the Great Patriotic War. If he is allowed to continue, Russia will become just another toady of America, like Great Britain or Germany. We cannot stand idly by and let that happen."

Paratov flinched inwardly. Kiroshenko's apparent hatred of the chairman did not come as a surprise. Paratov had been aware for some time that senior Soviet military leaders were less than happy with the country's new political direction. *Glasnost* took away their old enemies. *Perestroika* took away their new weapons. But Paratov was shocked to discover the disaffection had festered into mutiny.

"What are you proposing, comrade Marshal?" Paratov asked quietly.

Kiroshenko rose from his chair and turned his back to Paratov, staring out the window.

"In less than a week's time," he said, "the 104th Soviet Guards Airborne Division will seize the high ground above Bandar Abbas. At the same time, a complete tactical aviation army—led by you, Colonel Paratov—will occupy the air bases at Zaranj and Mazar. Together, they will sweep the Americans into the sea and these mercenaries from the skies."

Paratov was stunned. "I am surprised the chairman would permit such a bold plan."

"The chairman does not know." Kiroshenko spun around to fix Paratov with his gaze. "Even now, Illyushin's pleas for his life will convince the chairman's people that the matter is closed, and we will hear no more of you and your attacks against the Americans in Iran."

"But surely the chairman will..." Paratov said.

"He will be told when the time comes, when it is too late to do anything about it. What could he tell his friend the president then, eh? That it was a mistake? That he was sorry? No, Colonel. Not even an American would believe that! Besides, there is oil in Iran, and oil is money, and money will solve the chairman's problems. If he is smart—and he is, though misguided—he will go along with our plan of action. If he does not, well..."

Kiroshenko let the words hang heavily in the air. Paratov's mind raced with move and countermove, details of the operation, its complications and rewards. It finally came down to one word.

"Excuse me, sir. But what you say is treason."

"No!" Kiroshenko's immense fist slammed down on the desk. "We do not seek to depose the chairman, only to bring him back down to earth. We are not traitors, after all. This is *not* treason. This is patriotism."

"Whatever you choose to call it, comrade Marshal, you can still hang for it."

"That is true, Colonel. And so can you. So I would be very careful what you say and to whom you say it from now on."

"I am always careful," Paratov replied. "But you are taking a very grave risk. What is there to be gained by all this? Is it worth the countless lives of our soldiers who are sure to die in the invasion, possibly millions more in a larger war with America, just to teach the chairman a lesson?"

Kiroshenko settled back in his chair. "You ask me a question, Colonel. Now I ask one of you: Why should we settle for half of Iran? Have we not earned the entire country in blood? We have fought—we are fighting—a hundred times as many more in Tehran as the Americans are facing in Bandar Abbas. Without your intervention, the United States would have already accomplished its goals in Iran. And now, with your sacrifice, you have given us a reason to intervene. American pilots attacked and killed Soviet pilots over Bandar Abbas yesterday. However they try to distance themselves from their involvement with the mercenaries at al-Quaseem, just as you chose to distance yourself from Moscow, the fact remains that we are at war with the United States in the Persian Gulf.

"Remember, we did not start this war," Kiroshenko continued. "The Iranians began this madness. And the Americans brought us in, with an unprovoked attack on one of our destroyers in international waters. Now they compound their arrogance by shooting down your planes—our planes, as we can now tell the world, Russian planes, commanded by a Russian colonel. The U.S. cannot lie this time. The whole world saw it. We have a very strong case for intervention. The world has grown weary of the clumsy Americans, their high-handed meddling and trigger-happy diplomacy. It will not be difficult to present our invasion of Bandar Abbas as a necessary act of self-defense.

"No, Colonel Paratov, we did not start this war. But we are going to end it. And we are going to get something for our trouble and our blood. We are not going to limp out of Iran like we did in Afghanistan. This is the Russian Army, by God! The army that beat Napoleon and Hitler. To run from a pack of *mujahideen* beggars—that was beyond disgrace!

"This time we will not stay around to be dragged down, to have our soldiers die of sickness or loneliness or be betrayed by party bureaucrats in Moscow with no stomach for fighting. This time we are going to hit hard, take all we can, and then wait for negotiations."

"What makes you think there will be negotiations?" Paratov asked.

"Of course there will be negotiations," Kiroshenko said. "You cannot expect the Americans to lay down their arms and leave. They are much too proud for that. You have to give them an out. They will not be defeated in battle, but they do not seem to mind being swindled at the conference table after the shooting stops."

"No, I mean what makes you think they will not fight to the death?" Paratov replied. "They have long identified the Persian Gulf as an area of vital interest. What if they decide to defend it with weapons of mass destruction?"

Kiroshenko knew perfectly well what Paratov meant by *weapons of mass destruction*. The phrase conjured, in the language of the Soviet military, mushroom clouds over the Gulf, a nuclear exchange between the superpowers that would start in the Middle East but most certainly not end there. Kiroshenko brushed the objections aside.

"Are you telling me the president of the United States would risk the lives of his people so the Germans and Japanese can continue to power their cars with cheap gasoline?" he snorted. "America does not need the oil, so it does not need Iran."

Paratov had to admit the marshal was right. The vast majority of tankers cruising through the Strait of Hormuz never made it to the United States. Most veered right, to the Mediterranean Sea, to off-load the oil that kept the wheels of Western Europe turning. Another chain of tankers, thirty minutes apart, shuttled fuel to Japan. Those countries used Persian crude to power industrial machines that were slowly grinding down the once-mighty American economy. Yet the United States, and the United States alone, protected Western interests in the Gulf and around the world.

"But what if you are wrong, comrade Marshal?" Paratov asked plaintively.

"I am not," Kiroshenko shot back. "I am absolutely correct. I know this man in the White House. He will melt. And so will the Americans. They have had their first little bite of sacrifice, and it has left a bitter taste. Besides, you cannot lose what you never had. Less than a month ago, most Americans had never heard of Bandar Abbas. I think they will be quite willing to forget all about it."

"It does not have to come to that," Paratov suggested. "They could continue fighting with conventional weapons. What then?"

"I say good, let them fight! If we do not fight them now, we will have to fight them later. And I say fight while we still have the strength. If we wait long enough, that fool next door will disarm us completely. *Sufficient force!*" Kiroshenko spat. "What rubbish! He says we can no longer afford to defend ourselves, as if these ships and planes were merely toys, built to amuse generals and admirals. Do not tell me to cut back military production— tell the Americans! Do you know how much money they spend on weapons each year, comrade Colonel? Do you?"

Paratov shook his head, startled by the old soldier's anger and frustration.

"I could not tell you in rubles," Kiroshenko said. "There are not that many rubles in the world. And yet they continue to make more planes, more tanks, more ships. Now they are shooting weapons into outer space! I tell the chairman this, but he never listens. Perhaps he will listen now. Perhaps it is time he realized weapons are not a useless extravagance, as he obviously regards them. They are investments, very good investments."

"I am afraid I do not follow you, sir," Paratov said uneasily.

"Listen to me, Colonel," Kiroshenko growled. "In a single generation, the Soviet Union has grown to a position of world dominance. How did that happen? We did not do it with our industry or our banking. And we sure as hell did not do it *farming,* comrade. We did it by scaring the hell out of everyone. No one took us seriously until we took weapons seriously. Of all this country stands for, only our weapons—not our economy, or ideology, or culture—earn the world's respect. And now the chairman wants to take them away. For what? So we will have more money to buy tractors? People are not impressed by tractors. They may admire our forthrightness and vision. I could care less. Admiration is for the second-rate. The Japanese are admired. The Russians are feared! Which would you prefer?"

"I agree with you, comrade Marshal," Paratov said tenuously. "But the Americans have weapons, too."

"Ah, yes," Kiroshenko smiled. "But they have no resolve. It is like a gun with no bullets. Listen. The world is confused and frightened. People everywhere are looking for leadership. Whoever controls this situation in the Gulf will control the world in the next century, perhaps for centuries to come.

It is time the Soviet Union assumed its rightful place in the world. It is time that fool in the chairman's office..."

"Excuse me, Marshal Kiroshenko," Paratov said nervously. "Perhaps we should keep our voices down."

Kiroshenko spread his hands expansively. "Am I not among friends?" he asked. But he lowered his voice just the same. "The Americans are unfocused, undisciplined. Their system of government is hopelessly slow and inefficient, especially when it comes to making military decisions. Their resolve is weak. Their leadership will waver, as it has so many times before. Democracy! Hah! The freedom to jabber about all sides of an issue before finally deciding to do whatever the rich bosses had decided all along.

"They think democracy makes them superior. *Geography* makes them superior," Kiroshenko continued. "How could they fail? They were born between two docile nations and two limitless seas. Let them live like Russians, surrounded on all sides by generations of enemies. The Americans have oil floating underneath them, coal and iron and gold, and people they can work to death and then throw away. Who could not prosper under such fortunate circumstances? We have fought for everything we have gotten. It has only made us stronger. Stronger than them. They will see. We will make them see."

"This First Air Regiment, comrade Marshal," Paratov said doubtfully. "They do not strike me as weak."

"Individually, perhaps not. But they have nothing to fight for. They are *melochi,* a collection, odds and ends. If they are mercenaries, they will run," Kiroshenko said evenly. "If they are patriots, they will die. It does not matter to me either way."

"And what about the Iranians, comrade Marshal?"

"What about them?" Kiroshenko flicked an imaginary crumb off the desk. "They are tiresome little brown people of no consequence. A bloody nuisance. The world is sick of them. We will kill any *chernozhopy* who gets in the way."

"Iranians are actually not brown, comrade Marshal," Paratov said softly. "They are Aryans, most of them."

"Are they, now?" Kiroshenko said, genuinely surprised. "That is even better. We Russians are good at killing Aryans. I was. And so was Illyushin, before he turned into an old woman. Your father, Colonel—he was the best."

Paratov pitched forward with interest. "You knew my father, then?"

"Oh, yes," Kiroshenko said wistfully. "First in the Ukraine, then here in Moscow. You should be proud of him. He was a great flyer and a good man. But he chose his friends badly."

"What happened to him, comrade Marshal?" Paratov asked softly. If anyone knew, certainly the Soviet defense minister did. And since they were now coconspirators, bound together in a plot to subvert the government, what was one more state secret betrayed? At least Paratov, who had been burning all his life to discover his father's true fate, hoped Kiroshenko would see it that way.

"Surely you know," Kiroshenko said cruelly. "Illyushin killed him."

Paratov's face showed no emotion, though his hands clenched into quick fists.

"It is true," Kiroshenko said firmly. "Oh, Illyushin did not do it himself. He had grown too soft for that. But he killed your father just as surely as if he had pulled the trigger."

Kiroshenko raised his glass. It was empty. He lurched from his chair and across the room to the sideboard, almost staggering. Paratov could see the man was drunk and clearly accustomed to being so. Good, Paratov thought. Drunk men talk. And he wanted to know more.

"I cannot believe it," Paratov said. "Illyushin and my father were the best of friends."

"They were," Kiroshenko agreed. "That made it easy for Illyushin. You must remember, Colonel, times were hard here after the war. Everything was hard. In many ways, it was much like today. Then, as now, there were opportunities in paranoia, a name to be made in the panic," Kiroshenko explained. "Illyushin could not wait to leave active service. He made a great show of his 'secret' fear of flying, but it was the fighting that really frightened him, and the chance he might be killed himself. Like many cowards, he found his way into military intelligence. It was just the place for a man like Illyushin. The air was thick with plots and intrigue. There were so many things to be afraid of, so many things we just did not know.

"Quite on his own, Illyushin soon stumbled across an opportunity to make his name among the fearmongers. There was a traitor in Berlin, an American officer, willing to sell a secret we were desperate to have—the all-flying tail."

"Sir?"

Kiroshenko laughed bitterly. "It does seem a silly thing for grown men to worry themselves over, eh? It certainly was not worth the life of your father. But our Air Force people were scared to death of the American Sabre jet."

"The stabilator," Paratov remembered. "Before the F-86, most horizontal stabilizers were merely slabs or had at the most rudimentary ailerons. The Sabre's stabilizers actually moved on an axis, like giant ailerons. Quite revolutionary for its day."

"Yes, well," Kiroshenko continued. "All Illyushin had to do was report this to his superiors and they would have sent someone to Berlin to meet this man. A professional man for a professional job—that was the way it was supposed to be done, should have been done. But Illyushin was afraid someone would steal the credit. He was greedy for that cheap glory that passes for manhood among spies. If he had had any guts, he would have gone himself. But he did not. He asked your father."

"And my father accepted?"

"Why not? He had no reason to be suspicious when his best friend asked that he do his patriotic duty. He did not know the man Illyushin had become. In fact, your father thought it only logical that he be the one to go to Berlin. After all, Illyushin was a known intelligence operative. Your father was not. It would be easier for him to travel abroad without overly arousing the suspicions of American counterespionage agents. And he was a pilot. Who was better qualified to judge the quality of the aeronautical information he was buying?

"It was a trap, of course," Kiroshenko said sorrowfully. "The Americans were waiting for him. It seems two months before, a U.S. RB-47 spy plane was shot down over the Kola peninsula. The crew ejected, but only the pilot survived. The Americans needed someone to exchange for him. Your father was the perfect choice. The deal was made."

"That is unfortunate," Paratov said. "But I understand such exchanges were common before satellites replaced espionage aircraft. It is not a tragedy."

"No, you are right," Kiroshenko said. "Here is the tragedy: Illyushin had failed. But your father paid the penalty. Illyushin could not admit he had initiated his own outlaw operation, outside the center—a capital offense, even now, something you might keep in mind. And he had always been jealous of your father, jealous of his talent for flying, of his courage and leadership. Illyushin saw a way to save his own life while getting rid of a rival by telling his superiors the plan was your father's idea, that he knew nothing of it. He even offered to deliver your father personally to the KGB, which he did— the bastard."

Paratov sat silently, taking it all in. His blue eyes began to shine. For years he had wondered, worried, what had happened that day. He remembered it so vividly, in the stark, primary colors of childhood memory. His father, whom he idolized, had at last returned from a very long absence to Domodedovo, the air base outside Moscow where he was stationed as a test pilot. Illyushin suddenly appeared, suggesting to his father they take a ride into the city, an odd luxury with gasoline still scarce. Paratov's father had not come back from that ride.

"After Illyushin has served our purpose, he will, of course, be executed," Kiroshenko said softly. "I could arrange to have you kill him, if you wish."

"Perhaps," Paratov replied. "Thank you, comrade Marshal. But right now I have a better murder in mind."

"I am afraid I do not understand," Kiroshenko said, puzzled.

"Come now, sir," Paratov chided. "You are the minister of defense of the Union of Soviet Socialist Republics. There is precious little that escapes your attention, or your files. Surely you know who is commanding this First Air Regiment for the Americans."

"Yes, I do," Kiroshenko said, surprised. "The deserter, Robert Dragon. But how did you know?"

"I have known all along," Paratov said slyly. "You asked me before about my motives for attacking the Americans. You were right: This was never about Baluchistan. It has always been about Bobby Dragon."

"You still blame him for your..." Kiroshenko corrected himself, "for what happened in Vietnam?"

"Blame is an opinion, comrade Marshal. Burns are facts. Scars are facts."

"But you attacked the Americans long before Colonel Dragon became involved, before the First Air Regiment even existed. How did you..." Kiroshenko stopped himself in midsentence, confused and suddenly alarmed.

The minister of defense had come to see himself, in all his bureaucratic battles to the Kremlin summit, as the master manipulator, the man in control. Now Kiroshenko caught a glimpse of a larger plot, the dimensions of which even he had never dreamed or dared, one in which he was snared neatly, moved to another man's purpose. It was like a *metroska,* he thought, the folk-art dolls carved by Russian peasants—when you remove the doll's head you find another doll inside it, and another doll inside that one.

Kiroshenko did not know how many levels of the *metroska* Paratov had removed for him, or how many more were yet to be revealed. He did not know where Illyushin's plot ended and where Paratov's insanity began. Still, he was a smart man. Not quite as smart as he thought he was moments ago, perhaps, but he knew enough not to ask any more questions.

"Then we are after the same thing. To victory!" Kiroshenko raised his glass in mock salute. "And do me a favor, eh? Please, Colonel, try to do more than kill one man with the forces I give you. Kill enough to be a hero."

A Holiday in Hell

Bandar Abbas International Airport
Southern Iran Airport

Gray clouds rose from the morning haze over the coast and stitched themselves into a swift thunderhead over the city. The Persian *gaws* blew in from the south, whipping through the low desert, seeming to seek out whatever pitiful vegetation remained—bending the date palms along the coast road, shuffling through the mangrove in the swamp next to the airport, twisting the eucalyptus in the high mountains. When the wind met the rain, the sky cracked open.

Back at Fort Bragg, the cloudburst would have been noticed only for its brevity and severity. In the Persian Gulf, however, schools let out to watch sun showers. And in Bandar Abbas, it was a miracle. In Bandar Abbas, war was more common than rain. It was a holiday in hell.

The astonished troopers staggered out of the terminal and wandered across the runway, stripped to the waist, mouths upturned, dancing and sloshing in the sudden puddles. Sgt. Bill Willis leaned against the door to the terminal building and watched the giddy madness. He thought about stopping the party, getting the men back in ranks. It would not do to have the brass find his men cavorting like drunken Bedouins seeing rain for the first time. Willis decided to let the men have their fun. Screw the brass. Whatever they could do to him couldn't be worse than what they had already done.

The rain ended as quickly as it began. What little water that collected in the gullies and depressions did not soak in but immediately steamed away. The rain had only made the heat worse by adding to the already stifling humidity. Clothes stuck to the troopers' bodies in dank clumps. The moist hot air was difficult to breathe.

Willis caught a wing flash over the Gulf, a big plane lining up on final. He strode across the ramp to the runway, M16 in hand, his face screwed into the casual sternness of command. It was an expression he had learned from Casey. Poor Casey.

"All right, they're coming in," he bellowed. "Let's settle down and *try* to look tactical. You've only got to act like soldiers for another hour or so."

A cheer shot through the ranks, a cry of relief and genuine happiness. The noise was lost in the roar of the giant Starlifter that screamed onto the newly cleared runway. The gray-and-white transport rolled to a stop, swiveled around, and taxied back to the terminal. The men gathered their gear and stood stiffly at attention, single file in a line that barely stretched from one end of the C-141 to the other.

The aircraft stopped and shut down its engines. Gen. Curtis Coleman appeared at the opening doorway. At Willis's command, the men snapped a quick salute, then broke into cheers and whistles.

"Stand back, men," Coleman boomed. "I have a little surprise for you."

Coleman disappeared back into the aircraft. He emerged with another Army officer, who moved stiffly to the doorway with the aid of a cane. It was Steve Casey.

The men broke rank and ran happily to the Starlifter. They crowded around Casey, shouting, picking him up, and setting him down on the runway.

"Now, take it easy with him, men," Coleman admonished. "He just had surgery a couple of days ago. He's not even supposed to be here. I had to steal him out of the hospital at Wiesbaden when the doctors weren't looking."

The press poured off the aircraft in pairs, cameramen and soundmen, focusing on the celebration swirling around Casey. It made a good visual. They shouted at the troopers to stand back so they could get a better angle. The reporters were casually shoved aside.

More officers filed out of the plane, Beaufort Forest at their head. The president's national security advisor was surprised at how hot it was—hotter than al-Quaseem, although he hadn't thought that possible. He was also struck by how few soldiers remained from the Division Ready Force. Brick White hadn't exaggerated. The United States had been just one day short of losing Bandar Abbas and all of southern Iran. And the war. Yes, Forest thought. It was acceptable to call it a war now that it had been won.

Brick White followed, standing off to the side, getting his first look at the American soldiers he had fought so hard to save. The men had rearranged themselves in ranks, at attention, with Casey at their head. It wasn't the presence of high-ranking officers that made the troopers stand so stiffly in the sun. It wasn't even discipline, of the parade-ground sort. It was pride. They had done what no one else had, what no one else thought could be done. They had parachuted into hell and battled the demons there. Now they were going to fly out like angels.

The cameras were rolling. Coleman had the feeling that something was expected of him, though he didn't know what—public relations was an aspect of the modern general officer's life that Coleman was never comfortable with.

"I don't know what to say, men," Coleman began. "Words cannot express how proud I am, how proud your country is, of you, at this moment. The Free World, in fact will long remember your gallantry and heroism at...Bandar Abbas."

Coleman stumbled over the name for a reason. Since Napoleon's time, allies had often come to blows over what to name a battle. Bandar Abbas was theirs now, and to signify their victory, their presence, Iran's new beginning, the clearest message could be sent by changing its name.

Coleman had wanted to call it Camp Casey, but Casey had lived. Besides, the troops already had a nickname for Bandar Abbas. It began as "Bandar Armpit," in honor of its location, climate, and the regard with which it was held by the soldiers. It soon became shortened to "Armpit" and shortened still more to "the Pit," one of those grittingly appropriate labels that soldiers throughout the ages seem to be able to come up with instantly and endlessly.

But Coleman had the good sense to know the name was not his. He knew what the troops thought of outsiders—journalists and brass—who blithely tossed around the names of places soldiers had fought and died for and thus considered their personal real estate, paid for at the highest cost.

Coleman stood awkwardly before the defenders of the Pit. He had said all there was to say, and it wasn't enough. Something further was called for, a gesture, a token of respect. But what?

Suddenly, Coleman had an inspiration. Medals! That was it. Coleman had plenty of medals, but he was wearing fatigues. And soldiers don't wear their decorations on their fatigue uniforms. What to do?

He suddenly called to Brick White, who walked over, puzzled. The two men spoke briefly; then Brick smiled, picking off commendation ribbons from his dress uniform and handing them to Coleman.

The general stepped up to Casey. "Maj. Steve Casey, for conspicuous gallantry and leadership under fire, the United States Army awards you the Distinguished Service Cross."

He pried off the first cloth ribbon and handed it to Casey. Shocked and touched, Casey stepped back and saluted.

"Thank you, sir. If I may, I'd like to recommend..."

"I was just heading that way, Major." Coleman smiled.

He walked over to Willis, standing in the ranks. What he was doing was completely illegal, of course. Officers—even two-star generals—weren't allowed to just walk about, handing out commendations like they were candy. There were rules for such things, protocols and boards of review. But Coleman didn't think he'd have a difficult time getting these particular battlefield citations through channels.

"Sgt. William Willis, for conspicuous..."

"No thank you, sir."

"What, Sergeant?"

"I don't care for any medals, sir," Willis said, firmly. "Just doing my job, sir."

"I see," Coleman said, amused. And proud. "Then, perhaps, one soldier to another, you will accept my salute and commendation for a job well done?"

He stepped back and saluted smartly. Willis returned the salute with a snap.

Coleman walked back to the head of the ranks.

"We'd better wrap this up now, gentlemen," Coleman told the troops. "If we don't get off this landing strip soon, the Air Force will run us over. By the end of the week, thanks to your efforts, just about everybody in the Division will get to experience the joys of summertime in Bandar Abbas. Everyone but you."

Coleman waited for the cheering to die down before he continued.

"So that's it. There's nothing more to say, except to thank you once again for your..."

Coleman's unamplified voice was easily drowned out by the whopping rotors of a helicopter approaching from the Gulf. As if by reflex action, the soldiers brought their assault rifles up to firing positions.

Behind Coleman, Brick spotted the chopper hanging over the coast, a white-and-gold Sikorsky S-76. A commercial job, executive transport. Brick recognized it immediately.

"Don't shoot!" he screamed. "For Christ's sake, put those weapons down!"

Only Casey could hear Brick's pleas over the din of the whirring blades. He turned around and motioned for his men to lower their M16s. The troopers reluctantly complied. The helicopter spun on its tail rotor and set down smartly between the C-141 and the assembled troopers. The engine whopped slowly to idle. The helicopter's cabin door opened. A single figure, wearing a long, white, formal *aba* of the type favored by Iranian mullahs, emerged from the cabin.

"Jesus, that's Sheik Hassan!" Coleman gasped. "What's he doing here?"

"I don't know," Brick answered. "But he's lucky we didn't shoot his ass down. And so are we."

Hassan, quite aware that the eyes of the world's press were on him—indeed, the cameras had been locked onto the helicopter since it first approached—walked directly to General Forest.

"General, on behalf of the people of al-Quaseem, and my people here, please let me be the first to welcome you to the free city of Bandar Abbas."

The sheik extended his hand. Forest, standing dumbly, shook it, while cameras clicked and whirred.

"What does he mean, *welcome?*" Coleman griped. "We were here first."

"This whole thing is starting to smell," Brick said. He caught sight of a Western-looking man in a business suit climbing out of the sheik's helicopter. "And I think I know why. Excuse me."

Brick sprinted across the ramp and intercepted the man, who was hurrying to join Hassan and Forest.

"Mr. Schatz," Brick called out. "You should have told me you were coming."

"Ah, General White." Schatz recognized Brick and frowned. "I wasn't aware it was necessary to report my itinerary to my subordinates. Besides, the last time I visited, you seemed impatient to get rid of me. I didn't want to trouble you this time."

"Too late," Brick said. "You trouble me, Mister Secretary. You trouble me a great deal. What the hell is this all about?"

"I am sure I don't know what you mean."

"I'm sure you do, goddamn it!" Brick was livid. "The smoke has barely cleared, and here's the sheik dropping from the sky like some angel of mercy or something."

"Quite a nice image, General!" Schatz beamed. "I'll suggest it to Troy Damon—I'm sure he'll appreciate it. Now, if you'll excuse me, I..."

"No. Not until I get some answers."

Schatz glowered at Brick. "May I remind you that you work for me?"

Brick stared back, not blinking. "May I remind you that we both work for the president? Do I have to call him to find out what's going on? Or would you rather tell me yourself?"

Schatz sighed. "Very well. It's nothing really—just public relations. The caliph..."

"The caliph? Who's that? You mean the sheik? Did he get a promotion or something?"

"Sheik is a secular title," Schatz explained tiredly. "Caliph is an Islamic one."

"You sound like Hillary now," Brick smiled. "You guys wouldn't be so quick to get religion if these ragheads hadn't had the dumb luck to pitch their tents on oil slicks a hundred years ago. Where is Hillary, by the way? This little dog-and-pony show is right up his alley."

"He's back in al-Quaseem," Schatz said. "If you must know, Mr. Hillary had misgivings about the visit and backed out at the last moment."

"I'm not surprised," Brick said. "Hillary's a sleazeball, but he's too smart to get involved in something like this. Do you know what this is going to look like on TV? Christ! Alexander Haig comes off as an underachiever compared to Hassan!"

"Yes, well, that's your opinion, isn't it? Fortunately, this is all a bit out of your line. Your job is to..." Schatz paused, then added sarcastically, "You know, General, it's been so long since you did your job, I can't seem to recall what it is."

A pair of First Air Mirages, on patrol, screamed by, five hundred feet off the deck.

"Oh, yes, now I remember," Schatz continued. "Your job is to carry messages. Well, here's a message for you to take back to your little friends at that flying club across the Gulf: Knock it off. Cease and desist. No more combat air patrols. The war's over."

Brick was stunned. "You can't be serious."

"Oh, I'm *very* serious, General. We don't need your rootin' tootin' cowboys anymore." Schatz swept a hand across the airport. "Pretty soon, this place will be filled with *real* fighter pilots. The kind who know how to take orders."

"We risked our lives to capture this strip," Brick said bitterly.

"I'm sure we could have managed quite well without you and your outlaws. I regret we didn't try. If you hadn't been able to sell the president on your little scheme, I wouldn't be having this conversation now."

"You were all for First Air in the beginning."

"I was never for it," Schatz said angrily. "It's an expensive, dangerous precedent. Besides the fact that private armies went out of fashion somewhere around the seventeenth century, there are a number of significant drawbacks to your precious Regiment."

"Name one."

"I'll name two. First, this is an American show. We asked for international cooperation, and our allies told us to piss up a rope. You ask, and they make a big show of sending a couple of planes and a few pilots they were probably glad to get rid of. If First Air is perceived as the war winner, then those nations will want a piece of the pie. Well, they can't have it. It's our pie. No one died here but Americans."

Brick sighed. There were holes in that argument big enough to drive an armored personnel carrier through. But he decided to save his breath for the president.

"Two," Schatz continued, "your Regiment's run by Bobby Dragon. Oh, don't think we didn't know, General! What effect do you think that's going to have on our image, our recruiting and retention programs? The hero of Bandar Abbas a deserter from the American armed forces! What's next? Criminals running the government?"

"Well, now that you mention it..."

Schatz shot Brick a dark look. "Personally, I don't care what you do. But First Air has to be shut down. Cut out the patrols now. In a couple of weeks, when regular Air Force and Marine units get here, I want you to disband the Regiment completely. Do you understand?"

Schatz moved past Brick and began to stride toward the sheik's party.

"Wait a minute," Brick called out. "You can't order First Air around. Only the sheik can do that."

"He did," Schatz smiled smugly. "Those orders come from Hassan himself. The caliph believes the presence of armed aircraft on patrol over Bandar Abbas sends the wrong message to the world. People might think the city isn't secure. Or that the war isn't over."

"It isn't. Those MiGs are still in Afghanistan. In fact, they're being reinforced. The Russians are flying all sorts of tactical aircraft into Zaranj, and Mazar as well. They'll be back. You'll need First Air more than ever. If you don't let us CAP Bandar Abbas now, you'll just have to recapture it then. And with what the Russians are putting in Afghanistan, I don't think you'll be able to do it again."

"Are you finished?" Schatz asked mockingly. He put a hand out in an exaggerated motion, as if testing for raindrops. "Funny thing, General. You keep talking about MiGs. I don't see any MiGs. Nobody's seen any MiGs since those outlaws of yours chased away some harmless Afghan student pilots a couple of days ago—without too much of a fight, I might add. The sky's completely clear. It's a beautiful, sunny day. And you're out here selling umbrellas."

Schatz walked away. Brick, staring angrily as Schatz hurried after Hassan and the reporters, noted with grim humor that the secretary of defense managed to step right into the only rain puddle on either side of the Persian Gulf.

The Nightstalker Express

**Dar al-Harb Air Base
Emirate of al-Quaseem**

Maj. Dick Padgett had been in the U.S. Air Force so long he was slowly becoming Russian. The Air Force had taught him to speak Russian, read Russian, write Russian, be Russian. *Pravda* was more familiar to him than the *Washington Post*. Krypto knew more about Kiev than about Baltimore. If the U.S. armed forces' single-minded devotion to the Soviet threat bordered on paranoia, Padgett's diligence made him even more dedicated to finding out about a land and people he had never, would never, could never see. It was an irony common to all good intelligence officers—Krypto sometimes felt he knew more about his enemy than about his own unit.

Certainly it was easier to obtain information on the Soviets than it was to find out what was going on with the First Air Regiment, Inc. Padgett's small office at Dar al-Harb was cluttered with crates of Soviet data: intel reports, satellite photos, debriefings of defectors, stacks of papers dubiously labeled "human intelligence." The information ranged from the plausible to the ludicrous, but none of it answered the questions Krypto was asking.

He stared again at the pieces of the puzzle, neatly arranged on his desk in the middle of the cyclone of administrative chaos that was his office. Not much to go on—a pair of dog tags, some papers, a couple of pictures. Most of his proof existed only in his head at this point, which troubled Krypto no end. How much was real, and how much mere coincidence, animated by suspicion and faulty logic?

Of one thing, Padgett was absolutely certain—*something* was up. The Persian Gulf was bubbling with intrigue. The Russians—or maybe just *some* Russians—were part of it, but the plot went beyond that. Just how far beyond, Krypto wasn't sure. Like a scientist wrestling with a shark, he couldn't quite make out the details, but there was no denying the most important facts— whatever it was, it was large and unpleasant and a threat to further research.

"You wanted to see me, Krypto?"

Lost in his thinking, Padgett was startled to see Bobby Dragon standing at the door of the intel section.

"Yes, sir. Please, come on in. There's a chair around here somewhere."

Bobby picked his way through the clutter and sat down in a metal chair opposite the desk. "I'm surprised to see you still working, Krypto. As one of the Regiment's few presentable officers, I thought for sure you'd be getting ready for Hillary's party tonight. Didn't you get an invitation?"

"I think it's around here somewhere." Padgett waved a hand at the cartons and boxes and overstuffed shelves. "To tell you the truth, I'm not very big on parties."

"Neither am I," Bobby said. "Especially that one. But there's not much else going on around here, is there? I mean, we're grounded. We're just sticking around until the Air Force moves into Bandar Abbas. You might as well leave. A lot of guys in the Regiment already have."

"That's what I want to talk with you about, Colonel," Krypto said. "I don't think the war's over."

"I don't either," Bobby said, solemnly. "But we're definitely in the minority. The sheik has as much as annexed the Gulf coast of Iran around the strait—and with the backing of the United States, he seems to be making it stick. We've got ships sailing in every day off-loading supplies, planes coming in filled with troops. The MiGs haven't been back since *Private Lightning,* and that was more than a week ago. You could make a pretty good case for saying all's quiet on the Persian front."

"I know, but…" Krypto shifted uncomfortably. If he had proof, it would be easy. Padgett was not used to dealing without proof. "Let me just show you some things. I mean, it might not be anything—you can take a look and make up your own mind, okay?"

Bobby could see Padgett was upset. And Krypto wasn't the type to get upset over nothing. "Okay."

Padgett dug through the pile of photos on his desk and tossed one across to Bobby.

"This is Zaranj. Where the Fulcrums live," he said. "There's another base, Mazar, just south of it. It's actually bigger than Zaranj, but up until last week, there was nobody there except a troop garrison and some Afghan helicopter units. Now, both places are crawling with tactical aircraft—Fulcrum, Frogfoot, Fencer—enough for a whole frontal aviation army. Easily three times the size of First Air, even in our best days. Russian planes, too, with stars on the wings. No more of this Afghan Air Force nonsense."

"I've seen this," Bobby tossed the photo back. "Brick says the Russians are just beefing up air support for their operations in northern Iran."

"Do you believe him?"

"Well, the Soviets are having a tough time in Tehran. They could use all the help they could get. It's possible..." Bobby shook his head. "No, you're right. I don't believe it. And to tell you the truth, I don't think Brick does either."

"Good," Krypto said. "Because it's not true. The Soviets have a half-dozen tactical air bases around Baku that are hundreds of miles closer to Tehran and a lot easier to support. Those are the bases they're using now for air operations in Iran. Zaranj and Mazar are actually closer to Bandar Abbas than Tehran. Now, ask yourself why, in the middle of a desperate struggle in Tehran, when the Russians need all the help they can get, they suddenly undertake to establish two new bases in the middle of nowhere and stock them with their latest fighters?"

"Search me," Bobby shrugged.

"All right, then. What do you make of this?"

Padgett shoved a document across the desk. Bobby picked it up and examined it.

"Oh, come on, Krypto, give me a break. This is in *Arabic,* for Christ's sake. What's it say?"

"It's a treaty of friendship and cooperation between the People's Republic of Baluchistan and the Islamic Republic of Persia," Padgett explained. "Now, what's wrong with this picture?"

"Neither one of those countries exists?" Bobby ventured.

"Correct!" Krypto smiled. "Wait—it gets better. Steve Casey, the head of the invasion force, found this thing, sealed in a Quaseemi diplomatic pouch, in the wreckage of a 737 on the runway at Bandar Abbas. Now, the Navy wasn't supposed to bomb the runway, but some A-7 pilot with a dangerous sperm load went ahead and dicked it anyway, and the airliner along with it. If it wasn't for that, this thing would have gone on the last plane out. Which

means it would have been in the sheik's hands before the MiGs got there—
before the invasion even took place!"

Bobby stared blankly. "I still don't get it."

"Okay." Krypto picked up the pair of copper dog tags and handed them
to Bobby. "Take a look at these."

"Carlos Rivera," Bobby read. "Who the hell is Carlos Rivera?"

"He's not anybody anymore," Padgett said grimly. "He's dead. A couple
of our paratroopers picked those out of what was left of his MiG—it was
hit by an Iranian HAWK on the first day of Ready Eagle. When he was alive,
Rivera was a major in the *Fuerza Aerea Revolucionaria,* the Cuban Air Force.
He was also, under several other names, a key member of the *Direccion
General de la Inteligencia.* A Cuban spook, to put it bluntly."

"A terrorist?" Bobby asked.

"I have trouble with words like that," Krypto said with a pained expression.
"They're not precise. One man's terrorist is another man's freedom fighter.
The difference between a guerrilla base and a refugee camp depends on which
side of the border you're on. But in this case, yeah, you could call Rivera
a bad man. A very bad man."

"What did he do?"

"Hijackings, assassinations, gunrunning, dope smuggling—your usual
Third World decathlon. His main territory was Central and South America,
but he was also well connected in Europe and the Middle East. Rivera was
instrumental in marketing Cuban marijuana through the Colombian cartel.
That's very important to them. That's Cuba's only real cash crop, one of the
few significant means they have to get hard currency."

"Then I'm glad he's dead," Bobby said. "But what has this got to do
with our situation?"

Padgett looked around, furtively. The office, the building, and the area
for a hundred yards around had been swept, wiped, and flushed. Krypto knew
his business; there were no bugs or beamers, not unless Bobby brought one
in with him. And if he couldn't trust Bobby, Padgett thought, they were
screwed anyway.

"Ten years ago," Krypto began, "a Black Train was hijacked outside
Tbilisi. It was..."

"Excuse me," Bobby interrupted. "What's a Black Train?"

Padgett sighed. That was the trouble with secrets. When you finally got
around to telling people, they didn't know what you were talking about.

"The Soviets are very careful with their nuclear weapons. Probably more
careful than we are," Krypto explained. "Except for the strategic rocket forces
and some aircraft and SAM batteries on alert, the Russians keep their nukes
locked up tight, in igloos guarded by the KGB. On some special occasions,
such as a code-three exercise, which they don't do very often, battlefield

nuclear weapons—artillery shells, tactical missile warheads, and nuclear shapes for aircraft—are distributed by *Eskadriya Zveno,* KGB units flying black helicopters. But for routine delivery—from the weapons plant to the theater storage facility, for example—all fissionable materials are transported by the KGB on special armored trains, on clear tracks with roadblocks and armed helicopters riding shotgun."

"Black Trains?"

"You got it," Krypto nodded. "Like I said, one of these trains was knocked over about ten years ago, ostensibly by a Georgian terrorist group. It was a big operation, though, as you can imagine, and these guys used weapons you don't find in Russia, certainly not in the hands of some miserable little revolutionary cell that has trouble getting hold of a Xerox machine."

"Like what?"

"Like air support. Jet fighters, to chase away the helicopters and take out the engine and the tracks ahead. That's the way to do it, but..." Padgett shook his head, overwhelmed by the magnitude of the operation. "The Soviets were understandably pissed and worried, and just as understandably, they blamed the U.S., which is how we know about all this stuff. But, as far as I can tell, we didn't have anything to do with the raid. I'd be surprised if we had—I mean, we've pulled some pretty bonehead plays before, but *nobody* would be stupid enough to steal Russian nuclear weapons, certainly not in Russia."

Bobby sighed with relief. If Krypto Padgett couldn't find an American connection, there was no connection to be found.

"The hijackers were sharp, and they weren't greedy," Krypto continued. "They took just what they were looking for and melted into the landscape before reinforcements came. The Soviets closed the borders and the roads and pretty much strip searched the entire population of the Georgian Republic. They never found the hijackers or the stuff they took—two relatively low-yield nuclear artillery warheads. Until now."

Bobby felt his stomach tighten. "Go on."

"Nukes have a distinct signature," Krypto explained. "You can tell a lot about a warhead by examining the damage it's caused and the air it's contaminated. With the right equipment and know-how, you can determine the age, grade, and even country of origin by the way the stuff was processed. Some of our nuke pukes went into Baghdad with the Red Cross right after the bomb went off. They've just completed their report—I've got it right here."

Padgett held up a thin telex plastered with classified document warnings. "There's no doubt about it—the fissionable material in the Baghdad bomb was taken from one of the nuclear artillery shells stolen at Tbilisi."

"Jesus!" Bobby exclaimed. "So the Iranians hijacked that train?"

"No," Krypto said stubbornly. "No, it goes deeper than that."

"What do you mean? The Iranians admitted they were responsible for nuking Baghdad. Why would they lie about something like that?"

"Oh, of course they bombed Baghdad," Padgett said. "They're certainly capable of that, technically as well as morally. Delivering it isn't difficult, either, especially if you've got people who don't much care about making a round trip. And anyone can build a bomb. You can buy just about all the materials you need for the fusing and casing in a half dozen European countries. But what you can't get is the fissionable material. Certainly Iran couldn't have manufactured it. And they couldn't have pulled off that train hijacking and gotten away, either—Iranians are pretty suspicious-looking characters in Georgia. No, somebody gave it to them."

"Carlos Rivera?"

"You're getting warm." Krypto shook out another picture and placed it carefully on the desk. "That's Rivera. On the right. You'll recognize the other man, I'm sure."

Bobby bent over and examined the photo. It was grainy, with high contrast, obviously taken in low light from a great distance. But there was no mistaking the hawklike features of Sheik Hassan.

Bobby sat silent. It was almost too much to comprehend. There was always the possibility that the picture was a fake. He dismissed that thought— you couldn't fool Krypto. Then again, he thought darkly, *Padgett* could himself be a fake. Bobby rejected that line as well. He had worked with Krypto for years, checking out Soviet equipment in Dreamland. And though that was certainly no guarantee of trustworthiness, Bobby's gut feeling was that Padgett was a man he could trust. Besides, Krypto was doing all the talking. If he was a double agent, he was a very poorly trained one.

Still, there was no getting around the photograph and what it represented—Hassan, lounging in what looked like a hotel suite, calmly chatting with Carlos Rivera. An international terrorist. And a pilot in the unit the sheik was supposedly paying Bobby to destroy.

"Where was this taken?" Bobby asked softly.

"In Yemen," Padgett answered. "About a year ago. At the Pan-Arabian Islamic Conference."

"A terrorist convention, huh?" Bobby studied the photo more closely. He was not surprised that the United States followed and photographed Sheik Hassan. He did feel admiration for the professionalism of the person who took the picture—it must have been tough to get even that close, with the sheik's *Gahtell* lurking about. And Bobby felt a slight buzz of revenge and irony at the thought of Hassan being spied on for a change.

"The sheik has all kinds of connections in Iran, in power and out," Krypto said. "Don't forget, his family's from there. His great-grandfather was in line to be king of Persia until the real king kicked him out for trying to take over before his time."

"What are you saying? Do you think Hassan stole the nukes and gave them to the Iranians?"

"I don't know. It's possible, although I don't think he had any part in the hijacking itself other than financial," Padgett said. "The more I look at it, the more that operation looks like an inside job."

"The Russians stealing their own nukes? That doesn't make sense!"

"None of this makes sense, Colonel," Krypto agreed. He swept a hand across his desk. "Not yet, anyway. But it will."

Bobby stared at Krypto. He had no doubt that once the Superdog sunk his teeth into the problem, he wouldn't let loose until it was solved. That is, if there *was* a problem. No, Bobby thought, looking at the pieces of the puzzle spread out on Padgett's desk, Krypto was right. Something *was* going on.

"Okay, let's say the Russians did rip off their own train," Bobby asked. "Who did it? Why?"

"*Why,* I don't know," Krypto admitted. "That's the biggest question in all of this. As to *who*—here's your prime suspect. He was stationed at Vaziani, just outside Tbilisi, when the train was hit."

Padgett pushed a black-and-white photo across the desk. Bobby stared at the photograph with an expression of confusion and fear that was as unusual as it was unbecoming. The face in the photo was anything but frightening— a young lieutenant, smiling, standing proudly at attention in the snow by an airfield with a line of MiG-19s in the background. The picture was obviously a copy of an old photo, blown-up and grainy. It was hard to distinguish the features, but something about the young man with his new wings made Bobby feel uncomfortable.

"If there was ever such a thing as a fast mover in the Soviet Air Force, this guy is it. Listen to these credentials: Little Octobrists, Young Pioneers, Komsomol, DOSAAF, Suvarov Military Prep School, Chernigov Higher Military Aviation School for Pilots, Gagarin Air Force Academy, Military Academy of..." Padgett looked up from the dossier and noticed the troubled look on Bobby's face. "What is it, Colonel? Do you know this man?"

"I've never seen him before in my life," Bobby said uncertainly. "Or at least I don't think I have. I don't know. It's weird. There's something spooky about this guy, but I don't know what. Who is he?"

"That's Mikhail Paratov. He was a lieutenant back then. This picture was taken about twenty years ago, at a commissioning ceremony outside Moscow."

"Oh, Paratov..." Bobby sighed with relief. Now he knew why the face was so familiar. He must have seen it before, at some briefing, and forgotten it. "He's the guy behind Squadron 22, isn't he? If he's such a heavy breather, what the hell is he doing stuck in Afghanistan?"

"He volunteered." Padgett took the photograph and replaced it carefully in the drawer. "In fact, the whole operation at Zaranj seems to be his idea. There's no record of it going up or down through channels."

"You mean he dreamed it up on his own?"

"That seems to be how he works. Of course, there's always the possibility he's just following orders, but this Paratov has a very un-Sovietlike habit of doing things on his own initiative."

"That could be unhealthy."

"It's usually fatal," Padgett said. "But Paratov has two things going for him. One, he always finds a way to do what the Kremlin wants without officially involving the Soviet Union. That's important. And two, he's well connected. Paratov's father was a big hero in World War II. A pilot. Forty kills in the Ukraine. Peace was apparently too boring for him, so after the war he went into the spook business. Nobody knows what he did. Whatever it was, he probably did it too well and got somebody mad at him. He died right after Stalin."

"Executed?" Bobby asked.

Padgett opened his hands and shrugged. "Nobody knows, and nobody will. Nobody on our side, anyway. A friend of his father, Pavel Illyushin, took care of the boy, brought him under his wing. Illyushin's now the number-two man in the Soviet Air Force."

"Wait a minute," Bobby said. "Wasn't he that Soviet big shot who was in Zaranj just recently?"

"That was him," Padgett agreed. "But what fascinates me is that Illyushin visited the base *after* Squadron 22 attacked the 82d's transports, not before. It's almost as if he flew down there to ask what the hell was going on. And after *Private Lightning,* he and Paratov flew to Moscow to personally brief the Soviet minister of defense, Marshal Kiroshenko. Apparently this whole thing is almost as much a mystery to the Russians as it is to us."

"Are you telling me the Soviets didn't have something like this in mind all along?" Bobby asked. "You think this Paratov is making it up as he goes along?"

"It looks that way," Padgett answered. "Remember, Iran started this mess, not the Russians. Lucky for them, though, Zaranj is now strategically placed. If the Russians decide to come south, they're going to outrun their fighter cover, even if they can secure bases in Tehran. And Squadron 22 is in perfect position to cover a Soviet sweep to the Gulf. I don't know—maybe they *did* have the whole thing planned as a contingency, but there's no hard evidence the Soviets are even planning to move south. At any rate, Squadron

22 has yet to fly a mission in support of the Russian invasion. So maybe they just got lucky."

"Yeah, lucky," Bobby said ruefully. "We've got to fly three KC-10s halfway around the world just to bring in toilet paper. All the Russians have to do is walk across the street and they're in Iran."

"In Iran, yes, but not the Gulf, which is what they want," Padgett said. "They've got their own problems. Even if they could manage to get the situation in Tehran under control, they'd still have to cross the mountains to get to the coast. The key to this whole thing is Bandar Abbas. It's got the only ports and airfields for hundreds of miles. If we can hold onto it, the Russians will stay where they are; I'm sure of it. But if we can't secure Bandar Abbas, the Russians will come down and take it. It's their nature. That's the way they work. They abhor vacuums."

"Well, there's nothing to stop them now," Bobby said ruefully. "Have you been to Bandar Abbas? Nobody seems to be in any hurry over there. All the army's firepower is in crates or still aboard ship—they haven't really unpacked anything yet but cranes and bulldozers. They're acting like they've got all the time in the world."

"Don't think the Soviets don't know that," Krypto said. "It would help a lot if we could CAP Bandar Abbas. That would make the Russians think twice."

"You can forget about that," Bobby barked. "The sheik won't even let us CAP our own airfield. No kidding—he found out we were running a BARCAP out in the Gulf to protect Dar al-Harb, and he ordered the whole Regiment grounded. Except for a couple of guys going home, we haven't flown at all for the last couple of days. I don't know why he doesn't just order First Air disbanded."

The two men fell silent, thinking the same unpleasant thoughts: a large and powerful Soviet tactical air force already in place. Russian armor ready to sweep through the mountains to the Strait of Hormuz. American forces outnumbered and unprepared at Bandar Abbas. And First Air firmly on the ground.

"I'm a fighter pilot," Bobby said finally. He pointed to Krypto's desk. "To be honest, I don't understand any of this, but if *you're* worried, *I'm* worried. I've had a bad feeling ever since the MiGs ran away last week— that wasn't like them at all. Brick feels the same way. But we're back where we started from. We need proof. Brick needs a lot more than what you've got here to light a fire under Tweedle Dum and Tweedle Dee—Schatz and Forest would never be able to follow this, even if you could get them to sit still and listen. And we sure as hell can't go to the sheik with what you've told me. I don't even want to know what an Islamic jail cell looks like. And something tells me we wouldn't even get that far."

"You're right; I don't have any proof. But I think I know where to get it." Krypto checked his watch. "Feel like taking a ride?"

"Where?"

"Around."

Bobby shrugged. Padgett obviously had his own agenda. Well, why not? It was better than sitting around worrying. He followed Krypto out of the intel office, through the ops shack, and onto the ramp at Dar al-Harb. Padgett stepped to the middle of the runway and started walking toward the Gulf.

"Uh, Krypto, I know you're not rated, and I hate to bring this up," Bobby said, "but if you expect to take off, we're going to have to go back and get an airplane."

"Shh!" Padgett pressed a finger to his lips, then cupped his hand behind his ear. "Listen."

Bobby listened. He listened very hard and finally heard a faint fluttering, a mere suggestion of sound. Suddenly, a small black helicopter appeared as if from nowhere, settling gently at the very edge of the runway. Krypto ducked under the swinging rotors and approached the right side of the chopper. Bobby followed.

There were no doors on the helicopter. The pilot swung his head around and stared—two round beady eyes and a glass mandible! An alien! Martians had landed!

Bobby stepped back and gathered his wits. He realized now that the electric eyes were merely night-vision goggles. And the glass jaw was the maxillofacial shield that protected the pilot's jawline and directed cool air from the environmental control system into his face, a smart idea in the Persian steam bath. Bobby recognized the helicopter as an MH-6, an updated version of the Army's beloved Vietnam-era "Loach" scout ship. Only one unit was known to operate the MH-6, along with its armed sister the AH-6—the Nightstalkers.

The 160th Special Operations Aviation Group were the elite of the Army's elite helicopter pilots. They flew most of their missions under abysmal conditions and paid for it with abysmal loss rates—the small unit suffered more fatalities annually than the rest of the Army aviation community combined. The Nightstalkers, back when they were known as Task Force 160, were one of the Army's worst-kept secrets. Now that they had become "public," however, the Nightstalkers were one of its most secret overt units. It was known that they were based in Kentucky. There being little need for their special talents around the relatively benign environment of Fort Campbell, however, they often went other places. And did other things. Flying in unannounced to Dar al-Harb and scaring the hell out of Bobby Dragon was apparently one of the other things they did.

"Jesus, Krypto, where did *he* come from? Mars?"

"Close," Padgett smiled. "Bahrain. He's been sitting in the hangar of the USS *Jack Williams* since the bomb went off. The Bahranis wouldn't let the frigate leave at first, and now it can't get out because the deal with the Soviets prevents American warships from steaming in the Gulf. So these guys have been hanging around the dock in civilian clothes for the past three weeks—it didn't take much to convince one of them to go for a little ride."

The pilot flipped up his night-vision goggles. His eyes betrayed only slightly more expression. "Which one of you is Superdog 6?"

"I am," Krypto said. "You must be Captain..."

"Midnight," the pilot cut Krypto off, eyeing Bobby suspiciously. "Captain Midnight of the USS *Classified*. So who's this?"

"Jet Jackson," Bobby said. "Flying Commando."

The pilot's face never changed expression. He turned back to Krypto. "You didn't tell me there'd be two of you. I don't care, except I've only got one extra NVG set."

"That's all right," Padgett said. "I'll ride in back."

Krypto climbed in the small seat behind the pilot. Bobby clambered in the left side. The pilot handed him a helmet fitted with the ANVIS goggles, which looked like a miniature pair of binoculars. Bobby was trying to figure out how to operate them when the MH-6 rose abruptly and headed out to the Gulf.

"Don't forget," the pilot shouted back at Krypto, "you promised me gas on the way back."

"You'll get it," Krypto nodded vigorously.

"I hope so. There are things in the water down there worse than sharks." He shoved a clipboard back to Krypto.

"What's this?"

"I need authorization," the pilot answered.

Padgett looked doubtful. "Even on a secret mission?"

"*Especially* on a secret mission. This is the new Army. It's not just a job. It's a pain in the ass. Come on, Superdog. You sound like you know the drill. Give me somebody with a lot of stars."

Krypto thought for a moment, then scrawled something shakily in the dim light of the vibrating chopper. He handed the clipboard back to the pilot, who peeked underneath his goggles at the signature and laughed.

"Okay, General Forest, you're the boss. Where are we going, anyway?"

"Bandar Abbas," Padgett shouted. "A little ways north. I'll show you when we get there."

The pilot nodded. In the left seat, Bobby fidgeted nervously. Aviators always made bad passengers, and fighter jocks were the worst. They were easily conditioned to believe they were the greatest pilots in the universe, which meant anyone else with his hand on the stick was...less than perfect.

It was a comforting notion when you were zooming alone into battle against the godless swarm, but it made for some serious nail biting when you were mere baggage. And skimming fifty feet over the Persian Gulf into a war zone, at night, with a pilot from a unit known only for its high attrition, in a *helicopter*—damn! Bobby hated helicopters.

To settle his nerves, he pulled down the ANVIS goggles and fiddled with the controls. Suddenly the night became day. It was a surreal, gray-green day with significant portions of the visible light spectrum missing, but it was bright as day, nonetheless. Bobby looked around. Now that the veil was lifted, he could recognize familiar landmarks: The tip of Muscat rose from the bright green Gulf. Larak Island rolled by. They were in the Strait of Hormuz. Bandar Abbas was just ahead.

"Follow the road north, out of the city," Krypto leaned forward between the seats and shouted. "It'll curve around two mountains, the first one on your left, then one on your right."

The pilot's helmet nodded. The chopper swept across the beach at the dry river and hooked behind the airport to join up with the main road north at the fork. Bobby held his breath—nothing moved below, on the beach, in the city, at the airport. He was relieved that they were not going to be shot down, but he was also disappointed. Was everyone asleep? True, no one expected trouble, and how much trouble could a lone, unarmed helicopter be? And the Nightstalkers were experts at flying undetected. Still, Bobby felt a twinge of apprehension at the ease with which they had penetrated the airspace over Bandar Abbas. If First Air was allowed to patrol here, Bobby thought with perhaps misplaced pride, there would be one less helicopter in the world.

Genow Mountain rose swiftly on the left, a psychedelic slab in bright greens and ugly grays. He had to swivel his head to take in all its tremendous bulk—the goggles cut out peripheral vision and narrowed the field of view to forty degrees. The pilot jogged the chopper to the left, following the road. Khirou Mountain moved in on the right.

The pilot leaned back and shouted at Padgett, "This is it, sport."

Krypto bobbed his head vigorously and motioned for the pilot to make a wide circle. The helicopter banked to the left in a slow turn.

Bobby bent backward to talk in Krypto's ear. "What are we supposed to be looking for? I don't see anything."

The two heads changed positions—now Padgett was shouting into Bobby's helmet. "You *can't* see anything! It's a tunnel! Right below us!"

Bobby nodded. He leaned out and scanned the area. Sure enough, aided by the ANVIS goggle's subtle boost of the infrared spectrum, he could clearly see the arching entrance of the tunnel up ahead. He pointed it out to Krypto, who shook his head up and down in understanding.

They flew three times around the tunnel entrance before the pilot shouted back at Krypto, "Whatever you're looking for, I hope you found it. We've got to split now. We're running on vapors as it is."

Krypto held up a finger and then put his hands together in mock prayer. *One more time around, please.* The pilot shrugged. "Okay, but it's not going to look any different this time. And this is it, understand?"

Padgett gave the pilot an "okay" and leaned out, staring intently into the dark night. Bobby watched him in wonder. *What was he looking for?*

Whump! The chopper shuddered. Bobby spun around in time to see a man's face smeared against the shattered canopy. *What the hell?* The face, ghoulish in death and the distorted colors, looked just as surprised to have seen Bobby, in his Martian goggles, flying in a black bubble of air.

The air was filled with jellyfish, great green men-o'-war, with shrouds hanging down like tentacles. Paratroopers! Bobby leaned out the side door and looked up. The sky was black with lumbering transports squirting out more troops, like a guppy giving birth.

"Let's get out of here!" Bobby shouted.

The pilot spun the helicopter around on its rotor, heading for Bandar Abbas—and snagging another paratrooper on the tail boom. A third Soviet soldier met his fate, chopped to pieces by the main rotor. It was a Pyrrhic victory. The chopper's blades were fatally fouled. The engine raced. The MH-6 began to spin wildly around its rotor.

"We're going down!" the pilot screamed, frantically stirring the stick. Bobby braced himself and shot a glance at Padgett.

He was yelling something. Bobby couldn't make it out. He leaned back and strained to hear the words.

"I was right!" Krypto shouted, just before they hit. "I was right! I was right! I was right all along!"

Black Banner

Dar al-Harb Air Base
Emirate of al-Quaseem

Scooter! Look alive—bogie, two o'clock low."

Scooter Jeffries sat up straight in the ejection seat and peered over the F-14's long nose. "I got it! Daffy, can you get me a viz on the TISEO?"

In the backseat, Daffy Brewer struggled with the small joystick that controlled the target identification system—electro-optical, the Navy's term for a video camera with a powerful zoom lens, mounted under the F-14's nose. The image shook wildly, zoomed in and out, and finally stabilized.

"Perfect!" Scooter said, viewing the image on the horizontal display indicator. "Okay, Blade, we've got a visual. Hang on—we're sending it over!"

The microwave transmission took the tiniest slice of a second, as the image was encoded, beamed over via data link, unscrambled, and displayed on the screens in Blade Wilkinson's F-14.

"Great shot!" Scooter could hear the laughter of Blade's RIO behind his congratulations. "You guys are real killers!"

Scooter took another look at the image and laughed as well. It *was* a great shot—a woman's legs, wrapped in sheer nylons, frozen in the act of crossing.

"Hell, I wish we had infrared, Daffy," Scooter said over the intercom. "We could see what kind of panties she's wearing."

"If we had infrared, we could see what kind of panties *Hillary's* wearing."

Scooter convulsed with glee and hurried to repeat Daffy's quip to Blade Wilkinson. Brewer was bored with the game, however, and tuned out the radio traffic with a growing feeling of resentment and apprehension. He had come to al-Quaseem to fly, not to serve as a party decoration. He had joined First Air, at great personal and professional sacrifice, to fight alongside his friend and fellow Crusader Bobby Dragon in the holy war to rid the world of nuclear mullahs. But Bobby was nowhere to be found. And look at Daffy now—he was a *pinata!*

He scanned the whole surreal scene, the violent juxtaposition of two opposite worlds. There was the world he knew, the world that made sense— he and Scooter in the cockpit, Blade Wilkinson in another Tomcat beside them, pulling air defense alert duty in the Zulu shack at Dar al-Harb. That in itself would have been hard to believe a month ago, but at least it was within his frame of reference; the start carts, the humming APUs pumping power into the F-14s. Even the Zulu shack, zinc green and built like a fire station, was not unlike the alert barn at San Diego or Sigonella, where he had performed similar duties.

But what were these *people* doing here? Men and women like Daffy had never seen—except on television, perhaps. Come to think of it, he *had* seen many of them on TV, either interviewing somebody, being interviewed, or, the most common permutation, interviewing each other. These were the *beau monde,* the most glittering personalities of the generation. Brewer, not a violent man, really, was sorry he could not arm and fire the Tomcat's 20-mm cannon from the backseat.

Oh, there was a rational explanation for all of it, if viewed from Hillary's recently twisted perspective. Brewer could remember a day when Peter Hillary would have hitched a ride in a freezing, unpressurized tanker rather than share an airliner with these kinds of people. Now he invited them into the inner sanctum, allowed them access to the Most Butch aspects of First Air. That upset Daffy the most. Hillary was not a member of the Regiment, despite his title. He was an outsider. He was giving away what was not his to give, what he had not earned himself.

Look at them! Men in tuxedos and First Air baseball caps (where did *those* come from?), leaning against his airplane like it was the grandstand rail at Saratoga. Women in evening gowns, sitting on three-million-dollar Phoenix missiles, talking about clothes and adultery. Occasionally the cycloptic shaft of a TV light would add to the already glaring interior of the alert shack, as one or another illuminati would remember that they were *journalists* and had a *job to do.*

"Look left! Nine o'clock!"

Daffy responded to Scooter's voice over the intercom with a sigh. "Oh, come on Scooter, knock it off. I've had enough beaver shooting for one night."

"No, Daffy! It's that wonker Hillary. And he's coming up here!"

Brewer looked to his left and saw Hillary, his face distorted by the canopy, tottering on the crew ladder. Hillary rapped on the Plexiglas with his small white fist.

"Screw this guy, Scooter. I'm not letting him in."

"I'm with you," Jeffries answered. "Hillary's a real corndog. I'd just as soon—Hey! He's got Troy Damon with him. Canopy clear!"

Daffy groaned as Scooter raised the F-14's huge canopy. The frame jostled Hillary's arm, spilling champagne across the glass and down inside the cockpit. *Oh, bloody hell,* Hillary thought. It *would* be Brewer.

"Well, Don, we meet again after all these years," Hillary smiled. Brewer said nothing.

"Hey, isn't that Troy Damon?" Scooter asked, pointing at the tall man at the foot of the ladder.

Hillary turned to Jeffries. "It is indeed, Leftenant. I promised him he could sit in a real First Air Regiment jet. You wouldn't want to disappoint him, would you?"

"Troy Damon? Hell, no! Just a minute, I'll get unstrapped and..."

"We're on duty, Scooter," Brewer said sternly.

"Oh, come on, Daffy, the war's over! This is a victory party, isn't it? The war *must* be over." He leaned over the side. "Come on up here, Mr. Damon. I'll show you a *real* anchorman's chair."

Jeffries clambered out and squatted on the wing root, helping Damon up the ladder and into the cockpit. The two men fell into an easy, mutually fawning conversation.

Hillary tried again. "So, what's it like seeing Bobby again after so long?"

"Wouldn't you like to know?" Brewer grunted.

"Oh, come on, Don! You can't still be angry over what happened in Da Nang? That was almost twenty years ago. Actually, I should be the one who's angry. If you had told me the truth—if you had told me anything at all—maybe things would have turned out differently for all concerned."

Daffy looked up at Hillary and sighed. "No, that's not it. I still don't think you had any business asking questions like that, stuff about me and Bobby. But, hell—you were just doing your job. You were a *real* reporter back then."

"And I'm doing my job now!" Hillary said expansively. "The caliph wants to keep the Western press on his side, so..."

Hillary sloshed his champagne glass across the expanse of the alert hangar. Brewer could tell he was quite drunk.

"Okay, you want to throw a party, throw it in Sammarah. They really know how to do it over there." Daffy glowered. "We've got a real-world mission here."

"That's precisely why I wanted to hold the victory party here," Hillary said. "These people, Don—it's so difficult to come up with something new, something they haven't done. And, of course, if you can't amuse them, they'll ignore you. But this place lends a certain type of operational *ambience* you can't get anywhere else. They couldn't resist the chance to see the famous First Air Regiment at work. You should be proud."

"I don't give a damn about anybody here," Daffy said. "And I'll bet Brick would see it the same way. It's some kind of coincidence that you decide to throw this bash when you know he's over at Bandar Abbas trying to help the reinforcements get landed and sort themselves out."

Hillary's face darkened. "I don't need General White's permission. I'm the managing director of the Regiment. I sign everybody's paychecks—including yours."

"That's it!" Daffy exploded. "I've had enough! Get your drunken ass off my airplane—now! And get that sissy boy out of the front seat before I punch him and his haircut through that tin roof up there."

All conversation stopped. All eyes turned to the drama being played on the wing of the plane. Hillary was shocked. He turned to Damon, who had already zoomed down the crew ladder. The anchorman was heading, red faced, to the *hors d'oeuvres* table, trying to put as much distance as possible between his reputation and the messy scene.

Hillary scooted down the ladder so fast he almost fell. He sprinted for the bar and downed another glass of champagne in one gulp. That damn fighter jock, that *tradesman*, had embarrassed him in front of his guests. After all Hillary had done for him. He had *made* him! No one had heard of Daffy before *The Reluctant Dragon*. So much for gratitude. Very well—he would have a word with Hassan about Lt. Cmdr. Don Brewer.

Come to think of it, Hillary wondered, where *was* Hassan? After all, this was his party. At midnight, the sheik was to unveil the black banner signifying the return of the *mahdi*. Hillary had argued against it. It was one thing to call yourself God's soldier—*amir*, keeper of the faith. Certainly the sheik had a right to that title. It was quite another to proclaim yourself God's executive officer, which Hassan had done when he assumed the title of *caliph* that afternoon at Bandar Abbas.

Hillary had warned the sheik about that; the backlash from Islamic groups around the world when Hassan crowned himself *caliph* had been immediate and bitter and had proven Hillary correct. But now, instead of backing off, Hassan was going to take the final step. Tonight, before the representative eyes and ears of the material world, the sheik was to declare himself the *mahdi,* the new prophet, and the last one the world would see before mankind was destroyed.

Or maybe not. It was almost midnight, and still no sign of Hassan. Perhaps Hillary's arguments had gotten through, and the sheik had at the last moment thought better of the idea. Hillary hoped so. He was getting pretty good at public relations, but it would take some mighty spin control to sell the notion of a billionaire twentieth-century messiah in a double-breasted Armani suit to this crowd.

Hillary's reverie was interrupted by a sudden disturbance at the entrance to the Zulu shack. There was shouting, some Arabic, and an unmistakable English accent.

Dennis Nelson charged up to Hillary, carrying a manila envelope and trailing a parade of Quaseemi security men in his wake. Hillary nodded to his bodyguards, who had taken up station on Nelson's shoulders. They moved back.

"Dennis! How are you?" Hillary asked, anxious to change the mood from the ugly scene on the airplane. "You're looking well."

Nelson considered Hillary's new suit and his new friends.

"Obviously not as well as you, Peter," Nelson said, sullenly. "Do you know what you've fallen into?"

"I often ask myself that question these days," Hillary laughed, nervously. He had learned his lesson about public altercations—whatever Nelson wanted was best discussed away from the prying eyes of the popular press. He grabbed Nelson's elbow, spun him around, and marched him through the doors and out into the dirt median between the runways.

"Really, Dennis, you are out of line here," Hillary said angrily. "What do you want?"

"I want to know what's going on. I want you to tell me why you've been dodging me."

"Oh, come now, Dennis. I haven't been avoiding anyone. I really haven't had anything to say to you. You were at the press conference..."

"That's another thing!" Nelson shouted. "What the bloody hell were you trying to do, freezing me out like that? What's happened to you, Peter?"

"I grew up!" Hillary said sharply. "And you'd better, too. If you want to talk, we'll talk. But we'll talk like civilized people. Meet me in my office. Or come to my apartment, if you'd rather."

"No," Nelson said dimly. "Anywhere but there. Everything's bugged. And your phones are tapped, too, you know. All the Regiment's lines are."

Hillary coughed nervously. "Where did you get that idea?"

"I have a friend on the island. He knows all the Quaseemi secret service types," Nelson said darkly. "You know you're being followed, don't you?"

Hillary laughed. "Those are my bodyguards."

"Two of them are," Nelson nodded. "The other one isn't. He's *Gahtell*. He's writing reports on you every day. I'm surprised at you, Peter. You used to be more perceptive than that."

"And I'm surprised at you, Dennis. When did you become so paranoid?"

"Paranoid, am I? Well, this is the place for it," Nelson snorted. "I've *seen* the reports on you, Peter. You know, I remember when you used to tell *me* about these things. You're getting soft. You'd better watch out. This is not a good time to be soft."

"If you feel uncomfortable here," Hillary said coldly, "perhaps you should leave."

"I am. I'm getting out tonight. And you should, too, before it's too late. There's an RAF Hercules warming up at al-Quaseem International. I know the crew. They came in with a load of Harrier parts, and they're taking off with me. I'm not on the manifest. They're taking an awful chance. Do you know what the sheik would do if he found out? Normally, I wouldn't dream of taking advantage of friends this way, but I don't have any choice. It's the only way I'm getting off this island."

Hillary felt a hot, dry wind blow behind his neck. Nelson was not an alarmist. The two of them had been in tight spots in the past. And through wars and riots, Nelson could be counted on to keep his head. Maybe he was right. Maybe there *was* more to the situation than Hillary had been willing to see.

"Look, I know you made up that story about Bandar Abbas on your own," Nelson continued. "That was your first mistake. I think some poor dogface got to you, and you decided to do him a favor."

Hillary looked away in surprise. "So what if I did?" he said, defensively.

"Don't you understand?" Nelson shouted. "When you start screwing around with the truth, you're finished. Once you decide to become part of the story instead of covering it, you'll wind up like Troy Damon. Or even worse. At least he *thinks* he's telling the truth. But you knew better, and you did it anyway. I stuck with you out of friendship, but the other reporters were right to cut you out."

"They seem friendly enough now," Hillary said.

"Well, then, we've come full circle," Nelson spat. "They suck up to you now because they need a story, and you're all they've got. But I don't need anybody to feed me a story. I can find my own. Good reporters can do that. You used to do that."

Nelson stomped off in the sand.

"Good riddance!" Hillary shouted. "I've had it with your holier-than-thou attitude. I'm fifty years old, and what have I got to show for it? What's so wrong about thinking of myself, for once? Up until a couple of weeks ago, all I had were a bag of war clothes, a beat-up Olivetti, and a reputation. And we saw how quickly a reputation can be destroyed. The sheik did me a favor by giving me this job."

Nelson spun around, eyes wide with anger.

"Did you a *favor?*" he hissed. "He's *using* you; can't you see that? He moves his lips every time you talk. He's trying to sell a package, and you're the perfect pitchman, with your storied past and your Oxford delivery."

"Oh, come on, Dennis. Why does the sheik need me to sell First Air? What's in it for him?"

"Money, to start with."

Hillary laughed. "Hassan doesn't need any more money. He's the richest man in the world. Besides, how can the sheik make money off First Air?"

"By keeping his oil flowing, for one thing. Everybody else in the Gulf is shut down, and he's making a killing," Nelson explained. "And he's not letting General White park his planes here for free, either, not by a long shot. It's a very complicated trail. The cash is going from Washington to Wall Street to London and Hong Kong and Zurich and heaven knows where else. I haven't quite got it sorted out just yet, but take my word for it—there are some tremendous amounts of money floating around al-Quaseem these days, billions of dollars. Certainly enough to get even Hassan's attention."

"So why does he need me?"

"He doesn't need you. He just needs somebody *like* you," Nelson said. "You know the Gulf rulers never work directly with Westerners. They consider it beneath their dignity. Besides, they want deniability. And you're the perfect go-between. You speak Arabic. You have a reputation. Plus, you're honest, although in your case that seems to have become a synonym for naive. And you keep the attention of the press away from the sheik, which is what he wants."

"Look, Dennis, I don't have time for this," Hillary said hotly. "I don't know why you're so dead set against Hassan and First Air. So far you haven't told me anything that would make me change my mind about anything I've done."

"Take my word," Nelson said. "This whole business is going to come to a bad end, for you and for everybody else involved. Hassan has ambitions, Peter. He has his heart set on a larger stage than this tiny island; you can bet on that. Don't forget, he has blood ties to the shah's line. There's a vacuum in the Gulf, and he intends to fill it."

"That's not exactly a flash, is it?" Hillary smirked. "Don't you read your own paper? Hassan has all but declared himself the new shah."

"I know that!" Nelson spat. "But here's a flash for you. It's a good thing First Air chased away all the opposition at Bandar Abbas. Because the sheik was ready to take it one way or another and kill everyone who stood in his way—Iranians, Russians, even Americans."

"You're crazy!" Hillary gasped. "How could he do that? His air force wouldn't last a minute with those MiGs. And he doesn't have an army."

"He doesn't need an army, Peter. He's got the *bomb*. He's..."

The wind carried a sound, a vague *crump*, that froze both men in their tracks. It wasn't a loud noise—certainly not loud enough to stop Nelson's conversation in midsentence. It could have been a car backfiring in the distance, or a forklift driver dropping his load. But it wasn't, and both men knew it. They had covered enough wars to recognize the sound of aerial bombardment.

Hillary stared, transfixed, across the runway to al-Quaseem International. There were more explosions, and fires now, here and there. He could see no jets in the distance and darkness, but he could hear their roar, screaming at low level, dozens of them. And they were coming his way.

"Go wake up the tower! Sound the alert!" Hillary shouted at Nelson. "I'll take care of the party!"

Nelson stood stiffly, watching the bombs fall across the airport. Hillary had never seen him so frightened, had never before seen him frightened at all, as a matter of fact. Nelson shoved the envelope in Hillary's hands and sprinted across the pavement.

Hillary hurried back to the Zulu shack. The disturbance had already created a crowd at the entrance. Perfectly silhouetted by the bright light streaming through the square doors, the chic crowd stood, sipping *Bolly* and chatting gaily, watching their own approaching destruction.

Damon caught Hillary's arm. "Really, Peter, this is too much! I had no idea you were such a showman. That almost looks real over..."

"It is real, you fool!" Hillary shook his arm loose. A piercing siren rose above the pattering of the bombs—the tower's warning sounded like a mournful wail. Brewer pushed his way through the crowd.

"Hillary, get these people out of here!"

Hillary looked around frantically. Nelson was right—he *had* gotten soft. "Where?"

"I don't care!" Daffy shouted. He pointed to a low concrete hangar about a quarter mile away. "Stick them in that TAB-V—they'll be safe over there. Just get them the hell out of here!"

Leading and harrying like a border collie, Hillary moved the crowd out of the alert shack and down a dirt path toward the shelter. Brewer spun and waddled as quickly as he could in his G suit, back to the Tomcat. The maintenance drones, rousted out of the kitchen by the sudden siren, disconnected the hoses and wires that bound the F-14 to earth. There was no time for preflight checks.

"Let's go, Scooter!"

The big engines lit up as soon as Daffy hit the seat. Everything went everywhere. The barn was filled with flying plates, newspapers, flowers, beer bottles, tablecloths. The noise was deafening. The lowering canopy shut out the blizzard of party trash and cut the boom to a dull thunder. Scooter came off the brakes and nosed out of the hangar. They rolled out onto the short extension that led directly to the strip. Brewer looked up from his frantic attempts to align the navigation system and warm up the radar. And couldn't believe what he saw.

The crowd, distracted by the taxiing jets, had ceased following Hillary and had come back to watch the show. The strobing taxi light cut their movements into flickering pulses, like an old-time silent movie, as they lined the runway, waving, grinning, giving a thumbs-up signal to Brewer and Jeffries. Behind them, the attacking planes were tearing the heart out of al-Quaseem International. Daffy stepped on the intercom button to say something to Scooter, then raised his foot. There was nothing to say.

"Lima 2, Lima 1," Wilkinson's voice crackled over the radio. "We've got major FOD damage—looks like we sucked a folding chair or something in the right intake. We're going to have to abort. Suggest you do the same."

"Copy, Lima 1," Scooter answered. Then, over the intercom he asked Brewer, "What do you say, Skipper?"

Brewer wanted to say this was a nightmare that should never have happened. He wanted to say it was suicide to take off alone and take on what looked like an entire Soviet frontal aviation army. He wanted to say no one would blame First Air for not defending the base, not with the operational restraints imposed on the Regiment. But he didn't say any of it; Scooter knew.

"I say, go big or go home."

In response, Jeffries pushed the throttles into afterburner. The big jet lifted and roared down the runway, the rolling blast behind knocking Hillary's crowd into the sand. Two black shadows screamed above the canopy, dark dots falling from their wings. As Scooter raised the nose into a steep climb, Brewer cranked his head around to see the damage.

The Zulu shack was collapsed, on fire. A smoking crater punctuated the runway where, seconds before, they had taken off. There was no coming back to Dar al-Harb. Al-Quaseem International was even worse off—Daffy saw more holes than pavement there. There was always Bandar Abbas, but

Brewer had the feeling the airstrip there had received a similar visit. If that was true, the most he and Jeffries could hope for now was a safe ejection. Well, all right then. But they had business to take care of first.

Scooter, wisely, extended out over the Gulf, to gain speed and altitude and try to sort out the situation. Brewer got the radar up. The screen was crawling with shifting icons—all arrows, not a friendly half-circle to be found.

"Okay, here's the picture," Daffy said. "We've got eight missiles—four AIM-7s and four 'Winders. I count at least twenty bogies, but there's a lot more than that hiding down in the weeds. So what's our plan?"

"Surrender?"

Brewer laughed softly. "I don't think they want to surrender, Scooter."

"Then we'll just have to charge," Jeffries said. "Zoom on up to the stratosphere, ramp back down at about warp factor ten or so, and take whatever shots we can get. If we're lucky, by the time we pull out we'll be over Cancun. If you've got to punch out, I can't think of a better place."

Scooter pointed the nose at the blinking stars. Daffy looked back. The lights were out now. A dozen fires bloomed below, crossed by pairs of buzzing specks. The climb to altitude took too long for both of them. It gave them time to think.

"Daffy," Scooter said, "I'm scared shitless."

It was quite a confession for a fighter pilot. There was too much truth in the bar aphorism that said a real naval aviator would rather die than look bad.

"Me, too," Daffy said. "But look at it this way. We could have been in the Alert barn when it got hit."

Jeffries thought about that for a minute.

"Do you think Blade got out all right?"

No, Daffy thought. But he didn't want to worry Scooter with that now. "How long would you sit in a broken plane in the middle of an air strike?"

Scooter brightened up. "Yeah, I guess you're right."

Heavy with missiles and fuel, the Tomcat struggled in the high, thin air. Jeffries kicked it around. Al-Quaseem looked a long way down.

"You know," Scooter said, "it seems like we've been fighting these Klingons for years, doesn't it? And yet it's only been about three weeks or so. Up until about five minutes ago, the most important thing in my life was to nail one of the sumbitches. *Just one.* It seems like everybody's got a kill but me."

"You just haven't had an opportunity. You're a good pilot, Scooter," Brewer said reassuringly.

"Thanks, Daffy. And you're a real ace of gauges in my book," Scooter said. "But that's not the point. All of a sudden, I don't care about that anymore.

I just—I don't know—I want to do something *great,* that's all, something people will remember. Does that sound stupid?"

"No," Daffy said warmly. "That's probably the smartest thing I've ever heard."

Jeffries smiled under his oxygen mask. "Nice flying with you, Daffy."

"Same here, Scooter."

Jeffries nosed the Tomcat over and dove for the fires. In seven glorious minutes, Lt. Evan "Scooter" Jeffries earned a place forever in the golden log of combat aviation. He did everything exactly right. He was aggressive and cautious and inventive and professional, and any pilot in the world would be more than satisfied to fly the way he flew that black night—the night he and his backseater, Lt. Cmdr. Don "Daffy" Brewer, became First Air's first aces—and its first casualties.

The Battle of Bandar Abbas

**Bandar Abbas
Southern Iran**

One million or ten years ago, when Iran and the United States were actual allies, they might have taught English in a place like this. It was not difficult for Brick White to imagine that on that darker strip of wall above the blackboard there once hung those white-on-green placards of the English alphabet. He could, in fact, close his eyes and almost see the students, in their starched black-and-white uniforms, looking up from neat rows of desks and reciting happily as their teacher pointed to the American letters, first in block, then cursive, framed by dashed cheat lines and illustrated with apples and xylophones.

Someone, perhaps in this very classroom, had learned his lessons well. Setting up the new headquarters, after barely escaping with his life during the bombing of the old one, Brick had come across the slogan *Death to the American World-Devourers, please!!* in silver spray paint, still wet, in the main hallway. The graffiti—a rather standard, if unusually polite, Iranian epithet—was executed in the most beautiful handwriting Brick had ever seen.

It was more evidence that knowledge, skill, and cleverness were not the same as wisdom. Brick White did not need to be reminded of that, however. The men sitting glumly before him in the stifling classroom were proof enough.

"I'm real glad you guys kept telling me we weren't at war. Because if we were, we would have lost it last night."

Brick stepped up to a map of the region, pinned to the blackboard of the classroom. There was no power, so there was no relief from the heat of Bandar Abbas in the summertime. Portable generators for the communications equipment droned incessantly outside the open windows. The noise rose to a roar with the constant takeoffs and landings of helicopters on the soccer field beyond.

"Here's the situation, and it isn't pretty. I'm not going to say I told you so, but if we had capped Bandar Abbas and al-Quaseem like Bobby and I wanted to, this wouldn't have happened," Brick said bitterly. "You can blame it on the sheik if you want. He wouldn't let us, either. But I think we all know who's going to have to take a hit for the pounding we suffered last night."

He stared at each man in turn, and in their turn they each squirmed— Schatz with his tie loose and mousse unsprung, Forest in his Kevlar helmet with the absurd white stars painted on the brow. Brick knew the other two men present—Coleman and Casey—would realize the reprimand wasn't meant for them. He also knew he was being insubordinate. So be it. He had tried it the other way, and look where it had gotten them.

"Anyway, here's the damage report," Brick continued. "Al-Quaseem International is completely out of action and will probably remain so for the duration. So is Bandar Abbas International. Remember, they were commercial airports, not tactical air bases. They weren't built to take hits. The Russians used those dibbler bombs that bury themselves into the concrete before they go off. Both strips are cratered, end to end. At Bandar Abbas it goes all the way to the pipes. There's no way they're going to be repaired, even if we could get in there to do it, which we can't. The entire area is littered with delayed-action and motion-sensitive bomblets. You might as well turn it into a toxic waste dump. It's no good for anything else."

Brick looked at Casey and winced. He knew what Casey, now back in Iran as Coleman's aide, was thinking. To have fought so hard for the airport only to have it turned into a worthless concrete moonscape in three minutes— well, that was war. It could have been worse. Casey and his troopers could have been underneath the bombs. Brick wondered, as he had so often, why that had never happened, why the MiGs had not attacked the airport before. Certainly, in those last days before First Air came on line, when the Navy was played out and the Division Ready Force had their hands full fighting off tanks, Bandar Abbas International was theirs for the taking. Why had the Russians waited and let a week's worth of reinforcements land there before they put the airport out of action?

But that was that. Brick wasn't going to look too hard at a lucky break— they had had so precious few of them since the war began. He continued the briefing.

"The other two airfields were built for military use and are a little better off. The runway at NAS Bandar Abbas is cratered, and it's doubtful it'll be fixed in time to resume fixed-wing operations. But the rest of the facilities are pretty much intact, and we can, at any rate, base helicopters there.

"The good news, if there is any in this mess, is that Dar al-Harb is now operational. Apparently most of the Soviet strikers dropped their bombs on the first landing strip they saw, which was al-Quaseem International. The strip at Dar al-Harb *was* hit, which prevented us from scrambling immediately and going after them. The Zulu shack was completely destroyed, and the main runway took a couple of hits. But the sheik's people have been working around the clock to fix it up. The base is now operational."

Coleman shifted forward in his seat. "What about the planes, General? Can First Air still fly?"

Brick nodded. "The fighters, except for the ones on alert, were in hardened aircraft shelters. They're all right. Some of the attack aircraft at Bandar Abbas were damaged by bomb fragments, but we had built revetments around them that took most of the damage. It's not like First Air to leave aircraft lying around loose in the middle of a war. The transports, however, were parked out in the open. All totaled, one C-5, a couple of C-141s, and a bunch of C-130s were destroyed on the ground at the civil airports. I'm not even counting the commercial charters. Somebody's going to have to call American Airlines and tell them they're going to be short a couple of 747s next week. Probably forever."

Moving back to the map, Brick jabbed a finger at the coastline.

"The shipping situation is even more serious. There's a chartered bulk carrier sunk at the entrance to the new harbor. We're not going to be able to get any ships in there anytime soon. They hit the old port, too, but we didn't plan on using it anyway. The new port is the biggest loss. With that, and all the airports on this side of the strait closed, we're completely cut off from resupply."

"I know the feeling," Casey said softly.

Schatz cleared his throat. "I guess we'll just have to land the supplies and reinforcements at Dar al-Harb and shuttle them over in freighters. It'll be tough, but..."

Brick shook his head. "It's not going to happen. The sheik wouldn't let us park anything but First Air stuff there before the Russians attacked. What makes you think he's changed his mind now? They bombed his *country,* for Christ's sake! In fact, he'd probably kick First Air out of al-Quaseem now if he didn't need the protection."

"Then what about going back to Oman, or Saudi Arabia?" Schatz asked. "Things are different now."

"You're damned right they are!" Brick barked, exasperated. "You haven't been listening. None of the Gulf states wanted us here in the first place. They were afraid all along that something like this would happen. This just proves how right they were. No, we're stuck. We're worse off than we were before. Before, we just had a bunch of heavily armed hostages holed up at the airport. Now we've got a bunch of men and equipment—not enough to win, maybe, but too much to lose—hanging around the beach, waiting for a Soviet airborne division to roll down from those mountains and wipe them out."

"Just how much force can we muster, General?" Coleman asked. "I mean, I know where my people are, but the landings were so fast and so disorganized, I can't keep track of who's where and what they're supposed to do."

"Now I don't know if it was a blessing or a curse, but the geniuses who planned the deployment decided to make it easy on themselves by off-loading logistics equipment first," Brick smiled. "The Russians blew up a lot of bulldozers and portable maintenance shelters. Luckily, whatever combat units they managed to squeeze into their manifests had the good sense to run for the hills and dig in. We didn't land much, but they came through the bombing more or less intact. The tanks were already well north of the city, and the artillery was sited and dug in well away from the airport. The helicopters were just being unloaded when the Russians hit us, but they were crated up, and they look okay. And all the grunts, of course, starting digging for China when they heard the MiGs come in. We've got a lot of people on the ground, all around the city and the port, and they're all right, thank God."

"You can't kill dug-in infantry with airplanes, General," Coleman said. "They're like cockroaches. It only makes them meaner."

"That's where *we* are, General," Casey said softly. "Where are *they?*"

"The Soviets didn't land anywhere near us, tactically speaking. They didn't land anywhere near anything. According to the satellite pictures, they're up here..." Brick pointed to a spot on the map about thirty miles north of the city on the other side of Genow Mountain.

"What do they expect to get out of that?" Forest laughed.

"Iran," Casey said softly. "I'll bet they're all over the tunnel."

"Tunnel?" Forest asked. "What tunnel?"

"Genow Tunnel," Casey explained. "It's the only way through the mountains, the only way to get from northern Iran to the Strait of Hormuz.

Whoever controls that tunnel controls the route between Bandar Abbas and the rest of the interior, including Tehran."

"But that's crazy!" Forest argued. "They landed a whole airborne division up there. Why are they sitting on a bunch of rocks when they've got more than enough firepower to march down here and wipe us off the map?"

"Maybe they don't know that," Brick answered. "There's been so much stuff unloaded here lately—hell, *we* don't know what we've got. How could they know? They haven't run any recce flights since First Air became operational."

"But they've got satellites, too," Schatz said. "Surely they can get some idea from that."

"We've been off-loading around the clock," Brick answered. "Their satellites can't see through darkness and haze as well as ours can. They know we've got tanks, all right, but they don't know how many. And they've probably seen us unloading some attack helicopters, but they can't tell how many are uncrated and ready to fly, so they've got to assume the worst. That's what I'd do. Same thing with artillery. Tanks, planes, choppers, and guns— that's what paratroopers are afraid of. Even Soviet paratroopers. Right, General?"

Brick looked at Coleman, who nodded.

"So what are we worried about, then?" Forest asked with an idiot's grin. "We have the technological edge. Qualitative superiority in a target-rich environment—we couldn't ask for a better tactical scenario."

"That's what Custer said—just before he started collecting arrowheads," Brick shot back. "Besides, whether they know it or not, we've only got a few choppers and tanks. And maybe worse, we've only got a few bullets. And I don't see where we're going to get any more. There's no way we can run supply ships up the strait with so many Soviet fighters around. And there's no place to land cargo planes on this side of the Gulf."

"Excuse me, General," Coleman said, "but can't we airdrop supplies in?"

"Sure, we can," Brick nodded. "But not much stuff. And nothing heavy enough to make a difference. Bandar Abbas is still as far away from anywhere as it was when we started this thing. Besides, with those MiGs crawling all over the place, there's no way you can bring unescorted transports into the Gulf."

"Wait a minute," Casey thought out loud. "Logically, the Russians should have attacked when they first landed. In fact, they should have landed before we were able to bring in reinforcements. So why now? And why are they just sitting on those rocks? What are they waiting for?"

"Reinforcements, of course," Forest said, impatiently.

"But from where?" Casey asked. "I know in the briefings you've always heard the Russians had two airborne divisions near the border. But the truth is, in terms of air transport and resupply, they can only field one at a time. The 105th is a shadow division. They haven't moved out of their base in Fergana since this whole thing started. They can't—all their equipment is up at the tunnel with the 104th."

"Well, they're waiting for *something*," Coleman growled. "They're dug in up there, and it's going to be hard as hell to get them out."

"I don't think they're coming down here right away, General," Casey said. "I think they're going to stay up there and guard the tunnel until the Russians can get some of their armor down here from Tehran."

The notion of Soviet tanks in strength dampened the conversation.

"I've got to take what you say seriously, Colonel Casey. You've been in combat here, and you've always been right so far," Brick sighed. "But from what I understand, the Russians have their hands full up in Tehran. I just don't see how they're going to get out of there anytime soon, short of nuking the city. And even the Russians know we couldn't let them get away with that."

"There is another way, General," Casey said softly. "I've been talking with some of our intelligence folks since I got back. They've been getting reports of T-72s fighting their way out of the city center and lining up, track to track, along the ring road around Tehran—with the turrets facing *in*, not out. There's a train coming down from Tbilisi, high-priority, no other traffic allowed on the line. It's not KGB, but it's still getting the full Black Watch treatment. And lately the Russians have been very interested, even obsessed, with the weather around Tehran. Now, what does that mean to you?"

"Frankly, it doesn't mean a thing to me," Schatz said irritably. "Would someone please tell me what this man's talking about?"

Brick, Coleman, and Casey stared at the defense secretary blankly. Finally, Brick spoke.

"Gas, Mr. Secretary," he said, almost gently. "The Russians are going to use chemical weapons in Tehran."

Schatz went white. Forest stared back in disbelief.

"It makes sense," Casey added dreamily, as if talking to himself. "The last thing the Russians want is to get bogged down in another Afghanistan. Gassing Tehran would permit them to disengage and march south without having to watch their back. They could even use persistent chemicals—there's nothing in Tehran worth fighting for. Everything they want is down here. Right where we're sitting."

"Are you out of your mind?" Schatz exploded. "Has everyone gone insane except for me? Do you really think the world would tolerate the murder of millions of innocent civilians?"

"Oh, I don't think they'll have to go that far. They'll probably just have to gas a couple of isolated targets. The Iranians will get the message pretty quick," Brick answered. "And who said these are innocent civilians? They're Iranians. Don't forget who started this whole thing."

"Begging your pardon, sir," Casey said to Schatz, "but General White is right. World opinion, as far as that matters, would probably be on the side of the Russians. After all, they're here, ostensibly, for the same reason we are. Salting the earth is a military tradition that goes all the way back to Carthage. The Soviets just have a more sophisticated way of doing it."

"Besides," Brick growled, "they're not asking our opinion. If they want to poison everyone in Persia, there's not a damn thing we can do about it. Not short of nuclear weapons, anyway, and I don't think this president is willing to trade five American lives for every single Iranian dead. That's not how you win elections."

"When do you think they'll...do it?" Coleman asked worriedly. "And how long do you think it will take them to get down here?"

Casey closed his eyes and calculated, as if the question of mass murder was just another problem, no more difficult or serious than deciding how many steaks to fry at a cookout.

"About a week," he said finally. "If they get the weather they want and they don't have any trouble on the roads, they could be here in three or four days. If there's some problem, like a temperature inversion that keeps them from blowing the gas or partisan activities in the mountain passes, it could take longer. And if they travel like our Army, it could take even longer than that."

"What's that crack supposed to mean, Colonel?" Forest asked angrily.

"Oh, I meant no offense, General. It's just that it's a good three hundred miles from here to Tehran, over some of the roughest terrain in the world. And when we need to go across the street in an M 1, we have to put it on a trailer or move it by rail. Otherwise there'd be nothing left of it by the time you got to the battlefield. Moving tanks over the highway under their own power isn't good for the tanks or the road. And tanks break down when they have to move any distance cross-country. They break down a lot. They're not made for that, especially Soviet tanks."

"What if we blew the tunnel?" Coleman asked. "From what you said, there's no way tanks could get to us if we could close the tunnel."

"Wait a minute," Forest said sternly. "We're going to need that tunnel for our counterattack."

"I beg your pardon, General," Brick growled. "But let's get our plans worked out for this life before we worry about the next one."

"It doesn't matter anyway," Casey said. "Genow Tunnel is almost a mile long, and it's got four thousand feet of granite sitting on top of it. There's no way you're going to close that tunnel. Not with conventional weapons, anyway."

Casey didn't need to elaborate. Everyone knew what he was getting at: TacNukes. It was a textbook case for the application of battlefield nuclear weapons—an unambiguously military target, no civilian casualties, no collateral damage. And if the Russians chose to kill civilians in Iran with lethal gas, who could honestly object to the Americans moving a few mountains around?

The men sat quietly, thinking.

"Gentlemen, you are talking about Americans waging war on Soviet soldiers with nuclear weapons," Schatz said, his voice breaking. "I will hear no more of it."

"The secretary is right," Brick sighed. "The president would never go for that."

"I can see your point," Casey said, at once disappointed and relieved. "It's a pity, though. It would solve most of our problems. That tunnel is the key to this whole tactical situation. It's the only way in and out of here. There's no other way through the mountains, and there's no way anyone's going to build another tunnel anytime soon. It took ten years to build *that* one, and that was in peacetime."

"Hold on," Brick said. "Why would you have to collapse the whole tunnel? Why couldn't you just throw a Maverick or an LGB in the tunnel mouth and block the entrance?"

"It'd be a real bear to hit that small a hole, even with a laser-guided bomb, with half the 104th Guards shooting at you," Casey answered. "And even if you made it through and scored a direct hit, at that angle all you could hope to do is block the entrance with rubble and boulders. The Russians could move those rocks away in a couple of days."

Casey joined the rest of the men in a glum silence. He suddenly brightened, snapped his fingers, and added, "But not if we were sitting on top of them!"

"Have you got something in mind, Colonel?" Coleman asked.

"It's just an idea," Casey admitted. "But hear me out. We've got—what?—about a dozen tanks here? I saw a company laagered at the cannery yesterday. I don't think there are any more. We landed almost the same number of Bradleys before we were hit. I don't know where they are, but they couldn't have gone far."

"You've done a lot of sightseeing for a guy with a bad leg," Brick smiled.

"There's not much else to do around here," Casey said defensively. "Okay, let's assume that's all the armor we've got, except for the Marine LTVPs, and there are a lot of those running around. Okay, so they're really just armored tractors—they still make a lot of noise and churn up a lot of dust. From a couple of klicks away, they'd sure look like tanks, especially if that's what you were looking for."

Casey looked around, suddenly intimidated by all the stars in the room. "Go on," Brick said.

"Well, I was just thinking," Casey said. "The area around the tunnel's not that big. It's really kind of a bowl—you couldn't get much more armor than we've got in there anyway. And the Russians wouldn't know if we had any more behind it around the bend where they couldn't see. Especially with all the artillery shells and smoke going off and the helicopters all around."

"I think I see what you're getting at," Brick smiled. "Have we got enough helicopters?"

"There were about a dozen at the soccer field this morning," Casey said. "Most of them were Black Hawks, but I think we'll have enough Apaches and scouts ready by tonight to make a hunter-killer team."

"You're forgetting we're short of artillery rounds," Coleman said, doubtfully. "We couldn't sustain an attack for long."

"With what I've got in mind, that's not necessary, General," Casey countered. "We've got to put up maximum weight of fire for a minimum amount of time. It either works or it doesn't. If it works, we won't need any more ammo. And if it doesn't work...well, it won't make much difference."

"Now, wait a minute," Schatz interjected. "Let me get this straight. We're outnumbered, isolated, and short of ammunition and supplies—and you're talking about *attacking?*"

"I admit it's a gamble, sir," Casey said, "but I don't see any alternative. If we let those Soviet paratroopers secure the tunnel long enough for their tanks to get through, we might as well start swimming. At least this way we've got a chance."

"It doesn't sound like much of a chance to me," Schatz said doubtfully. "You're talking about a handful of tanks and helicopters up against two thousand elite Soviet *desant* troops."

"My boys are pretty elite, too, Mr. Secretary," Coleman snarled. "This isn't Europe. The Russians don't have any tanks. And I'd just as soon fight them before they get any."

"I didn't mean to disparage your men, General," Schatz said quickly. "But you'll have to admit the odds are against you. The Soviets are dug in, under cover. You'll be advancing across flat desert terrain. That would be suicide."

"You're right, Mr. Schatz," Casey said. "That *would* be suicide. That's why we're not going to do it. That's why we're going to put on the show with the tanks and the helicopters right in front of the Russians—to get their attention. Our men will sneak in from every direction, in small units so they won't attract attention. They'll concentrate only at the last minute, at the point of attack. There's *sarir*—dissected terrain, passable only on foot—all around the tunnel. The Soviets won't be expecting an attack from there."

"But what good are infantrymen going to be against troops in fortified positions?" Schatz asked. "They've only got machine guns and assault rifles. They can't shoot through rocks."

"Don't call them infantrymen," Coleman snapped. "Please. They're *Airborne*."

Schatz ignored him.

"We don't expect our men to wrinkle the Russians out of the rocks," Casey said. "That's First Air's job. Close air support is the only real combat power we have in this operation. Everything else is secondary. The tanks and the helicopters are there just to get the Russians' attention. Our dismounted forces are only expected to fix the enemy and keep their heads down so they can't fire back at the planes. They'll secure the tunnel once the Russians are pushed out. But the whole objective is to draw the Soviets out and pin them down so First Air can pound them."

Schatz shook his head. "I don't know. It sounds risky to me."

"Me, too," Forest spoke up. "I have to admit, Mr. Secretary, you and I don't often see eye to eye. But I agree with you completely—this is a very dangerous plan with little hope of success."

Brick spread his hands. "And what would you have us do, General?"

"Draw back everything we have into a tight perimeter around the city," Forest said, "and wait."

"Wait?" Brick exploded. "Wait for what? Withdraw into a compact, stationary target and wait for the MiGs to pound us into the desert? Wait for reinforcements that are never going to come? Wait for the Russian tanks to come down here and roll over us?"

"We don't know for sure that the Soviets are planning to move south," Schatz said calmly. He pointed at Casey. "All we have is this officer's guess."

Coleman snorted. "That's all you ever have in war, Mr. Secretary. Your best people's best guesses. Is it going to take treadmarks across your back before you believe him?"

"May I remind everyone that this proposed plan is predicated on the participation of First Air?" Schatz spoke the Regiment's name as if it were a dirty word. "How do we know this unit can handle such a job—they certainly botched their mission of air defense last night. In fact..."

Brick was livid. "You wouldn't let..."

"In *fact*," Schatz shouted over Brick's objections, "how do we know the Regiment still exists? Has anyone seen Bobby Dragon? For all we know he's deserted again. And without him, there is no First Air Regiment."

"Bobby will turn up. You'll see." Brick sounded like a man trying to convince himself. "You can count on him. And you can count on First Air."

"I don't care what you say. It still sounds imprudent to me," Schatz said. "I'm not going to let you throw away what little forces we have left on a reckless attack that is sure to fail."

"With all due respect, Mr. Secretary, it's not your decision," Brick said softly. "This is an operational matter. You don't have a say in this."

"No, but I do," Forest spoke up. "And I agree with Mr. Schatz. You've gotten a lot of mileage playing us against one another, White..."

"General Forest, I..."

Forest cut him off. "Now, don't try to deny it because we all know it's true. Seeing you in action now makes me wonder how many times the secretary and I have actually agreed in the past. Well, that's water under the bridge. The important thing is that you disabuse yourself of this rash notion of attacking the Soviets at the Genow Tunnel."

"I doubt the president would see it that way," Brick said angrily.

"General White!" Schatz said sternly. "I've had quite enough of your insubordination. General Forest and I have discussed the matter, and we are in total agreement that it's time for a change. We've given you complete latitude, and so far everything you've done has only dragged us deeper into this nightmare. In fact, we plan to brief the president on your miscalculations, just as soon as we..."

"You're setting him up for the fall, aren't you?" Coleman cut in, outraged. "You're going to make him take the rap for Ready Eagle and every bad thing that's happened since! You know that after last night's fiasco, the press and the politicians are going to look for a fall guy, so you got together and nominated Brick White. Well, that is really low, gentlemen. That really stinks."

"That's enough, soldier!" Forest shouted at Coleman. "It's about time you and everybody else in this theater learned how to count stars."

He walked to the front of the schoolroom and hiked a leg on a folding chair. "Pack your bags, boys," Forest drawled. "You had your chance and you blew it. You're out. The first team is taking over now. Mr. Schatz and I are assuming personal command of Operation Ready Eagle, effective immediately."

The buzzing of flies droned through the sweltering schoolroom. There was no other sound. Coleman's face was flushed. His hands clenched and unclenched in big fists. Brick didn't move a muscle. His mind was searching for solutions to the impasse, testing them, finding them inadequate, rejecting them, but searching for more; he looked like a computer presented with the concept of infinity, unable to accept that there *was* no solution and perfectly willing to search for one forever.

Suddenly the lonely sound of a pair of hands clapping broke the silence, echoing through the schoolroom like rifle shots. All eyes turned to see Bobby

Dragon, still in his soaking flight suit, leaning against the back wall with a crooked grin.

"So," Schatz smirked, "the shooting is over and the prodigal returns. For how long this time?"

Forest's eyes narrowed. "You got a problem, soldier?"

"Who, me?" Bobby pointed at himself in an exaggerated gesture. "No, sir. On the contrary, I consider myself fortunate to have witnessed the greatest tornado of horseshit ever to hit Iran. And considering what's gone on in this country in the past couple of decades, that's saying something."

"Pull yourself together!" Forest said furiously. "You're talking to a three-star general!"

"In whose army?" Bobby asked calmly. "Not *my* army. You've made that clear enough. Every chance you got, you tried to distance yourself from First Air. You called us mercenaries, consultants, scum. After we chased the MiGs away for you, you went on TV and acted like they ran because they heard Big Bad Beau Forest was in the neighborhood. Look, you want to hog all the credit, that's fine. You want to turn Bandar Abbas into another Dunkirk, go ahead; I couldn't care less. But I'm not going to risk the lives of my men on the whims and hunches of some fat-assed politician in a general's suit. I've tried that before. It didn't work then, and it won't work now."

Livid, Forest began to speak, when Schatz held up a hand for silence. "Pay no attention to this man, General. He has no part in this. He's just a hired gun."

"That's right, mister," Bobby said. "I'm not in the U.S. Air Force. And after what I've seen here today, I thank God for that. I'm a hit man, just like you said, hired out to the highest bidder. In this case, that's Sheik Hassan, your only ally in the Gulf, probably in the whole world at this point. Have you talked to *him* about your little plan?"

"We will, of course, consult with the government of al-Quaseem at the proper time," Schatz said flatly. "I really don't see how that's any concern of yours."

"Oh, you're right," Bobby said nonchalantly. "It's none of my business. I'm sure whenever you get around to telling the sheik that you're going to hang him and his people out to dry—for the good of America, of course— he'll understand. He seems like a very understanding man."

Bobby shuffled stiffly to the door.

"Well, I must be going. To us mercenaries, time is money." Bobby stopped and added, with fierce irony, "You know, that's what Krypto Padgett was saying just last night. Before he got killed, I mean. Well, that's an occupational hazard in our business, I guess. I'm sure you're used to facing death every day behind your desks."

"Really, Mr. Dragon, I won't..."

"Oh, don't worry, Mr. Schatz. Krypto knew what he was getting into. After all, he was just another hired assassin, in it for the money, just like the rest of us. Before I go, though, I'd like to ask you a question. That is, if you don't mind."

"Go ahead," Schatz sighed. "If that's what it takes to get you to leave."

"Can you swim?"

Schatz looked at Bobby with surprise and suspicion. "Yes," he answered tentatively, "quite well, as a matter of fact. But I don't see what that's got to do with..."

"Do you think you could swim seventy miles in ninety-degree water with sharks biting your ass all the way?" Bobby turned to Forest. "What about you, General? You're an old leg soldier—you probably didn't have the benefit of Mr. Schatz's summers at Cape Cod. That's okay. You can always hike to Pakistan. It's only about three hundred miles to Karachi, and it's the scenic route—mountains and deserts and plenty of sunshine. And just think of the fascinating political discussions you can have along the way with the quaint native folk whose country you've just invaded."

Forest's eyes narrowed. "What are you getting at?"

"Just this," Bobby said evenly. "Any road that's going anywhere—victory or orderly withdrawal, I don't care which—runs right down the middle of my runway at Dar al-Harb. You can't do a thing without First Air. We're the only thing that's keeping you from being bombed into the desert right now. And, like Colonel Casey said, we're the only real firepower you've got. If we leave, those Russians will come down from the mountain and push you into the sea. They won't even need to wait for their tanks. I call my planes home, you're screwed—that, gentlemen, is a true military fact. You can either choose to accept that reality or not. I don't give a gnat's ass either way."

Bobby leaned against the door, opening it slightly. Schatz and Forest carried on a hushed, anxious conversation at the front of the room.

"Just a minute, Colonel," Schatz called out. "Don't you think we should talk about this?"

Bobby turned around. "That depends on what you have to say."

"We'd welcome your help," Forest said a little too anxiously. "We're prepared to offer you a commission—a *real* commission—as a colonel in the U.S. Air Force. We'd forget all about that other...misunderstanding...in Da Nang. You could clear your name. You could be a hero."

Bobby looked at Brick and sadly shook his head.

"You were right, Brick. These guys aren't listening." He turned to Forest and Schatz. "No deal. It's gone way beyond that now. Don't you understand? This is *real*. People are getting killed. This is it, the Big Contingency—us against the Russians. It's not a question any longer of *if* but of *how*. We're about forty-eight hours from World War III, and you're still playing politics."

"What would you have us do, Colonel Dragon?" Schatz asked. He pointed at Casey. "We can't go to war based on this man's suppositions."

"We're *already* at war with the Russians! Who the hell do you think dropped those bombs last night? Federal Express?" Bobby sighed, exasperated. "And as far as what Casey says—Krypto Padgett was trying to tell me the same thing last night. I've never known him to be wrong. And, come to think of it, I've never known you to be right."

"Yes, but suppose he *is* right, just for the sake of argument," Forest said. "The thing to do is secure a perimeter, establish a fire base, and..."

"And get slowly bombed, starved, or bored to death," Bobby interjected. "Look, I don't know if Casey's plan will work or not. Nobody does. But I know this—it's the best chance we've got. I'm sure of it. So sure, in fact, that I'm willing to bet the lives of the men in the Regiment on it. You can't call that bet. I say we do it."

"That's not for you to say," Schatz declared. "You may exercise authority over your mercenary air force, but the men on the ground here are still under our command."

"Fine," Bobby shot back. "But whatever else you've got in mind, you can count First Air out."

The silence hung heavily in the schoolroom. Finally, Schatz spoke.

"So. It's a Mexican standoff. We need you and you need us. But we can't agree on a course of action. It's a no-win situation," Schatz sounded like a manager in the middle of union negotiations. "How are we going to resolve this dilemma?"

"Hey, I've got an idea." Bobby snapped his fingers, as if just stumbling upon the answer. "You know, every time something like this comes up, I always consult the U.S. Constitution. Call me a sentimental fool, but for deciding sticky questions like who's in charge and whether or not we should initiate hostilities with the most powerful nation on earth, there's no one better, I think, than the commander in chief."

"You mean the president?" Forest asked nervously.

"Ah, you've been reading up," Bobby laughed, a skittering chortle running on the edge of exhaustion and frustration. "That's right. That's what he gets paid for. Why don't you let Brick talk Casey's plan over with the president? If the White House okays the attack, then we'll do it. If the president says no, I'll try to square it with Hassan and protect you guys as well as I can, for as long as I can. What do you say?"

Forest tugged Schatz's sleeve. The two men whispered earnestly. Finally, Forest nodded and Schatz looked up.

"No," Schatz said firmly, then smiled. "No, I don't think it's wise to bother the president with this little disagreement. I'm sure he's much too busy at the moment to deal with tactical questions."

"Suit yourself," Bobby said. "Have a nice swim."

"Really, Colonel," Schatz sighed. "There's no need to be antagonistic. I can't see why you're getting so upset. I would hope you'd have been more open to input from all up and down the chain of command."

"Wait a minute," Bobby said. "Let me get this straight. Are you saying you authorize Casey's plan to attack the Soviets at Genow Tunnel?"

Bobby looked straight at Schatz. The secretary of defense held his gaze for two seconds, then dropped his eyes and looked at his watch.

"As General White has so rudely but accurately pointed out, as a civilian I have no authority over operational matters. As far as General Forest is concerned, like any good soldier, he delegates tactical responsibility to those subordinates he orders to carry out the mission. Isn't that right, General?"

Forest, out of his league, nodded sullenly.

"Well, I'm glad we understand each other," Bobby said. He wasn't used to dealing with someone as slippery as Schatz. He wanted to get it straight. "So Brick and General Coleman and everybody else will stay and handle this. And you go. Right?"

"Well, I would hope that what General Forest and I have contributed will get you thinking. What you do, of course, is your decision. We..."

"You go!" Bobby repeated. "Right?"

Schatz looked at Forest and nodded. They rose and headed for the door. On his way out, Schatz stopped, his face just inches from Bobby's.

"I'm not through with you, fella," Schatz hissed. "When this is all over, I'm going to get you and everybody else here."

Bobby laughed in Schatz's face. Schatz stomped out. As soon as he was gone, Bobby slumped down into the nearest desk. His back was covered with blood.

"Jesus, Bobby, you're hurt!" Brick hurried over to him.

"I'm all right," Bobby panted. The self-assured gambler who had faced down the secretary of defense and the national security advisor had suddenly turned into a tired, wounded man.

"I'll go get a medic," Coleman said. "Casey, get this man some water."

The two Airborne soldiers rushed through the door, leaving Brick alone with Bobby.

"What happened, Bobby? Where have you been?"

"Krypto had this wild hair," Bobby said weakly. "He thought the Russians were going to land up at the tunnel. He got one of those Army spooks to drive us up there in an MH-6. Sure enough, there they were, thousands of them. The rotor got fouled in some Russian's parachute shroud, and we went down. I jumped out before we hit the ground. I think the pilot did, too. I don't know what happened to him. Krypto was in the back, trapped. He couldn't get out. The chopper burned, just burned up."

Bobby shook his head in disbelief at the horrible memory of his friend dying in front of him.

"I..." Bobby caught his breath and continued. "I started back up the road. The Russians didn't see me. Or maybe they were too busy digging in; I don't know. Anyway, I walked and I walked and I ran into some of our guys in a Hummer. I told them who I was and told them to take me to headquarters. I got here just as Casey was coming up with his plan. It's a good plan, Brick. We ought to do it. I can't..."

Bobby slumped over, unconscious. Brick pulled him up gently and propped him against the desk. Casey and Coleman returned with a medic, who immediately went to work.

"What do you think, Doc?" Brick asked worriedly. "Is he going to be okay?"

The medic nodded. "Heat stroke and exhaustion. And that's a nasty cut on his back. It's not deep enough to be serious, but it probably hurts like hell. He'll be okay, though."

A couple of soldiers hurried in with a stretcher. Brick walked with them as they carried Bobby to the aid station set up in the school cafeteria.

Bobby's eyes flickered into brief consciousness. "We really showed those jerks, didn't we?" he smiled at Brick.

"We sure did," Brick answered. "But you ought to be more careful, Bobby. Schatz is a devious son of a bitch, and he never forgets. I'm sure he *will* try to get back at you, somehow."

"Then the joke's on him," Bobby smiled. "Does he honestly think any of us are going to live through this?"

The Greatest Gift

Dar al-Harb Air Base
Emirate of al-Quaseem

The wooden porch outside the Sierra Hotel thundered with the sound of dozens of heavy flight boots, as the members of the First Air Regiment, Inc., headed to their planes for what was, win or lose, shaping up to be their last mission.

Bobby Dragon, at their head, winced as he climbed down the stairs, the tight Combat Edge G-suit vest digging into the bandages across his injured back. The doctors said he shouldn't fly this mission. That was not acceptable to Bobby. First Air needed every man it could get.

Bobby turned around at the opening in the chain-link fence that led to the flight line, watching the remaining pilots file out of the Sierra Hotel. Well, that was one good thing about attrition. You didn't need to clear out a hangar to get all the men together anymore. You could brief the whole Regiment in the bar, like civilized fighter pilots.

Where had they gone? Home, most of them, called to roost, along with their planes, by nervous governments after the bombing of al-Quaseem. Bobby didn't blame them, though some had gone more willingly than others. All-out attack by the national air forces of the Soviet Union wasn't supposed to be part of the program. Those nations would need those men and those aircraft in the world war that might soon come—the war they had been sent to First Air in an effort to avoid.

And the rest? Bobby didn't need to look far to find out what had happened to them. It was there for all to see, scrawled in red on the pillars and cornices of the whitewashed porch, the proud record of the Regiment, its darkest days and finest hours. The dates of air-to-air victories and the call signs of the victors were stenciled into red outlines of enemy planes shot down. Losses were denoted simply by the name of the member of the Regiment who was killed stenciled in white over a black rectangle.

There had been some discussion when the tradition began as to whether it was a good idea to record losses as well as victories. Bobby had ended the discussion: *"This is a fighting Regiment,"* he had said, flatly. *"We're not going to pretend that nobody ever dies here."*

Bobby looked up at the names etched on the white walls now and wondered if it was such a good idea after all. First Air had saved the Americans' effort in Iran before the Russians came in force. And the Regiment was still the only thing keeping the Soviets from bombing the disorganized invaders into the sand of Bandar Abbas. But it had not come without sacrifice. Now, impossibly outnumbered, First Air was being slowly ground down.

The fact that he didn't know most of the men who had died for him and his Regiment cut into Bobby's soul. But of all the blows the list caused him, the worst was the first, Col. Daffy Brewer.

Bobby laughed to himself at the irony. So Daffy had finally made colonel. All the dead men were colonels. So were the living. What a crazy idea this whole thing had been.

He leaned against the gate and watched his men file past, nodded, smiling, saying, "good hunting" and "go get 'em" and all those empty, meaningless phrases men say to one another when they're about to go out and try to kill other humans for a good cause—without admitting that somewhere on the other side of the line someone else was saying exactly the same things at exactly the same time. And probably with the same amount of conviction, Bobby thought.

Daffy Brewer. *Why did it have to be him?* Well, at least Brick would see that his family got the pension, even if he had to declare war on the Navy to do it. Daffy's girls must be in college now. One was already born and another on the way when he and Bobby took off on those insane tiger hunts. Christ, how could a man with children fly fighters? A wife was bad enough, but you might as well go into combat with the kids in the cockpit, toddlers playing with the switches, infants tangled in the rudder pedals. They were never far from Daffy's heart. But he left them on the ground. An amazing man. A First Air man.

The pilots kept coming. They were not jolly men. They were not afraid, either, or resigned. If any great emotion moved them—bravery or duty or patriotism—they had left it behind at the bar. There was no room for great ideals in the cramped cockpits of modern fighters. These men knew it. It was one of the reasons they had lived so long. In the end, one common denominator bound the remaining members of the Regiment, the hard core, the heartbreakers, and the bar closers—they were all curious and stubborn sons of bitches who were sticking around just to see how bad it could get.

The Weasel brothers, uncharacteristically sporting full Nomex flight suits and chicken armor, were among the last to file out of the Sierra Hotel.

"Hey, it's the Dragon man!" Don said to Wally. "Were we glad to see *you,* guy!"

"Nice briefing—full of information, yet with that touch of dramatic irony that keeps us wanting more," Wally said. "Nobody gives good briefing like you, Bobby. I give it a thumbs up!"

"So when did you get back?" Don asked.

"This morning. I've been over at the Pit, working this thing out with the Army pukes," Bobby answered. "What have you guys been doing?"

Don's face darkened. "These are tough times for the Magnificient Several, Bobby. We've been in the barrel—MiGs on top and guns on the bottom. Extremely high pucker factor. Plus they've got a million of those piss-ant little shoulder-fired SAMs. They don't worry you fast movers too much, but in a flying mall like the Cannonball—well, let's just say it might not be as exciting as your wedding night, but it's probably more exciting than every night after that."

"*You* try going over Mount Ivan at three hundred knots in broad daylight," Wally added. "It'll definitely put a buzz in your shorts."

"That's not the only excitement around here, I understand," Bobby said. "What did you do during the bombing?"

"We weren't here," Don said. "We were over in Sammarah, playing *chemin de fer.* A couple of thousand bucks later, Wally gets this bright idea to crash Hillary's party. So we come back here, and it's raining MiGs. The lights are out, everybody's running around screaming—*major* dick dance. Wally's got the Cannonball wired to self-destruct, if it comes to that, so we just sat inside with a flashlight and played Rook, waiting for Russian paratroopers."

"Scary movie, man," Wally said seriously. "If those Bolsheviks want to fight, they should do it like real men, using high-speed digital computers and Doppler radars instead of guns and knives and crap like that. What do they think we are—savages?"

"Anyway, after a while the MiGs go away, and we realize we *aren't* going to be invaded after all," Don continued. "So the next morning, all the guys in the Regiment wind up in the ops shack, just standing around with their hands in their pants, looking for someone to tell them what to do. Brick calls us, tells us what happened to you, says the Army needs us, says you said it was okay. I didn't know what to say—we've never really had a command structure around here. You were gone. Brick was gone. Krypto was gone. We decided to ask the sheik. I mean, it's *his* country. But Sonny comes in, says screw it, let's go. So we went."

"You should have seen the kid, Bobby," Wally said with admiration. "I mean, this guy was like a combination of Ivan Lendl, James Dean, and George Patton."

"First he goes out and gets the repair crew off their butts and on the job," Don said. "We had a hole the size of a baseball stadium in the runway, and they had it fixed the next day. This is the Persian Gulf, Bobby—*nothing* gets fixed the next day."

"I think he mentioned something about castration," Wally added. "But my Arabic's not that good. He could have said total death."

"Then Sonny comes back in and starts giving orders—you do this, and you do that," Don said. "We were going to stop and ask him politely exactly who the hell he thought he was, except everything he said made too much sense. He got the CAP back up, on both sides of the strait. And the strikers have been sanitizing the area between Mount Ivan and the Pit, so the Russians can't come down and see just how much we *don't* have to fight them with."

"Don't get us wrong, Bobby," Wally cut in. "We're glad you're back. Faisal's just a kid, after all. But if it weren't for him, there wouldn't *be* a First Air Regiment now. Or any Americans left in Bandar Abbas, either, for that matter."

Bobby nodded. The sharp shot of cartridge starters in some of the older planes slapped across the runway. The white cloud of cordite rolled behind with its piercing smell. It would not be long now.

"So what's playing on the Cannonball today, boys?"

"Kind of a change of pace, today, Bobby," Don answered. "We're playing the part of the entire 101st Air Assault Division. The Cannonball's hauling a line of radar reflectors, broadcasting their radio traffic, laying smoke—it's Casey's idea. The real 101st is still floating on the ocean somewhere, but the Russians don't know that for sure."

"And if *that* doesn't work," Wally added, "we're going to jam the Soviet radio net with Yoko Ono tapes. We would have done it before, only it's outlawed by the Geneva Convention. But desperate times call for desperate measures."

Don looked at his watch. "We'd better get going, Bobby. We've got a little work to do. It's getting harder and harder to light up the Cannonball as it gets more holes in it. And even aboard the most advanced piece of technology flying, the ground and the whisky are still hard."

Bobby frowned. He had never seen the Weasels worried before. "You really think they can get to you?"

"Even a blind squirrel finds a nut now and then," Don shrugged. "There's always a chance they might luck out and throw something nontrivial at us. They're getting better."

"Then don't go," Bobby said. "You've done more than enough as it is."

The Weasels looked at Bobby as if he were crazy.

"Are you kidding?" Don said. "This is starting to get *interesting*."

Don patted Bobby on the shoulder. He and Wally strolled out on the flight line, whistling the Superchicken theme. Bobby turned back to watch the pilots leaving the Sierra Hotel. Faisal was the last one out.

"Got a second, Sonny?"

Faisal seemed surprised and pleased that Bobby wanted to speak with him. He and Bobby fell into an easy walk along the flight line.

"I just wanted to tell you how much I appreciate you stepping in for me," Bobby said. "There was a real vacuum there. You probably saved the Regiment. And everybody else under it."

Faisal smiled broadly. "I am glad you understand. Please believe me, I did not mean to take your position. No one could do that. And no one was happier to hear of your escape than I was."

"Even so, it could have been bad," Bobby said. "Someone had to give the order to scramble or else the second wave would have wiped us out."

Faisal nodded. "The men wanted to take off as soon as the runway was fixed. But the maintenance people and the workers in the tower—they wanted permission from my father. I told them I was in command and that I so ordered it. That seemed to satisfy them."

Bobby looked at Faisal. Sonny was young, but not that young. His brief life as a First Air fighter jock had put a few lifetimes on him. The playboy, the kid who zoomed through life pursuing fast cars and faster women—he was gone. Hassan must surely be proud of his son now. Faisal was a man. His orders would be obeyed.

They came to Faisal's F-16, squatting in the sun. The Paveway was already loaded, a laser-guided monster packing a ton of high explosives.

Bobby turned to Sonny. "Are you sure you want to do this?"

"No."

"No?" Bobby looked confused and worried. "But you *volunteered*."

Sonny sensed he had said something wrong. "I am sorry. My English is not that great. You asked if I wanted to do this. I said no, and that is the truth. I do not *want* to go on this mission. And neither do you, I hope, or

I am flying with a crazy man. But we have to go, whether we want to or not, yes? That is the right answer."

"Yes," Bobby smiled. "That's exactly the right answer."

Bobby ducked underneath the wing and patted the laser-seeker head on the huge bomb. "Now remember, Sonny. You've got to stay right with me. I mean, right on my wing—we've got to look like one plane on their radars. We've got to make them think we're just some recce aircraft coming in to take poststrike pictures."

"I know," Faisal said solemnly. He held two fingers close together. "Just like that. Just as you did with General White in Vietnam. The tiger hunts."

Bobby was stunned. "How did you know about that?"

"I know everything about you, Colonel Dragon. We studied your record in pilot training." Faisal, proud but striving to sound modest, added, "My instructors said I reminded them a great deal of you. It made me very pleased."

"Ah, thanks, Sonny," Bobby said. "I'm flattered you feel that way. But I'm just another colonel in the Regiment. Same as you."

"Oh, no," Sonny said, earnestly. "You are the best. Everyone says so. I spoke to Colonel Brewer, and he..."

Bobby felt a chill up his back. "You talked to Daffy about me? What did he say?"

Faisal shifted uncomfortably. "He said you were the greatest fighter pilot that ever lived. Only..."

Bobby stared into Sonny's brown eyes. "Only what?"

"You think too much." Faisal stared wide eyed as Bobby threw back his head and laughed. "I am sorry. Did I say something wrong?"

"No, you're absolutely right," Bobby chuckled. "It's just that my life would have been a hell of a lot more simple if somebody had told me that a long time ago, that's all."

It came in a shudder of laughter, an odd remark from a dead friend, solemnly repeated by a young man so very alive. Life was savage, strange, and sweet, but it made sense if you hung on long enough for the replay.

So here they were, Bobby thought, two decades later, hunting tigers again. History repeats itself—or does it? Did Bobby hate Faisal? Was he jealous? Did he want to see him killed? No, absolutely not. There were sound, tactical reasons for *this* tiger hunt. There was no other way to execute it, and Sonny was the perfect man for the mission. *Now, who did that sound like?*

The truths kept piling up, one after the other. Surely Vietnam was pointless. And surely Bobby wasn't the only one who thought so—Brick had often said as much while staring at the bottom of a San Miguel. Was that really why Bobby flew away that day? He could see now, his soul so illuminated in the Arabian sun. The answer was no. No real fighter pilot, not one on Bobby's aerie, really gave a damn about politics or anything else that happened on the ground. What drove a fighter pilot? Ego. And what did fighter pilots fear more than bullets and missiles? Failure. The fighter pilot's Kryptonite.

And he had failed. Brick had been shot down. *His wingman.* Shot down. It was Brick's own stupid fault. He could accept that now. But back then, young as Faisal, teethed on fables of his own invulnerability and true martial perfection—how was he to deal with it?

Bobby shifted uncomfortably. It was nice to get stroked so completely, especially from someone as young and gifted as Faisal. It was nirvana for a fighter pilot, a night in Vegas. But Bobby was through being just a fighter pilot. It was time to break the chain.

"Listen, Sonny, we've got a little time here. I haven't had a chance to talk with you much. When I was your age..." Bobby winced. He once swore to himself he'd never say that, and now it flew off his tongue like a missile. "When I was your age, I wished someone had taken me aside and talked to me, really talked, about flying fighters. About what makes a good fighter pilot."

Faisal looked puzzled. "Good eyesight, coordination, intelligence, and an aggressive attitude," he said, as if reciting from a book.

"No," Bobby sighed, "that's not it. Not all of it, anyway. Those things are important. Everybody here has all those qualities, in varying degrees. And everybody in the Regiment flies shit hot. Against normal pilots, there's nobody better. But they're not like us, Sonny. Something sets us apart."

"What is it?"

"It's kind of hard to explain," Bobby searched for the right words. "It's— I guess you could call it emotional, for want of a better word. Maybe even spiritual, although that's a hell of a word to use for people gifted in the art of murdering people in the air.

"There's nothing metaphysical about it. Flying—real flying, flying fighters—takes a peculiar set of physical, mental, and emotional skills. There's no computer smart enough or fast enough, no machine sensitive enough or tough enough, to do what fighter pilots do. What *we* do. What *you* do. You can call it the right stuff or the touch or the force or whatever you want to call it. Those things sound stupid because you're trying to describe in words something we don't have any words for. But whatever it is, it's real enough. And you've got it, kid. I've seen you fly."

"Thank you," Faisal said solemnly.

"Don't thank me," Bobby said sternly. "I'm not sure it's a good thing. It's like any other gift—you can use it to enrich your life and the life of the world, in however small a way. Or you can abuse it, hide behind it, make other people feel small. That's what I've done, up to now."

"I do not understand," Sonny said.

"No, I suppose you don't," Bobby sighed. "You're just too damn young. That's the way life is built. That's what Daffy was trying to tell me. You don't realize what's important until it's too late to do anything about it. Look, maybe I'm talking to myself, here. I just don't want you to do what I've done, what Brick did. I've spent my whole life flying fighters, and now I've come to realize, all along, it was the other way around."

A Near Run Thing

Genow Mountain
Sarzeh Valley, Iran

Steve Casey leaned on his M16 like it was a cane and lifted his binoculars. They were a new set, Zeiss, bought during his brief recuperation in Germany, and Casey was very proud of them. By zooming to full power and using yellow filters to cut through the haze, he could see all the way to World War III.

He scanned the area, west to east, from the low, rocky hills to towering Khirou Mountain. The brown, loaf-shaped peak had been dubbed "Mount Ivan" by the troops, because it was there where the Soviets' strength lay. The duke of Wellington had spent half of his life in uniform, he once said, wondering what was on the other side of the hill. Casey stared across the Sarzeh Valley and wondered the same thing.

He could see the whole battlefield from where he stood. It was an anomaly in modern combat, in which probes, feints, defense in depth, and deep strikes by mobile, mechanized armies could take hundreds of square miles. Because the forces on both sides of this line were paratroopers, however, for the most part short of any transportation but the airborne boot, this was to be a static battle. A set piece, not unlike Waterloo in geographic dimension though involving a tenth of the manpower and infinitely more firepower. For Casey, the question could hardly be more clear or portentous: *Was he Wellington? Or Napoleon?*

The sound of crunching gravel interrupted his reverie. Casey turned to see an HMMW-V roaring up the mountain trail to the command post. The Hummer was the Army's high-tech, high-cost replacement for the venerable jeep. It was bigger, more powerful, and not as dangerous, but the "Hum-Vee," as the soldiers called it, performed the same variety of tasks. In this case, it was performing a mission Casey had never seen *any* vehicle accomplish— it was carrying a general officer *closer* to the scene of an impending battle.

Casey shuffled awkwardly down the parapet of rock and gravel to the mesalike section of the larger mountain where he had set up his headquarters.

"General Coleman," Casey called, saluting. "This is quite a surprise, sir. I thought you'd be back at DivMain."

"I've seen about all I want to see of Bandar Abbas," Coleman said. "There's no point in standing around Khomeini Junior High listening to the RT when I can get up here and see things for myself."

Coleman climbed stiffly out of the Hum-Vee and followed Casey back to the small pile of stones that ringed the mountaintop. Casey noticed that the general, like the rest of his soldiers in Iran, now carried MOPP gear on a canister slung on his thigh. The mission-oriented protective posture equipment consisted of a gas mask, protective clothing, and a first-aid kit designed to treat victims of chemical/biological warfare attacks. The Americans had gotten serious about surviving CBW attacks the minute after the Soviets had gotten serious about delivering them. The Russians had used gas in Tehran just hours after Casey had sadly predicted they would. It had taken only a few limited demonstrations before the city had capitulated. And, as Casey had foreseen, Soviet armor was now rolling out of the capital and heading their way. If we lose this battle, Casey thought, we've lost the war. He glanced at his watch. "It should start happening soon."

Coleman grunted, unbuttoning his fly. He climbed up to the top of the stone hedge and began relieving himself over the side of the mountain.

"General, what are you doing?"

Coleman looked over his shoulder at Casey with an annoyed expression. "What does it look like, Colonel? I'm taking a leak. Jesus, I'm glad you're not in *intelligence.*"

"I can see that, sir," Casey laughed. "But, ah, shouldn't you wait for a more, ah, opportune time and place? Sir?"

"It's always a good time to piss on Iran," Coleman said, buttoning up. "Let me give you a piece of advice, young man. I may be an old soldier, but I know a couple of things about combat. And one of the things I've learned is that, when you're in a combat zone, the best time to take a leak is when it first occurs to you. That way, *you* make the decision of whether to go inside or outside. That option might be closed later on."

Thunder rumbled behind the mountain. Shells whistled overhead and impacted on the other side of Mount Ivan. Casey could see the flash and smoke. After a short interval he could hear the crash of artillery rolling across the valley. A few feet down the mountainside, a lieutenant with a finger in one ear and a headset on another peered through a stereoscopic viewfinder and called the fall of shot to the gun chief at the foot of the mountain.

"This is mostly for effect," Casey screamed to Coleman. "We don't have enough rounds to really lay down a barrage. And they're probably so dug into those rocks over there that it wouldn't do any good, anyway. But it will keep their heads down so the men and the tracks can get into position."

"I thought you said we didn't have that many guns." Coleman watched as the entire mountainside and the valley became wrapped in smoke.

"We don't have a lot of heavy artillery," Casey yelled back over the barrage. "But the Iranians had a bunch of four-deuce mortars. American made—the best kind. We just turned them around. They don't make as big a bang as the 109s. In fact, most of them are firing smoke. But mixed in with the big tubes, you can't tell the difference. Not with your head stuck in the sand."

Casey nudged Coleman's arm and pointed toward the valley directly below. A dozen vehicles shot out onto the hard-packed dirt and churned toward the tunnel. At the same time, a flight of AH-64 Apache helicopter gunships and OH-58 scouts moved into position just behind a sharp ridge facing Mount Ivan.

Casey turned and signaled to a radio operator standing in a trench looking at the sky. The man nodded and spoke into his handset.

"We figure we've got twenty minutes before the MiGs come," Casey said to Coleman. "That's how long it usually takes for these guys to call Zaranj and for the Soviet planes to scramble and fly down here. Hopefully, it'll all be over before then."

Coleman ducked reflexively as a pair of jets screamed overhead. He looked up. They were F-16s.

"There are more where they came from," Casey beamed. "Colonel Dragon promised me everything he's got. And we're going to need it. That's the key to this whole operation."

The Falcons swooped low over Mount Ivan, dropping a load of cluster bombs on the Soviet positions. Another pair of F-16s followed close behind, then four F-4s, a pair of A-10s...Coleman lost track. Aircraft were swarming all over the mountain. The Russians put up a tremendous barrage of antiaircraft fire. Sharp smoke trails betrayed the presence of hundreds of short-range infrared missiles fired from the ground at the attacking jets. Coleman had never seen such a cloud of steel and smoke. He wondered how any pilot could survive it, let alone press his attack.

Some didn't. An A-4 cartwheeled out of the inferno of fire and flares, crashing into the mountainside. A Mirage flew out of the battle on fire, streaming smoke, heading for the Gulf.

Coleman looked down in the valley. The tanks and tracks had taken advantage of the distraction to cross the dead ground between Genow Mountain and the road leading to the tunnel. The few M1 tanks and Bradley infantry fighting vehicles easily outdistanced the slow-moving Marine amtracs. They were already in contact with the Soviets dug in around the tunnel. Coleman could see the M1s, firing at high speed, zigzagging to avoid the tentacles of wire-guided antitank missiles zooming out from the rocks around the tunnel. Automatic fire from the Bradleys' 25-mm chain gun raked the hills on either side of the road.

"All right!" Casey shouted at the air-support fire coordinator. "They're as suppressed as they're going to get. Bring Colonel Dragon in."

The man shook his head and pointed to the sky. Casey looked up. MiGs! They must have already been airborne to have gotten here this fast. The Fulcrums lit into the strikers above Mount Ivan, only to be jumped by First Air fighters swooping down from above. Within a minute, the largest furball of the war boiled over the mountain. The air battle extended from horizon to horizon and reached from miles high to right down on the ground. Planes fell to earth everywhere. Some were MiGs, downed by ground fire from their own troops too scared to stop shooting.

"Get Colonel Dragon down here, now!" Casey yelled back at the man on the radio. "We can't wait. He'll understand."

Casey turned and looked south, over the Gulf. He saw a single dot on the horizon. The dot grew larger, sprouting two wings—no, four wings. As it roared overhead, Casey could see it was actually two planes, an F-16 and an F-15, so close together their wings overlapped.

As the flight cleared the mountain and headed over the valley, the F-15 peeled off, firing a missile at a MiG that was boring in on them. The missile blew the Fulcrum into pieces that scattered across the valley floor. The Eagle took off after another MiG rolling in from behind Mount Ivan, while the F-16 continued toward the tunnel.

Long lines of flak rose from the rocks around the entrance. Casey knew there was even more fire that he couldn't see. Dozens of surface-to-air missiles squirted up like bottle rockets at the F-16. Casey could see the Falcon was taking hits from the ground as the aircraft leveled out to give its computers time to settle for more accurate weapons delivery.

An infrared missile, not fooled by the flares dropping from the F-16, drove right up the jet's tail pipe. A ball of orange-and-black flame blew from the Falcon.

Ignoring the damage, the pilot flew on, releasing a two-thousand-pound laser-guided bomb. The LGB dropped through the sky as if on tracks, impacting directly in the tunnel entrance. The mouth of Genow Tunnel spit fire and smoke like a dragon. Then it disappeared in a haze of dust.

Casey heard himself cheering. The bomb brought tons of rock and debris down on the tunnel. There was no way Soviet paratroopers would open that tunnel by themselves without heavy equipment.

The F-16 flew on until pieces of flaming metal began spitting out from its engine. The plane dipped a wing. Something flew out of the cockpit. The F-16 crashed just beyond the tunnel. Casey could see the gray parachute blossoming now, and he knew the pilot had ejected. His elation turned to pity, however, when he saw the wind blow the chute eastward. The F-16 pilot landed right on top of the Russians.

Casey tried not to think of the fate of the brave fighter jock, who had probably saved Casey's life and that of every other American in Iran. There was too much to do.

"Call in the Cannonball!" he shouted at the radio operator.

"Are you going to encircle them?" Coleman asked.

"Hell, no, General!" Casey shouted over the growing din. "We have to give them somewhere to run to. The last thing we want to do is force the Soviets to fight to the last man. We'd never wrinkle them out of those rocks. It would be like Okinawa."

Somewhere to run to? Coleman frowned. These were *desant* soldiers, the cream of the Russian military. Soviet airborne forces were chosen for their self-reliance and loyalty. Almost all of them were Party members. If Casey expected them to run, Coleman thought, he was very much mistaken. The general wondered what other mistakes Casey might have made. It was too late to think about that now.

The Cannonball roared in, a dust devil of smoke and noise, towing a line of curious square and pyramid-shaped kitelike objects. The C-130 made a long, low pass, curving around the foot of Mount Ivan. The American helicopters rose from the ridge in front of the mountain, spitting rockets and missiles, seemingly at random. Fire chugging from the Apache's 30-mm chin turret kicked up dirt and knocked over rocks at the summit of the hill.

The First Air jets were still making slashing, diving attacks at the Russian positions on the other side of the mountain. Although not without losses, the Regiment seemed to have gotten the upper hand in the air battle. Casey could not see where the bombs were falling, but he knew the Soviet paratroopers were really taking a pounding.

A soldier rushed up to Coleman and Casey excitedly. "They're running, sir! Our forward observers say the Russians are heading for Bunny Mountain!"

Casey nodded. Bibi Sahr Banu was the mountain just behind the Soviet positions, the one Casey had intended to push them back to. It was isolated, well back from the road, and out of range of the tunnel. Bunny Mountain was also higher and craggier than Mount Ivan. It would be, if anything, tougher to push the Soviets out of their new position. But Casey had no intention of attempting it.

"Tell First Air to regroup and come in from the west this time," he told the radio operator. "We want to push any lost Russians off the road and herd them up into the northwest."

The soldier saluted and ran back to the communications trench. Coleman stared at Casey in astonishment and admiration. "How did you know?"

Casey looked distracted. "Know what, General?"

"How did you know your plan would work?" Coleman asked. "After all, that's an entire Soviet airborne division running for the hills over there. That shouldn't be happening. They're an elite unit. They outnumbered us. We should be wading in the Gulf right now."

"You're right, we should," Casey smiled grimly. "But we had a couple of things going for us, too, you know."

"Name one."

"For one thing, I don't think that's an entire division over there."

"It sure as hell isn't now," Coleman grinned.

"It never was. I think that was just the first wave. They don't have enough planes to land all eight thousand men and their equipment in one flight— not in the dark, anyway. The Russians probably figured there'd be plenty of time later to drop the rest of the division in, after they knocked First Air out of the picture—and they damn near did. But when First Air got back in action so quickly, it screwed up the Soviets' plans. They couldn't reinforce their paratroopers at the tunnel, not with Colonel Dragon's fighters around. So they were stuck with what they had. I think it's probably a reinforced airborne brigade. About a couple thousand men."

"Yeah, but that's still more than we've got," Coleman countered. "And they were dug in. Tactically speaking, it was a pretty stupid move to attack."

Casey looked at Coleman, surprised. "You sound like you agree with General Forest and Mr. Schatz."

"They had a point," Coleman admitted.

"Then why did you agree with the plan?"

"Because they were against it," Coleman laughed. "And because nobody else had any better ideas."

"Well, you're right, General. Tactically speaking, it was suicide. But one thing I learned in the Pit was that war is not logical. We tend to analyze this stuff to death, but that's no substitute for thinking. The Pentagon planners worry about how to defeat the Second Shock Army or the T-80 tank, or whatever. But they never think about the real issue, which is how to defeat the men inside them."

"I'm listening," Coleman said.

"Look, General, put yourself in their place. You're a Soviet *desant* soldier, the elite of the elite. They drop you into this strange place in the dark, but you're pumped up, you're excited, everything's gone like clockwork, and the general's coming down from Moscow any minute to give you a medal. Well, comes the next morning, and the rest of the division never gets here. Those American planes your air force said they destroyed are up there picking off the transports with your buddies in them..."

"I know the feeling," Coleman interjected.

"You and me both," Casey smiled ruefully. "Anyway, a couple of days later you're tired and hungry and thirsty and hot as hell. Remember, these are *Russians*. They're not used to this kind of country. It killed a lot of them in Afghanistan, just the heat. Okay, so you're bored, sitting on this stupid tunnel for no good reason—after all, it looks like your tanks are never going to make it, right?

"Then all of a sudden, all hell breaks loose—artillery, tanks, helicopters, the whole bit. Your commanders tell you the Americans don't have any heavy stuff to speak of, but they've lied to you before, hundreds of times, about stuff a lot more minor than life and death. The bombs are falling from those mercenary planes the *zampolit* told you don't exist anymore. But it looks real enough when your buddy is cut in half by a cluster bomb submunition. And in the middle of it all, this F-16 comes zooming in with a two-thousand-pound LGB and closes up the tunnel.

"Well, there goes your mission, your reason for being there. There's no point in sticking around to protect the tunnel when it's closed up anyway. All you know is that the bad guys—us, in this case—have tracks and artillery and jets and gunships, and you don't. You're a long way from home, and if you stay where you are, you may never get back. At this point, it happens. The survival instinct takes over. The soldier turns back into a man wearing a green suit. This whole operation wasn't meant to kill every Russian on Mount Ivan. It was only meant to force them to that point, to break down their discipline, to get the first guy to run for the hills. That's how battles are won. And lost."

Casey turned and waved a hand to the communications trench. The lieutenant picked his way up the rocks.

"Listen, Lieutenant, get on the horn and make sure the men are all well away from the tunnel by sunset," Casey shouted in his ear. The young officer nodded and scrambled back down to the command post.

"You mean we've fought all day for this tunnel, and now we're going to walk away from it?" Coleman asked, astonished.

"We don't have any choice, General," Casey answered. "When the Russians find out they can't hold the tunnel, they'll probably try to keep us from really wrecking it by dropping gas. They've used it in Tehran already. They won't think twice about using it here. First Air is going to CAP the valley to try to prevent that. But there's always the chance some Soviet plane will get through and drop a load of Sarin. I don't want any of my people underneath it if that happens."

"But what's to keep the Russians from moving back in and retaking the tunnel?"

"We're going to be between the Russians and the tunnel. They're going to have to come through us to get it."

Casey and Coleman turned again toward Mount Ivan. They could still hear the sounds of combat across the valley. The battle was over, but the shooting would go on for a long time. There were many men still to die today, on both sides. There were many men dying now. Through his binoculars, Casey could see the Black Hawk helicopters buzzing constantly, ferrying the groaning casualties to Bandar Abbas. Some men were lying silent, eyes open to the Persian sun. The medics were in no hurry for those.

"You know, Colonel," Coleman said softly, "the duke of Wellington once said the only thing sadder than the sight of a battlefield after a victory was the sight of a battle you had lost."

Casey looked up, surprised. "That's strange you mentioned Wellington. I was just thinking about him before the battle, thinking about how much this whole thing was like Waterloo. And it turned out just that way, the way the Iron Duke described it afterward. A near run thing."

Skeletons

**The Dasht-e-Lut
Southeastern Iran**

Are you sure this is the right location?"

The pilot nodded earnestly. He was as surprised as Hassan to discover that he had followed the directions explicitly and flown his sheik to the exact middle of nowhere. "I checked it against the VOR and the DME, Your Highness. These are the coordinates you gave me."

Hassan smiled tightly. There was no reason to doubt the pilot. He was a good man. It would be a shame to kill him.

The sheik unstrapped and stepped out of the helicopter onto the lunar landscape of midnight on the Dasht-e-Lut. Great hills of lava, cooled and hardened over centuries, cast eerie shadows in the blue moonlight. There was no sand, not much rock. Iran's western desert was hard as concrete, a natural parking lot paved with salt.

Hassan walked carefully. There were those spots—and only the *Quashqai*, the nomads, could tell by looking—where the underground rivers flowed dangerously near the surface. If a man stepped there, he would fall through the crust. The shards of hard-packed salt would shred his legs. From then on it was merely a question of whether he drowned or bled to death.

"You are alone?"

Hassan turned slowly, striving to look neither surprised nor frightened. "Yes. My helicopter and pilot are beyond that hill. No one could have followed us. I have done everything you have asked."

"No," said the voice in the shadows. "If you had done all that I had asked, you would not have had to come here, sneaking across the desert like the smuggler your great-grandfather was."

"If you would insult me, do it like a man. Show your face."

The man stepped forward. The beaming moonlight at once illuminated and exaggerated the grotesque features of Col. Mikhail Paratov.

"You are right. After having our destinies intertwined for so long, it is only fair we meet face to face at last." Paratov noticed the sheik's revulsion. "What is the matter? Carlos did not tell you what your precious Bobby Dragon had done to me?"

"No. That is, yes, he did," Hassan was not used to being surprised. "Colonel Rivera told me of your battle with Colonel Dragon and General White. But he never said..."

"What was there to say? That I was trapped in a flaming cockpit, plummeting to the ground? That the disfigurement of the burns was made even more unholy by the ravages of a desperate last-minute ejection?" Paratov said bitterly. "I had not realized how hideous I had become until I went to see this man, White, in a prison camp in Hanoi. I had assumed the sight of my vanquished enemy would somehow cheer me. I was wrong. He did not even recognize me as human. Now do you know what the death of Bobby Dragon means to me?"

Hassan felt a stab of panic. All his arrangements with Paratov had been made through middlemen. It had been a mistake; he could see that now. Paratov was quite mad. Hassan wanted to turn and run back to the helicopter, back to al-Quaseem and life as it had been before the bomb. *His bomb,* he reminded himself. No, it had gone too far for that. Hassan remembered the reason he had come to this place.

"Where is my son?" he asked quietly.

"Your son is here," Paratov answered, "alive and well, and he will remain so as long as you continue to cooperate as splendidly as you have in the past."

The sheik stared into the blue night, seeing only empty desert in every direction. "Where? Where is Faisal?"

Paratov turned calmly and spread an arm across the dark horizon.

"You know, one of the most satisfying aspects of my profession is the opportunity to explore other cultures, other lands," Paratov taunted the sheik.

"This one, for instance—Iran is a fascinating country. Who would have thought, to look across this vast, dry desert, that there was water running underneath? Or that clever shepherds have, for centuries, been digging holes 250 feet straight down into the crust—*qanats,* they call them—to suck out the water that runs down from the mountains? I had often flown over them. From the air, the long lines of perfectly round holes look like some giant octopus has dragged his tentacles across the desert. But as soon as I learned what they really were, I said to myself, *"Paratov, if you ever need to hold the crown prince of al-Quaseem captive, you could ask for no better place."* A nice cozy cell. Plenty of shade. We give him food and water—we are not barbarians."

"Ikhra ba yatak!" Hassan shouted. *A plague on your house!* "You will release him! You will bring him to me!"

"Of course I will," Paratov said smoothly. "Just as soon as you bring me Bobby Dragon."

Hassan boiled with anger and worry. "I have already done that. I delivered Colonel Dragon to you, just as you asked, during the Regiment's first mission over Bandar Abbas. And you ran away."

"I did not run! I was called away by my superiors. Very few of us are born to be absolute rulers of a nation. I have to obey orders if I am to remain in a position to fulfill my part of the bargain."

"I have seen how you honor your word!" the sheik shot back. "You attacked my country! That was never part of the arrangement!"

"It was not my idea," Paratov said, defensively. "I am a soldier. What did you want me to do? Tell the defense minister, *'Sorry, I cannot execute your orders because they interfere with a private arrangement I have with the sheik of al-Quaseem?'* As it was, I took a great risk in warning you not to go to the air base that night. And it was not easy to manipulate the plans to avoid hitting your airstrip at the palace. You could have been killed, if not for me!"

"Perhaps I should have been," Hassan sighed. "Perhaps it would have been better that way. We began with such a simple plan, such limited objectives—you give me the bomb, and I arrange to have you meet Bobby Dragon in combat. Suddenly the whole world is at war, and neither of us has any control!"

"And whose fault is that?" Paratov countered. "You were the one who gave my superiors an opportunity they could not resist. Your men in Bandar Abbas should have overrun the American paratroopers in the first few days after the invasion. Didn't you pay them enough?"

"They did not fight for money. They were *Salah al-Din.* They fought for the honor of the faith," the sheik shot back. "But I did give them weapons and support. Mostly, though, I gave them leadership, a cause to fight for in their shattered country. I even managed to find some tanks to send against the Americans."

"Whatever you did, it did not work," Paratov said firmly. "You failed your responsibility."

"How did we know the paratroopers would hold out so long at the airport? How did we know Bobby Dragon could prepare the Regiment for action so quickly, despite all my attempts to slow down its organization?" the sheik asked, defensively. "No, you cannot blame me for what has happened. It was the Soviet Navy—*your* people—who blundered into that stupid sea battle with the Americans. That was the crucial action. With the American naval aircraft out of the picture, I was put into a most awkward position. As it was, I had to stage a fake assassination attempt to rationalize my actions with my own people and placate the Americans, who were becoming suspicious of my motives."

Paratov reined in his temper. It was no one's fault. It was a good plan, but one with too many variables. It was now highly unlikely Hassan would ever accomplish his goal of ruling Iran. But Paratov was still determined to cash in on his part of the bargain. He had, literally, an ace in the hole—Crown Prince Faisal.

"Your Highness, listen to us." Paratov tried to sound warm and friendly. "We are arguing like schoolboys. Anyone who overheard us would think we were insane."

"And perhaps, Colonel, they would be correct."

"No. We had dreams; that is all. You wanted to rule a nation by any means necessary. And I wanted to kill one man on my own terms. Those are common dreams in the history of the world, although most men do not know how to make them a reality. But we did, didn't we? It takes power to make dreams come true. That kind of power can only come from the atom. I had the means. You had the opportunity. Illyushin brought us together."

Hassan sensed the change in Paratov's mood. He tried to hold his own temper in check. "I have often wondered how you managed to hide the stolen weapons from the KGB. And how did you get them to my people in Iran?"

"The bombs were hidden at my fighter base at Vaziani, the last place the KGB would look for them. I waited until the furor died down, flew to Iran, and dropped them at a spot in the mountains where Carlos was waiting with your operatives. It is a simple matter to slip across a border you are assigned to patrol. And nuclear weapons without fuses are, fortunately, steadfastly inert. But I, too, have often wondered about something. I gave you two bombs. Where is the other one? Surely you did not give both of them to the Iranians?"

"No." Hassan had a hole card of his own. The first bomb was for Baghdad. The second, if necessary, was to destroy Tel Aviv—that would surely have brought the Americans in. But the sheik was too smart to trust the Iranians with both nuclear devices. He could count on their hatred of the Iraqis to make sure the first would find its intended target. But he could not be so sure that, should he have given the Iranians both bombs, the second would not be used to destroy his own country, especially since the forces that were driving a wedge into Iran were based in al-Quaseem.

"You still have it, then?" Paratov asked.

"Perhaps."

Paratov ignored the sheik's attempt to be coy. "I must have it. The Americans already suspect where the material for the Baghdad bomb came from. If my superiors find out, I am finished. And so are you."

"You will get your bomb when I get Faisal," Hassan said firmly.

"You will get your son when I get Bobby Dragon," Paratov said. "And the bomb."

It was an impasse. Hassan briefly considered organizing an armed rescue mission. No, that would not work. Paratov's base was just over the horizon. Any military force the sheik could muster would have to come in by air—and would be chewed to pieces by Paratov's MiGs. Even if he could land a military force this close to Zaranj, where would he begin to look for Faisal? There were fifty thousand *qanats* spread over three-quarters of Iran. His son was dying in only one of them.

The sheik's mind raced, searching for options, pawns, pieces of the puzzle he could shove about, as he had so easily done before, to arrive at a resolution of his choosing. But that was before, when he was dealing with Americans and Iranians. And although they would rather die than admit it—*were* dying, as a matter of fact—those two peoples were very much alike. They were both true believers.

That they seemed to believe in entirely different things mattered only in the sense that it made it easier for Hassan to exploit their differences. Iranians would do anything in the name of Allah, including twisting the legacy of Muhammad and blaspheming sacred Islam for a secular victory. The Americans were the easiest of all. The key to manipulating Americans was pride, duty, honor, responsibility, or any of a dozen other euphemisms for vanity Hassan had become comfortable with over the course of his machinations. And if all else failed, there was always money.

But what to do about Paratov, a man who did not seem to believe in anything? His utter lack of humanity made him, no doubt, insane, but it did not make him weak—far from it. There was no way to get to him. He was invincible. Hassan felt nothing for Bobby Dragon—if Paratov wanted the American mercenary hanged in the roundabout of Quaseem City, the sheik would easily accommodate him. And as for the bomb, Hassan would be glad to be rid of it. If Paratov wanted it, he could have it.

But neither of those actions would bring Faisal back. Looking in Paratov's cool, crazy eyes, Hassan knew he would never see his son again. That sudden realization seized the sheik's heart until it squeezed out the final weakness. Now Hassan, too, was invincible. There was nothing left on the earth to care about. He could think clearly now about his new goal, the single remaining drive in his life: revenge.

"You shall get Bobby Dragon," he said, finally. "And your bomb."

"Fine," Paratov said. "Shall we say noon tomorrow? At this spot?"

"Yes," Hassan said. He added, softly, "Take care of Faisal."

With that, the sheik turned and walked steadily back to his waiting helicopter. There was much to do, many arrangements to make.

Paratov watched the sheik leave. He laughed softly to himself as the big white helicopter rose again in the blue night. Everyone had a weakness, even the Great Manipulator himself. Hassan's weakness, though he was not aware of it, was not his love of Faisal, but his love of himself. The sheik's own cleverness, his arrogance, and his feelings of superiority would catch up with him in the end.

They would catch up with him at noon tomorrow, Paratov thought, when Hassan would execute his brilliant, new plan. The single, savage stroke of vengeance that Paratov had been leading him to all along.

Moscow slept fitfully, as a man facing battle. A flat shadow moved across the office of the Soviet minister of defense. The dark shape settled itself in the chair with a slight sigh of satisfaction.

Illyushin swiveled Kiroshenko's chair to stare out the fine window. Nothing moved. He had never seen the courtyard so deserted, even at this hour.

The colonel general had chosen a perfect occasion to try the office on for size. The marshal was in Tehran inspecting the troops. The KGB palace guards who used to roam the armory like rude Alsatian dogs had been replaced by a forlorn pair of Moscow civil policemen, in another of the chairman's moves to make this military headquarters, this Soviet Pentagon, appear less warlike. The chairman was a fool, an idealist, the first Russian leader to grow soft with power. A visionary, yes, but too farsighted to see the enemies closing in around him.

Kiroshenko, Illyushin thought, was just the opposite. A nearsighted bully, jealous of his toys, meeting every challenge to his authority by lashing out with blunt aggression. The threat of military force was real power. But the act of military aggression, Illyushin knew, was an act of the powerless, a reaction of the unimaginative too vain to admit something, somewhere, had gone horribly wrong.

That left only one man in the Kremlin with the vision to see things clearly, to see the world as it was, not as how it used to be or might become. There was only one man in the Soviet Union—in the world!—who did not wish for war to end or begin. Because he, Pavel Ivanovich Illyushin, knew the long-dreaded clash between East and West, the Last War, would take place within the next twelve hours at a time and place that he had chosen many years ago.

This war, fought with mankind's most advanced weapons, was to have overtones of the primitive. A tournament. A joust. Single combat for the fate of nations. Illyushin cared little which champion emerged victorious. In the end, he would carry home the prize.

Illyushin leaned back in the marshal's chair and steepled his hands. Suddenly the room seemed smaller. The Finnish furniture looked cheap and shabby. No place for a king, he thought, and then smiled tightly as he remembered putting kingly visions into Paratov's head, where he had placed so many thoughts there was no room for Paratov's own. *The savage little puppet,* Illyushin thought. *My weapon. Even in thoughts of betrayal he is hearing my voice.*

Illyushin rose and walked to the door, wondering if, at this hour, there was anyone in the chairman's office. Surely his seat would feel more like a throne.

Hillary's War

Dar al-Harb Air Base
Emirate of al-Quaseem

You've got to help me, General White."

Brick White pulled himself out feet first from the wide hole where the starboard engine of an ex-Turkish Air Force F-4E used to be. The big J-79 power plant was spread in pieces across the floor of the hangar. Peter Hillary was going to pieces at the hangar door.

"This is a little early in the morning for you, isn't it, Hillary? It's not even noon yet," Brick whistled. "Christ, what have you been doing with yourself? You look like hell."

"I need to see Bobby."

Brick stepped over to the workbench and wiped his oily hands on an oily rag. It was really a job for specialists, but the sheik's contract maintenance personnel had been thin on the ground since the airfield had been bombed. Faisal had been good at keeping them in line, but Faisal was gone now. And Hassan seemed to have lost interest.

"Everybody wants to see Bobby," Brick sighed. "But Bobby doesn't want to see anybody. Especially you."

"Did he tell you that?"

Brick was silent.

"I must see him," Hillary insisted. "I think Bobby is in great danger."

Brick snorted. "Aren't we all?"

"Look, Brick, I'm on your side. I can help you. But I'm going to need more cooperation from your end. You keep me in the dark. You don't return my phone calls. They almost didn't let me on the base today."

"Maybe they don't know you're in charge," Brick sniffed. "Look, I've been busy, all right? I've got a sky full of MiGs just over the Gulf and a piss-ant group of our grunts and generals underneath who will probably die without our help. I don't have time to worry about your troubles, Hillary. I've got troubles of my own."

Brick turned to check out the Phantom's insides again. Hillary dogged after him.

"I don't understand. I thought we won the war. Didn't we bomb the tunnel? Didn't we chase the Russians away?"

"*We* didn't do anything, Hillary. I didn't see you there with an M16 in your hand, charging up Mount Ivan, or flying through that shitstorm of flak they put up," Brick spat. "But since you asked, no, we didn't win the war. All we did is buy some time, at the expense of turning a nice, little police action into Armageddon. The Russians will still come. It's going to take them a little longer to get here than before, that's all. We didn't close the tunnel; we just closed the entrance. The Soviets will open it up again. And by that time, the U.S. will have enough men and equipment in Bandar Abbas to really do it up right. Yesterday's battle was America's largest set-piece engagement since the Battle of Hue. But it won't even rank a footnote in the history of what's to come."

"There may not *be* anything to come." Hillary fingered a manila envelope he was carrying.

Brick looked at him quizzically. "What the hell are you talking about?"

"Dennis Nelson is dead. All he did was ask a few questions about Sheik Hassan, about the money and his motives. He found out a lot more than that. And they killed him."

"Who's Dennis Nelson? Oh, I remember, he's that other Limey reporter, the one who was asking all those stupid questions." Brick shook his head in disgust. "Look, I'm sorry, but that doesn't exactly make time stand still for me. A lot of people have died. And a lot more are going to die before this is over. What's one more reporter more or less?"

Hillary stared at the Phantom, bathed in the brilliant greenish-golden light of the hangar's sodium vapor lamps. It was the first time he had ever really seen a plane down for maintenance, seen its guts strung out over an acre of concrete. So many parts, so much to go wrong—he had never imagined. To see them zooming, to ride inside, as he had done so often, one got the impression fighters were made of solid magic, steel through, with bits of glass here and there. He had new respect for pilots. riding on this rocket of stressed parts screwed together by people they wouldn't even trust with their cars. Now he knew why fighter pilots put so much value on faith and loyalty. It was all they had.

"You know, Hillary, oddly enough, I used to admire you. Or, let's put it this way, I used to have a lot of respect for you. I didn't always agree with what you wrote. Hell, most of the time I didn't. But I liked the way you'd cut through the bullshit to get at what was really important. At least we had that in common."

"What makes you think I've changed?" Hillary asked.

"Look at you," Brick snorted. "Just look at yourself, will you? Somebody shoves some money in your hand and blows some smoke up your ass about how the world needs your towering talent in these troubling times, and off you go like some little puppy, eager to perform whatever tricks some gotrocks like the sheik wants to put you through."

Hillary turned to leave. He got three steps before he realized that if he left the hangar there would be no turning back. And he had to stay. He owed Nelson that much.

"Everything you've said is correct. I've been a bloody fool lately, and I deserve it. I don't know what I'm doing here. I should be covering this war instead of trying to prevent other journalists—*real* journalists like Dennis Nelson—from covering it. All right, then," he said firmly, "I resign. I'm a journalist again, as of now. And I've got to ask some questions."

"Welcome back, asshole," Brick said, smiling. "Now at least I know where you stand. Shoot."

"What if I were to tell you," Hillary said solemnly, "that Hassan was responsible for Nelson's death?"

Brick looked up, surprised. "The sheik doesn't go around having people murdered. That's not his style. He probably just had Nelson put on a plane to Abu Dhabi, which is where he was heading anyway. Why kill somebody when you can just deport them?"

"No, Nelson's dead, all right. He never made it to Abu Dhabi, much less London," Hillary said. "The *Gahtell* killed him. The sheik couldn't afford to let him leave the island alive. He knew too much."

"Look, Hillary," Brick said tiredly, "I've got too much to do here to stand around listening to unsupported allegations against the Free World's only friend for a two-thousand-mile radius. If you had any proof of all this, I'd..."

"I have proof." Hillary opened the manila envelope he was carrying. It was Nelson's story, the one he had died for. When the airfield was bombed and Nelson realized he would never leave al-Quaseem alive, he had pressed it into Hillary's hands, the only man he felt he could trust. It was that trust that had so tortured Hillary's long nights since the bombing.

He had hoped he would not have to show the story to Brick. There was always the chance that he was somehow part of the monstrous plot Nelson had begun to uncover. And if Brick was innocent, Hillary could be consigning him to death by sharing this knowledge with him. Well, Brick had claimed to have made his peace with the savagery of war. And this was a war of sorts— Hillary's war. The war of truth against everything else. He had been a deserter, even a quisling of sorts. But now Hillary was back at the front.

Hillary drew a photograph from the envelope and placed it before Brick. "You recognize this man," he said. It was not a question.

It was the same picture Krypto Padgett had shown Bobby—a young Soviet pilot at a snow-covered airfield—but a different print. This one was even more grainy, a copy of a copy, with "M.O.D.—Most Secret" stamped on the back.

"Oh, my God!" Brick gasped. The man in the photograph was only slightly younger than Brick remembered, his face smooth and undamaged. And this man was not Vietnamese. But those eyes! Brick swore he would never forget them. There was no mistaking the eyes of Colonel Doom.

"Where did you get this? What was Doom doing in a Russian uniform?"

"Nelson gave it to me. I suppose he got it from a contact in the Ministry of Defense," Hillary said. Brick had just confirmed his darkest fears. "That man is not the man you knew as Colonel Doom."

"You're wrong, Hillary," Brick said, though obviously confused. "This is the guy who came to see me at the prison camp in Hanoi, all right. I was there. I saw him with my own eyes. His face was all messed up—but it was Colonel Doom."

"Listen to me, General White," Hillary spoke very slowly. "The man you call Doom is actually a Soviet pilot named Mikhail Paratov."

"Colonel Paratov?" Brick said, blankly. "The guy who's running the MiG show at Zaranj?"

Hillary nodded. "He's also suspected of stealing a couple of nuclear artillery rounds—one of which destroyed Baghdad."

Brick sat down, suddenly aware of his age. And his stupidity. Last week, Padgett had tried to sell him something like the story Hillary was telling him now. Brick would have none of it then. *He wouldn't even look at the picture!* Brick had refused to look a gift horse in the mouth, not when that horse had the only friendly fighter bases in the Persian Gulf. God, how blind!

"Nelson had several good contacts in the British military intelligence community," Hillary continued. "They were able to determine that Paratov was in Vietnam at the time of the Linebacker raids serving as an instructor pilot at the MiG base at Kep. It was apparently quite common for Soviet instructors to fly actual combat missions over Hanoi and Haiphong. After all, there was little chance of the Americans finding out, since the MiGs never left North Vietnam."

Brick recovered slightly. "So Doom was a Russian. And we're still fighting him. What an amazing coincidence."

Hillary shook his head. "It's more than a coincidence, General. It's a proximate cause. Nelson believed that's what this whole war is about. Paratov is apparently more than a little bonkers. He's arranged everything that's happened in a concerted effort to gain revenge for what Bobby Dragon did to him in Vietnam."

"But that's crazy!" Brick protested. "That was war. You aren't supposed to go after people specifically. That's murder."

"You went after *Doom* specifically."

"That was different. That was in the air. You took your chances, win or lose, and that was that." Brick shook his head. "To hatch this plot, after twenty years, to start a world war for personal reasons—no, it's just too fantastic. No one could pull off something like that alone."

"Oh, he wasn't alone," Hillary said. "He had an accomplice—Sheik Hassan. Hassan has all kinds of contacts with the Iranians and within the various radical and religious movements they support throughout the world. The Soviets also sponsor a number of Third World revolutionaries. Some of them fly with Paratov. Carlos Rivera did. He was with Paratov when the nuclear bombs were hijacked—not far from Paratov's base near the Iranian border. Nelson thinks Rivera put the deal together."

"What deal?" Brick asked skeptically.

"The sheik wanted to blow up the Gulf and rearrange the pieces to suit himself. Paratov could get his hands on the bomb but not on Bobby Dragon. So Paratov stole those two nuclear artillery shells in Tbilisi and gave them to Hassan. The sheik gave one to the mullahs, knowing full well they would destroy Baghdad with it. And that set this whole chain of events in motion."

"You're grasping at straws, Hillary," Brick sighed with relief. "I have to admit, you had me going for a minute with that picture of Doom there. But there's no way Hassan would get involved with anything like this. Why should he? He's getting everything he wants now."

"Ask yourself why that is, General," Hillary pressed. "Whose idea was it to organize a mercenary air force in al-Quaseem?"

"See, you're already off the track. The Regiment was *my* idea from the start."

"Are you sure? Didn't the sheik come to you with the offer to base aircraft in his country as long as they were under his control?"

"Sure he did. That's what gave me the idea for First Air in the..." A light snapped on in Brick's head. *No, it couldn't be true.*

"And wasn't it Hassan who insisted that Bobby Dragon lead the Regiment? Didn't you think that was a little strange? Bobby was the last person anyone would choose for that position. He was a deserter, an outsider, a man with a proven record of resistance to authority. And how did Hassan know Bobby was still alive? Did you ever ask yourself that?"

"To tell you the truth, Hillary, I didn't stop to think about anything," Brick said. "Everything was happening so fast. Our paratroopers in Bandar Abbas were trapped. The Navy couldn't do the job. We had to get something going, and First Air was our only option."

"The sheik knew that. He counted on your drive, your pull, to ram the Regiment down your government's throat," Hillary said, almost cruelly. "The fact is, all your problems were imposed by Paratov's MiGs, not the Iranians, and not even the Soviets."

"Ah, that's where you're wrong, Hillary. Those were sure as hell real, live Russians on that mountain yesterday. That kind of blows your conspiracy theory out of the water, doesn't it?"

Hillary sat thinking. Nelson hadn't covered the Soviets' entry into the war along the Gulf. It was, in fact, the last thing he saw. Hillary could tell looking at Nelson's face in the glow of the Russian bombs that night that full-scale Soviet involvement was also the last thing he had expected.

Hillary, too, was stymied. Every piece of the plot fit together like a gun except that one. Why had the Russians arrived so late? That question had kept Hillary up for the past few nights until he had finally hit on the solution: It had nothing to do with the well-laid plans of Hassan and Paratov. Nelson was looking for evidence of a successful conspiracy. *He wasn't looking for a plot that failed.*

"I think the situation got out of control," Hillary said finally. "I think the Russians saw something too good to pass up. They saw how precarious the situation was, how little it would take to knock the Americans out of the Gulf, and how much they would stand to gain by doing so. The Soviets are opportunists. They're always ready to pounce on other people's mistakes. And this is the biggest mistake in history."

"We didn't start it, Hillary. The Iranians started it."

"No, they didn't, General," Hillary said. "Hassan and Paratov started it. And something tells me they're not finished."

Brick look troubled. He walked to the dismembered F-4 and pretended to examine the starboard intake. He didn't know whether to believe Hillary or not. But his story jibed so closely with Krypto's—a man Hillary had, to Brick's knowledge, never met—that he couldn't ignore it.

"Okay, let's say I believe you," Brick said. "Just for the sake of argument. You said Paratov gave the sheik two bombs. Hassan gave the Iranians one. Where's the other bomb?"

"Here," Hillary said ominously. "Nelson said Hassan has the bomb. I think it's on this island somewhere. And I think the sheik intends to use it soon while he still has some options left."

"Oh, my God!"

Brick held his head in his hands.

"What is it, General? What's wrong?"

"I just remembered something," Brick said. "During Private Lightning, I was up in the Cannonball with the Weasels. Don said he and Wally had looked everywhere for the other bomb. And the only indication of radiation they ever found was right over the sheik's palace."

Brick raised his head. "When you came in here, you were looking for Bobby. What for?"

Hillary stared at Brick, stripped of his self-assurance for the first time. It was like seeing him out of uniform.

"Because whatever's going on around here, he's at the heart of it," Hillary said. "From the beginning, this whole thing has been about Bobby Dragon. You know where Bobby is, don't you, General?"

Brick nodded. "When I got here this morning, I looked everywhere for Bobby. I even went over to the maintenance hangar. It was guarded by Quaseemi soldiers, which wasn't unusual. But there were *Gahtell* types there, too, which was a little strange. They wouldn't let me in, but I snuck around back and peeked inside."

"What did you see?"

"They had a two-seat Eagle in there, painted up just like Bobby's F-15," Brick said breathlessly. "It was all slicked up—no weapons. I didn't think anything about it at the time. I figured it was one of your ideas, to give the press joy rides, maybe, or to use for photo opportunities. I never thought..."

Brick slumped, silent, then pulled himself together. "What are we going to do, Hillary? There's no way we're going to get into the palace. That place is guarded like a fortress."

"We'll do what we do best, General," Hillary said, firmly. "My specialty is asking questions. And I've only got one left: Can you still fly fighters?"

Maximum Slick

**Quasir al-Quaseem
Emirate of al-Quaseem**

Am I a prisoner?"

Sheik Hassan's smile was the coldest thing in the Persian Gulf. Bobby could feel the chill from six feet away.

"Of course not," the sheik said. "These men are here to protect you."

"I feel safe enough," Bobby said. "Tell them to get lost."

"As you wish." Hassan nodded. The two *Gahtell* men moved back across the runway but, Bobby noted, were still within earshot. And within range.

"So what is this all about? If you wanted to see me, why didn't you just call me up? Why send these goons over and drag me out of the ops shack without even telling me where we were going? Why did they make me bring my flying gear along?" Bobby eyed Hassan dressed in a little-used flight suit and G harness. "And what are you doing in that getup? Are we going somewhere?"

"As a matter of fact, we are," the sheik said. "I apologize for the security measures, but it is imperative that this special mission not be compromised."

Bobby narrowed his gaze. "What *kind* of special mission?"

Hassan motioned for Bobby to follow as he walked a short distance down the strip to a spur leading off into an area encircled with savage-looking barbed wire and electric fencing. Bobby whistled. He knew, of course, that the palace had its own landing strip, long enough for business jets and the two Quaseemi F-16s that normally stood alert duty there. It seemed an extravagance on such a tiny island with a modern jetport—not to mention a tactical air base three times larger than it needed—but the sheik was indeed the man who had everything—including, Bobby could see, an alert facility more sophisticated than those found on the fighter bases of many countries.

A pair of Quaseemi guards in blue berets snapped to attention as Hassan led Bobby down an asphalt spur from the runway that ended in a hardened aircraft shelter. Built of solid, reinforced concrete with a rounded roof and heavy steel doors, the palace TAB-V was similar to the ones at Dar al-Harb, which had allowed the Regiment to ride out the Soviet bombing with most of its planes intact. But Bobby was surprised to find such a fortress amidst the stately elegance of the royal palace.

The sheik pushed a switch. The dark gray shelter doors rolled back electrically. The lights beaming down from the center of the concrete roof danced off the wings and fuselage of an F-15D Eagle. The two-seat D model was identical in every respect to Bobby's single seater with the exception of an added rear cockpit area in place of an auxiliary fuel tank. Outwardly, however, it looked exactly like Bobby's Eagle, even down to the same regimental markings and insignia. There was something else unusual about this bird, though. It shined in the TAB-V.

Waxed and gleaming, the F-15 was set up in what ground crews called "maximum slick" condition. The fighter was defenseless in that configuration—the gun port was faired over and the pylons removed, preventing the carriage of missiles. There were only two reasons to go maximum slick—speed runs and special weapons delivery. Somehow Bobby didn't think Hassan was interested in breaking any performance records today.

Bobby looked underneath the F-15. Sure enough, there it was—a single slick white bomb in the shape of an Air Force Mk-57 but bearing no markings. It was a rather innocent-looking piece of ordnance, compared with the arrowlike missiles and sinister precision-guided munitions he was used to seeing hung under aircraft. But he knew better. He was looking at a nuclear weapon.

Bobby stared at the bomb for a long time. Finally, he asked, "Where did you get that?"

"Does it really matter?"

"No," Bobby said. "I guess not. What are you going to do with it?"

"We," Hassan said, "are going to use it to destroy the MiG base at Zaranj."

Bobby shook his head. "Get yourself another boy."

"This is a vitally important assignment, Colonel. This mission could decide the fate of the war. And the world."

"Good, then you fly it. You're dressed for it," Bobby said. "I'm allergic to nukes."

"Come now, Colonel, aren't you being a bit hypocritical?" the sheik asked. "This is just another weapon, no different than the hundreds of bombs and missiles you have used in the past."

"Those weapons were air-to-air or air-to-ground." Bobby laughed nervously. "Not air-to-country!"

"So this one is perhaps a bit more efficient," Hassan said drily. "I should think you would like that. After all, you have constantly pressured me to equip the Regiment with the most advanced, up-to-date weapons in the world. I offer you the ultimate, and you seem displeased."

"I'm a fighter pilot. We're interested in quality, not quantity. What's the point of fighting with nuclear weapons? You don't even have to *aim* them."

A bitter smile played on Hassan's lips. "You pilots are an odd sort, really. You cling to this romantic notion that you are doing something more noble and dignified than any other soldier. You are not. You are all murdering other human beings. Yet you believe that, since you murder people in a different way, your war is some sort of chivalrous undertaking. And we let you live in that world because we need your skill and your initiative. And, after all, it makes no difference to us what lies you have to tell yourselves to do what we want you to do."

"You're wrong, Hassan," Bobby said. "We *are* different. It's not like we're in a ship, or a tank, or even a bomber. We're up there all by ourselves, just us and the ejector-seat handle. We can leave anytime we want. We have a choice. That's what sets fighter pilots apart. Now you're asking me to go Downtown with the Big One—that's where I draw the line."

Bobby walked toward the open door of the TAB-V.

"I knew you would run," the sheik called out. "It's what you do best."

Bobby turned and smiled. "Sorry. That's not going to work this time. I've kicked myself long enough, hated Brick long enough. Now I've come to realize we're all caught up in the same game. We love flying too much to look too closely at who's pulling the strings on our wings. Every generation it's the same story. Oh, the planes get faster, and the names of the air bases change. But guys like us—like Daffy and Scooter and the rest of the regimental heroes—we keep dying in the same old ways."

"Isn't this a little too late to be developing a case of morality, Colonel?"

Bobby looked at the nuclear bomb hanging on the center line of the bright Eagle. The sheik was right. It was just another weapon, like a knife or a gun. Or a Bobby Dragon. It was time to disarm the Hassans of the world.

"Maybe so," Bobby said with a sad smile. "But better late than never."

Bobby stepped out into the sunlight. Hassan screamed for him to come back. A burst of automatic-weapons fire ripped across the side of the shelter next to his shoulder. Bobby ran back into the TAB-V. "What the hell?"

"I warned you not to go out there!" Hassan shouted. "Those men have orders to kill you if you try to leave here alone."

Bobby stared at the sheik, shaking. This changed everything. Now he was a prisoner. He was being hijacked and forced to fly a mission against his will. And there was no chance of rescue by the authorities. Hassan was the authorities.

"Are you crazy?"

The sheik appeared to consider the question. "If you mean 'am I like normal men?' the answer is certainly 'no.' But my side has the guns, so that doesn't really matter. What matters is whether you are going to fly the mission."

"It's ironic that I was just talking about choice," Bobby said. "I don't seem to have much choice now, do I?"

"No, Colonel Dragon. You don't have any choice. You never did."

"What do you mean?" Bobby got the feeling Hassan was talking about more than just armed men outside the shelter.

"This war." The sheik swept a hand toward the Gulf. "You made it. This is not a struggle between the superpowers. Or, at least, it didn't begin that way. This whole war has been about one man. Bobby Dragon."

Bobby shook his head, frightened and thoroughly confused. "What the hell are you talking about?"

"You have to admit you shot down Colonel Doom that day over Hanoi."

"What's that got to do with anything that's happening here and now?"

"It has everything to do with it," Hassan said. He sighed. "There are so many things you do not know, Colonel. It is difficult to find a place to start."

"Why don't you begin with Doom? What does his death have to do with all this?"

"There was no death!" the sheik said angrily. "There was no Doom. The man you shot down was a Soviet pilot named Mikhail Paratov."

A light went on in Bobby's head. He remembered Krypto mentioning Paratov that night they had discovered the paratroopers landing. "You mean the Russian colonel commanding the MiGs at Zaranj? That's Doom?"

Hassan nodded. "You shot him down. But you did not kill him. Now you have to finish what you began."

So that's what Krypto was talking about! The whole, twisting scheme became clear in Bobby's mind, like the three-dimensional mental picture he could always maintain during dogfights. *Bobby, you fool!* he thought. *If only you thought as clearly on the ground as you did in the air!*

"You and Paratov dreamed this up on your own, didn't you?" Bobby spat. "He ripped off the bombs, and you sucked Brick in, and now half the Persian Gulf is about to follow the other half into hell. And all because you guys wanted to stack the deck in your favor. I know what you wanted. You wanted Iran—although I still can't see why in God's name you'd want to rule a hellhole like that. And this Paratov or Doom or whoever the hell he really is—you're telling me he's been carrying a grudge for twenty years because I beat him in a fair fight? He must be crazier than you are! You don't start a war for personal reasons."

"All wars are personal, Colonel," Hassan said, too calmly. "If you had ever read anything other than operations manuals, you would know that. Throughout history, tribes and kingdoms and nations have fought to the death for purely personal reasons. Often it's religion or money. There have been many wars over women. But the reasons put forth by rulers—strategic necessity, expansionism and hegemony, the domino theory—those are just phrases made up after the fact to rationalize the sacrifice to a wounded and wondering public. Dig beneath the graves of any war and you will find the skeletons of two men locked in combat, even after death."

"I can't begin to tell you how sick that sounds to me," Bobby said bitterly. "You actually sound proud of what you've done. What about those people in Baghdad? And Tehran? And what about those poor grunts over in Bandar Abbas, on both sides of the line? Don't you feel the slightest touch of remorse for what's happened to them?"

"They should be grateful to me," Hassan said. "They would have died anyway and been forgotten. Everybody dies. But I made their lives significant. I made them part of history, something they could never have accomplished on their own. I won't be ashamed for my capabilities, Colonel. At least I use them for the greater good. And if I had some hand in the killing, as you say, then at least it was for a cause I believe in. Myself. You don't even believe in that. You're like a police dog. You kill on command, because you're not willing to assume the responsibility for your actions. You just follow orders. You don't believe in anything."

Bobby took two steps toward the sheik, then stopped when he saw, out of the corner of his eye, the guard outside raising his rifle.

"You're wrong," Bobby said softly. "I believe in a lot of things, enough to die for. I believe in a guy named Krypto Padgett, who gave his life trying to figure out a war that doesn't make sense. I believe in a man named Don Brewer—homesick, airsick, and scared shitless, he tried to cover my butt through two wars and finally died in the attempt. And I believe in Prince Faisal, who sacrificed his young life in the service of his country."

Hassan's face was pale. "What makes you think my son is dead? The American soldiers say they clearly saw him eject and land behind Russian lines."

Bobby shook his head, firmly. "Sonny's dead. I've been flying fighters long enough to know that you don't bang out sideways at 9 Gs, a hundred feet above a mountain, and live to tell about it. He was dead before he hit the ground."

Bobby looked at Hassan. The sheik's control was slipping. This was not the confident, deferential host he had met in Sammarah his first night in-country. It was not as if Hassan had removed whatever mask he had worn that night. No, Bobby thought, this was even more frightening. The man was gone. All that was left was the mask.

"If he is dead, then you killed him," Hassan said bluntly. "You talked him into going on that suicide mission. He would do anything you asked. He wanted to be like you more than anything else in the world."

"Sorry. I'm not taking the rap for that one, either. If you want to blame someone, blame yourself. There wouldn't have even been a war for Sonny to get killed in if you weren't so greedy," Bobby said. "Sonny was young, but he was a lot older than some of those guys in the 82d that got killed yesterday in your war. He knew what he was getting into. He wasn't some kid following me around. Faisal was a man and a warrior, as good as they get, and the Regiment was lucky to have him. You should be proud of him. I am."

The sheik turned away. "I do not need you to tell me how I should feel about the death of my son."

"I'm sorry about Faisal, I really am." Bobby tried one last time to communicate with the sheik. "Look, I thought Doom was your ally. I don't know what you've got in mind, but let's just call it off, okay? If we nuke Zaranj, the Russians will start throwing *their* nuclear weapons around. I don't have to tell you what's going to happen after that. There's been enough killing already. Just let it go."

Hassan shook his head grimly. "It has gone too far for that. Besides, I don't believe the Soviets will retaliate. Zaranj is still officially an Afghan base, and I would guess the Soviet rulers are not willing to see their own country destroyed in its defense. There are witnesses who will swear that you took off, on your own accord and without authorization, to fly this mission. Your personal aircraft will be spotted on the way to Zaranj on both sides of the Gulf. You were not acting on orders from the United States, or even al-Quaseem. I will not have a difficult time proving to the world that you are a dangerous renegade, determined to win at all costs. Because, Colonel, you are."

"I'll just tell everybody the truth—how you forced me to do it."

"Somehow, I do not think people will believe you. Not with your past record."

And it's hard to explain anything if you're dead, Bobby thought grimly. "I suppose you're coming with me to make sure I don't just drop this sucker in the Gulf somewhere, huh? Gun at my back, hand on the ejection-seat override, the whole bit?"

"Something like that, yes," Hassan smiled. It looked like Bobby had resigned himself to flying the mission. *Maybe he could salvage the situation, after all!* "I had hoped we could avoid the more obvious cliches."

"I'm with you. I don't exactly relish the idea of doing warp six over the Persian Gulf with a cocked pistol in the backseat. I'll give you my word as a fighter pilot I won't try anything funny, okay?"

Hassan nodded.

"All right," Bobby began climbing up the ladder to the cockpit. "Let's get this over with."

The sheik put a foot on the ladder and started climbing up toward the rear cockpit.

"Hey, hey!" Bobby turned around and shouted. "Boy, it *has* been a long time since you're been in one of these crates, hasn't it? The backseater never boards until *after* the pilot taxis the aircraft out of the shelter."

Hassan eyed Bobby suspiciously.

"Why is that?"

"Because, Your Flaming Majesty, that way if there's an engine fire on start-up, only one of us gets killed." Bobby pointed to the TAB-V's concrete roof. "I mean, you can't really eject through *that,* can you? Why risk two lives? If *you* want to take this bird out onto the strip, be my guest, and *I'll* wait down there."

"No, that will not be necessary." Hassan moved to a corner next to the entrance. Bobby stood up in the cockpit and waved his arms tiredly.

"Look, I gave you my word; I'm not going to try anything funny, okay?" Bobby sighed. "I mean, there's a couple of soldiers out there with assault rifles and two of your *Gahtell* goons probably packing laser swords, for all I know. But if I did want to kill you, I could do it right now. I could turn on these engines and, where you're standing, you'd get sucked right into the intake. Instant sheikburger."

Hassan was surprised by Bobby's apparent cooperation. Bobby was right. He would have been killed.

"Then where should I stand?"

Bobby jerked a thumb toward the rear of the shelter. "Back there. That's where the backseaters go. And stay in a corner, so you won't get scalded by the jet pipes. And wear your earphones, too. It's going to be loud as hell in here."

The sheik gave Bobby a thumbs-up sign and walked to the back of the TAB-V. Bobby kicked the on-board starter to life, bleeding energy from it to spool up the starboard engine. He shut down the starter and cranked the port engine off the starboard one. Hassan watched intently. It was loud, as Bobby had said it would be. And, thanks to Bobby's warning, the sheik was well away from the main thrust of the engines. He was so happy the colonel had agreed to cooperate. The other means of persuasion were so...unpleasant.

A clear fluid began to trickle from two small pipes near the Eagle's wingtips. Hassan was only mildly concerned. All aircraft leaked in hangars. It was probably just hydraulic fluid. His old Hunter, he remembered fondly, used to leak like a sieve. Suddenly, a flood rushed from the pipes—it was fuel. Hassan could smell it. It sprayed across his flight suit. The sheik began to run for the entrance, sloshing in pools of fuel.

Too late. Bobby lit both afterburners. The fuel ignited in a fireball that blew the already accelerating Eagle out of the TAB-V and onto the ramp. One Quaseemi guard tried to block the way, shooting. He was drawn into the vacuum of the port intake, ground by the whirring turbines and sprayed out the jet nozzle in a red stream.

Hassan, on fire, staggered from the shelter shouting Arabic curses. The blast from the Eagle's big engines forced him back into the inferno of the TAB-V. He died there.

The *Gahtell* men raced to swing the red-and-yellow striped barrier across the ramp in an effort to prevent the F-15 from moving onto the runway. The Eagle, in afterburner, had no intention of stopping. One man was impaled on the F-15's long, sharp nose and slid, dead, to the ground. The other was crushed, along with the barrier, beneath the landing gear.

The strip was coming up fast. Bobby could hear gunshots in the distance. There was no way he was going to turn the corner on nosewheel steering, not at this speed. He snatched the stick up and slammed it to the right. The big fighter flew uncertainly and stalled. The starboard wing dipped and struck the pavement, dragging a long shower of sparks down the asphalt and spinning the aircraft around. Bobby seized the opportunity and brought the Eagle down again, slamming on the pavement with an impact that shoved the oleo struts all the way to the wings.

The F-15 rolled down the runway, gathering speed once again. Bobby could hear the pattering of gunfire around the plane. He made a silent prayer they had not hit anything vital. The Gulf was coming up fast. Bobby groaned. In his haste, he had turned the wrong way! He was trying to take off on the touchdown zone, the short end of the runway. If he had turned left, he told himself, he would have never made it past the antiaircraft batteries by the palace. It didn't really matter, though. He would probably die either way.

The Eagle zoomed over the threshold markings and out onto the Gulf.

Bobby instantly raised the gear for a belly landing in case he had to ditch. The airplane dipped slightly, almost skimming the flat surface of the water. Bobby resisted the temptation to lift the nose, which would surely have stalled the aircraft. The Eagle droned on. It reached rotation speed. Bobby pulled back on the stick. He was safe.

Well, maybe not safe, he told himself, but flying. That was always a good start. He should have been dead and wondered why he wasn't. By all laws of aerodynamics, he and his plane should be floating in pieces on the Persian Gulf. Then he remembered—this wasn't his usual Eagle, loaded down with fuel and weapons. He was lighter than air. He was a bird. He was maximum slick.

Instinctively, he flew northeast into the Gulf, heading for the Strait of Hormuz as he had so many times before. Bobby had no plans. He had fully expected to die in the TAB-V, to be incinerated in the explosion along with the sheik and his infernal bomb. It would have been a heroic final act. But it hadn't happened that way. And now Bobby Dragon was surprised and somewhat embarrassed to find himself still alive. It wasn't the first time he had felt that way.

So that was the situation—all bombed up and nowhere to go. Returning to al-Quaseem was out of the question. Even now he was grateful to be slowly flying out of range of the dead sheik's HAWK batteries. Bobby doubted he would be welcome anywhere else on the western side of the Gulf, not with the brother of the bomb that blew up Baghdad simmering on his center line.

Other possibilities? Bobby checked his fuel gauge. He might be able to make it to the Arabian Sea, maybe ditch and drown the bomb. And himself along with it—there were no airfields out there. And he didn't have the gas to go out to deep water, punch off the bomb, and then come back...and land where?

Bobby thought harder. There was always the desert. Iran's Dasht-e-Lut was huge and unpopulated, a surreal volcanic wilderness that looked as if it had absorbed many nuclear blasts before. He could drop the bomb there and then head back to the strait, call the Army, get a helicopter, punch out into the Gulf, get rescued, and then call Brick up and explain *this*. Even if no one believed the truth, whatever arrangements, excuses, or lies he would have to make up would be much better received without the bomb on board.

Okay, then, resolved: We're going to the desert to jettison this hellish ordnance. Bobby smiled. That bastard Hassan would get his wish after all. He was heading to Zaranj to drop the bomb. He would just drop it about two hundred miles short, that's all. *Pussies hit short*. Well, maybe Bubba Windham would forgive him just this once.

Bobby crossed the strait well east of Bandar Abbas. He did not want to face the flak or get picked up by a stray Fulcrum. The MiGs hadn't been up since yesterday's battle. In fact, the fighting between the American and Soviet paratroopers had lapsed into a delicate, undeclared cease-fire. Not that the battle was over. Both sides were simply exhausted, low on ammunition, energy, and ideas. It was merely an intermission. The final dramatic act would be staged when both sides received their reinforcements.

Bobby zoomed low over the Shahabad Valley. A quick beep reverberated in his headset—a lone MiG, dead ahead. He cursed and shut off the radar. No sense in broadcasting his presence when he was in no position to attack. Or defend himself, for that matter. Bobby didn't worry too much about the bogie. He'd have to have pretty damn good eyesight to catch a single aircraft screaming mere feet above the desert floor. No, more than that—you'd have to be *looking* for him. And no one knew Bobby was coming.

He checked the chronograph. High noon—well, how about that? There was no better time to turn sand into glass. Bobby saw a likely spot dead ahead. No roads, no trails, no lakes, no nothing. If Iran was nowhere, this was the exact middle of it. A great place for a nuclear weapon. It *belonged* there.

Now…how does one go about dropping a nuclear weapon? Bobby had always feigned boredom and ignorance whenever the subject was covered at George. It was expected of fighter pilots. Oh, he knew the mechanics well enough. Dive toss was his best bet—pull the Eagle up in a half-loop and fling the bomb out, letting its momentum throw it even further away while Bobby got a head start in the right direction.

Distance was the key here. Bobby had no idea what kind of bomb it was, how it was fused, how big a boom it would make. There was always the chance it wouldn't go off at all. It was a chance Bobby wasn't willing to take. Dive toss was the way to go.

He honked back on the stick to start the maneuver, a four-G pull that probably saved his life. The missile behind him tried to make the turn, but gravity and its own momentum buried the Alamo in the sand, where it exploded in a brown cloud.

Instinct took over. Bobby forgot all about dropping the bomb and searched the sky for the aircraft and pilot who had tried to kill him. He saw the Fulcrum skulking along the gray mountains on the horizon, probably the same one he had seen over the mountains east of Bandar Abbas. The lucky bastard.

Bobby went through his options. He had none. He had no missiles, no gun, no chaff, and no flares. No wingman or friendlies of any kind, he was carrying a nuclear bomb over Iran, and there was a MiG-29 coming in for the kill. It would make a great bar story, Bobby thought grimly, but there was just one catch—who would tell it?

There was only one thing on Bobby's side—speed. The bird he was flying could actually reach the top speed its manufacturers advertised. He doubted he could wind the Eagle, slick as it was, over Mach 2 in level flight at low altitude. But he could certainly outrun this MiG.

But could he outrun its missiles? No. His only hope was to deny the Fulcrum a decent shot. He turned into the MiG, trying to put him right on the Eagle's nose. The MiG repositioned, and Bobby pointed right at him again, keeping his speed up. A blast of gray smoke blew from the Fulcrum's left wing. A white ball headed toward Bobby, as if on rails—Alamo missile, head on. Bobby waited until he couldn't stand it. He waited even more. He waited until the little missile looked like the biggest thing he had ever seen, a telephone pole with wings, ringed in fire, coming straight for him. Then he pulled up.

Straight up. To an alert but not very bright Doppler radar, Bobby had ceased his movement along the forward axis, which meant his speed had effectively dropped to zero and he had ceased to exist. The missile zipped underneath and headed for Pakistan.

Bobby rolled over in an Immelmann. The MiG zoomed underneath, a beautiful aircraft, all gray with two black tails. *Black tails?* Doom's MiG had had a black tail. But Doom was...

No. No, that was Doom. Or Paratov. It didn't matter. It was death to Bobby, Hassan's final cruel joke. The sheik had planned to kill Paratov, to wreck the Soviets' plans in Iran, and to frame Bobby for the deed. But Paratov had double-crossed him. It was a set-up, an ambush. Paratov would get what he wanted after all.

But Bobby wasn't dead yet. He rolled over and headed for the coast in full burner. The zoom climb had cost speed and energy. But the MiG still had to turn around. Bobby might make it. He wouldn't bet on it, but he had no choice but to run for it.

He watched the airspeed slowly wind back up. Paratov had turned around. Bobby was gaining speed slowly, but not enough to offset the speed advantage of a Mach 3 missile.

Bobby wondered what Paratov was thinking. War movie pilots always exchanged witty repartee in this situation. In real life it was flatly impossible. There was no interspecies communication between modern fighter aircraft of hostile nations. Bobby's radio couldn't speak MiG, and Paratov's was probably glued to the GCI frequency anyway. Besides, what was there to say? *This sky's not big enough for both of us ghosts? Take that, Yellow Baron? Paratov, you red bastard, I'll see you burn in hell?*

Instead, they did their talking with airplanes, each maneuver an insult, each wing flip an obscene gesture. It was a dogfight that had lasted twenty years. And now it was ending.

Bobby watched as the Fulcrum zoomed into firing parameters. He was sure Paratov wouldn't fall for the zero-Doppler turn again now that he had

had a close enough look at Bobby's Eagle to know it had no talons. He could fling two or three missiles at Bobby. If, by some magic stoke of luck, none of them hit, he could still watch Bobby's energy slowly dissipate in his efforts to evade them and then close in for a gun kill. And there was nothing Bobby could do about it.

The MiG got larger. Its wings straightened. Paratov wasn't taking any chances. Bobby could imagine him in the MiG's cockpit, leisurely scanning the radar, checking the armament switches, *making sure*. Why not? Bobby wasn't going anywhere. He was MiG chow. Any minute now.

Bobby leaned back and looked over his shoulder. Better get ready for the Alamo that had his name on it. A white stick streaked in the sky behind the Fulcrum. A missile! A Sidewinder missile! A spike of black smoke erupted behind the MiG, spewing shrapnel through the sky in a thirty-foot radius. The Fulcrum dipped a wing and disappeared behind a mountain, trailing smoke.

Bobby looked up to see a big F-4 flying on his wing. The Phantom was green and tan, camouflaged for ground attack, with a big black First Air triangle plastered over its Republic of Korea markings.

"I don't know who you are," Bobby said over the radio. "But you just saved my ass."

"That's what wingmen are for."

Bobby's heart skipped. There was no mistaking that voice. "Brick! What the hell are you doing up here?"

Brick laughed. "My backseater had a wild hair, and we thought we'd come up and check it out."

Backseater? Bobby frowned. Who'd Brick get to ride in the pit with him?

"Tally-ho, Colonel!"

"Hillary? Is that you?"

"Roger that, old son. Peter Hillary, veteran war correspondent, former public-relations man, and master spy, here. I thought I'd try my hand at a new vocation. Say hello to the new stewardess on the Flying Brick Line."

Bobby laughed. "Watch out, Hillary. The guy's all hands."

"Hey, Bobby!" Brick called out. "Is that a nuclear shape on your center line or are you just glad to see me?"

"You got it, big guy! What should I do with it?"

There was silence for a moment, then Brick cut in again. "Ah, let's make Bahrain a nuclear power. What do you say? We don't have the gas to get to a real country, but those knuckleheads probably won't know what to do with it, anyway."

"All right, General. You're the boss. Lead on."

The F-4 turned slightly to the south. Bobby did the same, keeping in line-abreast formation. They were coming up on the strait again. It would be over soon.

"Hey, Brick," Bobby said seriously, "you know who that was back there, don't you."

"Yeah," Brick said. "Hillary figured it out. It was that fucking Yellow Baron. But I hosed him this time. I guess I shouldn't be so pissed at him, though. He made both of us aces."

"Yeah, he did," Bobby said. "Listen, Brick, there's something I want to say. About the tiger hunts, and Doom and all that. Now that I've had command, I can see...well, you were..."

"Skip it, Bobby," Brick said warmly. "Wait till we're on the ground, when there's other people around and I can hear it better when you tell me how wonderful I am and how right I was all along. There'll be plenty of time to..."

The flash was so bright it hurt Bobby's eyes. The back end burned off the Phantom, sending it in a flat spin, around and around. Both men were trapped inside, with no chance of ejection.

"Brick! Brick!"

"First Air, Bobby!" The voice over the radio was growing faint. "Go big or go..."

Bobby watched the faint flash of orange as the F-4 hit the desert floor. A tall column of dust and black smoke marked the graves of two more men who had given their lives so Bobby Dragon could live longer than he should have.

"Paratov!" Bobby screamed. It was a blood cry.

Paratov's MiG, riddled with shrapnel, rose over the Zendan Ridge. One engine was shut down, the other smoking. The Fulcrum leaned on one wing, flying shakily. *You couldn't kill the bastard!* Bobby thought.

Paratov's last missile flew off his unsteady wing, flying unerringly for Bobby. *So this was it. This was how it ended. Paratov is going to kill us all.*

No! Suddenly it became clear to Bobby what had to be done, why he had to do it. It made such perfect sense!

He nosed the F-15 down and pushed the throttles all the way forward, zone-five afterburner. He couldn't outrun the Alamo, but it would take the missile longer to reach him. And time was all he needed.

Airspeed picked up. Mountains rolled beneath the streaking Eagle. But the missile was gaining, and Paratov right behind it. *Give me time!*

There it was: the Genow Tunnel. The only link between the Americans and the Russians in Iran. Not the only reason for war, certainly, but the only means. *"No tunnel, no war,"* Krypto had said. And there was no one around it. Fear of a Soviet gas attack and American retaliation had driven both sides away from the tunnel. The Genow Tunnel. No tunnel. No war. No more.

Bobby dropped the bomb. He watched it fall right into the entrance. And...

Nothing happened. It was a dud. Bobby turned around to watch Paratov's missile finish its run, tear up his airplane, and end his life. Instead, he saw the sun roll across Iran.

Bobby didn't see the tunnel destroyed, the mountains pulled on top of it, and the whole valley sealed shut, smooth, with solid glazed rock. He didn't see anything. He couldn't see anything. The shock wave picked up the big Eagle and flung it out over the strait, end over end.

He was dimly aware there was something he was supposed to do in such a situation. His hands found a handle. He pulled it. Something kicked him in the ass. Something else jerked him up by his shoulders. He heard a distant voice, a voice from twenty years ago, a noise that had been floating around the earth only to return when he needed it most. And the voice said, *"Skirt up! Panties down!"*

What? *Skirt up! Panties down!* The voice of a survival instructor discussing the proper way to release the parachute harness—*pull up the cover and pull down the latch!*—before it dragged you, drowning, through the Persian Gulf.

Splash! Bobby found himself swimming. And remembering: sharks, and man-o'-wars, and sea snakes, savage little gray-green monsters that can kill with one bite. His head hurt. His eyes saw only yellow. He leaned back against the self-inflating life vest and wondered why he shouldn't just go to sleep...

No! Wake up! What's that sound? A helicopter. Bobby hated helicopters. He'd rather die than be rescued by a helicopter. *No! Wake up!* They're going away!

Come back! Come back! A chopper full of cameramen, come to look at Bobby's bomb. *Come back! I'll talk to you this time, I swear!*

Bobby felt the survival kit tangled around his legs. *Survival! Why? Let it end.* Hadn't he lived too long already? Bobby quit thrashing. Why fight it? The weight dragged him down, the warm water sealing over his helmet into a seamless sea.

No! I have to live! Bobby kicked out fiercely with his flight boots. He broke the surface, gasping, taking great gulps of steaming air. He wrenched off his helmet and struggled with the survival kit, pulling it slowly by the cord that bound his legs. Fingers trembling with exhaustion, he fumbled with the bindings. The bag was heavy and greasy with the water of the Persian Gulf. It slipped from his hands.

Bobby lunged for the sinking bag. His fingers grabbed something just before the survival kit disappeared underneath the blue water. *What was it? A flare gun! Some luck, at last!* Of all the things he could have snared—

rabbit traps, Morse code generators, silver dollars—here was something he could use! Now, if only...

It was suddenly light, as bright as the sun he had dropped on Iran. Brighter! *He couldn't see!* He fought the panic. What happened? He must have pulled the trigger when he grabbed for the flare gun. He must have been pointing it right at his face. He must be blind.

Bobby felt a burning on his chest, around his neck. Was he on fire? Impossible—the flight suit was Nomex. Then he remembered. *The scarf.* The stupid, romantic First Air scarf. Regimental issue. Black and gold, hopelessly dashing, and highly flammable.

Now, blind, drowning, and on fire, Bobby could think clearly. He could always think clearly facing death. Sometimes, he thought, he could *only* think clearly facing death. He had two choices. If he ducked underwater, he would put out the fire—and put an end to his only chance of being spotted and being rescued. He would drown and die there. Or he could remain on fire and hope the helicopter spotted the beacon and picked him up while there was enough left of him to pick up.

It was no decision. Bobby wrenched off the flaming scarf. Holding it aloft by the end still to burn, he waved it back and forth at the buzzing helicopter. The flames ate at the silk. Bobby watched the golden wings turn black and blow away, but he continued to wave the scarf. He waved it like a flag. A flag on fire, yes. But still flying.

Epilogue

ow the earth was made smaller, and there were two "dead zones" no living creature could inhabit: Baghdad and Iran's Sarzeh Valley. The question remained: What to do with the rest of the world?

The withdrawal of Soviet and American combat troops, supervised by the United Nations' newly created Pan-Arabian Peacekeeping Force, was accomplished quickly—both superpowers seemed only too willing to wake up from their Arabian nightmare. Pending the reconstruction of the country and subsequent free elections, Iran was split into four zones of occupation. The northwest, bordering Iraq, is administered by West Germany. France took central Iran, including ravaged Tehran. Paratov's cynical dream of an independent Baluchistan, ironically, came true, at least temporarily, when the British occupied the area. The real prize, however, was given to the Gulf Cooperation Council, a consortium of Arab states on the western littoral; the entire Iranian Gulf coast west of the Zagros came under its administration.

Although all the European countries had historic links to the areas they occupied, the consensus was that the old colonial powers looked forward to the day when they could relinquish their new Iranian colonies. Not so, however, with that stretch of Iran along what was now called, unequivocally, the Arabian Gulf. With its oily riches and strategic importance, no one believed the GCC protectorate—dubbed the "Republic of OPEC"—would ever revert to Iranian hands.

Soviet Defense Minister Feodor Kiroshenko was executed for treason, as were many of the Soviet high-ranking military, after a series of show trials in Moscow. The trials were conducted by the new Soviet government to demonstrate remorse and stability to the world after an internal power struggle in the Kremlin threatened to erupt into a second Russian Revolution. From the bitter and bloody battle between the Soviet left wing (who feared recriminations from the West for their country's massacre in Tehran) and the right (who welcomed the final confrontation) emerged a compromise candidate acceptable to both factions—Pavel Ivanovich Illyushin.

American Kremlin watchers were shocked at the rise of a minor Soviet Air Force functionary to the chairmanship of the Communist Party. The world was even more surprised when Illyushin, in an effort he said would "rid the Party of the miscreants responsible for the debacle in Iran," instituted a series of repressions and pogroms on a scale not seen since the time of Josef Stalin.

Secretary of Defense Kevin Schatz was sentenced to a three-year term at the federal minimum security facility at Eglin Air Force Base, Florida, after his convictions on multiple charges of embezzlement and extortion in relation to the diversion of U.S. funds earmarked for the First Air Regiment, Inc.

Gen. Beaufort Forest, forcibly and unpleasantly retired, authored, with the aid of a succession of ghostwriters, *Combat General: My War with Iran,* a book notable only for its vitriol and historical revisionism.

Adm. Sam Meredith, also retired, was thwarted in his bid for a congressional seat when a scathing report on his actions during *Ready Eagle* appeared on a television network documentary. His suit against the network is still pending.

Gen. Curtis Coleman assumed interim command of the American contingent of the Pan-Arabian Peacekeeping Force in Iran before retiring to his family farm in Bowling Green.

Lt. Col. Steve Casey stayed on in Iran, attached to the staff of the American peacekeepers. He has now returned with the 82d Airborne to Fort Bragg, where he is currently serving as a battalion commander.

Sgt. William Willis served in the occupation forces until the American withdrawal from Iran. He has repeatedly declined medals, honors, and promotions (other than those consistent with the normal enlisted career track) and is now 1st Sergeant, Alpha Company, 2d Battalion (Airborne), 325th Infantry, 82d Airborne Division.

Gen. William "Brick" White, Mr. Peter Hillary, Lt. Cmdr. Don Brewer, Lt. Scooter Jeffries, Maj. Krypto Padgett, Crown Prince Faisal al-Quaseem, and dozens of First Air Regiment pilots are dead, along with hundreds of Americans, thousands of Russians and Iranians, and countless Iraqis.

The U.S. government still lists Lt. Robert Dragon as missing in action, December 26, 1972.

FIRST AIR

REGIMENTAL ROSTER

FLIGHT	MEMBER	CALL SIGN	PARENT UNIT
Breaker	01 Col. Robert Dragon	Breaker	Unknown
Flight	02 Lt. John Engram	Rowdy	USAFE—36 TFW, Bitburg AB, FRG
F-15	03 Maj. Richard Foster	Spots	TAC—1 TFW, Langley AFB, VA
	04 Capt. Dallas Deeds	Spuds	PACAF—18 TFW, Kadena, Japan
Eagle	05 Chu. Hideo Mashuta	Minya	JASDF—203 Sq., Chitose AB, Japan
Flight	06 Maj. Lane Harris	Hoss	ANG—128 TFW, Dobbins AFB, GA
F-15	07 Capt. Dov Levi	Speedjeans	IDF/AF—133 Sq., Hatzor AB, Israel
	08 Lt. Col. Salem Taiba	King Rat	RSAF—No. 13 Sq., Dhahran, Saudi Arabia
Kitty	11A Cmdr. J. M. Wilkinson	Blade	VF-102 Diamondbacks
Flight	11B Lt. Phil Dobbs	Dogbone	CVW-1/USS *America*
F-14	12A Lt. Evan Jeffries	Scooter	VF-142 Ghostriders
	12B Lt. Cmdr. Don Brewer	Daffy	CVW-7/USS *Eisenhower*
	13A Lt (jg) Scott Newhouse	Paperchase	VF-213 Black Lions
	13B Cmdr. Gary Rix	Fang	CVW-11/USS *Enterprise*
	14A Lt. Cmdr. Alan Hyatt	Hotel	VF-32 Swordsmen
	14B Ens. Win Preston	Gameshow	CVW-6/USS *Forrestal*
Turkey	15A Lt. Dave Ramsey	Rooter	VF-111 Sundowners
Flight	15B Cmdr. Henry Carr	Smoothdog	CVW-15/USS *Carl Vinson*
F-14	16A Lt. (jg) Ed Keith	Buffy	VF-1 Wolfpack
	16B Lt. Hollis Robins	Rockin'	CVW-2/USS *Ranger*
	17A Lt. Cmdr. Elliot O'Neal	Stork	VF-41 Black Aces
	17B Ens. Ron Richards	Rickshaw	CVW-8/USS *Roosevelt*
	18A Cmdr. Terry Orr	Paddles	VF-103 Sluggers
	18B Lt. Nolan Gilbert	Fastball	CVW-17/USS *Saratoga*
Falcon	21 HRH Faisal al-Quaseem	Sonny	RAF/al-Quaseem, Dar al-Harb AB
Flight	22 Lt. Randy Dillon	Matt	PACAF—8 TFW, Kunsan AB, ROK
F-16	23 Lt. Gideion Katz	Garfield	IDF/AF—16 Sq., Etzion AB
	24 Maj. Todd Mallory	Spike	USAFE—50 TFW, Hahn AB, FRG
Viper	25 Capt. Darrel Amundsen	Dagger	KLu—323 Sq., Leeuwarden, RN
Flight	26 Flt. Capt. Christian Bruggen	Brewski	FAeB/BL—349 ESK, Beauvrechain
F-16	27 Maj. Gary Taylor	Hick	TAC—388 TFW, Hill AFB, UT
	28 Capt. Ivan Wayne	Duke	TAC—363 TFW, Shaw AFB, SC
Stinger	31 Lt. Steven Harper	Dots	USN Flight Demonstration Squadron
Flight	32 Col. Jose Martorell	Frito	EdA—ESK 211, Moron MAT, Spain
F-18	33 Capt. Gerry Francis	Hoser	CAF—419 Sq., Cold Lake, Alberta
	34 Flt. Lt. Ranier Siemen	Prince	KdF—18 Sq., Dubendorf, Switzerland

FLIGHT	MEMBER	CALL SIGN	PARENT UNIT
Cobra	35 Capt. Tom Ramsey	Smurf	USMC—VMFA 531, MCAS El Toro
Flight	36 Lt. Jean-France Larouche	Toque	CAF—433 Sq., Bagotville, Quebec
F-18	37 Lt. Greg Dunstan	Crock	RAAF—75 Sq., Darwin, Australia
	38 Capt. Mal Carrick	Rascal	RAAF—75 Sq., Darwin, Australia
Rhino	41A Lt. Col. R.J. Windham	Bubba	ANG—924 TFG, Bergstrom AFB, TX
Flight	41B Maj. Charles Combs	Thumper	
F-4	42A Col. Ned Flaherty	Bluto	PACAF—3 TFW, Clark AB, RP
	42B Lt. Larry Duncan	Dunk	
	43A Capt. Sun Pak	Six-Pack	RTAF—1 Sq. Royal Thai AB, Thailand
	43B Lt. Jun Nam	Jammer	
	44A Lt. Col. Mohammed Rish	Richie	EAF—88 Sq., Cairo West AB, Egypt
	44B Capt. Ahmad Kasim	Sneezy	
Phantom	45A Lt. David Hamner	Hammer	PACAF—51 TFW, Osan AB, ROK
Flight	45B Maj. John Walsh	Monty	
F-4	46A Col. Serif Sahap	Snapshot	THK—1Sq., Eskisehir AB, Turkey
	46B Capt. Umit Baban	Bozo	
	47A Mr. Tom Roemer	Radio	Lambert Field, St. Louis, MO
	47B Mr. Bill Giltner	Wildman	
	48A Capt. Walt Carver	Peanut	RAF—No. 43 Sq., Leuchars, UK
	48B Lt. Barry Gunston	Zipgun	
Rattler	51 Maj. Glen Reese	Rattler	USAFE—501 TFS, Bentwaters-Woodbridge, UK
Flight	52 Capt. Wayne Shannon	Bottles	
A-10	53 Lt. Al Driver	Nads	
	54 Lt. Chuck Templeton	Splash	
Hog	55 Maj. George Halbrick	Gaucho	
Flight	56 Lt. Lynn Griffin	Fruitloop	
A-10	57 Lt. Col. Rob Caine	Boss	
	58 Capt. Bob Nelson	Crash	
Frogger	61 Cmdt. Armand Guerin	Creamcheese	AdA—12 ESC, Dijon, France
Flight	62 Capt. Maurice Deulin	Dice	
Mirage	63 Lt. Michel Neville	Hobie	AdA—15 ESC, Orange, France
2000	64 SLt. Albert Gabriel	Taps	
Magnet	66 Lt. Col. Jim North	Oliver	USMC—VMA-331, Cherry Point, NC
Flight	67 Capt. Mac McPherson	Sticks	USMC—VMA-331, Cherry Point, NC
Harrier	68 Sqn. Ldr. Colin Worth	Samson	RAF—No. 4 Sq., Gutersloh, FRG
	69 Fl. Lt. Henry Gault-Prentice	Lighthouse	Royal Navy—No. 800 Sq.
Limey	71A Grp. Cpt. Gordon Pettit	Boney	RAF—237 OCU, Honington, UK
Flight	71B Flt. Lt. Reg Fraser	Blighter	
Bucca-	72A Sqn. Ldr. Charles Tate	Freight	
neer S.2	72B Flt. Lt. Cyrus Holcomb	Reaper	
Croc	73A Capt. Ian Wright	Kanga	RAAF—6 Sq., Amberley, Australia
Flight	73B Lt. Miles Anderson	Roo	
F-111C			

FLIGHT	MEMBER	CALL SIGN	PARENT UNIT
Adler Flight Tornado	81A Col. Karl Houk	Shakey	Luftwaffe—JABO 38, Jever, FRG
	81B Lt. Erich Frank	Hot Dog	
	82A Capt. Kurt Baum	BamBam	
	82B Capt. Ranier Hass	Rodeo	
	83A Maj. Jurgen Ruhl	Dracula	
	83B Lt. Erhard Huber	Choo-Choo	
	84A Capt. Hans Hauser	Hamburger	
	84B Lt. Ernst Stuken	Stuka	
	85A Maj. Richard Rehmann	Jager	
	85B Capt. Egon Schmidt	Screws	
	86A Lt. Fredrich Mathoffer	Rommel	
	86B Capt. Volker de With	VW	
Demo Flight Composite	91 Lt. Derek Richards (A-4)	Zipper	RNZAF—75 Sq., Ohakea, NZ
	92 Capt. Prepan Monday (F-5)	Tiger	RTAF—13 Sq., Don Muang, RT
	93 Tai. Kenji Komaki (F-1)	King Kong	JASDF—3 AW, Misawa, Japan
	94 Col. Mario Penna (AMX)	Mardi Gras	FAB—14 FG, Santa Cruz, Brazil
Rabbit Flight Composite	95 Cmdt. John Carbone (F-104S)	Pasta	AMI—28 Gruppo, Treviso, Italy
	96A Maj. John Moskowitz (FR-4C)	Bogie	ANG—117 TRW, Birmingham AL
	96B Lt. Cliff Turner	Burner	
	97 S. Lt. Jules Casale (RF-8E/FN)	Chops	Aeronavale—12F, RNF *Foch*
Cannonball Flight EC-130Q	99A Mr. Donald Smith	Don	Zen Light Industries,
	99B Mr. Walter Jones	Wally	Tonopah, NV

For the Regiment

Managing director: Mr. Peter Hillary
Commander: HRH, Prince Faisal al-Quaseem
Director of Operations: Col. Robert Dragon
Director of Intelligence: Maj. Dick Padgett
Air Adjutant: Gen. William White

Notes on Command Structure

All aircrew, regardless of their rank in their respective air forces, are given the honorary rank of colonel in the Royal Air Force of al-Quaseem. Operational command resides in the director of operations and is exercised through flight leaders, called "warlords." Warlords for their respective flights are listed first here.

The Author

In the course of his journalism career, Michael Skinner has flown in, ridden upon, or sailed aboard almost every major weapons system in the U.S. inventory. A former writer and editor for *CNN, The Washington Star*, and *The St. Petersburg Times*, he is the author of *USAREUR: The United States Army in Europe*; *USN*; *Red Flag*; and *USAFE: A Primer of Modern Air Combat*, all published by Presidio Press.